ALSO BY RACHEL KUSHNER

Telex from Cuba

The Flamethrowers

The Strange Case of Rachel K

The Mars Room

The Hard Crowd

CREATION LAKE

A Novel

RACHEL KUSHNER

SCRIBNER
New York London Toronto Sydney New Delhi

Scribner
An Imprint of Simon & Schuster, LLC
1230 Avenue of the Americas
New York, NY 10020

This book is a work of fiction. Any references to historical events, real people, or real places are used fictitiously. Other names, characters, places, and events are products of the author's imagination, and any resemblance to actual events or places or persons, living or dead, is entirely coincidental.

Copyright © 2024 by Rachel Kushner

All rights reserved, including the right to reproduce this book or portions thereof in any form whatsoever. For information, address Scribner Subsidiary Rights Department, 1230 Avenue of the Americas, New York, NY 10020.

First Scribner hardcover edition September 2024

SCRIBNER and design are trademarks of Simon & Schuster, LLC

Simon & Schuster: Celebrating 100 Years of Publishing in 2024

For information about special discounts for bulk purchases, please contact Simon & Schuster Special Sales at 1-866-506-1949 or business@simonandschuster.com.

Interior design by Kyle Kabel

Manufactured in the United States of America

3 5 7 9 10 8 6 4 2

Library of Congress Control Number: 2024003660

ISBN 978-1-9821-1652-1
ISBN 978-1-9821-1654-5 (ebook)

For Jason

Close, in the name of jesting!

Lie thou there,
for here comes the trout that must be caught with tickling.

> —Maria, from *Twelfth Night*

I

THE DELIGHTS OF SOLITUDE

NEANDERTHALS WERE PRONE TO DEPRESSION, he said.

He said they were prone to addiction, too, and especially smoking.

Although it was likely, he said, that these noble and mysterious Thals (as he sometimes referred to the Neanderthals) extracted nicotine from the tobacco plant by a cruder method, such as by chewing its leaves, before that critical point of inflection in the history of the world: when the *first* man touched the *first* tobacco leaf to the *first* fire.

Reading this part of Bruno's email, scanning from "man" to "touch" to "leaf" to "fire," I pictured a 1950s greaser in a white T-shirt and a black leather jacket as he touches a lit match to the tip of his Camel cigarette, and inhales. The greaser leans against a wall—because that is what greasers do, they lean and loiter—and then he exhales.

Bruno Lacombe told Pascal, in these emails I was secretly reading, that the Neanderthals had very large brains. Or at least their skulls were very large, and we can safely infer that their skulls were likely filled, Bruno said, with brains.

He talked about the impressive size of a Thal's braincase using modern metaphors, comparing them to motorcycle engines, which were also measured, he noted, for their displacement. Of all the humanlike species who stood up on two feet, who roamed the earth for the last one million years, Bruno said that the Neanderthal's braincase was *way out in front*, at a whopping 1,800 cubic centimeters.

I pictured a king of the road, way out in front.

I saw his leather vest, his big gut, legs extended, engineers' boots resting on roomy and chromed forward-mounted foot pegs. His chopper is fitted with ape hangers that he can barely reach, and which he pretends are not making his arms tired, are not causing terrible shooting pains to his lumbar region.

We know from their skulls, Bruno said, that Neanderthals had enormous faces.

I pictured Joan Crawford, *that* scale of face: dramatic, brutal, compelling.

And thereafter, in the natural history museum in my mind, the one I was creating as I read Bruno's emails, its dioramas populated by figures in loincloths, with yellow teeth and matted hair, all these ancient people Bruno described—the men too—they all had Joan Crawford's face.

They had her fair skin and her flaming red hair. A propensity for red hair, Bruno said, had been identified as a genetic trait of the Thal, as scientific advancements in gene mapping were made. And beyond such work, such proof, Bruno said, we might employ our natural intuition to suppose that like typical redheads, the Neanderthals' emotions were strong and acute, spanning the heights and depths.

A few more things, Bruno wrote to Pascal, that we now know about Neanderthals: They were good at math. They did not enjoy crowds. They had strong stomachs and were not especially prone to ulcers, but their diet of constant barbecue did its damage as it would to anyone's gut. They were extra vulnerable to tooth decay and gum disease. And they had overdeveloped jaws, wonderfully capable of chewing gristle and cartilage but inefficient for softer fare, a jaw that was *overkill*. Bruno described the jaw of the Neanderthal as a feature of pathos for its overdevelopment, the burden of a square jaw. He talked about sunk costs, as if the body were a capital investment, a fixed investment, the parts of the body like machines bolted to a factory floor, equipment that had been purchased and could not be resold. The Neanderthal jaw was a *sunk cost*.

Still, the Thal's heavy bones and sturdy, heat-conserving build were to be admired, Bruno said. Especially compared to the breadstick limbs of modern man, *Homo sapiens sapiens*. (Bruno did not say "breadstick," but since I was translating, as he was writing these emails in French, I drew from the full breadth of English, a wildly superior language and my native tongue.)

The Thals survived cold very well, he said, if not the eons, or so the story about them goes—a story that we *must complicate*, he said, if we are to know the truth about the ancient past, if we are to glimpse the truth about *this* world, now, and how to live in it, how to occupy the present, and where to go tomorrow.

My own tomorrow was thoroughly planned out. I would be meeting Pascal Balmy, leader of Le Moulin, to whom these emails from Bruno Lacombe were written. And I didn't need the Neanderthals' help on where to go: Pascal Balmy said to go to the Café de la Route on the main square in the little village of Vantôme at one p.m., and that was where I would be.

BECAUSE BRUNO LACOMBE had been positioned in the briefings I was given as a teacher and mentor to Pascal Balmy and Le Moulin, I was looking for references in his emails to what Pascal and his group had done, and what they were planning.

Six months ago, earth-moving equipment was sabotaged at the site of a massive industrial reservoir being built near the village of Tayssac, not far from Le Moulin. Five huge excavators, costing hundreds of thousands of euros each, were set on fire under cover of night. Pascal and his group were suspected, but so far there was no proof.

Bruno's emails to Pascal covered a lot of ground but I had encountered nothing incriminating beyond Bruno's assertion that water belongs in the water table, and not in industrial holding bays. Bruno lamented that the state had decided it would be a good idea to siphon groundwater from subterranean caverns and lakes and rivers, and to capture this water in huge plastic-lined "megabasins," where it would absorb leached toxins and be evaporated by the sun. This was a tragic idea, he said, with a destructive power that perhaps only someone who had spent considerable time underground might understand. Water, Bruno said, was *already* captured, in nature's own ingenious filtration and storage facilities inside the earth.

I was aware that Bruno Lacombe was against civilization, an "anti-civver," in activist slang. And that the rural, southwestern department Guyenne—and this remote corner of it to which I'd just arrived—was known for caves that held evidence of early humans. But I had assumed Bruno would be guiding Pascal's strategies for stopping the state's industrial projects here. It had not occurred to me that this mentor of Pascal's would have a fanatical belief in a failed species.

We can all agree, Bruno said, that it was the *Homo sapiens* who drove humanity headlong into agriculture, money, and industry. But the mystery of what happened to the Neanderthal and his humbler life is unresolved. Humans and Neanderthals might have overlapped for a good ten thousand years, Bruno wrote, but no one yet understood whether and how these two species had interacted. If, for instance, they knew of each other but kept apart. Or if there were so few people in Europe in the era when they overlapped, that amid rugged and impassable stretches of forest and mountain and river and snow, they weren't aware the other was there. Then again, Bruno said, geneticists have established that they mixed, and had offspring together—a sure indication that they knew the other "was there." Were these unions love? Or were they rape, the spoils of war? We will never know, Bruno said.

At first I wondered if these emails about the Neanderthal were a prank, as if Bruno had planted them for whoever had gained access to his account, to divert them from his actual correspondence with Pascal and the Moulinards. He covered a lot of ground but included nothing about sabotage, and he kept circling back to the Neanderthal—a species who, let's face it, could not hack it, or they'd be here still, and they weren't. They had vanished thousands of years ago, and no one seemed to know why, and no Neanderthal had come forward to explain.

Bruno pushed back against assumptions that *Homo sapiens* were simply cleverer and more adaptable, stronger, more indefatigable than the Neanderthals. In his treatment of these two species as opponents, I started to see them not in the diorama but in Ultimate Fighting Championship, with *Homo sapiens* a fighter who either gradually or all at once blazed into the ring on a winning streak.

It's tempting to picture the Neanderthal as a weak competitor, Bruno said, who was trounced by *Homo sapiens* (it was like he had access to my mental image of the two species facing off on Fight Night), but this was a cheap solution to the mystery, he said.

If there had been a war between them, it had been a soft war, a competition for resources, slow and relentless. The Neanderthals were skilled hunters, but as Europe warmed, the standards of excellence changed. The ice was gone, and a different body style was needed, lighter and built for endurance, along with new tracking methods, involving large groups in coordination, and different weapons and tools. While the Neanderthal bravely risked his life with a short-range thrusting spear, the *Homo sapiens* opted for a long-range throwing javelin. To kill from a distance was less valiant. It was killing without engaging in an intimate commitment to mortal danger, an embrace of gore, which Thal's weapon required. And yet, Bruno said, the concept of an air-propelled spear, a far more clinical approach to targeting game, was surely a winning method. Another advantage would have been *Homo sapiens*'s lighter frame, which required less food. And he—or rather she—was a more frequent propagator. Not by a lot. It was suspected that female *Homo sapiens* produced just ever so slightly higher numbers of offspring than female Thal. But after long stretches, thousands of years, these numbers would compound into huge population differences.

And yet many people carry Neanderthal traces, he said. Two percent, four percent, this measure of ancient life was stunning, given that there have been no living communities of full Neanderthals actively contributing to the gene pool for forty thousand years. It's as if our chromosomes cling to this old share, he said, as if it were a precious keepsake, an heirloom, the remnant of a person deep inside us who knew our world before the fall, before the collapse of humanity into a cruel society of classes and domination.

There are some who might say, "Two percent Thal, four percent Thal, why, that's not much, a rounding error. It leaves a whopping ninety-eight percent *sapiens*."

Indeed, Bruno wrote. Let us have a look at that majority share. Let us not deny that we are *occupied* by the *Homo sapiens*, and that we are, like it or not, ourselves *sapiens*, a figure who, we can all agree, has found himself in crisis. A man whose death drive is *in the driver's seat*.

H. sapiens needs help. But he doesn't want help.

We have endured a long twentieth century and its defeats, its failures and counterrevolutions. Now more than a decade into the twenty-first, it is time to reform consciousness, Bruno said. Not through isms. Not with dogma. But by summoning the most mystical secrets we have kept from ourselves: those concerning our past.

A psychoanalyst looks for clues of repression, of what a patient has hidden from others and, more importantly, hidden from himself. The deepest repression of all is the story of those who came first, before we did, long before the written-down. We must unpack what these earlier lives might mean for us, and for our future.

No, I'm not a primitivist, Bruno said, as if in swift answer to an accusation.

I face forward, he said, and any discussion of ancient history is only in regard to what is to come.

Look up, he commanded, in this email to Pascal Balmy and the group.

The roof of the world is open.

Let us count stars and live in their luminous gaze.

Which is to say, these stars' deep past, which is to say, our future, bright as Polaris.

THE ROOF OF THIS PLACE was not open, thank God.

But it leaked in two of the upstairs rooms. All of the roofing, which consisted of flat hand-chiseled tiles of slate, needed to be replaced, and there was a dispute between Lucien Dubois and his aunt Agathe over whether to pump money into the house and restore it, or cut losses and sell it.

The house was three hundred years old. Lucien had inherited it from his father, who inherited it from *his* father. I had asked him when his father's father's family had acquired the place and he'd looked unsure how to answer, as if the question itself betrayed a confusion on my part.

"It was our family house in, uh, the beginning."

Lucien's aunt Agathe was from the other side, his mother's family. Agathe was not a Dubois. She lived not too far from the Dubois place and had been looking after it. When Lucien was making arrangements for me to come here, he and Agathe argued on the phone about the roof and the future of the house.

I didn't care what Lucien decided. I was a temporary resident. The house was a perfect headquarters for my purposes here in the Guyenne Valley, despite the leaking roof. The location was convenient to Le Moulin, the group of people on whom I needed to keep tabs. It was protected, with a long private driveway. Any car turning onto the gravel from the little road far below would announce itself to me through the upstairs windows, which I kept open, alert to sounds. And it had a hilltop vantage. From the room I'd chosen on account of the fact it did not leak on this side of the house, I could see the entire valley. (It helped that I had high-powered binoculars with US-military-grade night vision.)

THE ROAD TO THE HOUSE led through dense forest canopy, discouraging anyone who didn't already know the place was here from investigating the turnoff, which I myself had missed while traveling the tiny and rural D43, upon my initial arrival.

There was no sign, no gate, no mailbox indicating I'd reached Lucien's family estate, just a narrow tunnel into the woods. As I turned up it, a large rust-brown raptor sailed low between trees in the half-lit undercanopy. I sensed it was accustomed to having this place to itself. Get used to me, I thought at it.

At the top of the road, I turned left, following Lucien's instructions. There was a row of tall poplars, tapered into points, like feathers. I like poplars. A straight line of them makes me think of driving, of going fast, into low Western sun, its rays illuminating their rippling leaves. Poplars remind me of Priest Valley, a beautiful non-place that I drove past with that boy who took the rap for Nancy. They are trees that remind me of a time when I felt invincible.

I passed the poplars and continued left, crossing through a walnut orchard, untended and ancient, which stretched out on both sides of the little gravel lane, just as Lucien had described.

I parked beyond the orchard, in front of the Dubois family manor, built of yellow limestone, large blocks of it that radiated daytime heat, although it was evening when I arrived, and cool.

The garden beyond the gates, now weeds, was where Lucien had thrown knives as a boy. Where he'd sifted the dirt for prehistoric tools while the adults drank eau-de-vie, water of life, a clear brandy distilled of this property's summer plums and autumn pears. (Eau-de-vie tastes the same—like gasoline—no matter what fruit it's made from, I didn't point out to Lucien.)

I'd had to hear all about his boyhood memories:

"Our report cards came in five colors: pink excellent; blue good; green satisfactory; yellow unsatisfactory; and red failing."

"My teacher at maternelle had beautiful long brown hair and a soft voice and she wore white sandals with little heels. Her name was Pauline."

"If I got all pinks, we could stay an extra week in the country."

It's the same, whether you're in a relationship with a man or pretending to be in one. They want you to listen when they tell you about their precious youth. And if they are my age, which Lucien is—we are both thirty-four—their younger boyhood, the innocent years, are the 1980s, and their teendom, the goodbye to innocence, is the 1990s, and whether in Europe or the US, it's similar music and more or less the same movies that they want to trot out and reminisce over, from an era I personally consider culturally stagnant.

I prefer to hear about the fixations of the oldest generation of European men, the ones whose youth involved encounters with war and killing and death, traitors and fascists and whores, collaboration and national shame: rites of passage into manhood, a true and real loss of innocence. Everyone has their type. And I'm okay with the generation just under them, the ones now in their sixties, because they at least know compulsory military service, or they know elective, extralegal refuge in the French Foreign Legion.

With Lucien and boys like him—who will forever remain mere boys—there is no war nor suffering nor valor. There is only some bland girl, some banal pop song, a romantic comedy, an August vacation.

August was around the corner, but no family was set to arrive. Lucien was grown, and those trips were long over. The trees from which fruit was made into liquor were still in the yard, gnarled, unpruned, their heavy limbs bending into the chest-high weeds.

Lucien had experienced his first romantic tryst here, with a much older girl, a university student from Toulouse, whose family had a place in the area. She wore a cashmere sweater and a heady Guerlain perfume. She had taken Lucien's virginity, he said, in an empty pig stall of an abandoned farm. I suppressed my laughter, laughed only inwardly, bearing witness to his adolescent memories as if they were not a cliché, and instead, as if they mattered.

Agathe had left the keys behind a dead geranium in a stone cubby next to the front entrance. I fitted a key into the lock in the heavy iron crossbar on the front door. The crossbar slid to one side. I opened both doors. The air inside was damp and cold like air in a cave.

I walked the broad uneven floor planks, my steps voluble, as if the weight of me was waking the floor from a long dormancy. I peered into rooms filled with furniture covered in sheets. Cobwebs wafted along the hallways, soft and dirty. I went upstairs and inspected bedrooms, opened shutters and windows to get a look at things and to dilute the smell of mold.

The ceiling plaster in half the rooms, under the leaking roof, was puckered and stained. Strips of wallpaper hung down like old movie posters dangling from a tack. On the floor of one of the rooms lay a rattrap bottom-up, a tail peeking from its wooden base. I picked up the trap with the rat strapped to it like it was his backpack and threw it out the window.

Each room was less inviting than the one before. They were crammed full of storage boxes and stacks of old magazines, *Paris Match*, the young faces on its covers water ruined. The largest bedroom featured neither leaks nor clutter but had been vandalized with children's stickers, cartoon babies, "Les Babies" was the logo, pasted onto the furniture and the walls.

I chose my room for its strategic view of the road, its working electricity, a lack of water stains, and a minimum of "Les Babies" stickers. (There was one on the bedside table, but I could cover it.) The sun had set, and from the windows next to the bed I could see a few stars initiating their night watch through the haze of dusk.

Downstairs, the kitchen had an ancient stone sink. The oven appeared to be fired by wood or coal. Next to it was a hot plate from the 1970s, its crooked burners caked white from use. The Dubois family had given up on ancient traditions and embraced this hot plate. Whatever. I was fine with a hot plate.

After surveying rooms, I ate a ham and butter sandwich that I had picked up in Boulière, light on ham and light on butter and mostly bad baguette, the kind that turns to crumbly powder when it goes stale. Realizing I wasn't hungry, I left the rest of the sandwich for the rats.

There were a couple bars of Orange.fr cell service so I texted Lucien that I had made it to the house. I didn't say that his family's beloved ancestral "manoir" looked like a scene from a horror movie. I said it was lovely here if rustic, and that I was meeting Pascal Balmy tomorrow.

Lucien had arranged this meeting.

He had expressed concern that I didn't have a career. He believed I was a former grad student who had lost her way. (I *was* a former grad student, but I had found my way instead of losing it.)

Lucien's idea of connecting me to Pascal (he believed it was his own idea to connect me to Pascal) was that I could translate into English the book that Pascal and his comrades at Le Moulin had written anonymously, since I had a facility with languages and a lot of free time.

—i mean, i will be meeting pascal if he shows up, I texted.

—He'll show up, Lucien texted back. For you, he'll show. He's curious about you. He's keen to work together. I talked to him about it. But I should warn you . . . he's charismatic.

Charisma does not originate inside the person called "charismatic." It comes from the need of others to believe that special people exist.

Without having met him, I was certain that Pascal Balmy's charisma, like anyone's—Joan of Arc's, let's say—resided only in the will of other people to believe. Charismatic people understand this will-to-believe best of all. They exploit it. That is their so-called charisma.

—are you jealous? I asked in reply.

Pascal was Lucien's old friend, and I'd be meeting him without Lucien there to mediate.

—It's not that. He gets the upper hand. Look at all these people who followed him down there from Paris. It's pretty weird. But that's how he is. I mean, I have known him forever and I still try to impress him. It's pathetic.

(I was already attuned to what, in Lucien, was pathetic.)

—he won't get the upper hand with me, I texted back, and for once I was being completely and totally honest.

BRUNO LACOMBE RECEIVED EMAILS from only one account, from an address that was used, I knew, by multiple people at Le Moulin, among them Pascal Balmy, certainly the main correspondent, although the queries sent to Bruno were never signed. They were always just a short question, open-ended, which Bruno answered in depth.

Such as the one they sent as a follow-up to Bruno's discussion of Neanderthals' depression and their smoking habits. Their question was about plant origins and tobacco: Was tobacco not a New World plant? they asked.

"Given how stringent we've been with our own farming techniques," they wrote, "and our approach to rewilding what might be native to this part of France, we are confused at the idea that tobacco, which we regard as invasive, could have always been here."

Bruno said, in reply, that without making direct accusations of anyone asking such a question, he could attack that person's conditioning and the external forces that had shaped their attitudes, leading to a profound misunderstanding of migration patterns and an abuse of the concepts "native" and "new."

No, he said, tobacco is *not* a New World plant.

And in any case, people have been in the Americas for tens of thousands of years.

The spread of people over the face of the planet was not a simple three-act play structure, of up and out of Africa (I), into Europe (II), and across a land bridge (III). Bruno said it was far more diffuse and mysterious how people had settled various corners of the earth. The idea that they flowed in a single direction, for instance, had to be false. Do you walk in only one direction? he asked rhetorically. Of course you don't, he answered. Over the parts of a day, a season, a year, a life, people move in many directions, as locus points with their own free will, though he put "free" here into scare quotes.

The more education a person has, the more scare quotes they seem to use, and Bruno was no exception (and neither am I, even as I deplore this habit in others). The less education, the more accidental quotes, whose purpose is the opposite of scaring, and simply to declare that a thing has a name but is being named by someone without a high level of literacy: "Corn Muffins," handwritten by a minimum-wage employee on a sign in a bakery case. "Sale," also handwritten. The not-so-literate and the hyper-literate both love quotation marks, while most people use them only to indicate, in written form, when someone is speaking. In my life before this life, as a graduate student, there were know-it-all women in my department who held their hands up and curved their pointer and middle fingers to frame a word or phrase they were voicing with irony, as a critique. They were fake tough girls who were not tough at all, with their fashion choices veering to chunky shoes and a leather jacket from a department store. They were getting PhDs in rhetoric at Berkeley, as I had planned to, before I abandoned that plan (and spared myself their fate, which was to subject themselves to academic job interviews in DoubleTree hotel rooms at a Modern Language Association conference). Listening to them prattle on and bend their fingers to air quote, a craven substitution of cynicism for knowledge, I sometimes used to imagine a sharp blade cutting across the room at a certain height, lopping off the fingers of these scare-quoting women.

IT HAD BEEN a long and tedious journey from Marseille to the Dubois place. Eight hours. I had made a lot of stops to try to keep things interesting. Then again, the trip might have been eight hours because I was doing that.

I was on toll roads, pulling over to drink regional wines in highway travel centers, franchised and generic, with food steaming under orange heat lamps, each of these travel centers offering local products. Lavender oils, for instance, always made at monasteries, as if the monks worshipped lavender instead of God. Or dried truffles, mustards, and glass jars of jellied meats that look like cat food, and which French people call a "terrine" and eat as if it were not cat food.

It all gets mixed up in your stomach anyhow, I heard no one say as people lined up to buy this stuff.

I sampled these wines from the vantage of plastic seating overlooking fuel pump and highway. I sipped rosé from the Luberon at a clammily air-conditioned Monop' off the A55, a chaotic place where children screeched and a haggard woman dragged a dirty mop over the floor. The rosé was delicate and fruity, crisp as ironed linen.

I found a Pécharmant from the oldest vintner in Bergerac at the L'Arche Cafeteria on the autoroute A7, a wine that was woody with notes of ambergris and laurel and maybe dried apricot.

I enjoyed a white Bordeaux of Médoc provenance en plein air at a roadside fuel stop where a trucker farted loudly while paying for his diesel at the automatic pump, the loose valves of his truck, like his own loose valves, clattering away. This white Bordeaux was smooth as a silk garment in a virgin's trousseau. I could have been a little buzzed by this point, five hours into my drive. This cold, dry white wine sent me dreaming about a world where all my clothes were white and I slept on white sheets and would never be traded for a dowry or violated by rough and unworthy men or forced to drink anything less than the finest French wines of the smallest and oldest and most esteemed appellations, and in a way I could say that I was living that life, right here at this gas station. At least in spirit I was.

I care about fine wine but not about food, and because the terrine is efficient—comes in its own container and can be consumed unheated—I stole two jars of it from one of these travel centers, the weight of the jars giving a new tug to the leather straps of my handbag as I purchased my wine.

It wasn't that I believed the wine I bought was payment enough for my jars of human cat food. Stealing is a way to stop time. Also, it refocuses the mind, the senses, if they become dulled, for instance by drinking. Stealing puts reality into sharper relief.

You're in a highway travel center, people in a great flux and flow, coming and going and milling and choosing, the cashiers in a fugue state of next and next and next. And in order to locate the precise moment when you can take unseen, you slow it all down. You make time stop. You insert into reality what composers call a "fermata," and while time is stopped, you put something in your bag.

In this way, I test my fitness. I test my ability to see. I gauge what other people see, and also, what they fail to see.

TREKKING AND HOBO WANDERING, Bruno continued, in parsing their question of Old World and New, was *not* how human beings had settled the earth. To leave Africa, to leave anyplace, and to go someplace else, in this false three-act structure, gave the impression of people walking arduous and long distances, like refugees or religious pilgrims, looking for a meal and a place to bed down. Taking off their heavy backpack with a "Phew."

In fact, he said, migration patterns were slow, and formed incrementally: not by trekking. Simply by *living*. People might stay in an area for a length of time, and when the seasons change, or the hunting stock is depleted, or the waters return to a flood plain or bog that had offered bounteous foraging, or when they stumble upon a place whose features seem desirable or track a herd of animals over a season, they might resettle in the new area where they find themselves, and it could be a short walk, a day's walk, or several weeks' walk, from their old area. Multiply these movements by tens upon tens of thousands of years, and that is the history of the settlement of the earth.

But how people had gotten from one landmass to another over the last half million years was not yet understood, Bruno said. Polynesians had crossed the ocean long before European navigators ever dreamed of leaving shore. On another occasion he would take up this subject but for now, he implored them to understand that nothing was how they might have thought it to be, and Neanderthals in Europe and Asia—*without question*—smoked tobacco.

They weren't even the first to do so, he added. That accomplishment goes to Thal's earlier ancestor *Homo erectus* (Rectus, in Bruno's parlance), nominally recognized for the rather low achievement of standing—it is in the name, Bruno said, Person Upright, but in fact, the true accomplishment of *Homo erectus* was that he was the first man to play with fire. And we must infer, Bruno told them, that the first man to play with fire was *also the first man to smoke*.

But where did Rectus *get* fire? We have all been taught the myth of Prometheus, Bruno said, in which is birthed this concept that man is an individual who was given, instead of a special trait, the ability to generate heat.

As the story went, Prometheus and his famously dumb brother Epimetheus were assigned the important job of distributing a positive trait to each of the animals in the kingdom on earth. Epimetheus plunged into this work, handing out traits—to bees, the ability to make honey, to deer, a talent for leaping and scampering, to owls, a head that could swivel 270 degrees, and so forth. But by the time Epimetheus got to people, he had run out of qualities in his quality sack.

It was at this point, when the sack was empty and Epimetheus had nothing to bestow, that his brother Prometheus stepped in, stole fire from the gods, and gave that to man as his positive quality.

But here is the catch, Bruno said. The catch is that fire is not always positive. And more crucially, fire is not a quality. It is not a trait that a life-form can possess.

It isn't night vision or silent wing feathers or a hinged jaw, a spring-loaded capacity to pounce. Man, bland and featureless in this myth, lacking in his own special trait, was condemned, instead, to ingenuity, to being a devious little bastard.

In his ontological featurelessness, different from the rest of the animals in the kingdom, man had to figure out how to work with fire to compensate for lack. Man would come to rely on fire as a crutch. His use of fire would stand in for what man was denied, the possession of a positive trait, as all the other living creatures were given.

This myth of the brothers, one dumb and the other crafty, Bruno told them, and the substitution of technology for traits, was, let's face it, not entirely mythical. In fact, it was accurate, he said, in explaining the miseries and devastations of the world, in accounting for the use of fire to do bad instead of good, to hoard, steal, ravage, pillage, and oppress.

The use of fire for harm instead of good seems to have taken hold, suspiciously, and damningly, just as the Neanderthals began to disappear and *Homo sapiens* rose up, an interglacial bully who shaped the world we're stuck with.

The culprit seems clear, Bruno said, but human history, the story of us, was still a great riddle. Examinations of the past, of dirt and DNA, could show us new ideas of where the entire project on earth *might* have headed. Currently, he said, we are headed toward extinction in a shiny, driverless car, and the question is: How do we exit this car?

I pictured a driver's helmeted tuck-and-roll from a Top Fuel dragster, his car in flames, his body in a flameproof suit, rolling and rolling in that interminable few seconds before the emergency crew comes running, crimson flags signal TRACK HAZARD, and track workers blast foam-up fire retardant.

But if it was all of us on planet Earth inside this shiny, driverless car, then what would we be exiting, besides reality? What would we tumble into, if not a void?

I AM A BETTER DRIVER after a few drinks, more focused.

Instead of trying to read my phone or put on lipstick, after several glasses of these regional wines I faced forward and held the wheel with both hands. Drink lulled me into doing only what I was supposed to: drive the car.

Except that I decided toll roads were going to put me to sleep, so I opted for a scenic route on secondary roads. I got lost winding through the Massif Central and its gear-grinding turns.

Sure, I was reckless with the clutch. But it's hard for me to feel that rental cars have value. This one, a small hatchback Škoda, cost eight euros a day. (They had given me a lump sum as travel budget, and so I'd chosen economy.) How did these companies make money? They had brand-new cars. You barely had to pay for them. And they didn't inspect the car before you drove it out of the parking structure.

The Škoda was "clean diesel," an oxymoron that was a metaphor for something, but I didn't know what.

Clean diesel, clean coal. Add the word "clean" and boom—it's clean.

My navigation was off, and the scenic route took me way too scenically over a summit. "Oh, come on," I said out loud as useless vistas, pink-hued Roman ruins and high-walled castles on jagged peaks, reared up left and right.

I passed a tower on a cliff, its top edges eaten away like a sugar cone, at that point when the ice cream is gone, and the child is contractually obliged to take bites of its tasteless container. "God damn it," I said.

These breathtaking vistas were unappealing because they confirmed I was lost. I wanted only an indication by this point that I was headed northwest, toward the city of Boulière, which Lucien had depicted as a cluster of crooked, dirty streets populated by ugly people in crappy cars, and a good place to stop at Carrefour or Leader Price, to stock up before arriving at the Dubois family estate. I saw no signs for Boulière. I was in remote forested highlands. I pulled off at the top of a summit, into an unpaved lot adjacent to a building, some kind of mountain inn, hoping for directions.

The inn was closed. It looked not to have been open in quite a while. Its windows were boarded. There was graffiti along its exterior walls, names and symbols fuzzed out in spray paint, writing that reflected no skill, added no beauty. This kind of graffiti, common enough in Europe, seems like little more than uglification. Certain crimes are natural enough, even serious ones. Murder is understandable when you think about it. It's human to want to annihilate your enemy, or to demonstrate to the world: *this* is how angry I am right now, even if you might later regret killing a person. But to spray-paint an inscrutable sloppy symbol on the outside of a building? Why?

It had just rained up here. The air was damp and warm and close, like human breath. The lot was crisscrossed with patterned ruts from truck tires. The rain had left enormous puddles that were the tint of milk chocolate, their surface silk-screened in sky. There were no trucks. Just ruts. A mist hung in the branches of the low trees beyond the lot, as if a cloud had descended on this mountain and left its ragged parts among the woods.

It felt like a place of aftermath, where something had happened.

I peed in the wooded area beyond the open lot. While squatting, I encountered a pair of women's Day-Glo-orange underpants snagged in the bushes at eye level.

This did not seem odd. Truck ruts and panties snagged on a bush: that's "Europe." The real Europe is not a posh café on the rue de Rivoli with gilded frescoes and little pots of famous hot chocolate, baby macaroons colored pale pink and mint green, children bratty from too much shopping and excited by the promise of the cookies, the ritual reward of a Saturday's outing with their mother. That is a conception of Europe cherished by certain Parisians and as imaginary as the pastoral scenes in the frescoes on the walls of the posh café.

The real Europe is a borderless network of supply and transport. It is shrink-wrapped palettes of superpasteurized milk or powdered Nesquik or semiconductors. The real Europe is highways and nuclear power plants. It is windowless distribution warehouses, where unseen men, Polish, Moldovan, Macedonian, back up their empty trucks and load goods that they will move through a giant grid called "Europe," a Texas-sized parcel of which is called "France." These men will ignore weight regulations on their loads, and safety inspections on their brakes. They will text someone at home in their ethno-national language, listen to pop music in English, and get their needs met locally, in empty lots on mountain passes.

The only mystery is where they find the women for these occasions, but even that isn't so hard to imagine. A girl or woman fallen on hard times, not French, and without EU documents, stuck in a rural outpost, picking her way out to the main road in impractical high-heeled shoes of flesh-biting imitation leather, aloe in her purse for rapid-fire hand jobs. She had left her underwear in these woods. Big deal. Her world is full of disposability. The panties hanging on a bush in front of my face are a package of three for five euros at Carrefour. They are like Kleenex. You sweat or leak or bleed into them and then toss them on a bush, or in the trash, or you flush them and clog the plumbing, someone else's plumbing, ideally.

I had been drinking, as I said. And I had to go. I was "making beer," as an unshaven Moldovan truck driver might put it. A foaming reservoir filled its makeshift banks on the ground over which I squatted, and then it overflowed those banks, streaming like advance troops sent downhill on a scouting mission. I was still peeing and watching my pee make its way down the hill when I heard footsteps.

I startled. Was someone here?

I AM TOUCHED BY YOUR QUESTION, Bruno told them, of why it is that we are alone here on earth, the only remaining human species. How did we go from multiple and thriving branches to measly *H. sapiens*, who faces no competitors, a lone runner on an existential racetrack, running and running, having somehow lapped the competition to arrive at species monopoly?

It is, to say the least, doctrinal to take at face value this idea that it is only us who occupy the earth, we runners on our lonely track, which we share with no other survivors, of all the populations of different strains of human who once thrived.

And I have been as guilty as anyone, Bruno said, of upholding this doctrine, of assuming that we are alone, and that there is no one else. And yet, just as we are so certain that it's only us here, to the point of wondering, as you are, why this has come to be the case, I would point out to you that every culture in the world has its legends concerning the continued existence of other human strains, stories that sustain various versions of a universal fantasy, that we are *not* alone.

There's the legend of Sasquatch, for instance, in the Pacific Northwestern mountain ranges of the United States and British Columbia, sometimes known as Bigfoot.

There's the "Soviet" Sasquatch of the Himalayas, sometimes referred to as the Abominable Snowman, or Yeti.

There is the tall and hirsute humanoid consistently if rarely spotted over centuries in the mountains of Nepal, known of as the "mungo."

In Gansu, they have the Bear Man. In Nanshan, the Man-Beast, with pleasing features and an agile gate.

In the Gobi Desert there's the Almas, or "Mongolian Bigfoot," a leggy and furred creature who is a fierce fighter and can run like the wind, and whose habitat maps to the same remote roaming area as Przewalski's horse.

Bruno went into a discussion of mid-twentieth-century Soviet cryptozoology scholars, who had worked without glory or compensation on this subject for decades, compiling oral histories concerning "wild men." The Soviet anthropologist Boris Nevsky, a specialist on revolts in medieval France, had come to suspect that peasant uprisings had been driven by peoples of Neanderthal heritage. Nevsky had hoped to research still-existent strains of these people in the Pyrenees mountains but was not granted a travel visa. Stuck in the Soviet Union, he was appointed to head the Commission to Study Relic Hominids, and redirected his field work to Central Asia, specifically the Pamir Mountains and Himalayas, where, for thirty years, he traveled and recorded sightings.

While Dr. Nevsky had at first allowed that the stories he heard on his travels, of fantastical sightings of wild men (and wild women as well), might be mythic, Nevsky could not deny that the details of the sightings—the pronounced and heavy ridged brow, teeth as large as a camel's, a sound these people made that was like the squeal of a rabbit at its moment of slaughter—were almost identical, in region after region.

Bruno said that the farther Dr. Nevsky traveled, the more convinced he became that these stories could not all have the same details by chance alone. In conducting his field research, Nevsky little by little lost his capacity to keep the stories of wild people within the territory of culture, of myth. The stories broke their corral, and the Wild Man, for Dr. Nevsky, became real.

From what I know, Bruno said, Nevsky's papers remain in the archives of Moscow State University, and thanks to Vladimir Kreshnev, who has catalogued them, and the research done since by subsequent cryptozoologists, we are compelled to cease resting on our laurels and assuming our own monopoly on human life.

Yes, take your sigh, Bruno wrote. *Bigfoot?* he asked rhetorically. *Real???* he jeered in repeated question marks.

I feel your skepticism, he told them. My own is voluminous, I assure you. Who knows if these Soviet cryptozoologists I speak of are not clinically insane. Who is to say that their "research" isn't hallucinatory, clownish, and faked?

But whether in Central Asia, or in the dark and wild heights of the Pyrenees, or here in the Guyenne Valley, in secret rock shelters—whether atavistically Neanderthal or some other strain of hominin, somehow living undetected on the margins of the modern world—such wild people already do very much exist. They do live. Guess where? That's right. *In our minds*, and in our culture, on account of these endless legends of a Sasquatch or snowman that we spin and dream of, hope for, and fear.

You can't get through your own childhood, Bruno wrote, without encountering a hairy, solitary, running man, or part-man part-beast, a creature that legend suggests might lurk in any woods you cross.

Every culture has wild regions, wild lands, whether forest or desert or steppe. Every wild land contains some wild person, human or humanoid of unknown origin, who lives separate from the rest, separate from the built world, the social world. I have come upon no culture without such a legend, of a man who lives in nature, whose life is formed of secrecy, of a vow never to join us.

Perhaps these legends, Bruno surmised, are meant to establish what is possible. To prove that somehow, someone—not us—has managed to evade the dominant reality (that we ourselves have failed to evade).

Perhaps it comforts us that there are stories—even if we don't believe them—that we *H. sapiens* are not alone. The breadcrumb trail of cryptozoology becomes a site of resistance to Big Science, and to crushing pessimism, this lore as a place where people can say, but . . . but . . . *but are you sure?*

THE PERSON I HEARD IN THE WOODS turned out to be me. I had stepped on some kind of crinkly food wrapper that made a noise.

I have quick reflexes.

The downside of my reflexes can be overreaction. (I had peed on my sandal and foot.)

Later that day I found Boulière, the largest town in this part of the Guyenne, with a ring road of car lots, tractor dealerships, and a couple of supermarkets. I stocked up on grocery basics and unrefrigerated six-packs and headed due west into a remote river valley, toward the Dubois family estate, which was not far from Vantôme and Pascal Balmy's radical farming cooperative, Le Moulin.

Vantôme was not on my way to the Dubois place, but I detoured to have a quick look around.

The housing stock was grim little dwellings of gray cinder block. There were no gardens, no signs of care. Many of the buildings looked abandoned, their windows broken, stone walls toppled, trees growing through caved-in barn roofs.

From what I'd gathered, the main industry in the higher elevations had been logging. The hills above Vantôme were scattered with bald areas, like the scalp of someone with an autoimmune condition. The nicest feature was a lake just beyond town, perhaps man-made, but pleasant, with a large and grassy recreational area. A few old men were dispersed along the lakeshore, still as statues, their fishing poles over the water.

I took a road that bordered Le Moulin and saw the commune's sun-singed squashes, their scraggly lettuces. Their land did not border a creek or river tributary and would be difficult to irrigate. The soil here was rocky. Only activists from Paris would take up subsistence farming in a place like this.

Much of the population had fled this region for its lack of jobs, its stagnancy, its disconnection from modern life. There was no future here, and so young people had moved to cities, to Toulouse or Bordeaux or farther, to seek jobs in factories or in the service sector, to get an education, try to find a pathway into middle-class life. There were still a few small dairy operations, but most of the locals who remained here had given up on farming, acquired satellite TV, and drank all day. With the butcher and baker in their villages long gone, the people in this valley had to drive to Boulière, to shop at Leader Price.

Corporations from outside the region were buying up land for large-scale farming of seed corn, as part of a state-led initiative to revitalize the Guyenne with a monocrop economy—corn, corn, and more corn. These operations needed water. The "megabasins" the state was planning would dedicate the region's water to megagrowers. Between Boulière and Tayssac I had seen this corn, vast fields of green, sterile as a Nebraskan Monsanto horizon. I had driven past the new megabasin where equipment had been destroyed. Construction barriers blocked the view, but the site was active. I heard machines. Dust clouds boiled upward. There were temporary trailers for security, and gendarmerie parked at the entrance to the site. The perimeter fencing was covered by sheeting printed with vague slogans, "no water without management," "no future without water," and "let's work together."

There had been rioting and violence over these megabasins in other parts of France, with serious casualties—people who lost an eye or a hand, and scores of police vehicles torched. What began as a peaceful demonstration tended to end with masked activists throwing Molotov cocktails toward a phalanx of armored riot police, who responded with ferocious volleys of pepper balls and beatings and arrests.

After the excavators in Tayssac were torched, Pascal Balmy had been suspected. An investigation was opened, but local residents did not give tips. The people around Vantôme and Tayssac proved uncooperative. They seemed to regard the anarchists at Le Moulin as friends, or at least not as their enemies.

Instead, the locals treated the corporate farming operations, the contractors building the megabasin, the police, the representatives from the Ministries of Agriculture and Rural Coherence as their enemies.

II

PRIEST VALLEY

MY INITIAL CONTACT with Lucien Dubois had been a cold bump. I had approached him in public, stranger to stranger.

That was six months ago, in Paris. He was at a bar near the Place des Vosges, playing pinball in a fedora like he thought he was in a French new-wave film from 1963.

I knew plenty about him, and that he had a kind of mannered affection for old Paris, that he conceived of reality as stage-directed in black and white. The truth is that even when Jean-Luc Godard and people like that were making those movies in black and white, with actors in fedoras who talk like gangsters, they were already an affectation.

I went into that bar near the Place des Vosges, sat down, and ordered a pastis. I was wearing tight jeans with suspenders. My white T-shirt was worn and thin and transparent, the suspenders framing my large breasts, which do not require a bra.

Are my breasts real?

Does it matter?

I sipped my drink. Lucien got an extra game. I sensed it was for me that he was playing so well, bringing his whole body weight into his command of the flippers, as he sent the little silver ball up the rails and watched it make its way back toward him like a loyal pet, before being shot back up to ricochet from bumper to slot.

He continued to play. I ordered a second pastis.

Watching Lucien work the flippers, hold this machine on either side of its narrow end in order to guide the ball and control the game, it seemed to me that this posture, of man and machine, recalled some ancient form: a man behind the box that he steers—a plow, perhaps, or cart. Boys playing pinball in pantomime of an old world where men drove plows over fields, steered carts that were filled with hay or manure. In this old world, those unlucky men who had no land to farm, no hay to cut, no animals to rear and abuse, pushed carts filled with junk for sale. "Tinkers," these men were called, the dreaded and wretched tinker, an outcast and thief who wandered the countryside pushing his cart and ringing his bell and selling his broken and stolen wares.

The pinball machine seemed to me some stationary and atavistic workhorse wagon, the old work reformulated as play. No longer a plow or a tinker's cart, this old box was now in a Paris bar, a game for boys and men to play. It enticed, with its pulsing lights: activate me.

I don't waste my time on games. I don't know if this is because I'm not a man, or because I'm not into games.

Lucien was out of coins.

The bartender, drying glasses with a cloth, asked him, "Is that it for today, boss?"

"It depends," Lucien said. He was staring at me.

I smiled shyly and looked at the bottles lined up behind the bar, and at Lucien in the bar's mirror.

He came over and sat down next to me.

"Hi."

"Hello."

"I'm Lucien," he said.

"I'm Sadie," I said.

I even had an American passport with that name.

REGARDING PROMETHEUS, we could ask if early man such as Thal, Bruno wrote to them, *had* been bestowed with special qualities. And if it was only modern man, *H. sapiens*, who lacked them.

The strong jaw, the big brain, the heavy bones and large face, these were positive traits. Perhaps Thal, he said, was a man graced with good qualities, and *H. sapiens*, in his plunder and advance toward the devastating dawn of agriculture, was a man with no such grace, a man without qualities, who substituted violence for the hole at the center of his heart.

But this business of Prometheus was of course a detail from the *Greek* account of human history. Here Bruno italicized "Greek." His emails, I noticed, contained quite a bit of italicizing, meaning either that he was *helping* them interpret his emails by *deliberately emphasizing* key components, or he had just discovered the shortcut key Command-I, which sent his words slanting rightward, and he found this combination of keys and their applied effects *fun*.

Bruno Lacombe was born in 1937. An elder's turn toward, his embrace of, technology is perhaps akin to the fresh perspective of a child: to misunderstand the adult world, and to misuse it, are the precursors to innovation.

While the members of Le Moulin were mostly people in their twenties and thirties, a generation pinned under the crosshatched straps of the technological harness that now held the world in place, Bruno was not pinned under those straps, and in his lack of computer proficiency, his accidental use of 24-point font, or a repeated resend of the same message or a blank message, such glitches were perhaps by-products of Bruno Lacombe's freedom from what enslaved most people. At the same time, he was an old person trying to use email.

I applauded Bruno Lacombe's technological fumbles, which were surely responsible for the footprint he left on a discussion board dedicated to Soviet cryptozoologist Boris Nevsky. Bruno had posted a question about Nevsky's archives, and whether any of Nevsky's papers had been uploaded to the internet. His username on this discussion board was his email address—which contained his full name, and so it had popped up in Google—a wanadoo.fr account whose password I guessed correctly on my eleventh try.

In the emails themselves, Bruno explained that the diaphanous and spectral nature of this form of communication suited him, but, he caveated, it was important to remember that every technology is blessing or disaster, depending.

Of that moment when man first sparked fire—if such a moment could be isolated, and more and more these days he believed it could *not* be, in the sense that to believe in an original moment you had to believe in clock time, in calendar time, and he was dispensing with those concepts—he told Pascal and the group that although he himself was a crudivore, meaning he forwent the cooked, he did not reject fire completely. He maintained a hearth and used it. He said he built small fires. He said only a fool makes a large fire. He repeated this in a few different emails he sent them, like a mantra, a slogan, a cryptic cue.

I assumed he meant that a fire is best kept discreet. In the ancient world, and in this one, too, a fire would signal a person's location. It might telegraph that a person had meat and was cooking it. A big fire was perhaps like a dinner bell, inviting unwanted guests to join you.

I took note of Bruno's proviso about fools and big fires, sensing it could be a warning to Pascal and the group, either to stay under the radar, in regard to Tayssac, or to plan acts that were more subtle and sly.

Bruno said it amused him that anthropologists had never figured out how our ancestors had built fires inside caves without suffering the mal-effects of smoke. Live in a cave for a while, he said, and you will know the answer. When the hearth is correctly positioned in the dead center of the space, smoke travels up, pools along the ceiling, and forms one tidy column as it exits. The smoke does not wander and linger; it knows where to go. The lower edges of the cave remain breathable, safe for sleeping, for preparing food, and for man's paramount art, which is thinking.

Bruno had renounced much of the baggage that came with man's ascent into the world of the cooked, but fire itself he regarded as mystical. It was fire that allowed the Thals to sleep for long stretches, warm and safe from animals, who were warded off by the plume of smoke exiting their cave. Protected from predators and from harsh climates by their fire, the Neanderthals had slept for longer and longer periods, from generation to generation. Sleep was key to thought, and to intellectual development. As man's thoughts became ever more complex, the longer he needed to sleep. The longer man slept, Bruno said, the more he dreamed, and the more penetrating and wondrous his waking thought became.

In his own cave, and its semblance of ancient life, Bruno said that he practiced sleep as a discipline. He had trained himself to sleep upwards of twelve hours a night. Sleep is time travel, he said. Sleep is revolutionary. And most importantly, he said, sleep feels good.

The more a person dreams, the more they imagine upon waking or before bedding back down, in those states, hypnagogic or waking, and hypnopompic or drifting off (Bruno had "pomp" and "gog" reversed, but I knew what he meant), which give us access to the invisible-real.

The point, he said, was that imagination and sleep and dreaming were the interwoven tresses of a single glossy braid, and this thick braid was a sign of health in a grand sense, of the heaven right here on earth, a garden of delights you should not wait for, pray for, but live in, occupy, and enjoy.

I pictured a braid that was a rope. I could not picture what it led to. All I saw was the rope.

LUCIEN AND I left the bar together and walked. It was a fresh and mild sunny day. We wound up side by side on our backs in the grass of the Place des Vosges.

Lucien pointed to a building along the square and said the writer Victor Hugo had lived there. He moved his arm so that it made glancing contact with my arm. I didn't move mine and he didn't move his. We lay with our arms touching.

After a while he turned toward me and ran his thumb over my face very lightly, and then he kissed me. I kissed back, but with a prim hesitancy. No need to rush this. Let him believe he's making every move and every decision. Let him be certain he is in control.

He sat up on an elbow and looked at me. I was aware that my hair was fanning out over the grass and that this was the repose of a woman in bed, her hair spread over the pillow, a man above her looking down.

"What," he said, smiling, detecting a spark in my eye, which he read as a spark of my happiness, my interest in him, presuming my emotions in this moment, us staring at each other, mirrored his own emotions at this moment.

I *was* happy. So happy I could almost feel my pupils dilate as I met his gaze. Things were going as I'd planned them to.

And then he leaned in like billions before him have done, acting upon a desire to kiss some woman. In such a scene between new lovers, a moment repeated everywhere all the time with no originality to it—none—Lucien surely felt that something singular and novel was taking place.

He pulled away from our shy kisses, gazing at me, thinking, deciding. And then he came down over me, shading my face from the sun, pushed his warm lips against mine, and thrust his tongue in my mouth with all the passion that his restrained manners, his effete bourgeois politeness, would have allowed him to muster.

For Lucien, what happened that day fit with how he saw himself, and who he wanted to be.

It felt right to him that he would fall in love with a stranger he encountered while playing pinball in an empty bar on a weekday afternoon, a mysterious woman with a cute American accent (my *R*s are unapologetic American *R*s) and a body he wanted to subdue but would be in no hurry to subdue, because he was well-bred (and on account of that breeding, inhibited).

I could sense him gathering a false hindsight that afternoon in the Place des Vosges, shaping a retrospective narrative, the thing a person tells himself about fate, about how everything had seemed fated, when the only evidence of this fate is *how things went*.

Something happens and people think, This was meant to be. The random nature of luck and of incident is too disturbing to acknowledge. I'm not the first to know this. It's in the Bible. Ecclesiastes declares that life has no meaning, that evil will be rewarded, and goodness punished. He says that even the most honorable man can be left in town to die in the street, while the greediest fool gets a eulogy and a proper burial. But either people skip that part of the Old Testament, or they never read the Bible at all, and instead they follow their instinct to mythify a sequence of random events and the stream of strangers they encounter in life: Good things happen to them or people they like and they think, "justice." Bad things happen to people they don't like and once again they think, "justice."

This is part of why a cold bump can be so effective: Lucien believed that he summoned me into his life by heart alone, by fate. He believed he deserved to fall in love (everyone believes they deserve this) and, in his specific case, with someone like me. His satisfied desire was a reward, as if it were part of a grand design based on birthright, on being from a good family, and making good choices, moral choices, and aesthetic ones too.

We took turns kissing and talking, lying on the grass of the Place des Vosges. Lucien was telling me about Victor Hugo, how Victor Hugo, exiled to the island of Guernsey in the English Channel, had heard voices in the waves, addressing him on the subject of the future of France.

As he spoke about Victor Hugo, I was hearing a voice in the waves of my own thoughts. What it said was that this thing with Lucien was a done deal. A done deal, the voice said. Which might also be, at least indirectly, about the future of France.

Three months later, we were living together.

LUCIEN DIDN'T ASK A LOT OF QUESTIONS, either before I moved into his apartment or after. He wanted to marry me and often told people I was his wife.

I said I made my income walking dogs, as this located me in far-flung neighborhoods like Vincennes, where I was in fact spending time, and had seen, in its large park, young people walking a jumble of random dogs that were not their own, and I had decided it was a good lie. Walking dogs was solitary and independent, piecemeal and part-time. Informal work that was impossible to verify, and from which Lucien would want to save me.

I said I was from Priest Valley, California. To French people, this sounds fine—poetic, even. Priest Valley. The name perhaps sent Lucien, a cinephile and aspiring moviemaker, picturing the casting ground for a Robert Bresson film, a land of rural pieties. A bare wood table, a tin cup, a flock of sheep, the clang of a church bell heard from a distance, et cetera.

In fact, no one lives in Priest Valley, California, not a single person. And not even people from California could tell you where Priest Valley is. Priest Valley is a signpost. Beyond it, on the left side of the road, are three ruined and vacant outbuildings and a row of untended old poplar trees that some settler must have planted a hundred years ago (trees that I had thought of when I'd first glimpsed the poplars at the top of the little road leading to the country home of Lucien's family). Priest Valley is on Highway 198, which is itself unknown to native Californians, a route passing between mountain ranges in the very center of the state, a rural two-lane byway traversing a valley of pure green, like you're gazing at the landscape through a Heineken bottle. There are no ranches, no developments, nothing but bottle-green hills.

The name Priest Valley exists on maps and was satisfactory to Lucien, as it would be to any of the people I might interact with at Le Moulin, Pascal Balmy or any of the others, if they inquired where I was from.

But my involvement with Lucien, childhood friend of Pascal Balmy, would reduce the number of questions they might ask, and curtail the usual paranoia you find with insurrectionary groups.

Lucien said he wanted Pascal to be a witness at our wedding, which was charming, in the sense that it's charming when I know a whole lot more about a stranger and how he thinks than his best friend knows: Pascal would never have agreed. Ritual bonds, to Pascal Balmy, must not be tainted by the involvement of the state, which is his enemy. There won't be a wedding anyhow, as by the time all the paperwork for such an affair might be completed, I will be gone.

But for now, I was the romantic partner of Lucien.

I was from Priest Valley, California.

I spoke French well, if not elegantly.

I was a thirty-four-year-old American, with a sex appeal that, for Lucien, was mysterious and could not be reduced to my looks. (And neither could it be reduced to my notable breasts, even as the novelty of them had not yet worn off for him.)

I had seen many of the films he cared about, talked about. This was important, because cinephiles like Lucien draw for their confidence to make films from their knowledge of film history, without understanding that the essential spark elevating a movie to art never derives from the low domain of "expertise." Cinephiles are accountants, but I could speak their language.

I was suitably cultured, with an education, as Lucien understood it, that I had never figured out how to apply. And until recently I had walked dogs part-time for a few rich families out in Vincennes.

What else would a person need to know?

As it turns out, *hardly anything*.

THE GENE FOR ADDICTION that many of us inherited from Neanderthals, Bruno wrote to them, a gene associated with depression and artistic temperaments, might have served a quite practical purpose for the Thal. (The Moulinards had sent Bruno a question about natural selection, and why we hold on to instincts that do not serve us and might harm us, even significantly.)

Addiction, Bruno told them, could have been the distorted expression of a quite useful trait: the instinct to move toward joy, and even to gorge oneself on joy.

To gorge on substances or behaviors that induced feelings of pleasure, of well-being and a certain "rightness" with oneself and with the world, might have aided the Neanderthal's survival in countless ways: to fall in lust, to fall in love, to bear children, to stay warm, to build reserves of fat for times of scarcity, to take intervals of rest, and to recharge and restore. Pleasure augers survival. Think of sexual pleasure, Bruno said, the very root of existence: we further our species with ingenious simplicity—by going toward what feels good, by letting things happen, by allowing our bodies to speak and to say: "This." To say: "Yes."

But of course, to embrace what feels good, to have a natural and quite strong instinct to do so, poses risks. Serious ones. Most notably, it leads to crippling attachments to drugs and alcohol.

I do not need to remind you, Bruno wrote to Pascal Balmy and the others, that the annals of history are filled with descriptions of gifted and charismatic people who wanted to remake the world, special souls with second sight, natural leaders who burned clean and bright, and who brought the promise of their vision to the masses, but who gorged on joy until it wrecked them.

Keep a list, Bruno wrote, of those who have been martyred to joy, lost to it.

Do not be on that list.

While many, as Bruno warned, drink because they have to, because they have become alcoholics, I myself drink simply for pleasure. Those who abstain as some kind of program are often recovering alcoholics, or acolytes to religions that ban it, but there does exist that rare breed of person with little natural interest in drinking, who doesn't like the taste or feel the pull, people who can *take it or leave it*. Pascal Balmy, by all accounts (according to the dossier in my possession), was a guy who could have just a single beer, or he might leave a beer on the bar half-full, and the fact that he didn't seem interested in drinking may have been one of the more pragmatic reasons why the old leftists like Bruno were so invested in him.

Some considered Pascal Balmy to be an heir to an earlier figure of French notoriety: the writer, filmmaker, and provocateur Guy Debord.

Bruno Lacombe had known Guy Debord well, or as well as anyone could have known him, moody and dickish as he seems to have been. In the uprisings of May 1968, Guy Debord had made quite a nuisance of himself to the French government, with his galvanizing charisma and his caustic tone. He had pointed out the ersatz value of consumer rewards and the inhumanity of wage work, which people should never do, as Debord had famously scrawled on the rue de Seine.

Debord rejected all official culture—the "spectacle"—which reduced modern people to imbeciles. He had a legendary status that seemed to endure even now. I could see why. Who wants to argue that consumer culture, whether it's fast food or franchised movies or duty-free cosmetics, is wholesome and beneficial? If people do not start out as imbeciles, they are made imbecilic by the corporate contours of their daily life, lulled into a sleep, a sleep which, according to Debord, prevents them from wanting a more authentic life. True enough. Which isn't to say I agree with Debord's insistence we should never work, or some of his other proclamations.

Debord himself never worked because he never had to. He had money from his family, if not a lot, and his critique of the world, and everything good in it that was lost and wrecked, might have derived, at least to some degree, from his anger about his own family's fortune, partly lost and mostly wrecked.

Pascal Balmy did not have to work either. He had family money, like Debord, and he was said to possess a Debordian charisma, wry and electric. It seemed that Pascal was modeling himself on Debord, but the "good" Debord—young and mysterious and magnetic—not the "bad" or "late" Debord, whose cult magnetism and talk of a better world curdled into bitterness and very heavy drinking.

Pascal was said to have Debord's sex appeal, back when Debord had sex appeal. (Late Debord's face had grown to resemble that of a dead goldfish clotted with scurf, and I am not being fanciful here, but forensic and precise, given the photos of Late Debord included in my dossier. At the end of his life, he looks like a dead goldfish floating in a dirty bowl.) And while Debord was considered "inimitable," Pascal had internalized his voice, his style of critique, in the essays and missives published anonymously by Le Moulin, writings that, as I suspected and Lucien confirmed, were mostly authored by Pascal alone.

Guy Debord had once bragged that he wrote much less than those who write but drank much more than those who drink. He had not changed the world. Instead, he had merely become famous.

Pascal Balmy had no interest in fame, drank little, and played a cat-and-mouse game with French authorities. These factors were no small part of why my contacts had me watching him.

I SAID PRIEST VALLEY is on the left side of Highway 198, but of course this is only the case if you are traveling northwest, as I had been when I saw a sign for that place, decided it would make a good origin story, and stashed it for future use.

On the single occasion I passed through Priest Valley, I was coming from Coalinga, a grim town that smells like pig manure and contains not a single family from the American middle class.

I was driving with an animal liberation activist in my passenger seat, a freckled boy aged twenty-three with a fringe of fluffy red beard-hair attached to his jawline like drapery tassel. If this outré facial hair gave hints of radicalization, I had just watched this boy purchase five hundred pounds of nitrate fertilizer from a farm supplier.

I had suggested to him that proceeding with this plan would be regarded by me as evidence of his viability as a romantic partner, that "direct action," in the form of sabotage, was a critical step in our courtship.

This was after many months of conversations between him and me, talk that was meant to lead him to speak freely of his plans to commit illegal acts in the name of his beliefs. The government agency who was my employer at that time had been convinced that this boy and his cohort of "green" anarchists were capable of violence. But the hundreds of hours I spent with him had not uncovered any evidence of such violence. This time together was mistaken by him for a deep personal bond between us. Pressure from my supervisor in those months was constant, to unearth plans for sabotage on the part of the boy and his cohort.

Looking back, I can only guess that pressure from my supervisor's own higher-up was also constant. This drive to prove that eco-activists were terrorists was so strong and so relentless that I began to feel I had no choice but to plant the idea of violence in the boy's head, since he was doing a poor job of coming to it on his own.

I don't blame myself. I blame the Feds and their obsession with scruffy kids, which laddered down the chain of command and all but forced me to act. It was easy enough. I made it seem that an ardent commitment to defending the rights of animals, and a possible romantic future with me, were one and the same thing, a future this boy and I might consecrate by planting a bomb at a research laboratory.

When the boy came to understand this, and to agree to it, he cried. He looked afraid, but he said he was very happy, and that he was so glad he'd met me. He was ready for the future, come what may.

I liked this boy. He was timid and earnest. He had the ascetic air of a devout person from a different century. We were never intimate. We touched each other only once, after he made the fertilizer purchase. He reached over and placed his hand on mine as we sat in the car, and his hand was ice-cold. It trembled.

The boy's role was to implicate someone else, a woman named Nancy who was the central focus of a federal investigation as a suspected militant in the animal rights movement.

Later that day, I observed the boy deliver the fertilizer to Nancy, who lived in a warehouse in West Oakland. I had never met Nancy. She wore Coke-bottle glasses and answered the door of her Oakland warehouse in a too-short kimono, flaunting bare legs that were stubby and blunt as sawed-off shotguns.

I try to be respectful of other women's shortcomings. The dumb luck of good looks is akin to the fact that it may very well rain on the sea in times of drought, and will not rain where it is needed, on a farmer's crops: grace is random, dumb and random and even a bit violent, in giving to the one who already has rather a lot, and taking from the one who has been denied, who doesn't have *a pot to piss in*.

And so it's nothing more than God's reckless scattering of grace that I am tall and have long legs, that I'm pretty, even if my face is bland.

I'm aware that iconic beauty involves some deviation from universal standards, and I don't have that kind of beauty. I wouldn't want it. My banal and conventional looks have served me well. People think I look familiar. Have I met you? they ask. But I'm merely what white women are meant to look like. Symmetrical face, small straight nose, regular features, brown eyes, brown hair, clear skin: these are not identifying descriptors.

BACK IN '68, Guy Debord and Bruno Lacombe had both believed, as many had believed, that an uprising, when it came, would happen first in cities, whose labor conditions, a density of factories and people who had little option but to work in them, were the necessary ingredients for change. Some event, such as the killing of an unarmed young man by police, would spark a revolt, and people would rise up, torch automobiles, occupy public buildings, and set up barricades to fight the state.

This sort of thing *had* taken place all over Europe in the half century since the 1960s. Part of my job is to be something of an expert on such events and the social movements that precipitate them (and how those movements can be destroyed, either from outside or from inside). But none of these eruptions had resulted in the overthrow of capitalism in any of the advanced industrial nations of the entire European continent—not a single one.

In the wake of the colossal failure of leftist revolt, many radicals went to the countryside. Guy Debord moved to a crumbling cottage in the Auvergne. His retreat marked the end of his revolutionary passion, at a point when Debord had convinced himself it was an insurrection to drink, over the course of a single weekend, an entire case of grand cru Burgundy, gifted by his wealthy banker brother-in-law.

It is not an insurrection to drink a case of grand cru Burgundy. And so Debord did the state a favor by nullifying himself in this manner. Eventually, he shot himself in the heart, but on account that he'd already destroyed himself with alcohol (he'd singed his peripheral nerves, the ones that control the hands, arms, legs, and feet).

Bruno Lacombe was part of this drift, the exodus from cities. He came to the Guyenne in the early 1970s, along with other '68-ers. Most of those who came grew disillusioned by the challenges of farming, the isolation of the region, the closed-off community of locals.

Of the '68-ers who had attempted to settle in the Guyenne, only one besides Bruno had stayed, a man named Jean Violaine, who had befriended many of the dairy farmers around Vantôme, and latched onto the notion that peasants, and not factory workers, were the real revolutionaries.

There seemed to have been some rift between Jean and Bruno, a falling-out, though my dossier did not specify what caused it. Rifts are good. Sectarianism among radicals—perhaps not unlike heavy drinking—can nullify threats to the status quo without the need for outside intervention. The state was keeping an eye on Bruno, and on Jean Violaine, but for the past forty-odd years, since those two had arrived in the Guyenne, the region had been quiet.

The Guyenne was no Larzac, for instance. That remote plateau in the Massif Central had become a territory of lawlessness in the 1970s. The state had tried to expropriate land in the Larzac for a military base. One hundred thousand people showed up to prevent it. There were hunger strikes and sheep let loose in courtrooms. Peasants, Occitan nationalists, cheese farmers in debt to the Crédit Agricole, and even a Catholic bishop had joined forces. The Larzac became a showcase for international troublemakers and an embarrassment to the French government, which was forced to abandon its plan to build the military base.

In the Guyenne there had been no such troubles. Not until the arrival—as my dossier suggested—of Pascal Balmy.

Pascal had used his inheritance to purchase a sizable tract of land just beyond Vantôme. (The land was not expensive, given that the village population had dwindled, as populations had all over the region.)

Young people, kids in their twenties, followed him down from Paris. They lived communally and planted carrots and had babies. Through Jean Violaine, the Moulinards were able to begin building connections to the local peasant culture. They reopened the village bar, raising their stature with the old-timers. They corresponded with Bruno Lacombe, but only, or so it seemed, by email.

In the second year after Pascal and his group settled in the region, the power cable of a TGV that crossed through the eastern edge of the Guyenne had been severed, causing huge delays and backups to an entire southwestern network of French trains.

Later, an electrical substation in that same area caught fire. The state was confident the cause was arson but had no leads on who had committed it.

Prior to the sabotage of earth-moving equipment in Tayssac, a new megabasin in the Limousin, a couple of hours northwest of Le Moulin, suffered a catastrophic pump failure, which led to the release, all at once, of that reservoir's water stores. Its pumps had been destroyed by an invasive shellfish, the zebra mussel. Pascal Balmy was known to have visited that part of the Limousin some months prior to this pump failure. Balmy was interviewed by police investigators, and a transcript of that interview was included in my dossier.

"Are you or have you ever been aware of the destructive properties of the zebra mussel?"

"Yes," Balmy replied. "It was described in the newspaper, after the pump failure."

He told the investigator that the Moulinards had made great efforts to propagate native plants on their own land and felt proud of the role they were playing to restore ecological balance, whose damage, historically, was the result of government interference.

Balmy told the investigator he was happy to finger the scofflaws responsible for dumping an invasive species in the water supply. "I will name for you who did this," he said. The perpetrators he named were trade, industrial farming, highways, tourists, commercial air travel, trucking, and shipping.

"Sir, we hoe a row," he told the police. "We plant potatoes. We don't use pesticides. We nurture pollinators. But here is how the state does things: They have a deer population that's getting out of control, so what do they do? They bring in lynx. When farmers get upset about the lynx, the government reintroduces wolves. The wolves kill livestock, so the state makes it legal to shoot them. Hunting accidents increase, so they build a new clinic, whose medical staff creates a housing shortage, necessitating new developments. The expanding population attracts rodents, and so they introduce snakes. And so far, no one knows what to do about the snakes."

WHEN FEDERAL AGENTS burst into Nancy's warehouse in West Oakland, Nancy and the boy with the chin-line beard were both thrown to the floor, their hands behind their heads.

Nancy understood. From her prone position, she saw me step back next to the invaders in tactical gear, and she glared. The boy, stunned, wept. Nancy did not cry and did not look stunned. She was reserved and dignified despite her too-short kimono, her undignified legs splayed out on the warehouse floor. No one dresses up for a surprise bust by an army of Feds with long guns, and only later did I understand that Nancy had dressed up for the boy.

These people stab each other in the back. They turn state's evidence. They give a self-serving account when interrogated.

I had assumed the boy would choose to become a witness for the state, which was mostly interested in Nancy, in exchange for a lighter sentence. He refused the state's deal. His case went to trial, with Nancy as his coconspirator.

My testimony in that trial was made under an assumed identity, as a federal informant. They had weak evidence against Nancy. Their evidence against the boy, while strong, mostly depended on me. If convicted, he'd get twenty years in federal prison. The boy's lawyer attempted to argue that he had been entrapped. By that point, this boy no longer believed he loved me, as it might be reasonable to expect, given that I'd set him up. He loved Nancy. They'd been through something together. They'd been screwed over by me, and this seemed to have bonded them.

Sure, I pressured him to purchase the fertilizer. Indeed, I lured him with promises of a romantic relationship. Yes, the money he used to buy it came from the FBI. But entrapment is a tough defense, difficult to prove. Recordings of my conversations with the boy, our text exchanges and emails, were not presented to the jury or turned over in discovery. I was confident he'd go to prison. I even felt a twinge of guilt about this. Twenty years is a long time! But after 9/11, the justice department was not merciful when it came to domestic terrorism charges.

My guilt over what I'd done to this boy evaporated when the jury read their verdict. The entrapment defense had worked. This boy was not predisposed to commit the crimes of which he was charged, or so the jury believed. In other words, he had been innocent until I came along. They did not convict on the most serious charges, only a couple of minor ones, which resulted in one year of prison followed by five years of probation. Nancy walked free for time already served, and also got probation. I lost my job. I had cost the Feds two convictions. The agency who had hired me more or less touched a button: their tinted windows went up, and that was it.

I started working in Europe, in the private sector, taking advantage of the fact I speak French, Italian, Spanish, and German. I'm fluent in all those languages, although I speak them with a strong American accent. (People think fluency is about having a good accent. It isn't. Fluency is about how well you understand the language, and how well you are able to speak it. Having a good accent is nothing. It's a consolation prize for people who aren't fluent.)

But why had Nancy and that boy entered my thoughts just then?

I could not remember. But then I did remember: on account of Priest Valley, my Heineken-bottle-green fatherland, my made-up fodderland, which I'd passed through with the boy, before he made trouble for me.

Priest Valley, where no one lives but I say I am from.

A valley with a sign on the side of a highway. Paradisical and empty. Soft with wild grasses. Grand with valley oaks. Its tall priest-like poplars, planted long ago, in hopes of colonizing this otherwise untouched place where a couple of outbuildings linger, their unpainted lumber collapsing back into nature.

PRIEST VALLEY
ELEVATION: 2,200 FEET
POPULATION: ZERO

A MONTH INTO LIVING TOGETHER in his apartment, Lucien and I traveled from Paris to Marseille, where he would be shooting a film based on a pulp novel about Marseille's criminal underworld.

I planned to stay for a week, as part of the contract of our romance, in exchange for which I would secure access to his family's estate, rent a car, and drive up to the Guyenne to establish trust with Pascal Balmy and his inner circle.

———

Lucien and I took the TGV from Gare de Lyon to Marseille, riding backward in a swaying first-class train car, a canister of modern French technology tearing through French countryside at three hundred kilometers an hour, farms and rolling hills and little medieval villages being pulled backward as if a monster vacuum cleaner was sucking the landscape into its unseen mouth.

The two of us riding faced in the "wrong" direction, Lucien began to feel queasy. The train car was full, so we could not move from our assigned seats. I watched as his complexion blanched. His forehead shone with sweat. I could see that he was suppressing the urge to vomit, as I read the newspaper and feigned concern.

I said I would get him some bubbly water, and I headed for the café car.

The core of my assignment and duties had been to infiltrate and to monitor Pascal Balmy and the Moulinards for proof they had committed sabotage and were planning more of it. But even before I'd pulled off the neat trick of sidling up to Balmy's oldest friend, my contacts had me tracking, in addition to Balmy, a French bureaucrat, an obscure deputy minister. I had been encouraged to study this man's activities and habits in Paris and elsewhere.

A message had come in, regarding him.

I read the message while standing at the bar of the empty café car, sent a short reply, ordered a glass of white wine, drank it, bought a sparkling water for Lucien, a package of mints, put a mint in my mouth, and made my way back to our seats.

Lucien looked greenish as I handed him the water.

I sat. He sipped the water and put his head in my lap. He closed his eyes and wrapped his arms around my waist.

I looked down at this head in my lap, Lucien's, foreign and heavy and warm, and then I looked out the window.

The trick of riding backward is to understand that this orientation of travel is time-honored and classical. It is like rowing a boat: you enter the future backward, while watching scenes of the past recede.

A high-speed train was approaching from the opposite direction. As it whooshed past our own, the effect of wind between the two trains stopped my heart.

I know perfectly well that each train has its own track. I know they won't collide.

THIS DEPUTY MINISTER'S NAME was Paul Platon. He worked in the Ministry of Rural Coherence, which was concerned with energy, ecology, and this ambiguous goal of so-called coherence. His area was security as I understood it, inside this ministry.

Deputy Minister Platon might not have been a public figure, but he had managed to make of his subministerial position something of a lavish mess, by stepping on the toes of senior politicians and energy tycoons, by always being in the wrong place at the wrong time. He was hated by powerful string pullers, and also by regular French people, who seemed offended that they should even be made to know who he was.

I had been watching him now for months, without any explicit instructions as to what I was meant to do except report my observations.

In the event of rural protests against new state projects—the building of a nuclear-waste storage facility or a new highway, a new prison—the Minister of Rural Coherence sent in Platon, who would rush to the site and make an unpopular statement, that the rural people of department X or Y should be eager for a prison, a landfill, a nuclear-waste dump. Now he was tasked with trying to drum up support for the megabasins, and promoting this new strategy for "rural coherence." The state plan was to squeeze out small farms and favor corporate ones, which would grow mostly corn.

After the excavators in Tayssac were burned, Platon had gone on television to declare that the construction of megabasins and the modernization of farming in the Guyenne were vital to the economic future of rural France. Whether this was true or not, this plan was vital to the economic interests of the people who had sent me here.

I had witnessed the meetings Platon had around Paris. I'd studied his habits. I had "gone along," unbeknownst to the deputy minister and his security detail, on various domestic trips he'd taken, and twice on trips to Spain, where he held long meetings with Catholic clergy. I assumed he was not talking to these priests about spiritual matters, although one could argue that those of poor character have more to discuss with their priest than those who are unassailable and good, and yet I was certain Platon was not hunkering in a confession booth, and instead involved in some racket connected to the Spanish Church.

In Paris, he had a mistress he visited regularly, out in Vincennes. This had been my sole reason for going to that suburb, in whose large park I had gotten the inspiration for my fictional part-time job as a dog walker. Platon's mistress, a wealthy blond divorcée with toned calves, herself had several small fluffy white dogs that I'd seen tugging her from a bouquet of leashes she gripped. Usually, her maid walked the dogs, and once, I saw her maid kick one of the dogs.

Platon made repeated visits to an aesthetic clinic in Chaillot, and one Saturday he emerged from its opaque-frosted doors with his head wrapped in bandages. Later, he had a fuller and thicker head of hair than he'd had before.

He dyed his new hair regularly at a beauty salon inside the Hotel Meurice. Perhaps the new hair was transplanted, perhaps from a dead man—I'm not up on how those transplants work, but they had to get the hair from somewhere.

The deputy minister had a static problem in winter, his pants clinging to his dress socks instead of draping as he wanted them to, and I could see that he had a temper in the way he stopped walking and jutted his leg to correct the static contact between his slacks and his socks.

You'll injure your groin by kicking your leg like that, I thought at him as I watched him do this repeatedly.

Platon argued with his staff. He yelled at his security guard for getting in his way. This guard had been assigned after Platon received threats to his physical safety. A deputy from the Ministry of Rural Coherence would not typically be assigned security, but Platon was. It seemed as if Platon, or someone near him, understood that he had something to fear.

His security guard was a young and muscular Serbian with a thick and pronounced brow bone. The Serb's comportment was clumsy, perhaps on account of his excessive muscles and the tight fit of his suits across his broad shoulders, his narrow slacks straining against his meaty thighs.

Platon also berated his assigned driver, an older man with a jaundiced complexion and hooded eyes that were the blue of mentholated cough drops. This chauffeur often glared at Platon with his menthol-blue eyes as if he detested his boss.

I knew why. This driver, called Georges, was the type who had worked his way up from the bottom. He played by the rules, respected hierarchies, and had spent his career in service to elites.

But Platon was not an elite, and so Georges did not respect him.

Platon had not been educated at any of the grandes écoles. His background was barely middle class, and worse, he wasn't even French. Platon was Spanish. His given name was Pablo Platon y Platon, which he'd gallicized to Paul Platon, nasal "on." The French tabloids called him Pablo. Georges, too, probably called him Pablo, at least secretly, to let off steam for the indignity of having to spend the final years of his professional life, just before his long-planned retirement, serving a low-class Spaniard subminister who pretended to be French.

And it wasn't as if Platon was from some grand Spanish metropolis like Madrid. He wasn't even from Barcelona. (Not that this would be acceptable either; one can imagine the outrage poor Georges felt about his boss's loyalty to FC Barcelona.)

Platon was from Palafrugell, a town that was basically a place to *fill up* before traversing wastes of saw grass droning with insect chatter on the way to the beaches of the Costa Brava, where Spaniards like him crowded the sand and not a single one of them was reading a book.

Georges the chauffeur didn't read books either, just racing forms, which I watched him study religiously.

EVERY CORNER OF MARSEILLE, riding from the train station to the hotel, looked like it had been recently jackhammered. Live electric wires grazed the sidewalk, setting off sparks. Graffiti covered buildings and retaining walls. Having never been there, this was exactly how I had imagined Marseille would be.

A motorcade of state dignitaries in Mercedes limousines rolled past in an uninterrupted stream as we were forced to stop, despite having the green.

Our taxi driver, an older lady with a gravelly voice, turned up the volume on Daft Punk's "Get Lucky" as she waited for the motorcade to pass.

This driver took us on an extralong loop to run the meter and show us more broken concrete, rebar, trash, a vehicle burned beyond recognition, but also villas with armed guards. In the driveway of one of the villas was a convertible Maserati blasting "Get Lucky." I knew she was taking us for a ride, but I didn't care. I said nothing to Lucien, who was too naïve to notice, or too in thrall to the anti-Parisian disorder of this place.

When the taxi driver deposited us in front of our hotel, she tried to sell us knockoff Patek watches from a display case in her trunk. Don't want a watch? I've already bilked you anyway, her sun-wrinkled face said wordlessly, as she tucked the money Lucien gave her into the pocket of the housedress.

I thought of it as *the* dress and not *her* housedress because my suspicion, not yet disproven with evidence, was that all these French matrons who were the sort to wear a housedress were wearing a single housedress. Faded floral print, a sleeveless shift with a zipper up the front and patch pockets, for carrying a few clothespins, a key to the mailbox, a token for the grocery carts at supermarkets. They shared this housedress. Passed it around.

Just as I had suspected that the Orthodox Jewish women in South Williamsburg, upon my initial introduction to that hermetic world, might be sharing a single wig, taking shifts wearing it for their occasional public sorties. This was in the course of my first foray into the private sector, after the debacle of Nancy and the boy. I was hired freelance by a tri-state security firm. The interview took place at an old-school steakhouse next to the Williamsburg Bridge, a place whose heyday was over. The clientele was not *Godfather Part III*; it was Men's Wearhouse. The job involved surveilling a politician who was trying to block the development of riverfront condominiums.

While lurking around Orthodox Williamsburg, I saw large groups of Hasidic men or Hasidic boys. I would see one woman, on the street or on a subway platform, in her shapeless long skirt and her orthopedic shoes, and I wondered if the reason I saw her at all was because she had dibs on the wig that morning.

The shared use of both the housedress by old French matrons and the wig by young Hasidic women keeps the riot potential down, making it so that these women have to emerge single file, or rather, one at a time.

If I witness an army of women in housedresses occupying town squares or breaking shopwindows with their rolling pins, I will know I was wrong, and I'll be amused to have been wrong, but those are scenes I have yet to see.

Which is not to say I sympathize with angry women breaking shopwindows. I do what I'm hired to. And yet, who knows, maybe I, too, could smash a big window with a rolling pin, were I a housewife tasked with using such kitchen equipment.

But I'm not a housewife, or an Orthodox subordinate in industrial pantyhose and a communal wig. And if I'm going to smash something, I'll use a sledgehammer, which, on account of its weight, does all the work for you.

IF ADDICTION WAS the unfortunate byproduct of a quite useful survival mechanism, what about depression? the Moulinards had wondered in an email to Bruno. Was it depression, to which Neanderthals were so prone, that led to their downfall?

Bruno replied that the depression suffered by Neanderthal man should be thought of as a spiritual mantle, and not all bad. Thal's tendency to anhedonic brooding had likely been the engine of his abstract thinking, and his stupendous preternatural capacity for a dream life.

Neanderthals had hunted in teams, had lived collaboratively, but were introverts by temperament and kept their clans small. They did not hoard supplies, or engage in a growth-at-any-cost mindset. Their brooding, Bruno speculated, may have aided their resistance to such a mindset, of greed and accumulation. And Thal's freedom from ambition for ambition's sake may have led him to the most refined and least practical of human drives: to art for art's sake.

Bruno said that the "standard story"—that art was the domain of the *Homo sapiens*—was flat-out wrong. Just because *Homo sapiens* was the first to leave rich evidence in pictures, most famously in Lascaux and other caves north of here, we must not deduce, he said, that *Homo sapiens* was the first to have a symbolic universe.

Pictures of hunting, Bruno said, show us *Homo sapiens*'s symbolic life, and it consists almost entirely of eating and killing.

If symbolism could be defined as the act of storing information outside of one's own mind, early *Homo sapiens* had chosen to store images that were *already abundant*, and by rendering likenesses of the animals he hunted, the *Homo sapiens* was attempting to exert power, and to own.

The Neanderthal, in contrast, wanted to record what he saw in dreams, to put into the world what otherwise did not exist. The marks that Thal was believed to have left, on cave walls, on rocks, on animal bones, were abstract codes of great mystery and transcendent beauty. Lines, dots, slants, cuts. And two colors: red and black.

These colors, red and black, were of course the scheme of the classic twentieth-century anarchist flag, Bruno didn't need to remind Pascal and the Moulinards. And while one would not want to draw a direct link between primordial contrasts of bright and obscure, of bloody and dark, with a modern symbol for rejecting statehood, nevertheless, what we find, he said, is that two essential chromatic hues were developed by Neanderthals: red and black.

This could have been retinal, and unconscious, that the eye is drawn to this opposition of hues, colors that stir us to commitment, to strength, to a longing for a better world, but Bruno counseled not to relegate such an echo to chance, because the enduring duality of red and black deserved more.

He had found in his own cave a small disc of black obsidian that had a cross grooved into its surface. His daughter, he wrote, had shown it to an archeologist from Bordeaux who said it was fifty thousand years old and certifiably Thal. Despite knowing its impressive heritage, Bruno had no plans to submit it to official state registries. He would not allow bureaucrats to requisition the beautiful palm-sized obsidian acrostic and relegate it to a museum for tourists, such as the hideous "cité troglodyte" up in the Périgord, with its Disnified prehistory. He said the evidence and study of our ancestors must be protected from such outcomes.

We need scholarship of prehistoric art, Bruno said, but mindful scholarship, and we do not have mindful scholarship.

In its absence, he could deduce the following precepts, pertaining to ancient art:

—The *Homo sapiens* was a *copier*. Despite his virtuosity in drawing animals and scenes of hunting, he depicted what was *already there*.

—The Neanderthal was a *conjurer*, and this act, Bruno said, to bring into being something new, was the fundamental kernel of true art.

To render the unseen seen: that is what an artist does, Bruno said.

And so the Neanderthals were artists. While the *Homo sapiens* were absolutely, definitely *not artists*.

They were frauds.

OUR HOTEL, THE RICHELIEU, was not a luxury establishment but happened to be, unlike all the other hotels in this part of Marseille, on the correct side of the Corniche—the waterfront side. The crew for Lucien's film had taken over the place.

Lucien's cinematographer and closest collaborator, Serge, and Serge's Italian boyfriend, Vito, were there when we arrived, but our rooms were not yet ready. Serge sat in dark glasses on a chair in the lobby.

I'd established something like a friendship with Vito, who was an extrovert, unlike Serge. As the two partners of the two artists, Vito and I had in common leisure time and a jokey attitude about the self-seriousness of our boyfriends.

Vito didn't do much. He was studying to be a Jungian analyst. Serge was the essential one. Our friendship had been forged from a shared understanding that we were inessential and therefore free. Vito didn't know anything about me, but I used aspects of my real self with him, and this came as a relief. I genuinely liked him.

I said I was hungry, and Vito chimed in that he was too. He wanted to go to the nearby Chez McDo', as he announced to Serge, who would never use that nickname for McDonald's, or eat at one.

"They've got a new ad campaign," Vito said as we walked in. The walls of this McDonald's were covered in slogans about tradition and family and togetherness. "We should take notes for our husbands."

(Despite acting like they were riding the crest of the new wave, Lucien and Serge accepted a lot of commercial jobs in between feature films.)

A woman with platinum upswept hair and diamond earrings sat eating french fries, daubing each slender fry in ketchup as if dipping a sable brush into a dollop of red paint.

"Oh my God," Vito whispered, squeezing my arm, "it's Zsa Zsa Gabor."

"That's just a Russian lady," I said. "They all look like that."

Vito announced that I had trampled on his dream.

I told him that's what dreams are for.

We brought our food back to the hotel. Serge complained that we made the whole lobby smell like McDonald's.

Lucien was more annoyed than I was about the rust-colored splotches on the walls and curtains of the room they gave us at the Hotel Richelieu.

The splotches were the dried blood of previous guests, who had been bitten by mosquitoes and had smashed them.

Mosquitoes tormented Lucien. They have never bothered me. I've always attributed this to character, and to the idea that it's sensitive people who get targeted. But the fact that mosquitoes are interested in some and not others might have to do with antigens and blood type, rather than weakness and strength.

Then again, it could be that blood type is connected to character. In Japan they have a system of personality traits that go with each blood type, which seems more interesting to me than the astrology that some depend on—women, usually—for life guidance. Blood personalities were developed by a professor in 1930s Japan. The Japanese military took up his theories as useful for discipline. Later, those who read about their own blood traits began to exhibit those traits by the power of suggestion. That professor either made the whole thing up or was inspired by the Nazis. In Japan there is still a problem with bias and judgment of blood type in the competition for jobs and romantic partners. A number one bestselling book there is called *A Handbook for Blood Type A*. Most Japanese people, thirty-eight percent, are type A. I'm O. Our handbook is not number one, but O has some winning traits: ambitious, intelligent, passionate, and independent. But also cold, arrogant, and conniving.

I opened the windows of the hotel room, which swung on hinges to reveal a panorama of misty blue, a horizon line intersected by a white ferry that flashed in the sun. Its horn sounded, a basso profundo that filled the room. Something about that horn, the white ferry splicing the blue, the huge window, sea air stirring the bloodstained curtains, which swelled like apparitions, the sound of water lapping the rocks of the jetty, in the ferry's wake, it all gave me a sense of calm, a feeling that everything was going to work out. I'd invested more than a year in this job, and the critical time was now: the next six weeks.

I lay down on the bed and opened the Marseille crime novel on which Lucien was basing his movie.

"This book," I said, "is written in short. Very short. Sentences. Pieces of thought. Phrases. Some, just a word. A single word."

Lucien was trying to assemble one of those little plug-in mosquito things.

Those don't work, I didn't say. Instead, I read out loud from the crime novel.

"'She tightened her robe. The robe that covered her body. The body he wanted. Under the robe. He pushed aside that thought. A thought that was new, but also old. Timeless. To want. To resist. So many memories. From before. Her smell. Her hair. Her skin. He reached under the pillow. He touched what was there. The gun. She'd left it. For him. And he knew. It was time. Time to kill.'"

"That's why it's ideal for adaptation," Lucien said. "The language doesn't carry abstract meaning. It tells you where the action goes."

Lucien showered and lay down, said he was taking a nap. I put on my bathing suit and a pair of shorts, intending to walk over to the nearby beach, the Plage des Catalans, take in the scene, and read some encrypted messages that had just arrived.

Lucien intervened, put his hands around my thigh.

I tried to pull away. He did not let go.

"I thought you were going to sleep."

I was never in the mood to have sex with him, so mood wasn't the issue. I tried to limit sex with him to times when there was no escape from it.

"I am," he replied, as he bent down to remove my sandals.

Couples and their routines.

We'd been together only a few months, and he knew nothing about me. He was in a couple with a woman who didn't exist. But still, we, they, that couple, she and he, they had their way of doing things. The removal of shoes was one of Lucien's.

I sat down. I told myself that relenting would buy me several days left alone.

He took down my shorts, and soon his warm breath was against my crotch. I knew what to expect. The tongue on my vulva was a prelude, a service that was mostly a request. It went on for only so long, and then there was the grand theatric of me wanting and begging for "the real thing." I was supposed to ask him to fuck me. Everyone needs something and that's what Lucien needed. And then there was the "Oh yes," portion of this scripted sequence, after he put it in, my reaction meant to make him feel like he'd been holding out on me, delaying the declaration that it was Christmas, and "Oh God!" it was Christmas, and he was piling into me.

Our script was boring and unpleasant. Sometimes, physically, it hurt. I was not attracted to Lucien, but that afternoon in the hotel, by closing my eyes and concentrating, by pretending I was masturbating with a tool, even if the tool was the body of another person, I came, which enabled him to do so, also, since he was "a gentleman," after which I was free to leave.

The Plage des Catalans was a few steps from the hotel, just around the curve of the waterfront. I ducked into a catty-corner bar, ordered a white wine, and glanced at messages concerning my subminister.

It seemed that Platon would be making an appearance in Vantôme.

I asked when and was told more details were forthcoming.

There would be a confrontation between him and the Moulinards, my contacts declared, suggesting without stating: it was my job to make this happen.

The wine was bad, but I ordered another, settled my bill, and crossed back toward the entrance to the beach. I could hear children laughing, people splashing in the water. "Get Lucky" wafted from portable radios, all tuned to the same station, forming one disco-scroll.

We're up all night to the sun . . . we're up all night to get some . . . And over it was the sound of someone shrieking.

CRS vans—the French riot police—were parked along the road above the beach.

As I approached the steps down to the sand, families were leaving. Or more like fleeing in a mad rush. People were snatching up towels and effects and racing up the stairs from the beach, coughing and covering their eyes. I started to cough also. More police vans maw-mee'ed their way toward the Corniche, lights flashing. The cars in front of them refused to budge. The police sirens wailed.

Several people were being arrested.

The Plage des Catalans is a proletarian beach, a family beach.

As I learned the next day on our hotel TV, two brothers, frolicking in the waves, had engaged for family fun in trying to drown a cop.

It wasn't clear how they got him in the water, but they were holding him under when more cops stormed the beach and gassed everyone, including babies.

That scene later stayed in my mind. The waves, the waist-deep water, the families, those brothers, and the riot cops who tear-gassed everyone. Cops whose vans were stationed at that beach, in order to harass and rough up beachgoers.

That environment helped me to understand something. It gave me an idea, a plan.

Paul Platon, my deputy minister, could be, for instance, the cop in the waves.

And the people trying to drown him, the Moulinards.

Pascal would be blamed.

It was time. Time to make something happen. Time to finish this job.

OUR SECOND NIGHT IN MARSEILLE we attended a dinner Lucien's producer was hosting, a woman whose family ruled a handbag dynasty in Paris.

We were at a private swimming club, walking distance from the hotel, and next to the Plage des Catalans, aka Tear Gas Beach.

Guests were gathering on the club's large terrace as we arrived. Lucien pointed out the Château d'If, a fortress of stone and caked concrete out in the blue. The air was sweltering, with just the faintest wind. The sun was dissolving into the watery horizon. The boulders and makeshift jetties that ringed the harbor glowed pink.

Lucien and I located Vito and Serge. They were leaning on the patio railing but turned inward, assessing not the sea and late-day light but the arriving guests.

The women, Vito observed, were dressed in expensive fabrics of muted colors, beige or gray, while the men were like peacocks, outfitted in explosive combinations of banana yellow and neon green, or melon pants with a turquoise polo shirt.

"These people," Vito said, as a man in a peach silk shirt and white slacks embraced a man in a pink linen suit, "they all look dressed to fly on the Concorde. While you, Sadie, look ready for Sunday dinner with the in-laws, in your little silk blouse and your fitted silk skirt. Tasteful, but sexy enough to pique the interest of the father-in-law, which is a French daughter-in-law's filial duty."

Luckily, I'd had no interaction with Lucien's family, since both of his parents were dead, and he was an only child. There were a couple of aunts and uncles and some cousins in Paris to whom he wasn't close, and I made sure I was "working" whenever any of them invited us over. He had his aunt Agathe, not too far from Vantôme, whom he wanted me to meet, but I intended to avoid her and maintain my winning streak. Relatives interfere, or try to, when a family member attaches to a stranger.

"My grandfather took the Concorde," Lucien said. "I remember him bringing me a model of one."

"Serge, did your grandfather take the Concorde?" Vito asked. The question was a taunt. Serge wasn't from money, like Lucien, and sometimes he made a stern point of this.

"My grandfather was born to French shopkeepers in Algeria," Serge said. "At eighteen, he joined the colonial army as a census taker. He roamed from village to village on foot, knocking on the doors of people's homes, sometimes their tent, and he counted their canned foods and recorded the number in a ledger. He counted the chickens pecking in their yard. He wrote down how many bolts of Berber cloth they possessed, and whether they sewed by hand or on a machine. How many pounds of rice they kept in dry storage. How many of their children they had buried so far.

"After his army service, he took over his father's shop, a tabac on a busy corner. In '62, when Algeria declared victory in its war of independence, my grandparents fled. Coffin or suitcase was the choice. A million people left. My grandfather abandoned his shop and the home he and my grandmother owned. They were French nationals who had never been to France, petits bourgeois who lost everything. They landed in Marseille by military barge, at the old port—there, where I am pointing—and were treated like stateless refugees.

"My grandfather was offered dock work. Later, he became a janitor at a hotel in Fréjus, where my grandmother cleaned rooms. Embittered over the lost colony of Algeria, he and my grandmother devoted themselves to reactionary politics and the National Front. When I read the novel that Lucien has adapted, which features wounded bigots who remind me of my grandfather, I signed on."

Dinner was lobster served in its bright shell, a labor-intensive saga that required guests to bend over their plates and toil with specialized tools, their napkins tucked into shirt collar or cleavage.

I talked to a woman across from me named Amélie, a location scout from Paris based here in Marseille.

As blancmange was brought around for dessert, each bowl containing a molded D-cup of stabilizer-thickened cream in a lake of berry glaze, the lead actress that Lucien had cast came over to our table to say hello. She was young and beautiful, her own D-cups jellying from her dress when she bent over to introduce herself.

Amélie and I ate our blancmange. "Get Lucky" came on over the swimming club's outdoor speaker system. Waiters replaced carafes of rosé in clear plastic bags of ice. The rich men in bright colors reached for the wine. Their faces had softened into drunkenness, their collars and lapels still starched. Lucien's producer was trashed, her makeup running, her words slurred, her hand on Lucien's thigh.

She was in her seventies. Old people should not drink, but watching her, and these men, their minds partly trained on the level of rosé in their glass, on how much was left in the shared carafe, their awareness of the waiter's location on the terrace, gauging the degree of his attention to their table and their need of replenished rosé, I had the thought these people were *gorging on joy*, as Bruno had described this ancient instinct.

THE NEXT THREE DAYS, while Serge and Lucien were busy prepping for their shoot, Vito and I returned to the private club to swim, with passes arranged by Lucien's producer.

Serge said that the primary function of clubs like this one, and those of the Côte d'Azur, where he had spent his childhood, was to protect the upper crust from poverty and from North Africans. "But go ahead and enjoy it," he told Vito. "My family would have done anything to join a club like that. Instead, they scrubbed floors and were mistaken for Portuguese."

The place had three swimming pools, but we chose the sea, where members lay on towels or canvas deck chairs on the jetty, or bobbed in the waves, tan as coconuts.

One lady, skeleton thin but with large, artificial breasts stationary on her chest, was dark brown, although by racial status white, like most everyone at this private club.

Despite its tight security and homogeneous clientele, the club's ambiance was slightly beat-up and ad-hoc, like everything in Marseille. The true power of the place, Vito and I agreed, the reason all these people were here, was not luxury amenities but the club's proximity to Tear Gas Beach next door, its exclusion of the kind of people who frequented that beach. Enhancing the facilities of the swim club was the visual reminder of how much worse things could be, right there at the other beach, the one we did not have to go to, where people were packed towel to towel on the sand, and body to body in the water, so many people it looked impossible to swim.

All day long, ambulances and CRS vans pulled up in front of the public beach, sirens blaring, either to intervene in violent altercations or to cause them.

Meanwhile, we left our valuables in our beach bags for long stretches of swimming and didn't think once about theft. We went back and forth to the café, which offered complimentary beverages and Häagen-Dazs bars. At happy hour, a waiter came around with beer and wine.

"This club is like the business-class lounge of an international airport terminal," I said, as we licked our ice cream. It was luxury offerings to a homogenous class stratum, people who were not going to steal your stuff.

"Serge only flies business class, by the way," Vito replied, as he picked the thin chocolate sheathing off his ice cream bar. "He's furious about the snobbery of rich Parisians but he refuses to empty a recycling hamper. Our housekeeper has to come every day, so that Serge won't have to touch bottles and cans. He's full of contradictions. I find that incredibly sexy."

Amélie joined us one afternoon, having completed most of her work securing locations. The woman who out-thinned and out-tanned the rest was there, as she had been every day, lying on her towel when we arrived, still there when we left, her skin the dark oily sheen of roasted hazelnuts.

"Like a nun marries God," Vito said, "she has married Apollo."

"Is that the name of her plastic surgeon?" Amélie asked.

I laughed, my own implants barely contained in the triangles of my white bikini. Mine were expensively done. But it could be on account of something more subtle—an assumption Amélie made about me, and about herself, that we were both too clever and naturally pretty to stoop to paying for shortcuts—that she would not suspect my breasts aren't real.

"She reminds me of someone," Amélie said. "A woman I once knew who was addicted to tanning, and always on some starvation diet. She was very tortured. She died from drinking too much water."

"What do you suppose got into her?" Vito asked.

"I think she mistook water for selfhood. Like those people who get into yoga and think you can just *breathe* and it will solve all your problems. Life is more than water and air."

"There's beer," I said, as I opened a fresh one a waiter had just delivered.

"If your tortured friend had chosen beer," Vito said, holding his up to mine, "she might still be alive."

My last day there a mistral came up, a cold and violent wind that ripped through Marseille with no consideration for anything not bolted down. Filming was put on hold. Lucien and Serge worked on scene blocking in our room.

I had private correspondence to deal with. I said I was going to the pharmacy and went out to find a quiet place to sit.

Plastic bags and other trash whirled at face level. Grit-laden gusts pushed at me as I walked. The restaurants had brought in their outdoor tables. Businesses were closed, their metal shutters rolled down. There were few people on the street, which felt dangerous with the possibility that the wind could knock me down or send a garbage can barreling into me.

The Plage des Catalans was empty, no one on the beach. The water was dark. There were no boats out.

I walked over to the private swim club. It was open. I flashed my temporary pass, went to the café, and ordered a Coca-Cola. It was just me and the bartender in his white waiter's jacket. The place was otherwise deserted. I took my drink to a table along the fishbowl windows facing the sea.

Below the windows the water churned. Waves hurled over the jetty, slapped the concrete, and burst upward. Trash pushed into a thick floating barrier, was sucked out into the bay, and slopped forward again toward land.

The jetty, usually crowded with families, was empty save for a single person, a lone sunbather: the roasted-nut woman.

I poured my Coke into a tumbler of ice and watched her.

She lay face-up on the decking, her fake breasts glistening in the cold light like twin copper vaults. Her body fell into shadow as explosions of surf burst over the seawall and onto the jetty. Her eyes were shut tight against the wind, her hands anchoring the corners of her towel as if to prevent it from carrying her away, or as if that had already happened, and she was mid-flight.

III

JOAN CRAWFORD'S FACE

BRUNO HAD STRESSED that the Neanderthal's large face was designed to accommodate giant nasal passages, which were themselves for warming cold air before it entered the lungs. The Thals had large orbital bones and huge eyes, for enhanced night vision. They had weak chins, he conceded, as could be ascertained from skulls in museums, or photographs of skulls, but he had once, as a boy, felt the eroding slope of this weak chin with his own hands, as he inspected the contours of a Neanderthal skull that was part of a display in a natural history museum, a model that visitors could touch and hold and palpate. It had been passed from child to child, as they sat cross-legged on the museum floor.

I pictured Bruno with this skull in his lap like the skull was a baby, his arms cradling its large head and weak chin.

Bruno said he had read about a skull found in a cave in southern Spain from which a stalagmite had formed. Stalagmites are a consequence of subterranean storage, Bruno said, mineral buildup from moisture, from water drips, and in the case of this skull, discovered in a sediment layer dated to thirty thousand years old, the stalagmite was *still growing*, shooting upward like the horn of that mythical if culturally exhausted creature, the unicorn.

Less explainable, he said, were the properties of a certain skull found in a cave in Croatia, which seemed to map, simultaneously, to two different eras of human time. The face had the broad features and strong jaw, the heavy brow and magnificent nasal passages, of the noble Neanderthal, and some had concluded this skull was Thal. But the skull's contours, its "occipital bun," had the angular features of Thal's earlier ancestor *Homo erectus*. (I'd read enough of Bruno's emails at this point to understand that this bun he referred to was not to be confused with any other kind of bun, such as the ballerina bun. The occipital bun was a protrusion at the back of the head with a steep drop-off—the lower rear skull.) The cranium of this skull had the features of Rectus, suggesting the brain it contained should also be Rectus. And yet its face looked entirely Thal. Which era was this individual from? Scientists debated, without drawing clear conclusions. The skull was some kind of hybrid, the coauthors of a journal paper argued, suggesting that developments took place unevenly, and that this individual had possessed a face that was one hundred thousand years more modern than his own brain case and brain.

There is so much we don't know, Bruno said. But a lesson in this curious hybrid skull, of Thal face and Rectus braincase and brain, seems somewhat obvious to me, he said. The lesson is that you cannot judge a book by its cover.

Because just as this individual looked like a Neanderthal but could have thought like Rectus, there may be modern individuals with similar developmental disjunctures, with modern faces but the mind and instincts of an older ancestor. Even if someone looks like you, they may not think like you.

New and complicating genetic evidence of how we have evolved is being sequenced all the time from bones, teeth, even the tiniest shards and splinters and bits of skeletal grit, Bruno said. New discoveries, such as the species called Denisovan, in Eastern Mongolia, and the Hobbit or *Homo floresiensis* of Indonesia, are reprising everything we once believed about early man.

This term, "early man," is itself a misnomer, Bruno said. Early man was Rectus, and before him, *Homo habilis*, or "handy man." While the *Homo sapiens* that some call "early man" in fact strode in two million years after *habilis* and was actually "late-arriving man," *Homo tardus*, or even *Homo tardissimus*.

If we think of time, of history, as a deep and long spike driving down into the center of the earth, into the earliest hominin life, *Homo sapiens* is right up near the surface, the mere head of this spike that goes a very, very long ways down.

And how bitterly ironic, Bruno said, that *H. tardissimus* strolls in at the end of a gaping stretch—unfathomable to the mind, so much time, lived by an enormous variety of people. At the end of an endless saga, *H. tardissimus*, aka "Tardie," arrives on the scene, only to destroy everything.

MY FIRST NIGHT at the Dubois country house I slept like a baby. I felt softly held, like that skull Bruno Lacombe had once cradled and palpated.

It helped that I'd taken two milligrams of Xanax and a slow-release Ambien. I'd worried that my long day of drinking and driving, from Marseille to the Guyenne, might interfere with my sleep, and so I'd subdued my cortex from two different directions with teeny pills.

I woke at dawn. I felt good. I felt strong. A zeppelin-shaped cloud hovered over the valley beyond the house, turning pink. It darkened in front of my eyes to fuchsia and then faded to plain old cloud color. For all its fame, rosy-finger dawn leaves no prints.

I went downstairs and prepared coffee that I'd bought at Leader Price in Boulière. I tore a hunk from a baguette I'd also purchased at Leader Price and found some vintage Nutella in the kitchen cabinets. It was ten years old but still sealed. Dead-stock Nutella. Nutella never goes bad, just gets a bit crystallized. I spread some on my bread.

As I ate, Vito sent me a selfie of him at the Calanques outside Marseille, on a rock above the transparent water.

I stamped his image with my digital thumbs-up.

—Serge wanted to be here by 7 am to film sunrise. We had to get all these permits. The road is narrow, the width of only one car. Serge was driving. He keeps honking. I said what are you honking at, why do you keep honking? He goes, I'm required to honk. You have to honk at every turn. Just in case. It's illegal not to honk. It's beautiful here. How is it there? What are you doing?

—eating bread w nutella. pride of your nation.

—That family are billionaires off this goo they invented. Wartime chocolate.

—do italians have a word like goo? because i can't think of one.

— . . . gelatina?

—that's not even close.

His thumbs-up brightened my screen.

—Europe's children are being raised on this goo and they don't know it. Because they don't have a wonderful word like goo.

I pressed a heart on that declaration.

It's rare for Italians to acknowledge their nation's cultural limitations. Vito is different, in this way and in other ways. Italians often want to tell you that the pasta and wines from their particular locality are the best. They want to pretend that different shapes of noodle are different culinary sensations. Spaghetti is made of flour and water and wherever it comes from it all tastes the same. Italian wines don't vary much either despite what Italians say. They call it Nebbiolo or tears of Christ and they claim the grapes are grown from volcano ashes or Sardinian sand, but to my palette Italian wine is more or less table wine. It is wine in a box.

Vito was not in denial of Italy's bland culinary offerings, and he had a sense of humor, which he steadily employed in this short-term friendship pact that he and I had formed. Its temporary nature was unknown to him, but no friendship, no contract of sympathy or trust with other people, comes with a guarantee of permanence.

Finished with my package coffee, my stale bread and wartime goo, I set up a satellite router. The router was new, had cost me two thousand euros, and could get a signal at the North and South Poles. It was the size of a small box of chocolates. I flipped up its antenna. The lights flashed from red to green. No more traveling with a clumsy dish I would try to mount and angle to get my signal. This little box was working perfectly. I took care of messages while toggling between various news sites.

A heat wave was gripping all of southern Europe. The newspaper headline that morning was "L'ENFER" over a map of the bottom half of France. Trains would be delayed on account of the conditions. A forest was on fire in Provence. The article included quotes from the directors of morgues, where bodies were expected to pile up.

I enjoy heat, personally. It's vivifying.

The Lucien phone came to life. It was Vito, texting to say they were leaving the Calanques. It was full of stinging jellyfish.

—as opposed to some other kind of jellyfish?

—I'm emphasizing the danger. This body of water is thirty percent jellyfish. Serge says it's global warming.

—did anyone get stung.

—the soundman, Attilio. He's getting some goop from the pharmacy right now ... Sadie *do not* ask if Italians have a word like goop! They don't. The French don't either.

I silenced that phone and tried to figure out where Bruno's place was. I had no address, only a sense it was in the hills above Vantôme. Bruno had lived there with a wife and their three children when the accident occurred.

He never mentioned this accident in his emails to Pascal and the group. I know the outlines of the story through the dossier I was given on Bruno, which included a news clipping about it (and was otherwise quite thin considering French authorities had been watching him for half a century).

The timeline was spotty, but it seemed that by 1973, he and his wife had relocated to this area and begun to have children. His last of three, a girl, would have been born in 1980, as I deduced from the news clipping, which was dated 1988. According to the article, Bruno had been teaching his youngest to drive a tractor. The tractor was on a grade—it was hillside property—and the little girl was trying to turn it. The tractor tipped over and crushed her. She was eight years old.

Bruno's marriage did not survive this tragedy. From court records, I pieced together that just after the death of the child, his wife had left, along with his surviving daughter and son. A divorce was filed in Souillac, on the river Dordogne, suggesting that the wife had relocated to that area, rural, like this area, but with a tourist economy.

Bruno's letters made it seem as if he had good relations with both adult children. The surviving daughter now lived on his property, in the farmhouse where the whole family had once lived, and where Bruno no longer lived.

It was after the tractor accident resulting in the death of his daughter, and the departure of his remaining family, that Bruno vacated the farmhouse and moved into his barn.

He talked about this personal history, his house-to-barn transition, in the emails to Pascal, by explaining that he had wanted to be closer to a more rudimentary diurnal pattern, and attuned to his animals. (He had a cow, several sheep, a pig, geese, guinea fowl, and chickens. His ducks, which he'd set on his pond, were quickly "reabsorbed into the greater chain of being," he wrote, in other words eaten by predators.) No mention was ever made, in these emails to Pascal and the Moulinards, of the death of his younger daughter, her life cut short by a tractor.

He wrote instead about the smell of hay, which has one thousand different permutations, he said, depending on season, relative humidity, barometric pressure, what the animals have been eating and drinking to influence the fragrance and pH of their urine. Stored hay, he said, when properly dried, creates its own microclimate, warm in winter, cool in summer.

He talked about the swallows' nests accumulating on the high posts of his barn like "mailboxes," one on every post, and the swallows, the mail carriers, darting in and through the barn in a sinuous tangle of swooping deliveries, bringing mud and grass to patch or improve their mailbox, or with leggy insects threaded in their beaks for the pink-orange maws of their peeping young. These birds, he said, had traveled all the way from Africa on their annual migration. They came to his barn from across the world and they brought the world to him, as much of the world as he would ever want.

In the emails, Bruno's life in the barn was treated as part of a long and involved process of altering consciousness and retreating from civilization, which he saw as the only solution to this stage of late capitalism. Revolution, which back in 1968 he had believed was possible, he now understood to be foreclosed. The world ruled by capital would not be dismantled. Instead, it had to be left behind.

From the barn, life for Bruno grew simpler still.

As he described in his emails, he gave up the barn for an ancient drystone hut that had been on his property for five hundred years. No one knows, Bruno said, what these peculiar huts, of which there were perhaps a dozen in the hills above Vantôme, were originally used for, whether to store tools, or for a shepherd to seek shelter in a storm, or for some other reason. They were a kind of halfway station, Bruno said, between man and nature, between farming and wilds. They had no door, just an open entrance, and they were low, forcing a man to stoop and crawl. Bruno said his stone hut had both reduced and expanded his mind. The hut had expelled him from the world he knew, but opened him to a different one, a realm that was nomadic and dirty and damp, but revelatory.

That hut was his final built structure, Bruno said, before he went into the caves.

He had always known the caves were there, he wrote to Pascal and the Moulinards, but the depth of them, their spatial complexity, had stunned him.

We never expect the true depth of a cave, he said, on account of our indoctrination, our enslavement to the aboveground, which is scaled to us and above us, scaled to trees, to high-rise buildings, to the industrial dreams of twentieth-century man, and to his military imagination, scaled to fighter jets, and to heaven, to our need to claim something in the blue beyond, a thing we might call "blessed."

This vertical arrow aiming from ground to sky constitutes modern man's entire spatial reality, Bruno wrote. It excludes the other direction, he wrote, the down-into-the-earth. This is an incredible blind spot, he said, and he himself had not understood how blind, until he one day squeezed himself into his own cave, on his own little property in the Guyenne.

When he had purchased the land, in the early 1970s, the previous owner had shown him the cave as a curiosity. That owner had kept a board over its entrance. Beyond the board was an opening, a cavern five feet shallow, at the end of which two rocks angled together into a narrow crevice. For years, the board remained there. One day, in the period after he'd left the farmhouse, and the barn, and was sleeping in his little stone hut, Bruno removed the board and went in. He put his hand through the crevice in the rocks and felt wind. He understood that beyond the crevice there must be a large open space. He returned with ropes and a headlamp and pushed through the crevice and lowered himself. He did not hit bottom for quite a while. When he did, he was in an enormous room, its ceiling perhaps three meters high. He found multiple openings off this main room leading in different directions.

One particularly magnificent discovery was a chamber that was flocked white like a snowy landscape. Is this a dream? he wondered. It was not a dream. The walls were coated with magnesium crystals. They were blanketed in sparkling white, a natural geologic phenomenon. Some call this moon milk, Bruno wrote. It coated the floor. In that moon milk floor were indentations that he believed were records of human presence, and in particular, shapes that looked, and felt, like the footprints of a child.

There were regions of the underground network where water ran through, he said. The water was very cold. In some places it was neck-high, he said, and in the water lived strange crustaceans with translucent shells that seemed to thrive in absolute darkness.

This entire valley he said, was laced with underground springs and rivers and lakes. Because Bruno's adult son studied hydrology and currently worked in that field, he had helped Bruno to better understand the caverns and the water table and especially how to remain safe, because in winter, he said, caves could fill and quickly.

One day my son took me to a lavoir fed by a spring, Bruno said. The water is clear, my son pointed out. When the water is cloudy, he said, you know that someone has been in the cave whose spring fills this washbasin. The underground waterway, my son explained, has thick silt in its bed. When it is disturbed by footsteps, silt is kicked up.

The cave in which Bruno slept was dry year-round, if a good deal cooler in temperature than a modern Frenchman might prefer.

He planned to stay in the home he had made for himself underground. Although he did exit the caves regularly, as he indicated in the emails. He got fresh air. He tended to his permaculture, having renounced modern farming techniques. He took walks on shaded forest paths. And he wrote to Pascal Balmy and the Moulinards at a computer terminal that belonged to his adult daughter, in the kitchen of the old stone farmhouse.

Bruno's son had pointed out to him that the French government had more than clouded the waters of the communal washbasins. They had desecrated the entire subterranean world of southern France with tunnels for their high-speed trains.

I can hear the Paris–Toulouse from down there, Bruno said. I sense its vibrations. I feel the faintest touch of its wind.

Bruno's son was of the opinion that the state's mad plan to leach out all the groundwater and shunt it into industrial bays would wreck the ecological balance of the Guyenne.

When the digging work began for the Tayssac megabasin, Bruno said he was convinced he heard the sound of the excavators. He felt a level of disturbance that seemed to come from multiple directions, and from which there might be no escape. One day, the sound stopped, he said. The subterranean world was quiet, left in peace. But peace was temporary. These days, he said, I hear again the distant groan of machines clawing downward.

And just when I thought we were at last arriving at the main subject—sabotage of trains and of earth-moving equipment—Bruno went off the rails.

He'd been in these caves twelve years now, he said, and still he had not gotten to any definable "end," the caverns' design instead calling into question the whole concept of an end.

I hear people, he said, whose voices are eternal in this underground world, which is all planes of time on a single plane.

Here on earth is another earth, he said. A different reality, no less real. It has different rules.

You won't understand any of this from me telling you about it, Bruno said. You might even dismiss what I say. The little I myself understand has taken patience, he said, and rigorous deprogramming.

For nine-tenths of human time on earth people went underground. Their symbolic world was formed in part by their activities in caves, by modalities and visions that darkness promised. Then, this all ceased. The underground world was lost to us. The industrial uses of the earth, the digging, fracking, tunneling, are mere plunder and do not count, Bruno said. Modern people who build bomb shelters, planning to survive some version of apocalypse, also do not count, he said. Yes, they go underground, but not in mind of a human continuum, a community. They think, I'll be the clever one, the one who survives mass death. But why would you want to survive mass death? What would be the purpose of life, if life were reduced to a handful of armed pessimists hoarding canned foods and fearing each other? In a bunker, you cannot hear the human community in the earth, the deep cistern of voices, the lake of our creation.

In my cave, he said, under my cave, welling up from deeper passages, I hear so many things. Not just the drip of water.

I hear voices. People talking. Sometimes it's in French, sometimes Occitan, or older tongues of the Languedoc, many languages I do not recognize, sounds of which I cannot understand a word, but I know that what I hear is humans, it is human talk.

Did we always have language? We don't know the answer to this.

Linguists try to chart what they call "glotto-chronologies." They picture language like a tree, with a trunk. The first language, at the base of the trunk, being simple and common, what some call "nostratic." This is a fantasy. But who can refute them? They cannot escape the chains of their telos, the sad idea that they are the logical outcome, the advanced form of human speech, and that what came before must have been simple and crude.

They never imagine that if language is a tree, they must look not at its trunk, but at its roots, which, like a tree's roots, might form an upside-down chandelier of extravagant complexity, reaching and spreading deep into the dark beyond. But most people are unable to grasp how far down the physical world goes. And they would not know that voices are stored in its depths, unless they were to hear those voices.

It is hard to explain, he said. You would have to have lived as I live, done what I have done, learned what I have learned, in order to hear what I hear. You would need a different consciousness, he said.

When you live underground, among the things you discover is that you are not alone. You're in a world richly peopled. Occupied by legions.

Homo erectus, who stood up and cooked, Bruno said, he is here.

Homo neanderthalensis, who huddled modestly and dreamed expansively: here.

Homo sapiens, gone into caves to paint, to render his capture with extra legs, extra horns, so that these beasts canted and ran over cave walls, or butted heads, clashed and fought, all in the light of a torch, *H. sapiens*'s underground cinema house: that resourceful and ruinous forbear of ours, he is here.

Cathars and other heretics, the few not slaughtered, gone deep, living in darkness: yes, present.

Cagots, after the war of 1594, hiding to survive. Surviving in secret. Here.

Cavers, nineteenth-century men and boys, killed by curiosity, fallen in, unable to make their way out: here.

The partisans, men of my own boyhood, who retreated underground to hide from rampaging Germans: they, too, are here.

For a long time, he said, you cannot tune in. Then, you might sense a current or buzz of telluric energy. This sound transforms, the more time you spend in caves. It becomes voices. You hear these voices but are unable to isolate them. It takes years to learn how to listen, to differentiate, to adjust your inner tuner to a position on the atemporal bandwidth of the underground world.

Remember shortwave transmission? he asked them. Probably you don't, he answered. Tuning into shortwave programming used to be an art, Bruno said. Depending on the bandwidth, it worked best at night, on account of how radio waves travel back from the ionosphere. There was a book, he said, that listed programs by calendar schedule and megahertz. Some of the programs came in stronger than others. You learned to listen for where to put the shortwave dial, between two points of static, and how to position your antenna, in order to hear a Bulgarian choir or news from Senegal or Venezuela's Radio Juventud.

Shortwave is real, of course, he said. It is also a metaphor. I bring it up not to reminisce over dead technologies, but to help you understand.

Cave frequencies, he said, are not three to thirty megahertz. Cave bandwidth crosses moments, eras, epochs, eons. You have to learn to get inside the monophony, to tease it apart. Eventually, you encounter an extraordinary polyphony. You begin to sort, to filter. You hear whispers, laughter, murmurs, pleas. There's a feeling that everyone is here. A wonderful feeling, I should add. Because suddenly you realize how alone we have been, how isolated, to be trapped, stuck in calendar time, and cut off from everyone who came before us.

I never want to be that alone again, he said.

I WOULD KEEP READING, to see if these "voices" Bruno claimed to hear were telling him the Moulinards should interfere with state plans. But for now, I shut the computer and closed up the Dubois house.

I placed on the front and back doors two lockboxes, which I programmed and set, preventing anyone but me, who knew their codes, from getting in.

This house was now my base of operation, and only I would be breaching its entrances. If Lucien's aunt Agathe made trouble, I'd explain to Lucien that I added the locks out of fear for my safety, as a woman, a foreigner, staying alone in this remote area. Agathe herself had told Lucien there had been break-ins close by.

Agathe had complained to Lucien about the inconvenience of driving over to deposit the key (Lucien could not find his own), since she lived over an hour away. Hopefully she'd stay an hour away.

The private road that the house was on crossed the walnut orchard and then led into dark wilds, land that belonged to the Dubois family but was untended.

I walked the road, which was graveled but too narrow for a car, under canopies of beech and oak, tall trees whose branches wove together and prevented direct sun from penetrating.

The dim light here converted the woods to a tangle of shadows and gave me an unpleasant feeling.

Bruno was some kind of lunatic, I considered, as I walked in the half-light.

At the same time, I could not help but see his discussions of cave frequency as a naked expression of grief. He was down there looking for his dead daughter, convincing himself he heard her voice.

I heard footsteps in the gravel just behind me.

I turned around. On the path was a large bird with long legs, a heron, its body dusty blue and floating like a petticoat. It stepped and restepped on the path's soft embankment, which collapsed under its large gangly feet.

"What's your problem," I said to it.

It moved in place, stepping on its thin legs.

Why was it not in a hurry to get away, I wondered, and then I saw why: it had a gopher in its beak. Its instinct to eat was overriding its instinct to flee. It took sideways steps, its large beak like gardening shears holding the gopher.

It aimed its head up to swallow the gopher and took off flying with a lot of frantic flapping.

Nature doesn't bother me. What bothers me in nature is the possibility of people. I get a feeling in woods, no matter how remote they are, that someone could be around. I was still on edge from that moment at the abandoned truck stop, flinching to think someone was approaching as I squatted in a vulnerable position, peeing next to women's underpants discarded on a bush, a scene I'd come to think of as the Tomb of the Unknown Hooker.

The woods gave way to a plateau with farmland on either side, fields of yellow grass, and large rolls of hay wrapped in white plastic like giant pills. No vehicles appeared as I walked along this road. I heard cowbells in the distance, and a soft nagging drone of farm machinery being operated somewhere out of sight.

On a hillside above the road was a little stone hovel, no windows, crudely built, with a dark and open doorway. It looked like a sad shelter for a nomad or vagrant. It looked like the sort of hut that Bruno had described and had lived in.

I passed rows of pruned vines, heavy with clusters of purple grapes. I stopped to eat a few.

Bruno had said the old Occitan name for this region, unknown to many, even those who studied Occitan, was the Aguienne Neire. "Neire" meant black, he said, and might have referred to black walnuts and black grapes. But more fundamentally, he said, this ancient name referred to the black of the caves.

It was curious to realize, as I tasted these grapes, how much I knew about this region, a place I couldn't care less about. I would not be here long, and when the job was finished, I would never see this remote little corner of France again. I would drive the rental car to Paris and meet my contacts and get fresh documents and then it would be a flight from Charles de Gaulle to my next destination. This place would all but cease to exist.

But because of Bruno's attention to local features, I had learned some of them. I knew this variety of grape I was tasting, the darkest by skin color, purple-black. The juice, Bruno said, was famously sweet, and here I was, tasting these local grapes, as sweet as he claimed.

And while I had not taken seriously his disquisition in one of the letters that the walnut orchard was a metaphor for wisdom, its filtering of light like the necessary filtering of truths, ugly ones hidden and useful ones highlighted, I had myself just traversed the Dubois property's walnut orchard, nuts moldering on the ground, their skins split and dehiscing. And while these skins were green, I knew they were a variety of black walnut, on account of Bruno.

Some kind of lunatic, a man who lived in a cave and ranted about cave frequencies, but his descriptions of the region were being confirmed one after the other.

I was on a high road now that was like the spine of an enormous sleeping animal. I could see Vantôme, and the scarred, logged hillsides above it, and down below, the glint of the lake. I could see one of the two rivers that crossed the valley, and various tributaries, marked by thickets of greenery in the folds where hills touched, forming natural hedges between tracts of land.

"Neire" could also have referred to the Guyenne's forests, Bruno had said, which are dense, at least those not defaced by logging.

I had just traversed that density. Released from it, I could see the defacement.

East of Vantôme was a series of low hills above the lake, where I suspected Bruno lived, based on his descriptions.

At the top of those hills was a castle. I could see its towers, the overlapping slate tiles glistening like fish scales in the sunlight. I peered through my binoculars. Four towers. This had to be the Château de Gaume, whose history Bruno recounted in one of his letters.

Below the Château de Gaume, closer to the lake, the land was all forested. Somewhere in there was Bruno, but all I saw through the binoculars was blurry and overmagnified green.

IT WAS TEN A.M. and getting quite hot. I consulted the iPhone (there was no cell service in this countryside but I'd loaded the map before leaving the house; I'd also brought a satellite phone in case I needed it). I realized I wasn't far from a connector to the D43, which would be the shortest route back to the Dubois house.

This steep connector switchbacked down to the D43 past huge walls of limestone. As I walked, the high sun illuminated uncanny colors in the limestone, colors so vibrant and bright they looked artificial. Some areas were lavender, but patterned with lichen that was gold-bright like ground turmeric. Other lichens were creamy white and stretched along the rock face like embroidery. I passed, on these switchbacks, limestone cliffs that were striped in lemon yellow. Aren't rocks supposed to be gray? I passed bands that were streaked the red of freshly butchered meat. Farther along this same section of rock shelf were drips of pale pink like candy hearts, and then thick vertical washes of baby blue. This had to be paint. I stopped to inspect. I touched the rock. It was warm as a body, from the sun. It wasn't paint. The color was inside the limestone.

As I walked, I passed an opening in the rock covered by a barred grate, like a little door. I thought about what Bruno said, that these caves look as if they end, but they do not end. The little barred door had a lock. Who has the key to these things, I wondered. I put my ear to the grate. I heard the very faint trickle of water and felt cool air against my cheek.

On the other side of the road, farther down, was a sign that said "lavoir" with an arrow. There were wooden steps leading off the road to a rectangular stone pool.

I sat on the edge and put a hand in the pool, to wash off the sticky residue of grapes. I studied the ripple the spring made on the water's surface. I understood that to put a hand in it was to touch what has been in the earth.

This kind of communal basin is standard in rural France, where women washed clothes, shared news, gossiped. I had an unsettled feeling of company, like other people, the women who had long ago come here to gossip, were here with me now.

I wasn't afraid of them, which I took as a possible sign the heat was getting to me.

AMONG THE MEANINGS OF "NEIRE," in the ancient name of the region, was bloodshed, Bruno said.

Neire was the history of violent struggle in this little valley of the greater Guyenne.

I here refer, he said, to the long and curious history of the Cagot, which you may not know much about, but should. For one thousand years in the Guyenne, Cagots were banished from community life, submitted to a range of untouchable-isms, and driven into the forests and onto high bluffs, where they survived secretly, in rock shelters and caves, sleeping in stone huts.

There are theories, he said, that these huts, like the one on Bruno's own property, are in fact Cagot architecture—Cagot design and construction—given that those deemed Cagot were forced into a nomadic and furtive life, traveling at night like escaped prisoners, to limit their contact with others.

These people were forbidden to keep farm animals. They could not enter taverns, or drink from communal cisterns, or wash in communal lavoirs, or shop in village markets. They were believed to live on black bread, roots, rodents, and creek water. If a Cagot came to town, he was forced to walk under rain gutters and downspouts. If one of them was caught violating the law, a strip of vertical flesh was removed on either side of his spine. It was not a crime to murder one of them.

The Cagots could not worship in church, or take Communion, with the single exception of the parish of Vantôme, whose tolerant and eccentric clergy offered these poor souls Communion from the side of the chapel, through a slit of a door that is still there. The opening was narrow so that clergymen were protected from having to look at the Cagots, as it was believed that meeting their gaze was dangerous. The priest held out a long wooden spoon through the narrow door, the host balanced in the spoon's ladle. Perhaps the most merciful acts in all of Christendom, Bruno said, took place in the little garden of the Vantôme chapel.

The Cagots were tall, sturdy of frame, with large faces and a heavy brow that gave them a brooding look. Many had red hair and pale complexions. Legend had it they were of rare and unique intelligence.

You may guess, he said, where this is heading, and indeed: there was an ancient rumor that the Cagot was a strain of earlier human, perhaps Neanderthal, which might account for why they had been barred from blending into the population.

Young people like yourselves, Bruno said, addressing Pascal and the Moulinards, are so often focused on 1871. The Paris Commune as our only flicker of something more, something better. I would like to point you toward a different date. I want you to look at 1594: the year of the Cagot Rebellion.

The Cagot Rebellion began here, he said. It was mobilized on the grounds of our local ruin, the Château de Gaume.

The Count of Vantôme, the feudal lord who controlled this region, had a barren wife. The village doctor could do nothing for her. The count's footman told him of a Cagot named Jacques who had magical powers to heal ailments.

Jacques the Cagot lived in a rock shelter above the creek (one could assume this was near the D79, Bruno said, before, of course, there was a D79). Jacques had jet-black hair and ice-blue eyes. He was two meters tall. For his striking looks, and his reputation for useful magic, Jacques had been afforded certain rights not normally given to Cagots. He was allowed to own a horse, and he had freedom of movement other Cagots did not enjoy. The name of Jacques's horse was Loli, a swaybacked mare that was much beloved and doted on by Jacques, who believed that his horse was the secret to his own power, that she was a magic horse.

The count sent for Jacques, who came to his manor riding Loli, his beloved mare. Jacques was brought to the bedside of the count's wife. She told her husband to wait outside, that she wanted absolute quiet while Jacques performed the magical rites that would heal her sterility.

In the days and weeks after Jacques's visit, the count's wife underwent a transformation. She was fatigued and nauseous and her belly began to grow. Her hair turned lustrous and thick. Her skin glowed. Her chambermaid gossiped, said she had begun hearing the count and his wife conducting loud and strenuous entanglements in the lady's chambers. My own interpretation of this, Bruno said, is that the count knew he could take no credit for his wife's condition, and thus he was trying to *overtake* her already-pregnancy, against all logic, by inserting a second seed, which would, in his own magical thinking, somehow replace the first seed, clearly Jacques the Cagot's. Jacques who was handsome, young, two meters tall, and given absolute privacy to cure another man's wife of a fertility impasse.

When the child was born, a baby girl, it had black hair and pale blue eyes. The count, in a rage—not his child, and even worse, a girl—threw the baby into a well. He cast out his wife, who had to be taken in by her own wet nurse. The count brought charges of sorcery against Jacques, who was burned at the stake with his beloved horse, Loli.

The brutality of the count's acts, the murder of a baby, the public burning of Jacques, the shunning of his wife, none of these, on their own, sparked what happened next, a revolt that convulsed the whole of the greater Guyenne.

There is always some tipping point, an incitement so outrageous among the smaller but no less hideous acts, that sweeps people into a full-scale insurrection, Bruno said. But we must not romanticize, he said. What made the peasants blind with rage was not the treatment of Jacques and of the baby. Remember, Bruno said, that Cagots were categorically subhuman. The count's wife, for her gender, was sub-man and a baby girl sub-baby.

It was Loli that was the final straw. A fiefdom that could burn an innocent horse at the stake was a fiefdom worth destroying.

A little background here, Bruno said, is important to understand: For thirty years the peasants had been conscripted by the nobility to fight the religious wars. For a peasant who had never strayed more than a half day's walk from where he was born, these wars were abstract, wars he was told he must die for and also must pay for, whether through taxation or extortion or land seizure. This situation and its discontents partly explains how it was that peasants and Cagots, historical enemies, suddenly conspired and came together to attack the nobles.

Peasants had targeted the Cagots for generations, and so this collusion between Cagot and peasant was shocking. It was as if, Bruno said, the poor white overseer and the Black man forced into chattel slavery had colluded against plantation owners in the American South, as if the poor white overseer all at once discarded his racial superiority, recognizing it as a dirty prize and little more, for his own servitude.

A peasant had been brought up to believe a Cagot would steal and slaughter your pig or good laying hen. A Cagot would poison your well.

He might kidnap your children, curse the weather, blight your crops, or blind a person who met him face-to-face on the road.

Suddenly, these strange people, with their white skin, their red hair, tall and strong and good fighters, were coming out of the woods to help the peasants plan their attacks against the local and regional nobility. And the peasant had to ask himself, Even if he looks a bit different from me, what is it that I hold against this man, the Cagot? Why have I believed he is my enemy, when my real enemies are the magistrate and the tax collector?

The local castle, the Château de Gaume, which had been looted and wrecked in the sieges of the religious wars, became the staging area of this unholy alliance of peasants and Cagots.

The roads to Vantôme brimmed with young and able-bodied men on foot, on donkey, on horseback, traveling to the Château de Gaume to join the rebellion. Some ledgers had it there was a ragtag army of twenty thousand, peasant and Cagot planning and plotting together on the castle grounds.

From the château, the peasants and the Cagots launched a series of attacks on the local nobility, whose armies were outnumbered. The skills of peasants and Cagots, Bruno said, were harmonious, because different. The peasants, for whom military service had been compulsory, used their training to plan their attacks. The Cagots were talented tree climbers with guerrilla tactics and night vision (legend had it that their eyes, like the eyes of a nightjar, glowed orange in the dark).

Working together they launched an offensive and captured nine nobles, who were brought to the Château de Gaume, where they were beheaded on the castle's open promontory. Centuries prior to the "humane" invention of the guillotine, these beheadings were accomplished with an axe, an imperfect instrument requiring two or three or four swings, making local woodcutters ideal for this assignment. The Cagots and peasants used the nobles' severed heads for games of pétanque, which the peasants taught to the Cagots. Given that Cagots had not been allowed the standard few rituals of leisure—dancing, lawn bowling—that a peasant was allowed, they were unfamiliar with the rules of pétanque, much less pétanque with severed nobles' heads.

So far so good, Bruno said. But do you even need to hear what comes next? You can imagine it. The rebellion was crushed, and brutally.

King Henry IV called in reinforcements, so many troops that their horses stirred up an enormous churn, a column of dust that could be seen from the tactical lookouts along the highest bluffs in the valley. A huge army was bearing down on their fortification in the Château de Gaume. As news spread of the imminent arrival of the king's armed troops, some of the peasants betrayed the Cagots, to try to save themselves in desperate acts of turncoatism, such as running toward the approaching army with their arms up, shouting surrender (many were trampled to death in the process). The army captured everyone, regardless, and herded them all onto the promontory of the château. Cagots and peasants side by side were slaughtered without differentiation, as one enemy. Hundreds were buried in a mass grave on the château's grounds.

As order in the region was reestablished, an amnesia set in, Bruno said. The peasants took up, once again, the social contract of their rulers, which required of them that they loathe those deemed Cagot, their own superiority over this wretched creature a paltry payment for serfdom, but a payment nonetheless.

Later, in the chaos of the monarchy's collapse, Cagots stormed local magistrates, burning birth certificates and other records of their low social status. Legally, they became French, and thus the Cagots—as a category, a trauma, a foreclosed victory—all but vanished.

The strange history of the Château de Gaume, Bruno said, has only reinforced this vanishing. In 1940, when nomadism was outlawed by the Vichy, the château became a prison overseen by German officers. Communists, teachers, trade unionists, and all manner of "undesirables," gypsies and Poles, "persons with no fixed address," were rounded up and held there. Many died of malnutrition or dysentery, or were shot while attempting to flee, and put in a mass grave. This is why no French leader has ever agreed to examine the castle's grounds, which have been abandoned for decades.

Relatives of those interred there in 1940 have asked for a monument. The descendants of Cagots have asked for no such thing. People of that lineage, Bruno said, do not announce it. Instead, Cagot heritage is a secret flame that is cupped and held and protected from the wind.

AS I TURNED UP the shaded gravel road to the house from the D43, eager to get home, take a shower, and drink some water (I didn't trust the water in the lavoir), I heard a car coming down this private road, from the direction of the house. And then I saw the car: a little white Citroën panel truck, an older man driving it. His windows were down.

"Sadie? It's Robert!"

I smiled as if I knew who this was.

"Your uncle!" he said in an aggressively friendly voice. "You don't know me. We've never met you. And Agathe said to me, why don't you make the trip, see if she's gotten into the house okay. Show her some hospitality. That's Agathe. She worries. And I knew, there's no settling this without driving over, to make sure you're okay. Never mind that Agathe and I have never even caught a glimpse of you. No one has. It's a bit odd!" He chuckled.

"But Lucien, he was always off the beaten path. I thought he was, you know. There's one in every family, right? We weren't offended not to get much warning he was having you stay in the house. But we were curious. It's natural to wonder. The Dubois name is quite . . . you know. These people are protective and even a bit snob if you want to know what I think. No one in that family does care what I think. But between us, Sadie, they have a point. I have to admit they have a point. The thing is no one seems to know anything about you. Our daughter did a bit of research on the internet. She said there wasn't much. A page she thought might be yours on some kind of professional network, but you needed to join the network to see the details."

Sadie Smith is what this man and his daughter would know to type in. But Smith isn't even a name. It's a placeholder. Smith is Anglo-American for Last Name, which makes me barely googleable, lost in a sea of Smiths. There's a LinkedIn page, nothing suspicious about it.

I stepped toward his window.

Robert was overweight and bald, with purplish-red blotches on his neck and face. His laugh was phlegmy and emphysemic; he rumbled. Behind his big smile and his loud voice, he looked ill. Not long for this world.

"I told Agathe, let the boy be," he went on. "It's a relief he's not, you know—"

"Lucien isn't gay," I said.

"Oh, I do not think he is!" He laughed, which sent him into a coughing fit.

You're headed for portable oxygen, I didn't say.

"And, you know, Lucien"—he was looking me up and down—"maybe he's done okay for himself."

There was something wrong with Robert's eyeballs. They were pointy. They bulged, as if trying to lurch toward what he was looking at, *get a head start*. Or like someone had stepped on his eyeballs by accident, squishing them out of round.

Is that a health condition? I wondered.

"I told my wife, go easy. Don't pry into Lucien's business. Technically it's his house. This American woman, sure, we don't know her, and she seems to have come . . . out of nowhere. Still, she's his girlfriend. We'll make the trip over to the house when they invite us."

"But here you are," I said.

"You don't know Agathe. She's asking about you."

I stepped closer to his car window. I was wearing just a cotton-stretch running bra, on account of the heat. Sweat was trickling down into the bra where it pushed my breasts together.

Robert's hideous eyeballs roved over me like the points of two pool cues, like he could probe me with them.

"I get here and see that you have put these locks on the front and back door. I wasn't able to use our keys."

"It's Lucien's house, as you just said. Perhaps you don't need keys."

"Yes, sure. It is Lucien's! Families hand things down, not over and across, right? Never mind that Agathe took care of this house for the last decade, making the trip on these little roads to keep an eye out, be sure it hadn't been burgled—over the last five years a lot of the old manoirs have been ransacked! Because people from Paris, they inherit these places, like Lucien inherited his, and they don't come down. The country? Inconvenient. Dull. Not much to do. 'Full of rednecks,' right, Sadie? They come two weeks a year, make a big display of their ancestral pedigree, play feudal lord, pack up and leave. People get wind of which houses are empty. They back up a moving truck. These are real thieves. Professionals, who know antiques, they know which books are valuable and all of that. They sift through everything and leave the junk behind."

There is nothing of value here, I didn't say. They can back their truck up and steal baby stickers and a hot plate.

"Agathe was always worried about this happening to the Dubois house. Didn't want it robbed. Didn't want its pipes to freeze or its roof to collapse. Always making the drive, making calls, trying to help out. Now, of course, the house has gone to Lucien, from his father's side, and not to my wife, despite all her work. We don't dispute that. Still," he said, "it's a bit peculiar that you would show up out of nowhere and lock everything."

He smiled, revealing a gold crown with a thick line of dark rot at its base.

"And the strangest thing," he said, "is something no one knows but me. It was sent to my wife, to an email account she never checks. And after I read it, I thought, Say nothing. You don't know Agathe. She worries. She has a heart condition and it is aggravated by stress. Her doctor said, keep the stress level down. I didn't tell her about this email. I didn't want to upset her. The email was about you."

"Is that right," I said. "What did it say?"

"That you aren't who you say you are." His pointy eyeballs roved over me.

I leaned down into his window. "Who am I, then?"

"Someone else," he said. He broke into his cough-laugh, but he could not sustain it because nothing was funny.

Lucien had told me that his aunt Agathe had married her gardener. Or her landscaper. She married down, was the point, way down.

No one in the family liked this man, although Lucien hadn't quite put it like that. The uncle didn't fit in, was what I understood from Lucien's coded language. (Then again, it could be argued that a good bourgeois family isn't truly good if their purity isn't marked a little by some bumbler from low-class stock marrying in: he reminds them what they are worth, and what they need to protect from people like him.)

I had done a little research on the situation. This Robert lived off Agathe, and he had taken out a quite beefy life-insurance policy on her, perhaps around the time they learned she had a heart condition.

I walked to the passenger side of Robert the Uncle's little proletarian vehicle and opened the door. I got in and sat down next to him. The woods were still and quiet. There were no sounds but Robert's labored breathing, which was ramping up, like he was excited.

Did he think this was going to be a date? A quickie?

"I have nothing to hide from your wife or from anyone in Lucien's family. But you, Robert, you do have things to hide. We both know that."

He shot me a look of fear.

I turned toward him, my head against the seat, like this was pillow talk.

"If you stay away from here, Robert, and mind your own business," I said in my most girlish voice, "I won't, for my part, say anything."

I mentioned the insurance policy. The name of the carrier. The amount. The date it had been taken out.

"You go home, and you tell Agathe everything is fine here. And when Lucien arrives, we will invite the two of you to dinner."

He stared at me as I got out. His look was dejected and childish, like I had just taken something that belonged to him, and broken it, and handed it back.

IV

LEMON INCEST

AN HOUR LATER, driving toward my meeting with Pascal Balmy, I found myself following a white Citroën panel truck as I entered a roundabout and took the turnoff for Vantôme.

Was this Robert the Curious? He should have left the area already.

This panel truck exited the roundabout at the turn before mine. The driver was a woman.

A few minutes later, another white Citroën panel truck appeared, traveling in the opposite direction, a young man behind the wheel.

A white Citroën panel truck is the most common utility vehicle in all of France, I reminded myself. I adjusted the volume downward on my mental alert for Robert the Unpleasant.

He might return. But for now, today, these vans were *not his*. And whoever had contacted Robert, whatever that was, I would fix it.

IT WAS TWELVE THIRTY P.M. as I arrived in Vantôme.

I parked my rental car near the village church and walked toward the Café de La Route, where Pascal had said to meet him.

The church was small and in disrepair, its plaster facade zigzagged with cracks, its main doors an unpainted wood that looked petrified. The doors were bolted shut.

I guessed that like so many other little parish churches across rural France, this one was long out of use. Its yard had thickets of stinging nettles and clumps of spear thistle, a dry fountain next to a secondary door in the side of the church, toward its rear, where the sacristy would have been. This side door was painted pale green, the powdery color of oxidized copper. It was warped and cracked and perhaps ten inches wide. A strangely narrow door, the width of a gym locker.

I pictured those people, the Cagots, young and old, men, women, children, waiting in an orderly line to receive the host on the end of a long wooden spoon. Not allowed in the church. Forced to pray at this little side door. I imagined them dressed crudely, in cloaks of rough burlap, these social outcasts without rights, who would come into the village to submit to the authority of the church. There was something moving about it, as if God and God's emissaries on earth were separate from the cruel feudal structure that deemed them "Cagot."

I had cross-checked some of what Bruno had written about these people, and it seemed they were real. They had different names, Cagot or Caqueaux or Gahet, Gotz or Quagotz or Bisigotz, Astragotz, or Gahetz.

In most versions of the story, it was believed they were afflicted with an "internal leprosy," an invisible taint, in addition to "maladies of brain," deliriums precipitated by full moons and other celestial turns. What Bruno had described regarding the lenient conditions of their worship in Vantôme, groovy priests who offered Communion to the wretched through a little door, was reiterated in various histories.

A big wind moved through the churchyard, stirring the tall and sturdy thistles, their purple tips bobbing like the needles of metronomes, and riffling the green stinging nettles that clustered around the dry fountain and grew right up to the old Cagot door.

Perhaps it was my own malady of brain, but I felt that the wind was moving through the churchyard in response to my thoughts, like it was an affirmation of my sudden awareness that this door was *that* door, and the wind was saying, "Yes. Yes it is."

The Café de la Route was on the main square, next to the mayor's office, a buff-colored nineteenth-century building fringed with paper flyers for community meetings. A sun-bleached French flag, tattered from exposure, hung in strips above the entrance to the mayor's office.

The leafed canopy of a huge plane tree, the bark of its trunk flaked in patches, arched over the square, creating a dappled light on the cobblestones as I crossed toward the café.

This café seemed to be the main life of the village. Its interior was two storefronts connected by an open doorway. One side was an épicerie, a little market that sold basic provisions, and the other a bar with an espresso machine, a couple of beer taps, a small selection of displayed liquors. The walls of the bar were dirty from tobacco smoke and hung with old photographs, presumably of loyal customers. The place was empty except for two old men in spirited conversation, their noses purple from the grape. (I tend toward white wine, in fear that red leaves such stains if you keep at it long enough.)

Behind the bar was a woman in her forties, topping off the old timers' drinks. She had thick dark hair pulled away from her face by a headband that showcased her dramatic widow's peak and even features. She was the kind of woman I'd call "handsome." She told me to take any seat. I chose a table out front with a good view of the square.

I could hear the two men inside, their raspy cheerful voices. Thanks to Pascal's strategy to augur goodwill by reopening the bar, they could escape their wives and sit drinking, undisturbed, on a weekday afternoon.

As I waited to order, two people appeared on the otherwise empty square. The man wore a torn safari vest and a faded Mao cap. The woman had black leather cuffs on both of her wrists. They carried overstuffed army backpacks, which they helped each other to remove and set upon the ground, the packs lolling like huge dusty crustaceans turned on their backs. They looked to be middle aged or older, in their fifties, perhaps, but the elements could have wizened them prematurely.

The handsome waitress approached them, asking did they want a table.

The couple shook their heads no, no thanks, and they stepped back warily from the outdoor seating area.

They were too old for this kind of vagabonding, this kind of penilessness.

They picked up their giant backpacks, carried them across the square, and took up a kind of squatting position against the exterior wall of the church, near that warped little door where a Cagot would have begged for his Communion.

What I didn't initially understand was that these two were also waiting for Pascal, even if he was not intending to meet them as he was me.

The sun was overhead and there was no shade in the churchyard. The way this couple squatted, they both looked accustomed to pretending that squatting is comfortable, that stinging nettles and spear thistles are not a problem. Their pretending was like the biker who pretends his ape hangers don't tire his arms as he roars down the highway (but later he relies on Icy Hot, and on me, to slather it on biceps and shoulder).

My biker and these tramps, as people who organize their life around some subculture or other: People can sometimes pretend so thoroughly that they forget they are pretending. At which point, it could even be said that they are no longer pretending.

Monitoring that biker and his crowd was such different work than what I do now. But in its difference, and because it was my earliest job, my first, it has stayed with me. It was basic policework, entry-level and crude. I had infiltrated a northwestern chapter of the Gypsy Jokers, as the "old lady" (his euphemism; I was twenty-four) of a member who was later convicted, with my help, of racketeering charges. For several weeks, this biker was my "old man," and now he's a truly old man and in prison in Washington State. It wasn't real intelligence work, but it led to everything that came after. All I did was wear a wire and wait for the right moment.

The waitress came outside to take my order. There was something about her that I liked, her even features, her thick dark hair and that widow's peak, her embroidered blue peasant's blouse. Her movements had a naturalness to them, a certain casual authority.

The man in the Mao cap removed from his safari vest what looked to be vaping equipment and squinted into the sun. The woman produced from a fanny pouch her own version of vaping equipment, and the two of them began to suck on these elaborate contraptions, large handheld objects with curves that reminded me of figureheads on ship prows.

I try to be sensitive to details, but the paraphernalia of vaping will forever remain oblique to me for the reason that I don't vape. I used to smoke, perhaps on account of some percentage of Neanderthal in my lineage, although I'll never know what percentage, not wanting my DNA in any database.

I watched as the woman stood to retrieve from her backpack her own faded black Mao cap, identical to his. She put it on and adjusted the brim and resumed her position next to him, the two of them leaning against the stone of the old church, gazing off, sucking on their vape contraptions.

Pascal Balmy was not late. I was early. The couple in their Mao caps was early. As we waited, a man rolled past the café in a convertible Chrysler Sebring.

"Lemon Incest" floated from its stereo. A Chrysler Sebring seemed like an unusual make and model for a tiny remote village in southwest France, a place where you would expect to see dusty little eco-carts, Renault Clios and Fiat Pandas. Citroën panel trucks. I watched as the driver of this Chrysler executed a clumsy eleven-point U-turn in order to park his Sebring, with "Lemon Incest" blaring.

There were two workers on the road beyond the square, unshaven young men in government-blue coveralls, sex symbols of the French proletariat, repainting a crosswalk with rollers on extender bars. You see these men all over Europe, on streets and highways, in their state uniforms, reflective silver material in a thick band around the cuffs of their pants. Such men on roadsides constitute "Europe" just as trucking and pallets and nuclear power are Europe.

The men painting the crosswalk paused and looked over, laughing at the Sebring driver's slow and impractical attempt to turn his car around.

The disco beat with sexual sighs of "Lemon Incest" continued, the famous father in this duet low and quavering, the young daughter joining in, not holding her notes, but in key, a soprano that was ice-cream-headache high.

The man parked his Sebring, interrupting the music as he killed the motor. He got out and crossed the square. He wore large, tinted sunglasses and a scarf at his neck.

One of the workers laying new paint called the man a French term for faggot. Lemon Incest responded by exaggerating his sashay. One of the other workers whistled.

I understood that he was not a woman to these men in coveralls, but they objectified and denigrated him as if he were a woman, as if their insult were a catcall. Before he reached the curb, he dropped his burning cigarette in the wet paint the men had just laid with their rollers. He stepped on it and pushed his foot around. The workers laughed as he ruined their painted stripe.

He said something to them that I didn't hear, as he tracked wet paint and turned a corner out of view.

Pascal Balmy showed up at exactly one p.m. He walked toward me in cargo shorts and Birkenstocks, a stack of books under his arm.

The anarchist kids in Paris who had followed him down here to build a commune would, I assumed, be in dirty black, not camp shorts and Birkenstocks. It made Pascal seem cooler than I'd expected him to be that he was dressed like a dork.

The couple in their Mao caps quickly extinguished or turned off their vaping equipment or whatever you do to it and excitedly walked toward him, calling his name. He semi-ignored them (glanced at them and, as quickly, glanced away) and headed for my table.

Pascal and I had not met before this moment. But he walked toward me gently smiling like we were in on something. We were at least in on the fact that he had guessed correctly who I was, or rather, who he believed me to be, based on Lucien's summary and the photograph of me that Lucien favored (it was the screen saver on his phone) and that Lucien definitely (proudly) would have sent to Pascal.

I recognized Pascal too, his boyish and kind face, round, wire-rimmed glasses lending him a patrician air that seemed out of place here in tumble-down Vantôme.

As he came closer, I looked at him as though unsure if he was the person I was here to meet.

I stood as he approached. "Are you—"

"Yes," he said, preempting the utterance of his name. "Yes I am."

He smiled.

I smiled back and we hugged like old friends.

THERE WERE FEW public photos of Pascal. His name came up in Google because of the Times Square incident. Journalists reporting on that case had circulated a photo believed to be Pascal Balmy that was not him. It was a Facebook profile photo of some guy with the same name. *That* Pascal Balmy was on a jet ski, wearing a life vest and wraparound sunglasses.

There were images of the real Pascal Balmy in my dossier. In one, taken in a Parisian bar among friends, Pascal's haircut looks to be an exact replica of the signature hairstyle of Guy Debord in the 1950s and '60s—short, even bangs over a high forehead. The faces, and the expressions, of Pascal and the younger Debord before his dissolution were similar: sensitive features, a supple mouth, a well-formed chin, a gaze that was both dreamy and penetrating.

The most curious photo in the dossier, which at first I took to be Pascal as a toddler, was of a beautiful baby about a year old. The baby gazes off to the right, with clear, bright eyes, a dark etched line around each iris. The curls of the baby's hair are as lustrous as a silent screen star's. His little pursed mouth suggests knowledge of things unsaid. The bottom of the photo is faded out, so that the baby seems to rise from a kind of ether—an intended studio effect. The ether gives the baby a diaphanous wisdom, as if it occupies not this earth but some eternal plane of peace and harmony. Later, I found this same photo online and its caption was "Guy Louis Debord, 1932." Either my contacts in Paris were interchanging their files, or Pascal had passed this off as his own baby picture, or it was no one's baby picture and everyone's baby picture, a kind of commons of innocent purity that could be borrowed and passed around.

Most of the images in the dossier of grown-up Pascal had been taken at long range, as surveillance, with a telephoto lens, from crowd scenes at a G8 summit in Genoa, back in 2001. Pascal during a street melee with Italian riot police, his figure circled in each image.

Another set of photos, which were my favorites, because no one in them has any idea they are being photographed (at a G8 summit, *everyone* knows they are being photographed), were profile views of Pascal and seven or eight other people walking down a city street in a loose group. These photos were of individuals from a network of climate activists who had converged for a "meeting" in Times Square of New York City in 2008. Pascal Balmy had entered the United States at the Canadian border, having been driven from the border down to New York City by a "comrade" who was in fact an undercover agent for the UK police, and this comrade had tipped off the FBI about the meeting, whose purpose, this undercover agent said, was to plan an act of terrorism to take place in Times Square.

The photos show young men in sunglasses and army parkas with cool haircuts walking on a brisk morning down 44th Street. Pascal is there, in a horsehide leather jacket and checked scarf, his wire-rimmed glasses. He's holding the hand of a petite young woman in a Fair Isle cap and a peacoat. They are seen walking past bodegas and pretzel carts and delivery trucks, passing under construction awnings, stepping over steam-exhaling sidewalk vents. You can see that it's cold from the amount of steam being generated but also by their body language, the way they are bent forward, as if to conserve warmth, their hands in their coat pockets, with the exception of Pascal, who holds the girl's hand. The girl is nice-looking in a meekly bourgeois and Parisian manner, but she gives the impression, in her knit cap and her peacoat, her unwashed hair tumbling down her back, that she has tried to distance herself from her pedigree and good looks, from the luck of wealth, of being "from a good family."

It is obvious that none of these people on 44th Street have any idea that a slow-moving vehicle is snapping images of them. They think they alone hold the key to the meaning of their purpose, the key to their association as a group. They believe they have a secret, and that their secret is safe, an electricity only they can sense, invisible as winter static as they walk through the dry cold on a bright morning in Times Square.

But their secrets have already been shared by the UK undercover agent who is in the photos, right behind Pascal and his petite chérie. They are on a stage as they walk down 44th Street, their secrets already known to four governments—French, British, American, and Canadian.

The UK undercover agent reported, after the meeting, that disagreements among the group led to a cancellation of plans for action. (Curiously, he said his hidden microphone stopped working when they began their meeting.)

A few days after that meeting, an army recruitment center in Times Square was bombed. No one was hurt.

Arrests were made, but not of Pascal Balmy or his female companion. Those two had reentered Canada and from there flown back to Paris before the bombing occurred. They had been stopped and searched at the Canadian border, either by random luck or on account of the communications between the UK police and Canadian authorities. Photos of Times Square had been found in Pascal Balmy's backpack. Pascal told authorities he was a tourist.

"Why were you photographing Times Square?" Canadian border agents had asked him.

"For the same reason as millions of other tourists who go there," Pascal told them. "To take pictures of the most photographed tourist site in the world."

It was just after this incident that Pascal decamped from Paris to the Guyenne and took with him the most committed of the young anarchists from the little scene he'd cultivated.

It turned out that this UK undercover agent who had tipped off the FBI about the meeting was himself the bomber of the army recruitment center, and that he had acted alone.

That agent's name was Marc Cutler, though he had been using the name Marc White while undercover.

Marc Cutler, aka Marc White, was apparently in love with Pascal Balmy's girlfriend (I mean Pascal's girlfriend at the time, the one in the Fair Isle hat; in the file there are short biographies of thirteen women with whom Balmy has been romantically associated in the last few years). Cutler sued the UK Metropolitan Police for failing to protect him from ultraleft indoctrination, and failing to protect him from falling in love.

Because that girlfriend of Pascal's was the daughter of a high-ranking official in the Ministry of Justice, she was scrubbed from French police files.

I had figured out her name. It wasn't difficult.

She was married last April at Sainte-Chapelle with a reception afterward on the banks of the Seine. I had seen on the internet a spring fête of refined-looking people who own country estates and dabble in charity work, ladies in big hats, men of all generations in soft linen blazers, the older ones smoking their pipes, the younger gleaming with good looks and bright futures.

The groom graduated from a grande école and works as an EU consultant. The bride is an assistant editor at the venerable and snobbish old publisher Gallimard. Her wool cap is in a landfill somewhere, her hair as shiny and fresh as her dossier.

THE CASE OF MARC CUTLER, the British agent who was himself the bomber, erupted into a public relations nightmare around the same time as some other calamities for UK intelligence. The stories were building into something like a backlash against police spying across Europe, and were causing a lot of paranoia, well-founded as it was, among subversives like Pascal Balmy and Le Moulin.

The first undercover officer ensnared in public scandal had been a married British professor named Bob Lambert, who was outed by multiple women with whom he'd had affairs while surveilling them, in one case fathering a child with an activist under an assumed identity and then disappearing. That child, now an adult, had filed a lawsuit against the Metropolitan police, citing psychological distress after learning that his father was a fictitious person.

A female agent by the alias Lynn Watson had been exposed on "Cop Watch," an online database with Vimeo footage of her with a theater troupe of "climate clowns." She's wearing clown makeup and protesting outside the perimeter fence of a coal-fired power plant. To me this Lynn Watson looks quite obviously like a cop under the clown makeup: straitlaced, and with an ROTC physique (fit, tall, square-shouldered), but apparently she had managed to slip away from the climate clowns before they confronted her.

This is what agents do—slip away, disappear, move on to their next assignment. Afterward, those they infiltrated come to believe that this person who showed up out of nowhere and later melted back into nowhere either: (1) fell in love and ran away, (2) had a mental breakdown, or (3) was a cop all along.

While Lynn Watson's real name was not made public, her visage was. I doubt she was a valuable agent. She was scamming a paycheck by pretending that people who dressed as clowns were a threat to the energy sector. But she won't be able to work undercover now that everyone knows what she looks like. Even with the clown makeup, it's obvious.

Marc Cutler, it turned out, had become romantically entangled with eight different women from various groups in the UK and Germany that he'd surveilled, by the time he'd gone to New York with Pascal, in 2008. It seemed he could not help himself. These women had begun sharing stories, information, and some of them were suing both Cutler and the UK police.

When you work for government entities, as Cutler did, as I once did, there are rules about how you conduct yourself. You have a boss, a supervising officer, and a logbook. Every time Cutler bedded down with some activist, his supervisor was listening to the whole thing.

Just as my supervisor heard me suggesting to the boy with the chin-line beard that he and I should be a couple, but that first we had important work to do together for the movement.

After the boy unexpectedly got off with an entrapment defense, someone involved in that undercover operation had to be sacrificed. It wasn't going to be my supervisor, and it wasn't going to be the Feds. It would be me, but in many ways, it was a relief to be in the private sector now, where there are no supervising officers, no logbooks, and no rules.

When Marc Cutler had first glommed onto Pascal, back in the Paris years, the mid-aughts, before Times Square, Cutler was what Lucien described to me as an eco-hippie: ponytail, earrings, Guatemalan surf pants, a dopey tattoo of a sun in sunglasses in the middle of his chest. But overnight Cutler had renovated his appearance in accordance with international black-bloc-style anarchism: short hair, black clothes, kept his tattoos hidden. Lucien said he found this weird, but a lot of people around Pascal were sycophants, and Cutler discarding his old style and adopting the look of his new milieu would have seemed to Pascal like a person coming to his senses. Plus, Lucien said, a lot of them had come from other social milieus and had tattoos from earlier lives, since people who change affinities are the same kinds of people who are attracted to the permanence of tattoos.

Cutler had used as his alias his real first name. Like those breeds of little dog who don't have the mental capacity to respond to their name, perhaps Cutler was afraid he would forget a made-up one on emergency reflex. This kind of small-brained intelligence officer might say their birthday is January 1, or that their birthday is Boxing Day, or Christmas. As if it is beyond them to memorize a date. I have never experienced these issues with names or details or birthdate or astrological sign or place of origin or family background or anything else I've manufactured to convince. If you have a good memory, and if you don't get in the way of your constructed self, it's not hard, even under duress, to remember who you are supposed to be.

Often, the sloppier undercover agents are obvious to the activists, who later say, "We knew." They suspected, they sensed a cop in their midst, but they staunched their suspicions for one reason or another, despite shadowy backstories and unfurnished apartments, despite unexplained absences and access to abundant cash with no clear source. Marc Cutler had all those things, plus a van, among people who were always having to borrow some car that turned out to have a dead battery or a blown radiator, and here was this new guy with a late-model van, and money for gas, and energy to pursue direct action, to *do* things.

I knew some of this from Lucien. Lucien explained Pascal's fears and his secrecy as personal, and the betrayal of Pascal by Marc Cutler as also personal.

According to Lucien, after the story about Marc Cutler became public, Pascal began to see that Cutler had been too eager, too assertive. Always volunteering for projects, taking everything Pascal uttered as gospel. Only in retrospect did Pascal and the Moulinards recognize that Cutler's hunger for acceptance was driven by the fact he was a narc, and not because he was obsequious and loyal. Forever after, they would keep an eye out for signs in outsiders: too much zeal, not enough backstory, too many unanswered questions. Anyone who showed up wanting to attach might be a Marc Cutler.

And this was why Pascal was so keen to work with people who were carefully vetted, who came from inside, people like me.

PASCAL ASKED ME RIGHT AWAY about Lucien, as I expected he would. They were still close, even as they'd gone in different life directions.

Their biographies overlapped in crucial ways. Same social class (Lucien's father was a banker, Pascal's a lawyer). Neighborhood (sixteenth arrondissement). Family structure (only children). Ancestral country homes in the Guyenne. Elite education (Lycée Henri-IV). Academic promise followed by disappointment (intelligent boys who were uneven students). And finally, they shared in their teenage years an obsession with film, although Lucien said that Pascal would dismiss that now, might not admit he ever cared about this bourgeois art form. But once upon a time they had cut class for ten a.m. showings of John Cassavetes and Marguerite Duras, lined up in the rain with old women in plastic bonnets and rubber galoshes designed to fit over their block-heeled shoes, dowagers married to avant-garde cinema.

Lucien had wanted me to understand that Pascal, despite his infamy as a left-wing subversive, was a person who came from somewhere, who had a past, had been, like Lucien, a boy who loved movies, even if it was a movie that marked a turn for Pascal away from all that. Pascal and Lucien had gone to see Guy Debord's *Society of the Spectacle* in the Latin Quarter. Lucien found it grating and pompous. Pascal was electrified by the scathing tone, the use of film clips and advertising and seduction to excoriate cinema and advertising and the promise of sex. By the time Lucien went to film school, Pascal had decided that throwing yourself into any project in this society was useless, except for the project of destroying this society.

I told Pascal that Lucien was shooting a film in Marseille, and Pascal made a dismissive comment about entertainment.

Lucien had said he would do that. "He likes me on account of loyalty. Movies are marketplace trash to Pascal."

I had read a bit of the script of Lucien's film, and I could confirm for Pascal that it *was* marketplace trash, but I refrained from doing so, since I was supposed to be in love with his friend. (While reading Lucien's script, I'd thought of what Bruno said about an art that shows you nothing new, *H. sapiens* as copier and fraud.)

The handsome waitress came over. She addressed Pascal by name. He inquired what I wanted, ordered a coffee for himself and another for me.

"You know each other," I said as she left.

"We all know each other here. The commune no longer runs the café, but we did all the work to reopen it. We stepped back and Naïs is in charge." He gestured to the woman. "She's a local, the daughter of Bruno Lacombe, and it was important that the café be run by someone with deeper ties here."

"Sorry. Who?" I asked this as if I had no idea who Bruno was.

"Bruno Lacombe. I brought you his book, because it is quoted in ours, which I also brought you, of course. For translating quotes, you'll want our sources."

Pascal handed me Bruno's book, *Leaving the World Behind*, as well as the book Pascal referred to as "ours," which had no declared author on its cover, a little sky-blue paperback titled *Zones of Incivility*. I'd already read it. It was meant to function as a kind of handbook for insurrection, or so my contacts suggested.

"We are not concerned with how to live in this day and age," the book begins, "but how to live *against* this day and age."

Chapter headings offer directives like "form communes," "create territories," "employ silence," and "plunder and obstruct," but the language stays vague and philosophical. The basic idea is that there are people everywhere who might be ready to reject the insult of their commodified life under late capitalism, and that these people need, first and foremost, to find each other.

I thanked Pascal and looked at both books like they were new to me.

"That is the last thing Lacombe published before he stopped writing."

"Why did he stop writing?"

It was a question to which I genuinely didn't know the answer.

"Lacombe feels no need for a public role," Pascal said. "At this point he writes only to us. He's developing a unified theory of life and it's something quite esoteric, to be shared with those who are on his wavelength. Things read by the wrong people can be misunderstood."

Understood to be the eccentric ideas of a man who has lost the thread of reality.

"The origins of what he's developing now are in this book. There was a split between him and various Marxist comrades after May '68. Lacombe alone argued that the proletariat was no longer capable of destroying capitalist society. Instead, the proletariat had become part and parcel of capitalism, a cornerstone of the very world, according to Lacombe, that we must leave."

I turned over Bruno's book and looked at the photo of him on the back. It was an image I'd examined, a book I already owned.

"Lacombe sees no point in class-based organizing. His argument is that the wedge between human beings and nature is far deeper than the wedge between factory owners and factory workers that created the conditions of twentieth-century life. That's a blip, to him. He has gone back to what he considers a fundamental estrangement, which he's convinced we must address in order to transform consciousness. We draw from his ideas, but only in part, I should say. There are some disagreements."

In the photo, Bruno is leaning against a country fence post. There is something lamblike and gentle but also hearty about him. He is short, maybe five foot eight (I am also five foot eight, but because I'm a woman I am "tall"). His chest is barrel-like. His face is broad and mild and browned by golden sun. His hair is soft and white, in dramatic contrast with his sun-browned complexion. His white locks fall to his shoulders and are combed over from a deep side-part. His comb-over seems not borne of vanity. It is not a dishonest comb-over meant to falsify, to hide what he has lost and to pretend he has not lost it. Instead, Bruno's comb-over seems like a guileless celebration of what remains.

Because I spend so much time reading the emails that he sends to Pascal and the group, I go back to this photo of him leaning on a fence post to make the voice come alive. I can't say that examining Bruno's photograph or delving into his private correspondence with Le Moulin is promising at this point, as a lead for uncovering Pascal's plans of sabotage. But I'm driven to keep reading the letters. I get a boost when I see that Bruno's sent box has a new one.

Naïs Lacombe (I was guessing, with no idea if she shared her father's surname) came back to the table with our drinks.

I thought I glimpsed what was pleasing about Bruno in the symmetry of his daughter's face.

Pascal introduced us. She was not friendly. She nodded hello and went back inside.

"She isn't involved with the commune. Sometimes these very politically active people, critical figures like Lacombe, they live these crazy lives of triumph and failure and sacrifice, surviving on the margins, and they have children who grow up to be completely normal and apolitical. Without the same drive, without even what you might call the need for a symbolic life. Lacombe is someone who has been close to revolutionary movements since the early sixties. And when you talk to Naïs it's, *Have you seen that the price of petrol is going up? It might rain Saturday. My new hens are not good layers.*

"His son is the same," Pascal said. "Country. Works with his hands."

"Does he live around here also?"

Pascal shook his head. "He's in the Lozère, east of here. Works for the state."

I pictured those proletarian hunks painting the crosswalk. They had packed up and left.

"He comes around, now and again."

I hope I get to meet him, I did not say.

I wanted to ask about the other daughter, the one who had died. In a rare lapse, I had to remind myself that I should appear to know nothing about Bruno.

Pascal will bring it up on his own, I thought. But he didn't.

He had moved on to the topic of Le Moulin's own book. A translator, he said, wasn't just rendering language word by word and sentence by sentence. A translator was a full collaborator, he said, a comrade.

As we chatted, the older sun-grilled couple in their matching Mao caps approached us. The man leaned sideways to read the spines on the other two books Pascal had brought, works of continental philosophy by some Italian. The couple both had notepads out. They began writing down these two books' titles.

Pascal addressed them in a familiar manner that was not polite. The man asked if Pascal had read something by some other Italian, and Pascal said yes and then quickly, but with some annoyance, summarized what he thought of it.

This sent the couple madly scribbling, each of them nodding and writing down what Pascal said.

The leather cuffs on the woman's wrists gave her note-taking a guerrilla flair.

Whatever Pascal said, they both wrote down.

He could have said, "There was an old woman," scribble scribble, "who lived in a shoe."

He could have said, "A penny saved," scribble scribble, "is a penny earned."

He turned toward me in a way that all but commanded them to get lost. "I'm talking to Sadie here."

They looked at me with awe and envy and backed away.

The couple had resumed their post among the stinging nettles and spear thistles next to the church, when I asked Pascal about them.

"A lot of people have been showing up recently. They want to escape their life, and word has spread about Le Moulin. They quit their jobs and come down here. Or they've been with some other collective, and for one reason or another, they are looking for a fresh start with us. We believe in small societies. We can't absorb all these people. Those two came up here from the Susa Valley, where there's been a movement to fight against the construction of a high-speed rail. We told them there wasn't housing for them, which is the truth. But also, we have to go by feel, in deciding who fits."

I looked over at the dejected couple squatting in the nettles.

"I don't want to give you the sense we're closed off. But the composition of the collective has to be considered. And farming is hard work; not everyone is suited to it. Plus, we do have a housing shortage. We need people with construction skills. And there's a question of trust. At this point, we don't trust most people."

Pascal segued to the subject of Marc Cutler, told me stories I already knew in detail, and I shook my head in dismay at such betrayal.

The couple in the churchyard stood. Pascal kept talking as they helped each other with their big dusty backpacks and trudged off the square.

PASCAL TENDED TO SPEAK in priestly aphorisms, which I found convenient for mental note-taking.

"Democracy is for predators."

"To live is to live through something to the end."

"Those who understand extinction is coming can transform the future."

"A saved humanity will be a mystical humanity."

Naïs brought out our lunch, two regional salads with fried pieces of heavily salted duck organ.

The duck organ was delicious. I said so.

"It's the best thing on the menu. Naïs gets her foie gras from a goose farm run by three generations of women."

Was Pascal not opposed to the foie gras industry here? I said I'd read it was controversial—not traditional Guyenne fare, and requiring yet more sterile corn to overtake the landscape.

"I used to believe that whatever wasn't a deep tradition here was a mistaken direction. But I'm starting to see that it's unrealistic not to be open to change, if change is what allows older modalities of life in the Guyenne to continue. So people grow corn instead of grapes. They raise geese instead of cows. They mechanize, instead of keeping to an old way of farming that is less efficient and more picturesque. Still they live with seasons, in preservation of agrarian life. That's Jean's perspective, anyhow.

"You'll meet Jean," he added, before I could pretend to ask who Jean was. "This is the main split between him and Lacombe. Jean is focused on pragmatics. On the farmers finding some way to survive. They have bills to pay. Equipment to maintain."

Naïs came back with a basket of bread and an oil-and-vinegar caddy and went back inside.

"She lives with her father?"

"On Lacombe's property, yes."

The same property where her little sister died. Maybe that event had made her how she was. *It might rain Saturday. My new hens are not good layers.*

"Does she have children?"

If I knew who lived there, I could see the place better.

He shook his head to indicate she didn't, but his "no" also seemed a dismissal of this line of questioning. He wanted to focus on his aphorisms and not on Naïs.

"The key question for Jean is not *how* you farm. He believes that working the land is fundamentally anti-state, because the state's true lifeblood is the city."

"Cities are a false world, and one that convinces its denizens there is no other."

"The culture of cities rose in the East. It is setting in the West. Coming to its end, in a condition of slow but certain collapse."

"'Occidere' means to kill, to tear apart."

As Pascal made these statements, I studied this childless daughter of Bruno's, who stood in the doorway with a hand in her apron pocket.

Perhaps she's like me, I thought. I had no interest in other people's children or in having one of my own. I had an IUD, and at most another decade to be careful. The only scenario I could imagine in which I'd become a mother was if I found a baby, orphaned, crying, maybe in a dumpster. In that scenario, I am walking down a street in some city, and I hear this "waaah, waaah," issuing from a helpless little bundle of warm life in a heap of trash.

I have imagined that. It's a mental tic. It has no meaning. But it has created this uncomfortable feeling that someone, somewhere, is going to need me at some point.

Pascal said that it was Bruno Lacombe who had drawn him to this area.

"But your family had a house down here, no? That's what Lucien told me."

"Near La Grèze. It was sold long ago. My parents used to come to the Guyenne. Like Lucien's. But we stopped visiting when I was ten. I came down on my own, as a young adult, in hopes of talking to Lacombe. I knew he had been close to Guy Debord. I contacted him and we struck up a correspondence, but when I tried to meet with him in person, he put me off. I knew there was another old leftist in this area—Jean Violaine. Since I could not see Lacombe, I went to see Jean instead.

"That visit with Jean changed everything. I knew the Guyenne from my childhood, but I knew it as a bourgeois, as someone who used the countryside as a site of leisure, and then returned to Paris. Jean connected me to the people of the Guyenne and their peasant traditions, to something that is stubborn and fierce. He taught me a lot. I have also learned a lot from Lacombe. And the irony is they don't speak to each other."

I nodded as if absorbing this for the first time.

The two old men emerged from the bar interior, shouting goodbye to Naïs. There was a pandemonium as they greeted Pascal.

"Still sick over your heifer?" one of them asked Pascal, sending the other into a fit of laughter.

The broken capillaries on their faces seemed to have traveled from their noses to their cheeks and ears.

"It's tough, but this is how it goes." The man patted Pascal on the back. "She's 'in a better place,' as they say."

"You were white as a ghost, Pascal!" the second man said, continuing to laugh.

His friend scolded him for teasing Pascal, and the two of them commenced a lighthearted debate.

As they left, continuing their boisterous talk, I realized I could not understand what they were saying. I later figured out they were speaking Occitan.

Pascal explained to me that they'd had a milk cow at Le Moulin with a breast mastitis. Jean Violaine had suggested calling Mr. Crouzel. That was the name of the man who asked Pascal if he was still upset. Crouzel was a local elder who could be relied on for help with animals. He came to Le Moulin to make an assessment. He had bent over their poor cow, who was lying on her side, her udder distended, and while Pascal waited for Crouzel to examine the cow and make his recommendation—perhaps he would suggest massage, heat, antibiotics—Crouzel had taken a revolver from his coat pocket, placed it at the cow's head, and pulled the trigger.

The church bells rang two times for two p.m., each ring a clanging sortie that reverberated over the village and its blue banner of cloudless sky.

Pascal had been saying something about violence as the bells rang. When they stopped, he continued.

He declared that some acts, Crouzel's, for instance, were borne of pragmatic sympathy. But the purest and most logical violence, he said, was without sympathy, and also without antipathy. He talked about a mysterious tribe on an island in the Indian Ocean. This tribe, he said, had killed a fisherman illegally poaching. They had threatened to kill every anthropologist who had tried to study them, had attacked every ship that grounded on their reef. Pascal had seen a documentary about the tribe, who were one of the last "uncontacted" communities on earth. He told me the title of the documentary, and he spelled the name of its director, in expectation that I would want to go and watch it later. He'd been naming books and thinkers and stopping to make sure I wrote them down. The couple in their Mao caps, with their eager scribbling, seemed to be what Pascal expected and was habituated to, in response to his talk. I was happy to comply.

The poacher, who had been fishing for mud crabs, got drunk and drifted into a lagoon of the island. Tribesmen waded out and pierced him with arrows, dispatched him like a French farmer might dispatch a wild hog that was threatening his tubers.

"The most innocent man in the entire world," Pascal said, "is the person who aimed the arrow that killed that poacher."

Perhaps he meant to shock me, but I could not resist making him understand I was not shocked. It seemed a good opportunity to encourage a space, eventually, for franker talk.

"Violence is a reasonable response to a certain kind of threat," I said. "In the case of the tribe, the threat of annihilation."

"That's right."

His enthusiasm seemed a little performative, and later I wondered if my contacts weren't overplaying their focus on Pascal, who could not even handle the scene of an ailing cow put out of her misery.

Lunch was over. We settled our bill (we split it) and got up to walk to Le Moulin.

"Is the commune far?" I asked, pretending not to know. (It is 2.2 kilometers on a footpath that follows the river before veering up to a plateau, as I'd already mapped on Google Earth.)

Naïs nodded a curt goodbye.

"After you moved here, did Lacombe ever agree to meet?"

We were crossing the square under the leafy shade of its giant tree.

"When I made that trip down to try to talk to him, there was a lot I didn't know. For starters, that Lacombe had stopped seeing people in person twenty-five years ago."

I did a calculation. After his child died, the other daughter.

PASCAL AND I CROSSED an iron bridge that spanned a slow muddy river. After the bridge, we turned onto a narrow footpath of powdery dirt that was lined on both sides by waist-high grasses and wildflowers.

We rose in elevation and skirted under the limestone overhang of an enormous rock. It was not colored like the magical rocks near Lucien's house. These rocks were gray, with curious notches that looked man-made, little squares carved into them like hand-sized cubbies.

I said the notches were curious.

"They used them to attach the skins of animals. They hung down like this"—he gestured to the lip of the cliff—"and functioned as walls. We are standing in people's rooms."

I got a funny feeling I didn't like. As if the ancient people Bruno talked about were here with us. Not contained in my mental diorama, with their big faces and their weak chins, but invisible and everywhere, ghosts run rampant.

We ducked out from under the rock shelf. There was a steep hillside above us, covered in dense trees.

"Do you see that place up there?" Pascal gestured to the top of the hill. He was pointing to the Château de Gaume.

"What is it?"

Pascal gave me his summary of the Cagots, the religious wars, the persecution, the uprising and the slaughter, the château's later conversion to a prison. He was unaware, of course, that I knew all this history. In fact, he had some of the dates and details wrong.

Pascal said the Cagot was both real and a kind of myth, but that when people believe a myth, that, too, is real. It is a real belief.

"Lacombe says there are remainders from another world that might still be here," he said. "Figments of an older species that never integrated."

Or figments of someone's imagination, I did not say.

"This is among Jean's disagreements with Lacombe. Jean deplores Lacombe's interest in prehistory, his talk of species. And so we're like the children of a divorce, at Le Moulin. It is on account of these two figures that we came here, and in the ashes of their split, we sift to find our own direction."

The river was far down below us. I could hear people in kayaks and canoes, voices calling to one another, and the hollow sound of oars knocking against fiberglass hulls. Some of the people in the boats had gotten out to pull them through the shallows.

"You might have heard about the water issues here," Pascal said. "The government wants to divert our river, which is already so much lower than I've ever seen it, because of drought, and because the big growers irrigate from it. If they cut off this river, they will rob this entire region of its life."

I asked what could be done.

"It will be up to the people of the Guyenne to answer that. I consider myself an outsider. The problems here have to be resolved by the locals, not by anyone at Le Moulin."

He'll admit nothing to you, Lucien had said of Pascal.

For Lucien, this secrecy on Pascal's part was a referendum on their friendship. Lucien found it hurtful that Pascal didn't trust him, and it did not occur to Lucien, as he talked to me about his feelings, that I might have a vested interest in the question of Pascal's guilt or innocence, an interest that was quite separate from Lucien's feelings.

My own feelings were neutral; I do not care what people do. It was my job to find evidence that the Moulinards were a threat. Whether they were a serious threat was irrelevant. Either I would locate evidence, or I would locate a way to implicate them, so that police could raid this backwater and shut down their little commune.

We were at a river bend where the water was deep, a beloved local swim hole that Pascal said might be gone forever if the state had its way.

We paused to watch a group of boys taking turns on a rope swing looped to a branch of a massive plane tree. Each boy climbed up short boards that were nailed into the tree's trunk, while holding on to a rope. At the highest step, each was given instructions by a boy on the ground, who seemed to be the leader.

"Push off as hard as you can. Don't let go of the rope too early," this boy hollered. "But don't let go too late, or you'll swing back and hit the tree."

His hair was in two French braids that went past his shoulders, and he was the tannest and smallest and looked to be the youngest. He wore a necklace made of white beads. He kept touching the beads, bringing them to his mouth.

One by one, the boys pushed off, swung out over the river, let go, and dropped into the water. One or two seemed skilled at this activity, but most of them let go of the rope awkwardly, flailing as they plummeted, hitting the water at odd angles. One of the boys did not disengage all the way and burned the insides of his legs from rope friction. He emerged yelling in agony. The others laughed at him.

The boy in braids and the beaded choker, who had been instructing the others on where to stand, when to let go, took his turn last. He climbed up without the rope, and at the highest step in the tree, he grabbed a tree limb and began going higher and higher, moving from branch to branch until he was at the highest tree limb over the river. He must have been forty feet above the surface. He touched the beads at his neck, crossed himself, and jumped. His body was still and straight and upright, like a person riding downward in an elevator.

The boy shot up from the river's dark surface, sunlight forming a veil of diamonds in his braids.

"He was one of the students in the open-enrollment school we started," Pascal said, "but we had to ask him to leave."

I'd read about their school. Modeled on some crazy place in England in the 1960s, no rules nor hierarchies. Children as young as four designing their own curriculum. Everyone sitting on the floor.

I asked what happened.

"He impregnated his schoolteacher," Pascal said. "It's been a drama. At first, I'll admit I defended her. When does childhood end, and adulthood begin? Age eighteen? Age sixteen? Puberty? What love is adult love? But the precepts we are raised on are difficult to shake. People felt she'd crossed a line. She was asked to leave the commune.

"The boy's parents are not part of Le Moulin. They're locals. His father maintains some of the vacation homes closer to Boulière, and the parents run a market booth selling crêpes in the summer. We are trying to solve our own problems here, through dialogue and compromise. The boy's parents agreed not to go to the authorities if the teacher gave up the baby and let them raise it. The teacher is young. She wasn't ready to be a mother. She could have faced serious charges, and she agreed. In a way, the boy's parents were quite humane and reasonable about the whole thing. They sent the boy to his grandparents and took in the teacher until she was ready to give birth. They are raising that baby now. They said she could visit, and she told them she had no interest. We never saw her again. I heard she moved to Corsica."

"How old is the boy?"

He was pussyfooting up the river's bank, stepping over rocks and tree roots. Water streamed from his tan, slim body as he high-fived his friends.

"Now he's thirteen," Pascal said. "This was a couple of years ago. He was eleven."

I'D RECENTLY SEEN an Italian documentary from the 1980s that featured a child with alarming sexual confidence, a boy of nine named Franck. Vito had recommended it. If Vito and I agreed that Italian foods and wines were subpar, we also agreed that Italian films were superior, but we partly insisted on this as a way of challenging Serge's and Lucien's bias toward French cinema.

"Does this ship take passengers," Vito and I would say to each other, in emulation of Monica Vitti in *Red Desert*, a despairing housewife clutching her coat, looking for an escape from her neurosis. Does this ship take passengers? she asks a sailor from a docked boat. There is no vessel that can remedy what ails her, but the sailor cannot understand her question, doesn't speak Italian, and responds in untranslated Turkish.

My favorite work of Italian cinema is *La Dolce Vita*, for its bleak ending, Marcello Mastroianni jaded and lost, won over by the void of a shallow life, and numb to the call of the angel smiling at him from across the beach. This documentary that Vito recommended (he gave me a thumb drive; it wasn't the kind of thing you could stream) was unknown to me. In it, various subjects talk about love, including this nine-year-old, Franck, who leans on one elbow and chews gum with rhythmic and casual machismo, as he recounts a recent sexual pursuit.

"We began to kiss each other," he says. Chew, chew. "And we touched each other's bodies. I asked her if she wanted to make love."

"She was also nine?" This was the off-screen voice of the filmmaker, behind his camera.

"Yes," the boy said, "same as me."

"And what did she say?"

"She had never, you know, been with somebody. Been with a man, I mean. But she wanted to try it, with me. I was her first. Afterward, she told me she had never felt anything like this before. We were both very happy."

Chew, chew. Leans, to get more comfortable on his propped elbow. Lets out a sensuous and long sigh.

"We made love," chew, chew, "and then we went outside to play. We were playing together, simple fun, a boy and a girl, just as we had played before we had started to kiss. Our game was the same, but we, how do I say it"—he repositions his propped elbow, overgrown bangs falling in his eyes—"we were different. We played better with each other, after making love."

As little Franck talks about why he thinks adults are afraid of children's sexuality, someone in the background rides by on a loud motorcycle. Franck turns his head to look. He's nine, but his body language is that of a teenager: he wants to know what's going on around him, to be on the scene, to not miss out, while he's stuck talking to this documentary filmmaker. But at least he gets to talk about his sexual pursuits and libertine values. He tells the filmmaker that grown-ups are full of fear. Children should not be in school, Franck says into the camera. They should be out in the world, traveling around, experiencing joy.

"What do you imagine your life will be like when you're older?" the filmmaker asks him.

"I'll get home from work. My wife and I will take a shower together and soap each other's bodies. A nice long, hot shower. Then we will dry each other. We will eat dinner, watch TV, go to bed. In bed, we will make love. It'll be nice for both of us. The next day, it will be the same. *Giusto?*"

He says "giusto" throughout, to mean, Right? You with me? Understand? Giusto?

I wondered what had become of him, which is what we say of people who have made an ominous impression. If you wonder what became of someone and they turned out normal and undistinguished, it is disappointing. Asking what became of Franck could be suitably answered only with scenarios like:

Franck was killed in the commission of a bank robbery in Milan.

Or Franck works with the Catholic Church in sub-Saharan Africa, preaching abstinence.

Or Franck became a leftist insurgent in central-southwestern France, and masterminded the kidnapping of the Franco-Iberian subminister Pablo Platon y Platon, who was never seen again, his body never found, and Franck is now in prison, possibly for life.

While those answers might be okay, the most satisfying answer, the only answer that would not disturb the early impression of Franck and his terrifying sexual confidence at age nine, would be:

Franck never grew up. Franck's precocious sexual appetite resulted in the magic trick of permanent youth. Franck looks now as he did at the time he appeared in this film—button face, brown hair with overgrown bangs. Franck continues to be nine years old, to chew gum and say "Giusto," and to talk about the relaxing and healthful benefits of sexual intercourse among children.

After watching that documentary, I'd looked up Franck. I found his Facebook page. As a non-friend, I could see only the profile photo and banner image he had chosen. The profile photo was his face, a grown version. It's painful what happens to children's faces when they get older. In my sole fantasy of motherhood, where I raise a baby that I find in a dumpster, the baby has no awkward phase. As the baby grows, it retains the blurry softness of perfect youth, but in fact people lose that as they mature. They take on the hardened lines of adulthood, which blurs them in a different way, into the vague category of grown-ups banished from their own youthful cuteness.

We should destroy all the photographs of the awkward phase. Put the ugly photos in a common incinerator and release the smoke of our traces into the higher atmosphere. I myself have already done that. I did it for professional reasons. But everyone should do it, for aesthetic reasons. Save only the most charming and angelic of baby pictures, like the one of Guy Debord that I found in Pascal's file. There could be one universally shared image, a photographic commons, that becomes the symbol of our perfect beginnings.

The banner photo on grown-up Franck's Facebook page was of a race car. It would be acceptable to me in the what-became-of-Franck genre if he were a race car driver. But this was a commercial photo, an advertisement for Lamborghini, a make whose broad fan base has never owned and will never own actual Lamborghinis. Lamborghini fans own a poster or calendar. They have a T-shirt.

Franck had thirty-one Facebook friends. His interests and hobbies included Nescafé, Burger King, and a Facebook group called I Love My Daughter. Adulthood had sanded him into someone profoundly unremarkable.

But what did I expect? As he had made clear on film—it was all there in the record—Franck's plan for adulthood had been: go to work, come home, shower, eat your dinner, watch TV, fuck your wife, go to sleep, and the next day, do it all over. Work, eat, fuck, sleep, over and over and over.

Grown-up Franck is driving an Amazon delivery van right now, in his Lamborghini baseball cap.

WE HAD LEFT THE DIRT TRAIL next to the rock shelter above the river and were on an open road that led to the commune.

I heard a car coming from behind. I turned around, relieved to see that it was not a white Citroën panel truck.

It was a beat-up old Renault sedan, coated in country dust, all of its windows down, a woman driving. She pulled up next to us, so that there was little room to walk.

The woman's brown hair was gathered into a lopsided bun. She had a faded tattoo on her neck, a gecko or some other creature. It looked like it had been moving toward her hairline but got stuck in its tracks. She directed angry looks at Pascal, driving the speed of our walking and struggling with the clutch.

"Here we go," Pascal said.

"Everything he says is a lie!" she shouted.

Pascal did not turn his head to look at her.

"Where were you, Pascal, when they raided the Chat-teigne, when they tried to burn us out of the Rohanne Forest? Ten thousand were blasted by water cannons! Four hundred farmers on tractors blocked the police from entering Notre-Dame-des-Landes! Where were you, Pascal?"

He kept walking, a slight smile at the corners of his mouth, as if to suggest that the nuts were out of the nuthouse.

Her skills with the clutch were wanting. She revved. Stalled. Started the car again and restarted it by accident after it was already idling, gnashing the teeth of the flywheel.

"I have been fighting cops and holding my ground since you were being pushed in a stroller in the Jardin des Plantes, Pascal. Pushed by your nanny! No doubt an 'uncouth,' someone like me! Hired to wipe the ass of someone like you!"

Pascal never once looked at her.

She had clumsy features, a large nose, a broad forehead, a chin that disappeared into her wrinkled neck. Coarse strands of gray escaped her careless bun like live wires. I understood that her unkempt appearance, the sweat pooling on her upper lip, her middle-age fury, these details made it easier for him to keep walking as if she weren't here.

She over-shifted and lurched away.

We kept on. I said nothing about her. In my silence, Pascal would feel obliged to explain.

"That was Nadia Derain. It's kind of a long story. She showed up here last fall. And it's like she said. She came down from Nantes, where they've had a very successful movement. They stopped the government from building a massive airport, and they pushed out the police and declared the land an autonomous zone. Nadia was a committed participant with a lot to say. In fact, too much. Her insistence on her activist bona fides began to grind us down. She argues about everything. You have to hear a million stories that feature her. Some of it has to do with origin. She's from Brittany. It's a different culture."

You simply don't like her, I didn't say.

"The affective layer of the person," he went on, "how close to the surface that layer is, this is how we all communicate. You can feel who people are."

He gestured to the bare skin of his own arms, his own affective layer. (They were rather fleshy arms, and I guessed that Pascal did no farming, no manual labor, just the thinking as his contribution to Le Moulin.)

"We tried to work with her. But her energy was not a good fit. A vote was taken. People wanted her gone. Now she's off our land, but she won't leave the area. It's become this campaign of harassment. I can't go anywhere without that car showing up. I might have warned you, but I'm always optimistic that she will locate her dignity and move on. Go where people respect her as a veteran of various movements. Why not return to Nantes? The insistence on hanging around, it's made some at Le Moulin wonder if she's an informant. Jérôme is convinced she's a cop. But I don't think Nadia's a cop."

I don't think she is either, I didn't say.

"She is alone. And that's hard. We are social creatures. People don't have a lot of tools to deal with rejection. And the ones who come here, they tend to be estranged from their families, from the dominant culture; they come to us as if to a family, for acceptance, and so what is next, after rejection? Nadia is mourning her expulsion. And the form her mourning takes is anger. My hope is that her anger will burn itself out and she'll find something else to channel her energy into."

"Where did she go, after she moved off the commune?"

He puffed air through his lips and shrugged, a gesture that said, But who cares?

V

THE RED AND THE BLACK

BRUNO'S MOST VIVID MEMORY of the war, he wrote to Pascal and the group, was of picking up an enemy helmet from the forest floor at the age of seven.

The Moulinards had asked a question about the Resistance and the French Communist Party. Bruno answered them, or didn't, by delving into his wartime childhood.

He had been scavenging the rural landscape of the Corrèze with a ragtag band of boys when he'd come upon the helmet, and the dead soldier next to it.

Bruno told them that this memory could be considered a *screen memory*, in the Freudian sense—a recollection that functioned to cover his own trauma, to obscure it behind a different incident, one that was less significant. The enemy helmet and the aftermath of its discovery was always with him. In contrast, the more extreme consequences of the war on Bruno's life, and what, exactly, he had understood of those consequences as a seven-year-old, had remained vague, something he was blocked from recollecting in any detail.

Even as we do not choose a diversion from pain in the form of a screen memory, Bruno said, on account that *it* chooses *us*, we might retroactively heighten that memory, in our recognition of what it means.

I regard my childhood encounter with this enemy helmet, he said, as a stutter or shift in the axis of my existence, one that has been critical to who I am, and to what I have come to believe.

But I will start at the beginning, he said, by which I mean, with my earliest memory, which emerges from the gauzed sensations of toddlerhood, when I am three. I am at a medical clinic with my parents because my older brother, Maxime, has just broken his arm. He has fallen from a tree at a playground. His arm is sagging from his shoulder like a length of aged sausage. The shoulder is dislocated, and his elbow is shattered.

They didn't have modern medicine in 1940, but already that profession was attempting to put people back together with pins, as if our bodies were machines. They inserted a metal plate into Maxime's elbow, to secure the two moving parts of his arm. In the weeks after the accident, he complained that he could no longer bend the arm. The plate, counter to the doctors' hope, had fused the two bones into a fixed position. But later, Bruno said, that metal plate did serve a useful purpose: it allowed the authorities to identify Maxime when they found his body at Buchenwald after the war, along with fourteen of my other relatives, including my mother.

Bruno confessed that the extreme difference in fate between him and his older brother was a lifelong vexation that eluded his grasp.

In the summer of 1942, Bruno and Maxime were both sent to the country from Paris by their parents, who each held bureaucratic positions in their municipal chapter of the Communist Party. His mother's parents, their name was Kouchnir, were Jewish, having come from Odessa, at least that was what Bruno had been told, and there was no way to verify much, Odessa being a kind of black hole for a Jew, a place no Jew could truly be "from," as the fact of a Jew's survival in imperial Russia was proof that this same Jew did not linger any place too long. His father's parents, the Lacombes, were Communist Party militants who ran a little bakery in the Parisian suburb of Malakoff.

Rumors had spread of children rounded up with their parents, for the purpose of keeping families together (uniting them in doom), or so Bruno's parents had heard, and they felt it was safer to split the brothers up. Maxime was sent to Burgundy. Bruno to the southern Corrèze. Maxime was twelve. Bruno was five, and transported under cover of night, in a truck bed with other children, all of them hidden under a tarp. These children were housed with elderly people on farms to keep them safe from deportation.

Bruno did not understand until much later that his parents were in the Resistance. He had no knowledge of his father's arrest by the Gestapo in 1943, nor of his death in 1944 at Fresnes Prison, a place where Bruno himself later spent time, though for a silly collection of charges, robbing parked cars—nothing so exalted as resisting tyranny, but he would delve into that perhaps another time, he said.

In those years, 1942 to 1945, he was in a little village in the countryside, in relative idyl. He didn't know the fate of his mother, his father, his older brother, until after the war. He had not even a sense that he was half-Jewish, no understanding there was any mark of vulnerability by which he should be burdened. Instead, he proceeded within the parameters of how life, for him, had gone so far: you were with your family in Paris, and then you went to the country, while your parents stayed behind. You lived with an old woman who was not your grandmother but hugged you tightly and told you to call her grandmother.

Bruno's own grandparents the Lacombes rose before dawn, and on Sundays, when the bakery was closed, they visited Bruno and Maxime, bringing with them a sack filled with pastries. This woman in the Corrèze had no pastries, and no grandchildren of her own. She was widowed. Her sons, both grown, had joined the Resistance.

Bruno spent his days roaming with a group of boys, some his age, some older, others mere toddlers—ambulatory, as Bruno put it, but not yet into language. They threw rocks at one another or stole apples from orchards or searched the ground for discarded weaponry and other excitements.

Located in a pocket of the Corrèze known for its red limestone, the village had been erected over seams in the earth of this special red rock. Everything, the churches and farmhouses and barns, the old train depot, had been built of red limestone, its color velvety and appealing, also durable and strong and insulating. Its smooth surface was what Bruno's little feet touched first thing each morning, bare, as he pattered into the kitchen to greet the old woman, who poured hot milk in his bowl, when there was milk. The old woman was always in the kitchen, waiting, as if the clock of the day would start with Bruno's appearance in her midst.

Bruno described this little village as a rose-red valentine nestled among golden fields of hay. The village existed still, he said, looked now as it had then, except that tourist buses groaned loudly on the main road that bordered the town, spewing diesel exhaust, and the houses were more tidy and prosperous than they had seemed to Bruno in the wartime years of his childhood.

When German troops rampaged through the area, the old woman and Bruno took refuge in the hayloft of the barn. They spent several nights there. Bruno could still recall the feeling of being clutched against the woman's bosom, the terrifying sounds of war near and distant, explosions and the report of rifle fire. At one point, they heard German being spoken right outside the barn. They heard boots, people going in and out of the house, someone shouting, a commander, perhaps, and then people driving away.

Quiet descended. The only sound was an old, galvanized water bucket on the ground, sent rolling by the wind. The Germans were gone.

To this day, Bruno said, I can hear that sound, a water bucket rolling on its side. It is the sound of danger's retreat, and also a signal that is more complex for me, he said, because in the absence of an enemy, an "other," we become, ourselves, responsible for good and evil. This too, he said, I shall take up later.

After the elders had established that it was safe to come out, Bruno and a band of other boys yelled and tumbled and ran through the woods beyond the village, elated that their forced quiet and cooped-up days were behind them, and curious to see what was changed, for the landscape bore the scars of war. Burned homes. Burned woods.

If they were told to be careful, Bruno said, he had no memory of this. The Nazis left and the boys ran free, ran wild.

When they came upon a soldier in a field just off the road, the sight of this body on the ground had seemed a game to Bruno. *An enemy!* one of the boys whispered, and they all hid behind a row of trees. The man was facedown, his body twisted wrongly.

One of the boys threw a rock. It bounced off the soldier's side. His body stayed still and inert. An older boy, proving his mettle to the little band, stepped forward and nudged the soldier with his foot. He declared the man dead, and the others crept forward.

The soldier was German. His eyes were open. He looked as if he had been puzzling over some question at the moment of his death, trying to solve an unsolvable math problem, and he would travel into eternity that way, with a thicket of half-tabulated numbers lodged in his mind.

His weapon and his ammunition were gone. His boots were gone. One boy took the soldier's canteen, looped it to his own belt. Another claimed his case of medical bandages.

Bruno was afraid to get close. The dead body scared him. He picked up the enemy soldier's helmet, which lay on its own like a giant walnut shell, empty and discarded.

The boys heard a truck coming down the road and scattered from that scene.

They wandered through the woods, Bruno wearing the scavenged helmet, holding it so it would not fall off. The helmet's weight, its reduction of his visibility—it rode low—felt to him, he wrote to the Moulinards, like the intrinsic burdens of men and war. He was trying on those burdens, which was the essence of play, to rehearse the dramas and terrors of adulthood.

Etched into the black-painted metal of the helmet over the brow was: "Blutgruppe 0."

"Blut" is blood, one of the boys declared. This was the soldier's blood type. He'd scratched it into the helmet.

That boy wanted the helmet. Bruno said no and held tight to it. They all wanted it.

Bruno marched along in the coveted helmet, chanting. Blood type O, blood type O. The other boys took it up. It became a shorthand for bravery, for victory, a celebratory mantra, blood type O. As if they themselves had just vanquished this enemy soldier, had driven out the Germans.

The things you do when you don't know what reality you've come to occupy, Bruno wrote to Pascal and the Moulinards. When you don't yet know that your fun is over.

His brother was dead. His mother was dead. His father was dead. It was not clear in his memory, Bruno told them, when he learned the news of their deaths. What he remembered, instead, was rampaging over the retreat of the enemy. He saw the forest and heard the whoops and shouts of boys, and he felt the loose fit of a Nazi's helmet, bobbling against his ears as he ran.

The sensation of movement on his head wasn't immediate, he wrote to them. But within a matter of hours there was an unpleasant feeling of life behind his ears and along the nape of his neck, his scalp sending him new and unsettling signals in the form of an itch.

He had caught a dead man's lice.

The lice were in the helmet because their host had died, and they were in search of a new host. Bruno had volunteered his own head, had given these lice a new lease, a reason for being. They roamed happily, exploring their new home, the continuation of their raison d'être. It was wretched to inherit the lice of a dead Nazi soldier, and yet an experience that he later turned to, again and again.

These lice were real, Bruno said, but he had come to understand that they were also a metaphor: they stood for the transmigration of life, from one being to the next, from past to future.

Bruno said that transmigration, what some called metempsychosis, wasn't magic in the degraded sense of taking place outside physical laws or as conjured by people draped in wizards' cloaks. Transmigration, he said, was the entire story of people and their long history, archived as chains of information inside the bodies of every living person. No man was not the product of such a chain. Every human was a child of a child of a child of children of mysterious mothers who once lived, and whose secrets we carry. This was our genome, Bruno said. Science and technology are embattled terrain among those who reject capitalism, he acknowledged, but the new discoveries in the study of ancient DNA were stunning and consequential. They have to be dealt with, Bruno said.

I am linked, he said, to ancient people not as a vague and baggy "idea" but as little pieces of string examined under an electron microscope.

We have material proof, Bruno said, of transmigration, of the way in which everyone who came before us left a mark on our genome, adding to the story of our ancestry and evolution.

Spirit travels, he said, from the dead for centuries, for millennia, into the living. Each of us inherits code, blueprints, a set of instructions—call it what you want—from those who came before us, all the way back into the deepest sediments of time. These codes, Bruno said, are genetic lice, which crawl from ancestors to descendent; they travel from the many to the one, right on through human history. How do they make their way? They take a transmigrational highway, he said. The lice had helped him understand this.

He had discarded the helmet before returning to the village. Over the days that followed, as the itching on his scalp intensified, he told his "grandmother" he'd caught lice. He did not say where they came from, and neither did she ask. Lice to her were no mystery. She told him to lean over a tree stump where she beheaded chickens (when they had had chickens, which they no longer did, and now ate potatoes with salt, when they had salt).

Bruno put his head on the stump. The old woman treated his scalp with kerosene, which she glugged from a metal can that had lost its nozzle and splashed unevenly. The kerosene was for refilling a lantern that the Germans had smashed.

The vapors from the kerosene made young Bruno ill. Its noxious effects did not kill his lice.

The lice ranged over his head as the Germans had ranged over the Corrèze. They did eventually leave, having explored, as he now put it, the *limits of possibility* on his scalp. In this way, he tangented, lice have yet a second metaphorical meaning: The bromides marketed to us to fix our problems, like kerosene was once believed a remedy for lice, these posited solutions tend to give us hope more than material benefit. In reality, problems leave when they are ready to go, when they have exhausted their stay, just as these lice did.

Then again, Bruno said, perhaps no one could declare with confidence the reason for the departure of lice. As I have raised three children, he said, I have had plenty of experience with lice and scabies and cradle cap, all manner of bug and bacteria that thrive on the scalps and bodies of the young. (Reading this, I realized it was the single instance I had encountered in these letters of Bruno acknowledging the lost daughter.)

Lice decide on their own when to retreat, Bruno said. The true remedy for them is not poison but patience.

The effects of the kerosene, he said, remained. Thereafter his vision sometimes had a tremble at its edge like a ruffle or pleat that crimped his field of sight. This crimp came and went. It was happening now, he wrote to them, as he was composing this very email, and it was this visual phenomenon that had precipitated his boyhood memory of the soldier and the helmet and the lice, his foolish joy at the death of the enemy, a joy that displaced the memory of learning his family had been murdered.

Because of his exposure to the kerosene, at the outward periphery of each of his two eyes, Bruno's vision periodically degraded in a vertical line. The line quavered as if a zipper had riven the seen world at this outer periphery, riven it and then sewn it back up, but unevenly, and the living parts of the riven world were vibrating, sutured badly, and leaking something from under the sutures—an unseen, untouched absolute. It was at the quavering edges of his vision, he told them, that the truth of the seen and unseen was attempting to break through, to communicate, to coalesce. A *critical point*, as a terminology of chemistry, he summarized, was that moment when gasses and solids had the same valence. Perhaps the two trembling seams at the edges of his vision were the destabilized place where two worlds were reaching equilibrium, attempting to find balance where each did not annihilate the other. He regarded this tremble as pertaining to the riddle of history, and to a dream of forging a future that did not negate the past, a dream that honored reality without occluding its own verso, its counter-reality.

Reading these descriptions of the vertical pleats at the edges of Bruno's vision, I suspected that he was prone to ocular migraines. He didn't catch them from kerosene, or lice, or an enemy helmet. I myself happen to suffer from ocular migraines, and so his inspired descriptions of this para-phenomenon, a visual fluttering or disturbance that is both pronounced and diaphanous, were quite familiar to me, although "suffer" is too strong a word.

The ocular migraine is not that big of a deal. On occasion, there's something at the edges of my vision on both sides, if I am tired, or have had too much caffeine or too much to drink. An eye doctor told me this was a *vascular event*, and when I asked what that meant, he said it meant I could ignore it.

Bruno found in the crimps to his peripheral sight something meaningful. I did not find the crimps to my own sight meaningful. I ignored them as the doctor advised. If the crimp was there, it lasted maybe thirty minutes, and I waited for it to subside. I never could later recall the moment when it did subside. I only noticed that it was gone.

LE MOULIN COMPRISED eleven hectares that the group had been developing. There were forty-five of them living there now, give or take a baby or two, Pascal said. They believed in a loose head count for the purposes of kitchen prep and work assignments, and no records were kept, as they were against records. Pascal said he liked to think that when people took up residence at the commune, they fell off state surveillance and also self-surveillance, in the form of social media and the various sorts of digital tracking that were inescapable in city life.

When they had first acquired the property, there'd been a failed Christmas tree farm over there, Pascal said, pointing to a hillside that still had fuzzy evergreens dotting its slopes. The Moulinards were now trying to redevelop the hill into a stepped fruit orchard, mostly quince.

I asked what they did with the quince, a fruit that to me has always seemed useless. Quinces look like apples puckered with blight, cannot be eaten raw, and when cooked have no flavor.

"Some of the women are making preserves and selling them at the Saturday market in Sazerac. Everything we grow is for our own use, and for our elder assistance program, delivering food around the village. The rest we sell at market. Our biggest operation is walnuts. We are refurbishing old machines for crushing them and expelling oil, which we also sell. Everything we generate in income is pooled and shared."

They also pooled checks, he said, that came in for those who qualified for state assistance. There were times, especially in winter, when some at Le Moulin had to seek work beyond the farm to keep things going.

We passed three young people weeding between rows of squashes, two women in sun hats and a guy with a T-shirt wrapped over his head as a makeshift visor. A man on a tractor tilled soil in an area that had not yet been planted. Over the roar of the tractor, Pascal told me that the local farmers had helped them learn how to fertilize naturally, what crops should be planted next to other crops to decrease infestation, how to irrigate without losing topsoil.

He said that Lacombe, whose book he'd given me (reminding me who this was, in case I'd forgotten), was against the use of tractors.

This made sense: it was the weapon of his child's death.

Lacombe, Pascal said, felt that tractors destroyed too many of the dirt's microorganisms. He had renounced even the violence of the plow, if you could call that violence, Pascal said, and he himself didn't. They had to till the soil. They had people to feed.

I sensed that Pascal had no awareness of the animating reason behind Bruno's rejection of tractors. Bruno who had once owned a tractor, driven his tractor, believed in it, until the accident, terminating his association with tractors. But Pascal had no dossier, no news clipping, and perhaps he was a less sensitive reader of the emails, even as they were written to him.

We were going to see the woodshop, run by a man named René with a helper called Burdmoore, who was apparently American.

I hadn't been informed of an American and was eager to cross-check for intel when I had the opportunity.

The woodshop was in an unfinished barn with a poured concrete floor. Near the entrance, Burdmoore was cutting lengths of board with a circular saw. He was a man of about seventy, his face and arms and bald head stamped in large, square freckles. He had a big round belly, the kind that looks hard rather than soft, which the French call a bidon.

Pascal introduced me.

"Where you from?" he asked, as he blotted sweat from his face with the neck of his T-shirt.

I told him California.

"Right on. That's cool," he said, as if "California" meant something specific, instead of a huge assortment of different terrains inhabited by forty million faceless people.

"You gonna be around much, California? I get tired of frogs, even if I love these guys. Pascal might have told you I'm not fluent in frog talk." He had a strong New York accent that flattened out and flared the ends of his words.

Pascal said that Burdmoore was working on housing. "But he's not working fast enough," Pascal added.

"Says the man who never cut a board in his life. When I first showed up down here," Burdmoore said, addressing me, "I was in a canvas tent. On shipping pallets. No floor. Sleeping in a puddle of rain. I started helping out in the woodshop. Not 'cause I'm good at it. I was hoping to jump the line for a dry place to bed down."

The shop smelled of heated metal and fresh-planed boards. It was a drafty structure, with a warble of wood pigeons coming from its eaves. Sun angled in from a dirty skylight, sawdust floating in its shaft.

A shirtless man with a cigarette in his mouth minded a huge machine, his smoke mixing with the airborne sawdust. This was René. His arms and chest were lean and tanned. He had pronounced cheekbones and white-blue eyes like a wolf's, which filled with light when he looked up. He looked at me with total indifference, spoke only to Pascal.

"I could do this job better without him here," René said to Pascal in quick French, confident that Burdmoore could not understand him, and not caring if I did. "He cut everything to the wrong measurement this morning."

Oblivious he was their topic, Burdmoore turned to me.

"Jean speaks a little English, luckily. Although he doesn't live down here at the Mill, as I call it. You met Jean?"

I said Pascal had talked about him, but no.

"Oh, man. You don't know Jean?" He smiled, amused by my purported ignorance.

"Me and Jean, we've been through similar stuff. Jean was underground. I was underground. I was involved with a group in New York. Jean in Paris. Same years, late sixties. Then a whole bunch of shit happened to me, three decades of trouble with the law, trouble with women, money woes. I fall in love with this French chick, move to Paris. She dies. I'm alone. The saddest I've ever been. I'm sitting in a bar feeling sorry for myself when I meet this guy. We start talking. Turns out we know some of the same people. We keep talking—this is Jean—and he says, Come down to Vantôme, and my friends will look after you. It'll be better. It'll be a home for you. Up there in Paris, I was working lousy jobs, doing demolition and for peanuts. I split. I've been here three years."

Three years, and he had managed not to learn more than a few phrases of French.

As Pascal and I left the woodshop, Burdmoore groaned about having to go back to work. I could see he would have been happy to spend the afternoon talking in his New Yawk accent. René was at his machine, some kind of band saw, which let out a deafening shriek.

Next on this tour was the communal kitchen. Lunch was over and a crew was cleaning up. A slight boy with dark curly hair was washing enormous pots with a high-pressure sprayer on a hose that hung from the ceiling and snapped upward like a Poma lift when he let go of it. The room was suffused with the close, humid odor of drain-trap food scraps. Women were carrying dirty plates from the dining area. The plates were dipped into two side-by-side tubs on a stainless counter in the kitchen, one tub presumably soapy and the other for rinsing. The expression "food-borne illness" floated across the surface of my thoughts like the stray bubbles that floated on the surface of the tubs.

Behind the kitchen was an outdoor area with a sandpit and a crooked old metal swing set. A little girl in nothing but loose underpants was pumping away on a swing like she was training for something, or trying to get someplace by swinging there, back and forth, back and forth.

One leg of the swing set popped out of its hole in the ground as she surged forward, and sank back in its hole as she swept back, the entire rickety apparatus strained from her athletic pumping and threatening to topple over.

Three young women sat at a table ignoring the children in their midst. One was hand-rolling a cigarette. Another was smoking a factory-rolled cigarette. The third had a toddler in her lap and another toddler standing at her knee, crying. The diaper of the crying toddler sagged heavily. His face was flecked with some kind of food residue. I felt sad for this child, who didn't know that his lament was being undermined by how ridiculous he looked, with crud caked around his mouth. I had the thought that public embarrassment starts at the beginning, before a person even knows to feel a sense of it.

Pascal was explaining how the crèche functioned, that everyone at Le Moulin volunteered.

"Childcare is challenging from zero to five," he said. "And here, no one is alone in parenting. Children can look to any adult, they are not stuck with the destiny of two people."

I'd been with Pascal for three hours now and he hadn't once mentioned his own children. He had at least two that I knew of, neither of whom he was raising.

"In cities, there is no support for parents. They're stressed and isolated and exhausted. Their children absorb that stress and enter adolescence in a state of repressed rage. The health of a society can be read through kids' emotions."

Le Moulin's book (Pascal's book) *Zones of Incivility* contained a short section on "the gratuitous acts of children." In rich countries, the book argued (Pascal argued), you find trends of children who snap. In Japan, this phenomenon had a name, "kireru." But it was America that was the capital of "kireru," where kids committed murder or suicide, or shot up a school. These lost children, by erupting into acts of extreme nihilism, were unconscious actors in an imaginary army, according to *Zones of Incivility*. They were symptoms of society's ills. Reading the anonymous authors' analysis (Pascal's analysis) of school shootings as logical responses to modern alienation, I had the thought that you'd have to be French, and fairly sheltered, to develop such a fetish for American violence.

Two little boys sat in the sandbox, throwing handfuls of sand at each other. Flung sand has weak momentum. The little boys kept at it, until one of them scrunched his eyes and put his hands to his face. After a moment of quiet, he wailed. The boy who'd thrown the sand that hit its mark looked bored and uncertain as the other boy cried. Would he be in trouble?

Pascal barely noticed, so intent was he to sell me on the idea of this collective day care.

"There have been, here at Le Moulin, people who have advocated for 'the abolition of the family.' I'm against that; I find it silly, to be honest. Familial bonds are a source of independence and ethics, a harbinger against the state, against its predations. Still, children are better served when they aren't limited to the nuclear structure, and instead are part of a larger family, their community."

The little girl on the swing had stopped pumping and sat still, her bare feet in the sand. With one hand she held the chain of the swing. Her other rummaged in her own underpants. She had a pensive and private look on her face, as if the feedback from the hand in her underwear had muffled the cries of the boy with sand in his eyes.

The young woman rolling her cigarette was now licking the seam of glue on her rolling paper with patent finesse. She stood up and strode over to the two boys, the rolled unlit cigarette between her fingers. She wore the timeless hippie look of an old random faded men's T-shirt of no particular size over an ankle-length skirt and no bra, her breasts stretched tragically low for someone her age, so young—and pretty too—but with these long breasts swinging around under her shirt.

As she attended to the boy with sand in his eyes, and admonished the other, the two women at the table spoke in low and serious voices and never once glanced toward the sandbox.

I was certain these women were not discussing children, even as one had a toddler in her lap and another at her knee. They were criticizing some man or assassinating the character of a commune sister, hashing out some intrigue or annoyance among the piles of annoyances that would crop up for people attempting to live communally.

Children who were not yet school age could be dropped off here, Pascal was explaining, and there was a sheet on which people signed up for shifts.

"These women are volunteers? The kids aren't their own?"

Pascal looked around and said that these women who happened to be here right now *were* the mothers of the children who were also here, but this was incidental. It was a day care, collectively run, even if those here at this moment were the parents of the kids who were here.

"It's better for everyone, than being isolated at home."

This way the kids could throw sand at each other while their mothers smoked and complained.

I pointed out that it was all women volunteering here. It's good to be a little skeptical. It can arouse suspicions to be too credulous. Real people have judgments.

"That's true," Pascal said. "And we are not the first group to discover that a division of labor between the genders reasserts itself when you try to live in a communal structure. Middle-class wage earners in cities, of course, can delegate their own domestic labor—the childcare and the housework—to nannies and maids. Well, we have no nannies and maids. And nor do we believe that it's a true feminism to pass off your domestic work to people who earn less than you do, and are more exploitable, who clean your house plus their own house.

"We are doing everything ourselves here. Someone has to split logs and maintain farm machinery, while someone else looks after children. The men end up attending to the blown head gasket on our delivery truck, while the women are canning tomatoes. Both types of work must get done. We don't have a magic solution. It's a challenge we face, with no easy remedy."

We had left the crèche and crossed a walnut grove toward a set of outbuildings where they pressed nuts to make oil. I followed Pascal through these buildings as he told me about the walnut harvest, explaining the sorting process, the various machines for grinding and expelling the nuts, the three grades of walnut oil they produced. The tools they had fabricated in order to repair their own machines, which were one hundred years old and came from Bordeaux, equipment slated for obsolescence that they were reviving.

He kept talking as we exited the final outbuilding, but I had stopped listening. The heat was suddenly getting to me.

As we passed back through the walnut grove, I looked into the lacy shade and wished I could lie down. The trees were spaced in a geometry that was pleasing and regular, each with enough room to stretch, but not too much room. On their trunks were irregular patches of purple-brown moss, thick as sheepskin. Bruno had written that the base of an old walnut tree is the best place to daydream. Carpeting the ground under the trees was chartreuse baby grass. With the exception of Pascal's voice, it was quiet here in this orchard. I could not hear the racket of the walnut sorting machines, or children crying, or saws from the woodshop.

I didn't know what to make of the growing evidence that Bruno had insinuated himself into my thoughts, Bruno whom I called Bruno, and Pascal kept referring to as "Lacombe."

Lacombe. Pascal said it as if they didn't know each other. As if Bruno wasn't even a person, a man, with feelings, a first name. Pascal said "Lacombe" like he was referring to someone absent or dead. He said it like he might say "Hegel" or "Marx."

A breeze stirred the limbs of the walnut trees, whose shadows made frolicsome patterns on the ground.

I looked up at their leaves, so bright, a pure, chlorophyll green. They shook and twirled like silk ornaments. They seemed to be vibrating.

As I stared at the vibrating leaves, I understood that I was having one of my vascular events, here in this walnut grove.

The flutter and play of light and leaves was breaking down along the edges of my vision. It would pass, I knew, as it always does. But it had not yet passed. It was happening now, as if proving that Bruno, whom I had thought of here, as a presence in this orchard, was somehow actually here, in the confetti of light and shadow, in the tremble of the leaves.

LE MOULIN'S LIBRARY, a former barn with rough walls of stone and mortar, metal floor-to-ceiling bookshelves bolted to them, was cool and dark. An electric fan riffled the pages of Clairefontaine notebooks, which lay open on a large table in the center of the room. The notebooks belonged to the four young men seated around the table.

Pascal pulled up two more chairs for us, and at my request he got me some water to drink.

My vision had calmed. I guessed that the heat had brought on the disturbance. And a touch of dehydration. All that wine I'd had yesterday, on my drive north from Marseille.

Pascal introduced me to these four who worked on the collaborative writings. They were all about the same age, early thirties, and all four had short stylish haircuts and glasses, and they wore a polo shirt or a clean, plain T-shirt, dark jeans, a watch on a thin, delicate wrist. Nice boys—like Pascal, like Lucien—from nice Parisian families.

A young woman, still in her teens, or twenty at most, with long blond fine-grade hair and a gloomy manner and too much kohl eyeliner, came in with a tray of coffee for us. No one introduced her. She set the tray down and adjusted the fan so that it no longer squeaked.

"Thanks, Florence," Pascal said quietly as she left.

From a window I could see a group of men working in a garden behind the library, sweat-soaked as they installed fence posts with a huge postholer, heaving each time they drove it down into the hard ground with a dull metallic "clunk." It did not sound like they were making progress.

I had the thought that the boys in the library were like higher-status monks in a medieval monastery. And that Burdmoore and René and the ones driving the postholer into the earth, they were the lower-status monks, the ones who do the backbreaking labor, forgo sleep, and endure inclement weather and unpleasant tasks. They dig irrigation canals, or carry stones up a hill, while the educated monks stay inside where it's cool in summer and warm in winter, recopying Bible passages, a monk who cannot read running their tea tray like Florence ran ours, although I was sure that Florence could read.

We discussed the translation of their book. I would work here in the library, with Alexandre (a dirty blond in wire-rimmed glasses) gathering sources for me, so that I could see what they quoted from. Jérôme (with dark hair, in horn-rimmed glasses), whose English was very good, would look over my work and flag sections that might call for discussion, for nuance of transposition.

With their plain and preppy look and their soft serious voices, these people were different from the West Coast eco-warriors with their piercings and their food-coloring hair dye, T-shirts whose logos were supposed to help define some micro-split in movement ideology. Nor did these boys resemble the anti-globalist window smashers of Genoa, the milieu in which Pascal had been radicalized, among people who wore all black. (Then again, Pascal didn't look like that either.) But whether people cultivate an exterior meant to signal their politics, or they cultivate, instead, a strait-laced appearance that does not signal their politics, their self-presentation is deliberate. It is meant to reinforce who they are (who they consider themselves to be).

People tell themselves, strenuously, that they believe in this or that political position, whether it is to do with wealth distribution or climate policy or the rights of animals. They commit to some plan, whether it is to stop old-growth logging, or protest nuclear power, or block a shipping port in order to bring capitalism, or at least logistics, to its knees. But the deeper motivation for their rhetoric—the values they promote, the lifestyle they have chosen, the look they present—is to shore up their own identity.

It is natural to attempt to reinforce identity, given how fragile people are underneath these identities they present to the world as "themselves." Their stridencies are fragile, while their need to protect their ego, and what forms that ego, is strong.

The boy with the chin-line beard who had delivered the fertilizer had told himself he was taking a stand to protest the cruel treatment of animals. He wasn't a poseur. But still his real motivation was libidinal: he did it for the promise of love. Love confirms who a person is, and that they are worth loving. Politics do not confirm who a person is.

People might claim to believe in this or that, but in the four a.m. version of themselves, most possess no fixed idea on how society should be organized. When people face themselves, alone, the passions they have been busy performing all day, and that they rely on to reassure themselves that they are who they claim to be, to reassure their milieu of the same, those things fall away.

What is it people encounter in their stark and solitary four a.m. self? What is inside them?

Not politics. There are no politics inside of people.

The truth of a person, under all the layers and guises, the significations of group and type, the quiet truth, underneath the noise of opinions and "beliefs," is a substance that is pure and stubborn and consistent. It is a hard, white salt.

This salt is the core. The four a.m. reality of being.

When I came to understand this, it was literally four a.m. and I was staring at an actual mountain of salt. I had been in northern Spain, tracking subminister Platon.

The subminister had traveled to a village called Cardona, where he met with Spanish investors. That day, we (he and I, though he had no idea we were "together") had been in Girona, a city of fanatical Catholic architecture and fetid standing water, where daytime mosquitoes hovered around the bare legs of tourists. While Platon ducked into a side door of the main cathedral to meet with side-dealing Catholic clergy, I blessed myself irreligiously that mosquitoes do not bite me.

After Girona we had driven through the dust and heat to Cardona. From the highway, tall craggy mountains stretched across a section of horizon like a diabolical curtain, sharp and jagged, frozen black flames against sky.

In Cardona, Platon had spent the night in a castle above the village, next to the famous salt mines of that region. The castle had been converted into a hotel, one of the state-run paradors (luxurious for government-run hotels). My own room was across a courtyard from the subminister's. From my exterior-facing windows, I could see the salt.

I looked out, unable to sleep. It was, as I said, four a.m. The moon was full, and the night sky was rinsed in the brilliant blue of indigo dye. The moon shone down on a mountain of salt, which wasn't white, it was a dirty reddish, coated in clay particulates.

The salt of Cardona had been mined for thousands of years, but now it was a tourist attraction. It came up from deep inside the earth. This mountain of it would somehow replenish forever, according to the brochure in my room. It would keep emerging as if by magic. In Roman times, salt was so precious it served as money. It is the source of the word "salary."

I stood at the window at four a.m. and told myself: You, too, have a core of precious salt. The human core of inner salt, like this salt of

Cardona, comes from the deepest part. Human salt, like this salt, is everlasting. Mine it, use it, and it will not deplete.

In my own salt, my own core, this is what I knew:

Life goes on a while. Then it ends.

There is no fairness.

Bad people are honored, and good ones are punished.

The reverse is also true. Good people are honored, and bad people are punished, and some will call this grace, or the hand of God, instead of luck. But deep down, even if they lack the courage to admit it, inside each person, they know that the world is lawless and chaotic and random.

This truth is stored in their salt. Some have access. Others don't.

A gift or a curse, that my salt is right here, with me all the time?

A gift.

I'd rather be driven by immutable truths than the winds of some opinion, whose real function is to underscore a person's social position in a group, a belief without depth.

These boys in the library would profess to share beliefs. But eventually, they might become enemies—of those beliefs, of one another. They will adopt new beliefs, new personas.

It is better to be steadfast.

Me, I adhere to my salt. I draw strength from it, use it. I keep watch over my salt, and when it serves me, I keep watch over other people's salt. I mine my salt, and sometimes, I mine the salt of others. Which is to say: I cooperate with the part of them that they can't reach, are not in touch with, cannot see, but that sometimes, when I am lucky, I can see quite well.

After the night "we" spent in the castle overlooking the mountain of salt, I followed Platon into the grubby medieval village of Cardona proper, which was below the castle, down a set of steps. I walked, while the subminister was driven, not by Georges, but by a driver based in Barcelona. To drive from the castle down to the village took longer than walking, so I paused, gazing at the salt mine over the wall of the open-air medieval steps, waiting for the car to appear. When it did, Platon emerged, and I followed at a comfortable distance.

This village, though in twenty-first-century Europe, reminded me of war-torn Kabul or the slums of Benghazi, with its jerry-rigged electrical wiring and a population that looked to be suffering from rickets and other diseases you don't see in the developed world. Platon went into a municipal building. I feigned tourism and read the plaque on the exterior of a shabby Romanesque church. It had been built in the eleventh century, and it looked like it.

As I pretended to read, a woman crawled on her knees along the ancient, grimy cobblestones—either physically disabled or disabled mentally, such as by a religious zeal, I could not tell. She was pulling herself on a thick slab of cardboard.

The front doors of the church opened. A priest emerged, dressed in stained white robes belted with a dingy braid.

He lit a cigarette, the vapors of its smoke heavy in the air of this dank and narrow street.

He watched the woman, in his dirty vestments, his cigarette pluming away.

She slid past the church, over the cobblestones, on the cardboard, on her knees.

She was still inching along on her hands and knees when the priest finished his cigarette and flicked it into the gutter. He went back inside the church.

Platon reappeared. He ("we") went in the opposite direction of the struggling woman, toward his waiting driver.

PASCAL INVITED ME TO STAY for their communal dinner. I said I was tired. I wanted to return to my rented jalopy on the town square, drive back to Lucien's family's moldering estate, drink bad beer I'd purchased in Boulière, and do some research and planning.

Pascal asked if I remembered the way, or would I like someone to accompany me?

"Florence can walk you," he said.

But before he could summon her, I assured him I was fine to walk alone.

It was seven p.m. and the hottest part of the day, the peak temperature spike, at least forty degrees Celsius, maybe 105 in Fahrenheit, and by any measurement hot as balls.

Up ahead, something dropped from above and landed on the road. It was a snake. Snakes in heat waves don't coil up on tree trunks. They sleep hanging down from a branch; it's a tactic for staying cool. Sometimes they fall, which is what must have happened to this snake. It slithered into a drainage ditch.

I walked in the middle of this road, instead of in the shade of overhanging trees, in order to avoid falling snakes.

I heard a car coming from behind and turned around. It was Nadia Derain in her dusty Renault.

This was the stretch of road she patrolled. I moved over. She drove up alongside and coasted the speed of my walking.

"Hi," I said.

"Are you fucking him?"

I laughed. "I'm married to his childhood friend."

"Is that a Canadian accent? You sound Québécois. No offense."

"None taken."

"He's got an insatiable hunger for fresh meat. New girls. You're too old."

"Could be," I said.

"No one talks about this thing of Pascal and the girls."

I'd had the thought while sitting across from him, at the Café de la Route, that it would have been interesting if Pascal bucked the trend, broke the cliché, and was in a committed monogamous relationship, and with someone his own age. But Lucien had already suggested this would not be the case.

"They talk about their supposed ethics," Nadia said, "but none of it applies to him!"

"That doesn't seem right."

I could see the tension that was straining her face start to release a little, her features smoothing in reaction to my sympathy, which she had not expected.

"Did he try the whole 'the affective layer of my Parisian buddies can be felt,' while a shrew from Brittany, her 'affective layer' is hidden?"

"He did try that," I said. "I wasn't convinced."

I personally found her affective layer—if that means "feelings"—boiling away right there on the surface.

"Well," she said, unsure how to respond to this validation. "I could tell you things that will not make Le Moulin look so idyllic or nice."

"Okay," I said.

"What do you mean *okay*?"

I stopped walking.

She put on her brakes. The car stalled. As she restarted it, I glanced back at Le Moulin to see if anyone was observing us.

The fields were empty of people. They were all in their dining commons, taunting a food-borne illness.

"I mean, I'd like a ride," I said. "But your passenger seat is piled with crap."

She began tossing dust-coated items one by one, books, a half-eaten apple, an old sweater, gardening shears, onto the floor behind her seat.

"Happy now?" she asked.

I said that I was, and got in beside her.

EVEN WITH ALL THE WINDOWS DOWN, her car had a pronounced agricultural smell, teeming and microbial. The back seat was piled with milk crates full of limp vegetables, soggy lettuces, their edges brown and gelatinous, and rotten melons, their faces caving in.

I moved a mud-caked boot off the passenger-side floor and put it in the back.

"You think this is a mess? Wait until you see my trunk!"

She stalled as she put the car in drive, started it again, then restarted it without realizing the motor was already running.

Setting off, she let out the clutch too quickly. She was in third instead of first. The car lurched forward, the engine pinging. She realized her error and downshifted to first, redlining the motor. She shifted by accident to fifth, causing the car to sputter, then back to first, the engine screaming.

She found third gear. We were on our way.

I started to tell her where I'd left my car, but she interrupted me.

"I'll take you to your *blue Škoda with the rental stickers*. Your blue Škoda which has been parked on the north side of the church since quarter past noon today."

She looked at me proudly. "I know what goes on. I see everything. The bar closes from two to five. Naïs locks up and goes home for lunch. Afternoons, it's dead around here, until Naïs comes back and the locals can start up again with their drinking, since Pascal believes it's revolutionary to supply them with beer and wine. The long afternoon while the bar was closed and no one was around, that blue Škoda was still there and I told myself, Nadia, something is happening."

"You're correct," I said.

"Of course I'm correct! I came down here from the ZAD. To pull off what we did up there, we pushed out the cops! We won! To do that, you have to notice and observe. I've been at this twenty years. You learn to sense things. I knew something was up when you appeared on the square today."

But how had she seen me? The square had been empty except for the tramps with their backpacks and the two workers painting the crosswalk in their state-issue uniforms. Who else had been around? Briefly, the man in the convertible. Had she been in the bar? I'd made a visual sweep of the bar's interior and seen only the two old farmers, Crouzel and his purple-faced friend.

"I didn't see you," I said.

"That's right, you didn't see me, Québécois. Because I was in the church. That's something I've learned over the years. Churches are open. Even when they're closed, they are open. There's always a way to get in. A church is a nice place to stay out of the sun. Plus, I happen to believe in God. Do you believe in God, Québécois? Or just in Pascal?"

She didn't wait for me to answer. "He doesn't *claim* to be a god, of course. That would be *vulgar*. And yet his disciples, Jérôme and Alexandre, treat him as one."

She drew out the syllables of "Alexandre" in mockery, as if that name demanded to be pronounced in a stuffy lilt.

"Boys who have never worked a day in their lives. Have never prayed, never needed to. Never been humble. Up in the ZAD, we were on the front lines defending the land with country people who can as easily face off against the state as they can slaughter and dress an animal, and no one up there is talking at them in some bullshit theory-speak. I come down here and it's, pfff, Nadia, she's too loud, too boastful. She's coarse. Nadia, she's got a lot of opinions no one cares about. Do you get what I'm saying?"

Once again, I wasn't meant to respond.

"'You're always talking about your status, your role, the part you played,' they tell me. 'Victories aren't about credit,' they say. By Pascal's rules, everything must be an invisible 'we.' Well, you know what, Pascal, some of us were born an invisible 'we.' Some of us are from a nameless nothing, and we want a name. When you're one of six mouths to feed and your parents can no longer work because their bodies are broken from labor and stress, you want a name and a place and respect, as part of a movement. Pff. Renouncing individuality, that's for rich kids. Pascal can go ahead and get rid of himself. But me, thanks, I'll stay me!

"Did you know he thinks he's Guy Debord, reincarnated? Why would you emulate someone like that? A megalomaniac who was fucking his own sister! That's the truth of things. Everyone knows it, but they hide that part, the part where Guy Debord was having a sexual relationship with his sister, and she wasn't a half sister either—not that it would excuse things—but she was a *full-blood sister*!

"The day I brought this up, that was the beginning of the end for me and Le Moulin. Pascal looked at me with hatred. This is in the dining hall, at lunch. Burdmoore is telling some story, and no one can understand him, even the ones who are good in English. Pascal signals him to quiet. Everyone is supposed to stop what they're doing and listen, and Pascal says:

"'I realize, Nadia, that it's difficult for you to leave anything unspoken. So be it. Let's address this. If we concede that Guy Debord was a sadist and sexual deviant, which, yes, sure, let's concede these might be true. But then we must also concede, Nadia, that the world is chock-full of sadists and sexual deviants, numbering no doubt in the low billions.

If we take Freud half-seriously—I know this is a stretch, Nadia, especially for those who haven't read Freud—we might suggest that sadism and deviance are part of the human psyche, as archaic and ever-present pressures that enter into contradiction with other psychic pressures and forces.'"

This sounded about right to me, but my thoughts on the subject were private, and irrelevant.

"And he continues like that, lecturing me in front of everyone. Well! Nadia's read some Freud. I read the part where Sigmund says cavemen urinated on the first fire because they thought the flames were penises, excuse me, 'phalluses,' challenging them about their own dick size! They pissed on the flames and put them out in order to win the dick-measuring contest. That's Sigmund's full account of human history."

Freud's arguments in *Civilization and Its Discontents* were a little more involved than Nadia's summary, but the point was that she was hurt. She was angry. Her salt was bitter, and I might want to see about mining it.

WE WERE BACK AT THE TOWN SQUARE. The sun had gone behind the hills. The air was cooler. Dusk was coming on. I thought about the Dubois house, locked up and waiting for me. It would be dark when I got there.

Nadia pulled over next to my rental car and shifted into what she thought was neutral. The car shuddered and the engine died. We were next to the church, its garden of nettles and thistles deep in shadow. But for Nadia, we were still in the dining hall, where Pascal had just upbraided her.

"And then he says, 'So here is my question for you, Nadia: Why is it, that among legions of sadists, *exactly one* wrote *The Society of the Spectacle*? Could it be the case that Debord's sadism might have had something to do with his greatness, Nadia? That the very success of his organization *depended* on his sadism? Could it be that vice becomes, in the historical and political space of the "sect," a virtue?'

"He goes on and on, and his entire point is: billions are sadists but *there's only one* Guy Debord!

"Le Moulin will fail if they continue this way. Up in Nantes, we stopped the government from their plans to build the airport. We defended the land. The reason for our success is that we had no leaders. Pascal doesn't want a movement; he wants a fiefdom. Some of them at Le Moulin should have defended me. René, for instance. He's not from their world, you know. Only Florence still talks to me. The quietest among them, and yet with the most integrity."

We were standing next to her car.

I asked where she was staying.

"Up at this ruin. It's an empty castle on the hill behind the lake. I broke in to one of the buildings."

"The Château de Gaume?"

"I don't know if it has a name. It's a ruin. If Pascal finds out you were talking to me," she said, "he'll cut you off."

"I'll keep our conversations between us," I said.

"You're married to his friend?"

"Lucien Dubois. He and Pascal went to school together."

"And before that?"

"I was in California. I had to leave. I had some trouble with the law." She nodded.

I was not on stable ground exactly but I took a step.

"Why don't we talk in a few days. I'll come up to the château."

"Okay." Her expression was guarded, but I felt her inner conflict. Part of her was distrustful of me, but she was too lonely to listen to that part.

She started telling me how to find the place.

I let her explain, even as Bruno had debriefed me on the coordinates of that property, and what was under it—who was buried there, and why. Not intentionally, of course. Bruno didn't know he was debriefing me on the long and bloody history of the Château de Gaume. He didn't know I was his student, or what a good student I was, that I could recite the year of the Cagot Rebellion (1594), the incident that sparked it (the execution of Loli the horse, burned alive in the square of Vantôme), the historic compromise between Cagot and peasant that fueled this rebellion. The pétanque they played with nobles' heads. The defeat, the dead, the potter's field, the castle later used as a prison for undesirables. Some of those undesirables added to its potter's field.

"The castle gate looks locked," she said. "But the gate is held with only looped chain. Take the road up to the top. You're on the promenade, in front of the main building. Opposite is a chapel and an orangery, and beyond the orangery is a little one-story building with a black door. That's where I'm staying. When you come up, can you bring some food? Things have been tough for us."

"Us?"

"Me and Bernadette."

"Bernadette?"

"You can meet her."

She went around and opened her trunk.

There was a live pig in there, pinkish, coated in white bristles. It began to scrabble at the sight of Nadia, grunting and sniffing with its sheered-flat pig nose.

She clapped her hands one time and pointed.

The pig hurled itself up and over the lip of the trunk and landed on the ground, not on its feet like animals are supposed to, but it righted itself from its inelegant side-flop and stood watching her as if for further commands, sniffing with that nose that looked molded into the shape of a cup.

"Bernadette is in training. She's learning to hunt truffles. You can make a good living with a truffle pig. Isn't that right, Bernadette."

The pig watched her.

It can't speak, I didn't say.

"A farmer near Sazerac traded them a weaned piglet in exchange for vegetable deliveries and their plan was just, fatten her and eat her!"

She tossed a couple of the old lettuce heads from the crate in her back seat onto the ground. The pig nudged its face into the rotten lettuces and began chewing their slimy leaves.

"A babe as young as she was when they got her can be trained to earn thousands. By the time the season starts this fall, she'll be ready.

Take our yield to the gourmet markets. People will pay a fortune for just a few ounces of black truffles. The Moulinards have no imagination beyond converting animals to food. Eat your pig in winter, then be hungry and broke."

Bernadette had finished the lettuce. Nadia commanded her back into the trunk by banging twice on the rear quarter panel, a signal in a language the animal seemed to know.

It leapt up but missed its mark. It took a couple of tries, plus Nadia helping with a boost to its hindquarters, for the pig to clear the lip of the trunk, because it had quite a long body, as I suppose all pigs do. They haven't been bred to hurdle over barriers.

It lay down in a pile of hay she had back there, snorting and grunting.

"Black truffles," I said. "In this area?"

She said yes and closed the trunk lid.

"So that's also Neire," I said.

"What?"

"Neire," I said. "Black. An ancient color. The secret of this place."

She looked at me like I was crazy, but she was the one who was crazy.

BACK AT CHEZ DUBOIS, my aristocratic flophouse, I had forgotten to put the bad beer from Boulière into the refrigerator, so it was very warm bad beer, almost hot. I drank it, its carbonation a fraying patter on the tongue instead of the sharp pop of cold bubbles filling the mouth and throat.

I lay on the bed in the upstairs room I'd chosen, the open windows letting in cool night air and allowing me to detect any sounds as I researched this unexpected American, Burdmoore.

If a single pebble on the gravel shifted, I would hear it. I heard nothing. The lockboxes had been undisturbed. There had been no Citroën panel truck waiting for me upon my return.

It was not a common first name, and with my guess of his age, and his New York accent, my yield on him was low effort, high reward.

Burdmoore's rap sheet was stunningly long: vandalism, petty theft, felony theft, check fraud, mail fraud, possession of stolen property, fencing of stolen property, battery, violating the terms of a restraining order, driving a stolen ambulance, driving a stolen box truck, driving under the influence, a host of other convictions and bench warrants and parole violations, various weapons charges, and deep into the record, from 1977, a guilty plea of arson and second-degree murder, for the death of two people trapped in a burning building.

The details painted a portrait.

My impression, upon meeting him, had been that he was something of a joke and a novelty, a geezer taken in by the Moulinards out of charity. But from his criminal record it looked to me like Burdmoore was the actual heavyweight among them—perhaps the only serious one.

I was on my second "hot one" and relaxing, as I sifted through a stack of Bruno's emails that a word search for "Neire" pulled up. I found one I had not read before and downloaded it.

Caves are uniquely black, he began this email.

Unaided by a fire or a torch or a flashlight, in a cave you encounter a blackness that is much more extreme than what in normal life is thought of as "black."

Bruno said that what most interested him about the dark of a cave was the way in which outer darkness seemed to spark an explosion of activity inside the mind.

In absolute dark, he said, you turn inward. It is in true dark that one's mental scenes are most full of light and color and movement, as if the dark of a cave were the secret pathway to our own inner world, the same path taken by our hominin brothers and sisters, who went down into the earth where no light leaked in order to *see*.

Bruno had gone into the nether chambers of his own cave without any artificial light. He arranged food and drink around him in an assembly he could locate by touch. He was committed to remaining fourteen days.

He wrote to the Moulinards that in his darkest hour—and he meant that literally, the apex of extreme dark, which occurred on the first night, when he was unaccustomed, rather than the expression's more common and figurative usage, to describe a psychological crisis—it was in his darkest hour that he began to see.

An image in his mind, he told them, came into view: it was a black-and-white silver-nitrate studio portrait of the American icon for the blind, Helen Keller. She was seated, noble, in a black high-necked dress, and holding in her lap an enormous magnolia blossom. Her pose emphasized her beautiful upright posture and her handsome profile. Her gaze was of pristine beatitude, blessed and transparent.

He understood that this image he could see in his mind of Helen Keller was a real photograph that he had once looked at in a book. The power of this portrait of Helen Keller was to conjure, without having to explain, her sense experience as a blind person, her communion with this magnolia blossom in her lap. She cannot see it, but its lemony and delicate fragrance is rising to her. She can feel the thick and spongy consistency of its petals, and the sturdy structure of its leaves, which frame the flower like the points of a star. Leaves that would be slippery on top, fuzzy and soft on their undersides.

In the darkest region of his cave, in absolute blindness, Bruno had pictured a blind person apprehending beauty by smell and by touch.

To Bruno, the meaning of this paradox was self-evident: to not be physically blind, as he was not, was to be blind to what it means not to see.

He put this another way for them, in an attempt to clarify: He could not abandon his own capacity for sight, he wrote. Even if he wanted to.

I see in the light, he said. I see in the half-light. I see in the dark. And it is imperative that I embrace this capacity. That I give in to it. That I insistently see.

Some of what he pictured that fortnight in his cave was testament to the kaleidoscopic talents of the mind to make patterns, to make art, even as his own visions, he told them, were strikingly similar to late 1960s and early 1970s psychedelic poster art—a graphics style, he said, that was inescapable for those who lived through that era. He said that poster art might itself point toward, and even establish, a common counter-reality, the swirls of color that people see in heightened states, a lake-in-the-earth in which we all swim, he said, whether induced by hallucinogens or by extreme dark.

The good and the bad of this counter-reality, he told them, our "inner seeing," was that it sometimes lifted debased fragments from the commodified world. We are all sieves, he said, and we catch and hold on to all sorts of things, and not just the images we want to return to. Take an inner trip, and it will not be just the beautiful and the sacred that you find. From the depths of my own mind might come a jingle I heard on the radio as a child, advertising tooth-whitening powder, or I might see Tintin's dog, Milou. We pick up things along the way that are of no use at all. The trick, he said, is to acknowledge these images, and to let them float past.

My iPhone rang. It was Lucien. He knew reception was bad, which gave me a perfect excuse to be unavailable, but I was expecting his call and ready to answer.

He asked about Le Moulin, but I understood that what he wanted to know was what Pascal had said about him, where he stacked up in Pascal's judgments.

I invented quotes about how much Pascal respected Lucien and the choices he'd made.

Satisfied that he was not a sellout in the eyes of his radical friend, Lucien moved to the topic of the house. He said Agathe was being overbearing, constantly texting him details about the property, details that he would spare me, but that she might show up there.

I was prepared for this. I said I had met Robert. I was sorry to have to inform Lucien of what happened, but his aunt's husband had been inappropriate. I had gone out for a walk and encountered Robert parked on the road. He was touching himself in his car.

"Oh my God, Sadie. Are you okay?"

Lucien seemed to think this was my first lesson that men masturbate.

I said I didn't want to make a big deal of things, but I didn't feel safe thinking I might encounter Robert again. I was afraid of him.

"I should come up there," Lucien said. "But everything is permitted and arranged for the shoot, and I can't leave. I feel like I understand why I've never liked that guy. No one in the family can stand him." He said he would call Agathe and tell her they should both leave me undisturbed. It was his house, and it was time to put his foot down. He might even tell Agathe the truth, that Robert had a problem.

Robert would be incensed, naturally. He would deny the accusation, but he would get the message. A message from me to him, to leave me alone. And Agathe would keep him closer to home, to keep an eye on him.

As we ended our call, Lucien said he could not wait to join me when the shoot was finished, six weeks from now.

"I'm thinking about you," he said. There was an audible sigh. "I need you here," he whispered.

A noisome image of Lucien naked flashed into my thoughts. This image was attended by a smell, or a memory of a smell (and what is the difference): the rankly sweet emanations from his armpits. His hot breath. His warm hands.

In Marseille, as we lay in the hotel bed, my back to him, pretending I was asleep, he said into my hair, "When I'm inside you it's like I'm home."

I'd shivered in disgust. Sensing my shiver as if it were a tremble of love, he squeezed me and whispered, "Sadie."

His utterance of that name, using it without knowing who I am, didn't function as it should have, to remind me this was all an act, temporary.

"Sadie."

He had said it a third time as he rolled me toward him, summoning more physical strength than I might have expected him to have.

Perhaps with similar strength, but a mental kind, I forced myself to submit.

For several weeks I had patiently allowed Lucien to unbuckle my sandals and take off my jeans and my underwear and breathe all over me and slow everything down to the tempo of some song or movie he thought he was living in. I let him roll me toward him and look for home. I'm not all that different from Narc Cutler, except that I'm strategic, and Narc Cutler wasn't.

Lynn Watson, with her ROTC shoulders, her CIA strut, she probably didn't fuck anybody. But to her detriment, I'd wager. No one had liked her, she'd raised eyebrows, she had never effectively embedded herself, and at their first opportunity they'd pounced and ruined her.

With my long-ago and very first undercover assignment, wearing a wire for my biker and his associates, I had not found it a significant challenge to fake things. I had not had issues of internal resistance like I felt with Lucien.

Physically, I had suffered on that assignment. It had rained the entire job. I was constantly soggy and cold. I'd ridden hundreds of miles on the back of a chopper, on a hard and tiny seat, my tailbone absorbing every bump. I'd burned the inside of my leg on a motorcycle exhaust pipe, a burn that left a large brown bubble, which turned into a scar I still have. In our various travels, my biker seldom agreed to stop and by the time he did I had to pee so badly I would walk toward the bushes or toward a gas station bathroom hunched over, as if normal steps in an upright posture might produce a great involuntary release from my bladder of what I had been forced to retain.

My biker had a pocked complexion and a goatee whose prickly feel I never got used to. He had a long white scar up his belly like someone had tried to gut him. He was a good deal less considerate than Lucien. But unlike Lucien, he didn't badger me for intimacy and acceptance. Whoever he believed himself to be was coterminous with his performance of who he was. He didn't need a woman to make him feel whole.

I would be gone, my work here completed, before Lucien was done with his film shoot in Marseille. His plan for an eventual "honeymoon" (his expression) in the Guyenne would vanish like his delusion that he'd known me.

But these thoughts, my own actual thoughts, of Lucien breathing all over me, might remain. I might be stuck with the memory of him rolling me toward him at the hotel in Marseille, overpowering me and pinning me down in a manner he was convinced was right and good for both of us.

Revisiting that, unable to block it, I wondered if I was getting paid sufficiently for this work.

Things can be renegotiated, based on the unexpected, the challenges that crop up. I have always been a good negotiator. What amount would be enough?

Know your worth. Know your salt. Know their salt.

Proceed accordingly. Few could do what I do.

Name a price, I told myself.

But thinking of Lucien's hands all over me like I was a book of Braille and he was a blind man insisting on reading this book, running his hands up and down my arms and legs and over my stomach and breasts, not to read me, but to force me to pretend I wanted to be touched like that, I could not come up with a number.

THE ITALIAN DOCUMENTARY that Vito had recommended, with nine-year-old Franck sharing his sexual philosophy while chewing gum, propped on an elbow, had also included an interview with a prostitute from Rome who worked the Termini train station.

I know that station a little. I once had to meet a contact at Termini, and afterward I had passed on foot through the sleazy neighborhood adjacent, composed of bleak and homogeneous postwar apartment blocks, lines mounted out every window and hung with flapping laundry—the international flag for anonymous women's work.

Termini station is edged with another kind of anonymous women's work, but the train station prostitute in the movie is interviewed at home, in her own kitchen. She's in her forties. She does not suggest she's retired from her streetwork but she's not aging well. She has dressed primly for the occasion of this interview, in a high-collared synthetic blouse and an acrylic vest, garments that are the color of Nutella, the goo Italians are raised on despite lacking a word like "goo."

Or she has not dressed for the filmmaker, and this is the real her. A woman who, if you glimpsed her at six a.m., bustling around her tiny apartment, would already be in these clothes, stiff and dowdy, and sitting at her kitchen table like a foreigner in her own apartment, even with no camera on her. Her kitchen is tidy and airless, everything put away, wiped clean. Domestic order is her solution to the rangy feel of the train station and its squalid and prisonlike perimeter, its concrete watchtowers, chain-link and barbwire, discarded needles, cigarette butts, graffiti on every surface, graffiti even on the vestiges of crumbling Roman wall.

Her brown hair is dull and short and set in a permanent. Her brown eyes are small and beady and reflect no light. Her eyebrows are drawn on, but I would not expect a woman like this to have any natural eyebrow left, at this point in her life. Her brows have been lost long ago to over-tweezing, casualties in the war of her life.

She's not pretty but she's confident when the voice behind the camera, it's the same guy who interviewed young and horny Franck, asks her, "How do you please a man?"

She tries to summarize but falters. Her hesitancy is the kind you'd find in any expert speaking to a layperson, trying to locate the simplest language to explain a complex skill.

He presses her for details.

"You have to caress a man gently," she says.

"What is a gentle caress?"

She rolls up her blouse sleeve to demonstrate on her own bare arm.

"Very, very lightly," she says. "You have to use the lightest touch on the sensitive parts of their body. Like this." Her fingers trace up and down her arm.

"How do you prepare to go to the train station at night?"

"I bathe. Set my hair. Put on makeup."

"Could you go with a fifteen-year-old boy?"

She shakes her head no. "He would remind me of my son."

"Who was the youngest you've gone with?"

"Eighteen or nineteen. And totally naïve about sex."

I wonder if the filmmaker is thinking of Franck, in asking her if she could go with a fifteen-year-old. But Franck is much younger. And Franck doesn't pay for sex.

"How do you pick up clients?" the filmmaker asks her.

She answers as though he has asked, How do you manage psychologically to do it, even as he has not asked that.

"Every day, the first client I'm with, it's difficult. It anguishes me. It's very hard. But after the first one, I do okay with the others."

"What would you like to say about your life?"

She pauses, searching her mind for how to answer.

"I once fucked a man with a screwdriver." She emits a sharp laugh, but her laughter seems false, as if a devil is forcing her to laugh at a joke she doesn't find funny.

"He wanted me to tap his balls with something and that's what I had in the car. It worked. I made him come with the tools of the trade." More laughter. The tools of the trade. She's told this one before.

The filmmaker asks her what she dreams about.

Dead people, she answers.

"I dream I'm talking to them. They tell me about simple, everyday things, like their house chores or how long they waited for the bus. But I want to know other things. I have so many questions. And as soon as I start to ask them, they recede. The dead disappear and I don't see them anymore."

The laughter is gone now. She's turning inward, to these dead people in her dreams who won't answer her questions.

"What do you want to ask them?"

"So many things. What it's like to live on the other side. If paradise exists. I want to know about hell."

"How do you imagine hell?"

"A place where you cannot see God."

Her eyes redden and water. She looks to the side. And up. And again to the side. People do this to try to dissipate sadness, to cast it from their own face, by looking here and there to avoid crying. It doesn't work.

The boy with the chin-line beard had done this.

In his filmed confessions, they tell him that Nancy has already turned state's evidence against him. (She has not; they are lying.) The boy doesn't want to believe them, but he's not seasoned. He doesn't know that cops lie.

He blinks, looks at the floor and into the corners of the room. Looks up. Tears crest, roll down his cheeks.

I betrayed this boy. It was my job to betray him. But it could also be said that he betrayed me, by mounting that entrapment defense, which got me fired. Still, I blame Nancy for my exile, more than I do him. It's not logical, exactly, it's emotional. We all like to find a person to hate, and for me that person is Nancy.

The boy, as a type, is one of the lost and the weak. The rudderless. Nancy is among the strong and vengeful, as I could see from the character test of the surprise raid at her warehouse.

She and the boy were still together from what I could tell. They had lawyers working to clear their names. Nancy gave interviews to left-wing journalists blathering on about the agent who set them up. No one had discovered this agent's real name. Instead, they used the alias the boy knew her by, which was Amy, and they always put the name in quotes. "Amy" this and "Amy" that. They had no photo of her to match the name.

"TELL ME WHAT YOU THINK OF MEN," the filmmaker says to the prostitute in her tidy kitchen, she and her kitchen both reeking of despair.

"Men are all the same," she says. "They try to get what they want. And after they get it, they change. They're completely different."

The screen goes black.

Words come up:

The day after this interview, the woman killed herself by drinking bleach.

I had watched that film in Lucien's apartment in Paris, which had become my apartment as well.

The next night, I was in the bar of the Hotel Meurice with Lucien and Serge and Vito.

Is her death the filmmaker's fault? I asked Vito.

"I don't think it's his fault," Vito said. "It's her life, her decision to end it."

We were in a dark corner of the bar, but that bar is all dark corners.

"He didn't give her that life. But I can promise you the filmmaker never forgot her."

I could see from the bar into the lobby, the same lobby my subminister Platon passed through to the hotel's salon, to have his hair dyed (or someone else's hair dyed, or synthetic hair dyed). Platon had brought his mistress from Vincennes to this hotel, but not regularly. The rooms were quite expensive.

Lucien was on his third martini. I was counting. One more and he would pass out when we returned to the apartment. Meaning I could work or sleep unmolested.

I was also on my third martini, but I hold my liquor fine (except I get a bit of insomnia from overdrinking, nothing that can't be fixed with American sedatives).

Lucien and Serge both looked over as a group entered the bar: an ancient man, a middle-aged woman, and four young adults.

"It's Claude Perdriel," Lucien said, as the man came over to say hello to him.

There were polite introductions. He and his family were here for a late meal in the bar, having just flown in from the Maldives.

Family friends, Lucien explained as a waiter seated them on the other side of the room. Claude Perdriel had started a magazine, Lucien said, *Le Nouvel Observateur*. He was in his eighties. His wife was in her forties.

The idea of living one continuous existence for that many years baffled me. He looked vigorous and healthy despite his age, despite having just flown in from the Maldives.

"What's his secret?" I asked.

"Money," Vito said.

"His money is no secret," Serge said. "He made it in bathroom fixtures."

"A tub and toilet man," Vito said.

Vito said this was what he loved about the Hotel Meurice. You never knew whom you'd see. Politicians—last time it was former prime minister Lionel Jospin—and shady neocon pundits, Bernard-Henri Lévy with his shirt torn open to the waist.

"He gets them tailored without buttons," Serge said. "A shirt, for Bernard-Henri Lévy, is just two shiny draping panels of fabric that pool together at his navel."

"The Hotel Meurice is like a theater stage," Vito said, "where we watch the important men of France order a very expensive hamburger."

"That's what Pascal ordered when I met him here," Lucien said.

"Pascal Balmy hangs out at the Hotel Meurice?" Vito asked. "He's supposed to be jumping turnstiles in the metro. Or smashing bank machines. What was he doing here?"

"The same thing we're doing here, my love," Serge said. "Watching Lucien greet the captains of industry, otherwise known as his people."

"It's the same for Pascal," Lucien said. "He and I were sitting here, and two judges and a minister walk in. They come over, shake hands with Pascal, cordial and familiar. Friends of his father's. None of these people are strangers. The most powerful people in France come in here. And Pascal's connected to them whether he likes it or not."

I looked over at Claude Perdriel, just in from the Maldives, eating with his good-looking family. I watched the impeccably suited older men in club chairs, leaning forward, conversing in pairs.

These men ran industrial conglomerates. Any of them might have bought up land in the Guyenne, which could turn them a huge profit. Or cause them a huge loss, if the state's infrastructure project was halted.

The men in this bar were exercising their social connections to the judges and ministers who also came here, to advance their economic interests. And no doubt these men advanced their interests in other ways too. By hiring consultants and spies. By keeping close track of those who threatened their interests, like the contacts who had hired me were keeping close track of theirs, contacts who were concerned with the remote Guyenne Valley, so curiously concerned with a minor bureaucrat who was not of their league.

I looked around the Hotel Meurice bar at these various men, casual, discreet, with an air of refinement, of insulation from harm. My thought was that any of them could have been behind this job, could have been my true and actual boss.

And if my secret bosses were not here in this bar tonight, right now, they might as well have been. Because this was what the people I was working for looked like. This was who they were.

VI

GET LUCKY

IN 1939, LOUIS-FERDINAND CÉLINE, writer, physician, war hero, invalid, anti-Semite, and author of novels full of grammatical ellipses (a punctuation mark meant to simulate, or so he claimed, the sound of "hissing"), was hired as a ship's doctor on a French passenger vessel requisitioned to transport troops between Casablanca and Marseille.

This was before France surrendered to Germany. Céline loved Hitler and secretly rooted for the Germans, but he was bored and so he signed up to help the war effort against them.

I'd read about this one morning at the kitchen table of the Dubois house, from a torrid biography I'd found in a cupboard, a six-hundred-page volume that was puffy from water damage. On its cover was a garish photo. It was Céline, but he looked like an actor in a made-for-TV movie about some swashbuckling historical figure.

Céline was on his third round-trip excursion, performing medical duties on the passenger ship, when it rammed a British torpedo gunboat near Gibraltar. Céline's ship was going full speed as it plowed into the gunboat, which exploded in a fireball. The collision was an accident; the torpedo boat was piloted by France's official allies.

Does it matter to the consequences if something is "an accident"? The torpedo boat sank, and everyone on board drowned. Céline's passenger ship was fine and kept going.

That is what I would call *very good luck*. It was the kind of luck one could never count on or expect, to T-bone a gunboat and, boom, keep going. But I seemed to be having pretty good luck myself.

I'd been on watch for Robert the Terrible, with no new encounters, thinking I'd effectively scared him off. I imagined him trying to find a way to mention to Agathe that he had taken out a life insurance policy on her.

And then Lucien informed me that Robert was in a hospital in Limoges, in some kind of diabetic coma. Lucien had spoken to Agathe, who reported this.

I thought of his pointy eyeballs.

It was true he had not looked well, I said, adopting a compassionate tone.

Agathe told Lucien that Robert had been in kidney dialysis. His health was now in a state of collapse, and Agathe didn't know what was next. A priest was being summoned to the hospital.

I almost felt God was smiling down on me. A coma. Limoges (Limoges was hours from here). But since there is no God, it was luck, pure luck.

Robert was gravely ill. And Agathe would be tied up at his bedside.

This turn of events put to rest my fears regarding whoever had contacted Robert. They had done so to warn me, whoever they were. It could have been my own contacts for this job, letting me know I was disposable. Making sure I was aware they could blow my cover while I could not blow theirs, not knowing even who they were.

In any case, what trouble could Robert the Incapacitated make for me now?

The poor man was in a coma. It was practically like being dead.

SOME OF MY LUCK WAS MORE MEASURED. Not good or bad. My presence at Le Moulin was fairly well-accepted after the first week, although no one shared any hint to me that they were planning acts of sabotage, or suggested they had committed any, and certain people there seemed to regard me coldly. This was normal and expected. I knew to be patient.

The trust I was building was primarily with the upper-class monks, Pascal and the boys in the library. We sat around the table, debating things. I was free to disagree, since having a few contrary opinions, within limits, was the persona of authenticity by which they were coming to know me.

―――――

We broke for the Moulinards' communal lunch at one thirty p.m., meals whose offerings hovered in the genre of the enchilada despite this being France.

I often pleaded American workaholism and skipped lunch. I either stayed in the library or lay under a walnut tree.

"Off to your daydreaming," Pascal would say.

He was not wrong. I lay and watched patterns of light, recalling ideas of Bruno's about the hallucinatory effects of nature.

After lunch, Florence with her pale complexion and her smudged eyeliner would bring coffee to the library. I observed her on account that she was maintaining contact with Nadia Derain, whom the rest had relegated to the status of a leper.

I knew from Nadia that Pascal assigned Florence to care for his two children when they came to visit. The mother of those kids, a former Moulinard, had gone back to Paris, and Pascal saw the children two weeks a year, in the summer. This past summer he had imposed nannyship onto Florence, who was burdened with these two little brats, whom Pascal all but ignored. But secrets and discord were, for now, to be observed and not acted upon.

After Florence delivered the coffee tray, the cups were passed around as if this coffee had miraculously appeared, or as if we were well aware that "unwaged labor" had produced it (meaning someone completed a task without being paid to do so). We accepted as a given that someone had to make coffee and wash cups and that, as Pascal had said to me, the old division of labor between men and women reasserts itself when people attempt to live on a commune.

That the labor of thinking, reading, and writing fell to men was not discussed in the library. That my status seemed to be something on the level of an honorary man was also not discussed. My connection to Pascal's personal life, combined with my academic training, put me in a special category. And I was from the US, which to the library theorists was a mythical place of social extremes and gun violence. They asked a lot of questions, and I played a certain role, as an expert on savage life in America, pointing out their own naïveté as people from a country with a civil fabric, a social safety net, which reinforced my status as separate from the women of their commune.

When the concept of "unwaged labor" was discussed openly, it was treated as an abstraction. Housework, childcare, and "emotional labor" (which meant listening to someone's problems or offering advice) should be considered real work, the Moulinards argued, because this work had to be done, in addition to the work that people did for an employer. Like a woman cooks meals and launders clothes for a husband before he heads to the factory or the bank, depending on his class level, and this woman does the same for their children, who are reared either to join the workforce like their father or to be conscripted themselves into unwaged labor like their mother.

Pascal talked about the radical icon Melva Blumberg and a treatise she had written on gender and housework, in which she addressed the fact that domestic chores fell to women even as women had, by the time she wrote this text, in the late 1970s, left the home and were working waged jobs, which meant that these women were forced to do double duty, to moonlight as chambermaids for themselves and their families. Melva Blumberg suggested that just as automation was reshaping the American factory, robots might be assigned to do housework, a civic task that would be like a huge public works project, sponsored by and managed at the level of the state, like nationalized health care, Pascal summarized. Nationalized home-cleaning crews would go house to house with specialized robotic machines developed to do this work, and no one would have to clean their own house.

"Come on," I said.

Voices rose. Jérôme and Alexandre were on my side of this one—the state, they asked, we want the state in our homes?

Pascal quieted the furor, gesturing to take things down a notch.

"These proposals of Melva Blumberg's were for a different world than this one," he said. "She's a brilliant thinker. And you embarrass yourselves, frankly, by looking for the dumb argument inside her bold one. She's talking about a realm in which property won't be privately owned.

"The state entering is not the same specter you imagine now, in terms of a violation of so-called privacy. This is not about being raided by the gendarmerie! It's not a social worker coming to inspect your home and consider taking your children away. You don't know what a shared world will feel like. Everything will be different. Including your own emotions and biases and judgments."

Pascal was so determined to convince us that he seemed to vibrate with belief in his own rhetoric, practically trembled under his own powers, self-seduced.

These people were always repeating a maxim about the end of the world, that it was "easier to imagine the end of the world than it was to imagine the end of capitalism."

The point of this maxim was that bringing down capitalism would require a more robust imagination. But just because something is harder to imagine does not mean it's correct.

In terms of which of these two will end first, capitalism might be more insidious and durable than the blue-green miracle of planet earth and its swaddling of life-giving ether.

Bruno had declared in his letters that capitalism wasn't coming to an end. The only option was to leave the world. An abstruse idea, as he didn't mean leave the blue-green earth. He meant leave our world on it, cast off an entire manner of inhabiting reality.

At first this idea struck me as lonely and hopeless. But maybe it is only by admitting that some harmful condition is permanent, that you begin to locate a way to escape it.

BRUNO WAS "LACOMBE" TO THEM, and not a man you'd ever sit down with or see. Their other mentor, Jean Violaine, I met my second week at Le Moulin.

Jean hugged everyone upon greetings, even me, a stranger to him, and as he did, I smelled the volatile fumes of liquor wafting from him. He was in his seventies and alarmingly thin, his arms roped in veins. More veins crept up over his temples and head, as if there were no spare flesh to mask the essential wiring that kept this man alive. He wore a ratty sleeveless T-shirt. His trousers were belted way up high.

In one of the letters, Bruno had written about Allen's rule, which postulates that people and animals from colder climates will have shorter limbs than their equivalents from warmer climates (accounting for the sturdy legs of the Thal, and the breadstick limbs of *H. sapiens*, who began to flourish as temperatures thawed).

My rule is that the older the Frenchman, and the more rural his location, the higher his pants will be belted. Jean Violaine's were up at his sternum. This style is typically complimented with five-euro supermarket espadrilles. Jean's disintegrating pair, their soles as thin as matchbook covers, looked to have been walked in all the way from Boulière.

In fact, Jean had just come from Boulière, where he had attended a meeting of the Federation of Milk Producers of greater Guyenne. We were at the table in the library, listening to him talk.

"Morale is low," he said. "The wholesale price for milk is less than what it costs to produce. Dairy farmers are desperate. Up in the Dordogne, a breeder just committed suicide. In Normandy, it's happening regularly."

He had gone to this meeting to discuss with the dairy farmers the movement against megabasins in the Guyenne. Some union members said they were ready to give up farming and sell their land to one of the big companies coming in to grow seed corn. Let them do what they want, these farmers had argued. It was time to give up on the old ways. Others shouted them down. A vote was taken. By just a hair, the union members took an official group position: they were against the megabasins.

This was treated as a victory by those in the library, but after Jean left that afternoon, an argument began. Alexandre and Jérôme objected to some of the politics of the people Jean aligned himself with.

"He drinks with these guys who are yelling about Arabs and foreign workers," Alexandre said.

I kept my face blank, to suppress my amusement. Refined and Parisian Alexandre had never been forced to associate with the sort of lower-class white people who might feel threatened, if misguidedly, by immigrants and nonwhites.

This was more or less what Pascal said to him.

"Perhaps that's true," Alexandre conceded. "But when you sit down with some of these people to find out what they want, it's 'We want more supermarkets. We want cheap gasoline. We want Catholic neighbors.' And when they say Catholic they mean French, and by French they mean white."

(Everyone at Le Moulin was white, or at least they looked white to me, but they were white people with the burnish of good language, who knew not to be coarse and racist.)

"They want to use pesticides," Jérôme chimed in. "They want to be able to shoot wolves with impunity. They don't want environmental regulations."

"When you put it like that, it's all rather dubious, isn't it," Pascal said to them, shaking his head in mock disapproval. "Crude and ignorant people who want to dump poison in the earth! But that's not what a farmer wants. That's not what he wants at all, and I would expect you, Jérôme, and you, Alexandre, to be more sensitive in your perceptions."

Pascal was shifting into high oratory. A farmer wants to be able to tend his land, he said, just as his father and grandfather and his great-grandfather had done before him. He wants to impart what he's learned to his own children, so that they can inherit the land and preserve it, instead of abandon that world and move away. But suddenly, some pencil-neck in Brussels, a bureaucrat in a high-rise building in a foreign country, a person who has not even been elected, a nameless appointee who has no relationship to this land or these people, is telling the farmers that how they do things is *wrong*, that it must stop, and, according to this nameless policymaker who is not a farmer, they must start doing things a *different* way.

And it just so happens, Pascal said, that the huge corporate operations have the scale and the capital to *easily* make the changes that the man in Brussels is demanding, while the small farmers will no longer be able to survive, and so they will have to give up farming, give up everything they are.

"We are talking about environmental policies that only faceless agro-business can implement. Does that seem right or fair to you?"

I WAS SPENDING LONG HOURS in the library, listening to these debates (Pascal always won), and working on translations, which also involved debates—over what to do with certain words, "puissance," say, or "événementielle." The first, in their usage, would be more or less "potentiality" but not quite, and the second, almost impossible to transpose, something like "eventness," having to do with an event in the sense of a political or social rupture.

Sometimes we dedicated whole afternoons to a single paragraph. In addition to that work, I was focused on studying the Moulinards, in order to learn what they might be doing in secret.

I made visits to the Tayssac megabasin project, in search of clues that someone from Le Moulin might be watching that site. At its entrance was a gendarmerie trailer and a few police vehicles.

Once, as I drove the perimeter, I recognized Lemon Incest, his convertible Chrysler Sebring parked on the side of the road. He stood speaking to a couple of police officers who seemed to regard him as a curiosity. I chalked up this scene to a local eccentric who flirts with proletarians, as he had flirted with the men painting the crosswalk in Vantôme.

The heavy security presence at the megabasin, the gendarmerie trailer, the officers standing around, suggested to me that sabotage of this site was past-tense. It had already taken place. I didn't know what the Moulinards were planning next, but it wasn't here. There were too many cops.

———

I was putting in long days and had no time for "unwaged" domestic chores in my off hours. And since the Dubois house was not my own, and I would be leaving it soon enough, never to return, I let it devolve into a mess, with no regrets and no need for robots to come in and clean things up.

I used up all the drinking vessels that had clotted the shelves of the dining room's various bureaus and sideboards—these Dubois people were hoarders of glasses and cups of different styles and sizes, for various uses and occasions.

The water in the kitchen sink never got hot and I could not find dish soap, and so I drank from the less dirty cups when I made my morning coffee on the crusted hot plate. My process for selecting an unwashed cup to reuse became a kind of beauty contest that I judged. Like that New York real estate buffoon and his Miss Universe pageant, I stood before the dishes crowding the sink, assessing. Most of the cups had a tar of old coffee hardening in their base like bunker oil. Who will be the winner, I'd wonder, as I looked for a less-dirty cup.

I had changed bedrooms upon realizing I could see farther and in more directions from the corner bedroom I'd originally rejected on account of its defacement by children's stickers.

Now I was ensconced in the Les Babies room, the Salon des Babies, whose images were the last thing I saw before drifting off, and the first upon waking.

Some women sleep in rooms of wallpapered toile vignettes, little repeated pastoral scenes that might come to upholster their dreams and moods. Me, I lived with the babies. Every night, and every morning, it was cartoon babies in oversized sunglasses, with oversized feet, like puppies.

The baby stickers had grown on me. The babies were cute and cheeky, as if knowingly playing the role of babies. They held the hands of even smaller babies. Their conceit was a mimicry of adult life. Les Babies drove trucks. Piloted airplanes. Declared love to one another with bouquets of roses. Les Babies delivered mail, flashed police badges, wore stethoscopes.

The theme of the stickers was an adult world that had been invaded, taken over, by babies, babies who had renounced babyhood and instead pantomimed grown-up life, but playfully, and mockingly.

I took a picture of the baby boy declaring love to the baby girl with his bouquet and texted it to Lucien.

—What is that from, he asked, after hearting the picture.

—your house.

—Upstairs?

I pressed thumbs-up.

Dots followed. Lucien typing.

—This is Agathe.

—putting up these stickers?

—I think she rented the place out last summer without telling me. Families with kids, just letting people have the run of the place, for her own gain. This is unacceptable. Can you take a video of the rooms?

I said I would. I didn't. A couple of times Lucien re-requested this video, but since such a video would show him that whatever Agathe had done to the place was small potatoes compared to what I had done to it, I said I had tried to send it and the file was too large. The telephone service here was spotty and so he took on faith my reasons for not sending him a video and stopped asking. (I had my satellite router and high-speed internet, but I sent texts to Lucien on the single bar of Orange.fr that was available in the area.)

I had transferred my stocks of beer to the refrigerator, and in the evening, I would fetch a cold one and manage exchanges with my contacts and with Lucien, although he was preoccupied with his film shoot and becoming less needy, less communicative. I checked Bruno's account daily, which was partly work and partly for my own personal interest.

As I lay on a couch and read Bruno's emails (I reread old ones if there wasn't a new one), I pitched my empties into a corner of the living room. My years of living lives that weren't mine had conditioned me not to concern myself with domestic spaces that were also not mine. I took care of my own things—nightly, I hand-washed my T-shirts and underwear and socks, and hung them in the bathroom connected to the Salon des Babies—but I never took care of other people's things and didn't see why I should. When the recycling accumulated a fermenty stink, I rolled closed the pocket doors of that room and switched to the other living room. (There were two, and they were equally cluttered but usable.)

Robert the Sick was resting in his coma, but I remained vigilant for unwanted visitors. I pushed desks and tables against the back door and a side door, so that I could manage security in case someone attempted a breach. These pieces of heavy old furniture left deep grooves from being dragged, as if cave bears had sharpened their claws on the floorboards, had *added their signature*, as Bruno would put it.

Bruno had discovered an artwork, possibly Neanderthal, on a wall of a cave linked to his own though distant, closer to the lake, under someone else's property, someone unaware of this cave. If the art was Neanderthal, it was rare for its depictive qualities. It was an image on the rock wall of a cave bear's face and head. This artwork was atypically figural for the Thal, and yet playful, practically avant-garde.

Much of the Thal's art, Bruno noted, was patterning. Geometric designs on bone and rock, in ocher red and a black dye whose exact ingredients were still unknown but were charcoal mixed with some kind of animal fat.

Bruno said that what charmed him about this image of a bear's head, which he inspected regularly by firelight, was that it was a *collage*, of "mixed media." There was a natural convex eruption to this portion of rock surface, which resembled a bear's muzzle. There was a natural concave dip or dimple in the wall, he said, which resembled a bear's eye. These elements came together, he said, by the addition of a sweeping line, in that mysterious black dye, delineating the bear's brow and the line of his snout.

Over this likeness of a cave bear's face were deep grooved scratches, he said, which by their size and depth had to be the work of an actual cave bear, adding a "signature," or attempting to scratch out this likeness of a bear such as itself. Or, the most probable scenario, these lines were from an animal behaving like an animal, by sharpening its claws with no regard for art. Scratching, as a cave bear is wont to do, and in doing so, leaving its mark.

The effect of the scratches over the surface of this image, Bruno said, was not unlike the effect of craquelure glaze on the surface of a Rembrandt painting: it allowed us to see time, to apprehend the massive interim from a then to a now.

This image on the wall of his cave had three authors, Bruno told them: bear (scratches), man (charcoal), and wall (bulges and dips). It was a work of art that must be read, he said, as a collaboration.

The mind's eye has its way, and what I pictured, while reading Bruno's description of bear claw marks, was a white paper bag, the kind bakeries use, its paper dampened by translucent grease spots, the bag weighted with something butter-dense and fragrant, sugary, golden and drizzled in glaze, flaked with thin slices of almond, a paraffin sheet enfolding it, for lifting it from the bag without stickying the fingers: a bear claw.

I miss bear claws. I miss donut shop coffee. I miss California, where I once lived and would like to live again. But I would happily live in Texas. I would live in Virginia.

I miss being at home in a culture. Using English with other native speakers is what I might miss most. For nuance and verve, English wins. We took a Germanic language and enfolded it with Norman French and a bunch of Latin and ever since we keep building out. Our words, our expanse of idioms, are expressive and creative and precise, like our music and our subcultures and our street style, our passion for violence, stupidity, and freedom.

The French might have better novels (Balzac, Zola, and Flaubert) and they have better cheeses (Comté, Roquefort, Cabécou). But in the grand scheme that's basically nothing.

BETTER NOVELS AND BETTER CHEESE, and more annoying men, or so I had decided, until I revised this assessment, happy to have been wrong.

I was leaving Le Moulin one evening when René, the woodshop manager, approached me as I walked toward my car.

"Mademoiselle," he said in his low voice, emitting little puffs of cigarette smoke as he spoke, "pardonnez-moi, mademoiselle."

Where had they gotten this guy?

"*Mademoiselle?*" I said back, in light mockery. "I'm not your schoolteacher. It's Sadie."

His beautiful eyes narrowed. "Yes," he said. "Not a schoolteacher. No. A girl with things to learn."

"Is that right."

"Yes."

We locked eyes. When it was clear that neither of us was going to look away first, something shifted in his features. He dropped the cigarette. Stepped on it, smiled, and said I should get in my car and go to the lake. That I should park at the lake.

I was amused by this forward behavior, his stern manner, which added to his considerable sex appeal. I'd sized him up right away, that first moment in the woodshop. Perhaps by ignoring me he'd sized me up too.

He was, according to Nadia, different from the others. Could he be turned against Pascal? I weighed risks. Pascal had gone to Paris for a few days, supposedly to see his children. Le Moulin was having a "work party" tonight, to shell beans. It was a Monday, and there was a town festival in Sazerac on summer Monday evenings that the locals all went to. The lake of Vantôme would be deserted.

Dusk was coming on when I got to the parking lot. There was one old guy, fishing with a rod as long as a felled utility pole. The fisherman's little Citroën, an old-fashioned Deux Chevaux, was the only car in the lot. I got out of the Škoda and sat on a park bench.

I was there a long time, watching this old man watch the lake. Periodically, orange-bellied fish flipped up out of the water, and then slapped back down, as if the lake were speaking in a language of splashes and ripples. Two cars passed on the D79. Dusk deepened, turning the water surface silver. The fisherman sat in his lawn chair sipping from a thermos, his pole out over the silver lid of the lake. The fish kept jumping to eat insects. The man was still, with no tug on his line.

How much of fishing was fishing and how much was something else, a way to empty the mind, to stop time.

I heard the rough idle of an old truck, recognized the utility vehicle shared by the commune. René was behind the wheel.

He parked, walked over, sat down next to me on the bench.

We watched the old man.

"It's for carp," René said of the very long fishing pole. "They catch fish this big." He held his hands out.

"Do you fish?" I asked.

"Black bass." He said this in English.

René, I was aware, didn't speak a word of English, and something about the way he said "black bass" made me laugh.

"Why do you laugh?" he asked.

"No reason," I said.

He reached over and put his hand on my shoulder, and then he brushed my hair back and stroked my exposed neck with his fingers. He was staring at me as he moved his hand to the back of my head and neck and pushed a little. And like that, he guided me down toward his lap.

Wow, I thought. This is how it goes? I just service him, right here on this bench?

That was what I did, while keeping an eye on the old fisherman, who never once looked back, as if his job were to face the lake no matter what. As if he would turn to salt if he looked away from the water, if he glanced back to where I was giving René an unhurried blow job on a bench in the grassy field behind him.

René made no sound, not even a sigh. His hand stayed on the back of my head, not rough or forceful, just lightly placed there, as I used my mouth and my hand, surplus spit. I liked his body, his directness. I liked his silence. He wasn't going to lose himself. He stayed in character, his breathing even and controlled, a slight increase in weight from his hand on the back of my neck when he came, filling my mouth.

———

We watched as the old man packed up his gear. That pole was telescopic. He compacted it and rolled his cooler and chair to his little car. He loaded his gear and drove off, the dim halogen bulbs of his Deux Chevaux barely illuminating the road.

"The old guys around here all want to go to America to fish," René said. "They want to go to Oklahoma."

"What's in Oklahoma?"

"Catfish you catch with your hand. They trap the fish like this," he said. He made a fist and held it up. "They put their hand in a hole and wait, and these enormous catfish think your hand is food. They lock on, and you let them, grab their gills from inside and pull them out of the water. I saw a video. I would not have believed it."

He moved that fist down and rubbed it over my jeans. We kissed. He tasted like someone who lived on cigarettes and beer.

He unzipped my jeans, and I shifted my weight so he could pull them down. He put me on his lap, facing forward, my back against his chest. He reached around, his hand between my legs.

With that fisherman gone, and just us here, it was my job, now, to face the lake, to watch the lake, which had lost its reflective power in the oncoming dark. I did not turn around to get a look at René, not because I would turn to salt but because I didn't need to see him, I could feel his fingers, and he was doing his job, doing it well, surprisingly skilled for someone so gruff, and since I had no stoic's role to maintain, I was plenty audible.

I HAD BECOME USEFUL TO NADIA, by bringing provisions up to the abandoned château, a miserable place where she was more or less camping, she and her pig, while they prepared for truffle-hunting season. We had a rapport (me and Nadia that is; I stayed away from the pig). I was hopeful I might cultivate her for something.

The gate of the Château de Gaume had no lock, just as Nadia had indicated, but the road leading up to it was not maintained. While I didn't care about the Škoda, rented under an assumed name, I didn't like the feeling of branches flopping against its windshield and pressing along the sides of the car. Thwacking the exterior, as if to say, You're not wanted here.

At the top of that rough road was a flat promenade, bounded on one side by the castle, a mean-looking fortress with four tall towers ending in spires sharp as meat skewers. The towers were of thick gray stone, their proportions ugly and crude. The castle looked like a military armament, not any kind of home, even for a feudal lord. Its windows were all broken, curtained by spiderwebs, the interior bare and open to the elements through its rotten roof.

In one of his letters, Bruno had said that before their retreat in 1944, the Germans had attempted to burn the castle down, but the cold damp stones of the Château de Gaume had refused to catch fire.

Opposite the castle was a little chapel, in similar disrepair, with old vines like tangles of barbed wire smothering its facade. A reflecting pool occupied the center of the promontory, with spouts at either end. The spouts were the tiny penises of marble cherubs, facing each other as if they were meant to piss in an eternal loop. The cherubs were headless. The reflecting pool was dry.

Nadia was camped in a maintenance shed next to the greenhouse, where she had a makeshift pen for Bernadette. I brought her subsistence provisions: rice, cooking oil, canned tuna—dry goods, as I knew that she got produce and eggs at the open-air markets, whatever she could beg off the sellers as they packed up.

She had a propane camp stove and a laundry line. There was a spigot, but no working plumbing. She seemed comfortable living in the sub-squalor of this creepy old château. She was a Zadiste, as she reminded me, a hard-core movement veteran, though she never said why she had left the ZAD. I imagined that her strong personality had been, as they say of such personalities, divisive.

One afternoon, as I dropped off two bags of groceries I'd purchased for her in Boulière, and she sorted through the bags bossily, as if I were her shopping assistant, she said, "There's talk about you among them."

Had my tryst with René been discovered? I quickly worked through the complications it might cause. He had a family who lived with him on the commune.

"Florence says you curry favor with Pascal's inner circle and ignore everyone else. You need to be careful," she said with a superior air. "Get acquainted with the people who do the actual work there."

They didn't know about René. I covered my relief with an expression of worry, and Nadia began advising me on how not to get purged, never mind that she herself had failed to avoid such a fate.

I left the abandoned château with a mental short list of the people Nadia named, whom I should get to know.

BRUNO SAID THAT AS SCIENTISTS were becoming more sophisticated at mapping ancient DNA, they were locating genomic traces of undiscovered people who had left their mark. These mysterious ancestors were called "ghost populations."

We've found their genes in our genes, Bruno said, but we don't yet know who these people were. We have not found traces of them in dig sites, neither their own bones nor the bones of what they ate.

What this means, Bruno said, is that we haven't found their trash, and we will not name them and define them, they will stay "ghost," until we do stumble upon their trash. But their trash might never be found.

Don't underestimate the power of time to erase, he said. Much of life, and what matters most to a culture, consists of what a visual artist would deem "fragile materials": Wood, say, and wax. Feathers, flowers, fish bones. Plants and unstable pigments. Ice. Emotions, and their transmission from one person to another. Blood, tears, tenderness, joy. Very little of what comprises culture can be found at a dig site. Stone can be found. And this, Bruno said, is the level of logic we are dealing with: the stones are all that is left, and so let's call them *stone* age!

I don't fault you—it's not a character flaw that you've used this parlance in your email to me. (The Moulinards had sent him a question about "stone age technologies" as predictive, or not, of later and more destructive technologies.)

Rocks endure, Bruno said, and they give us this mistaken idea that human lives revolved around them, when it is merely that rocks are what is left. Which proves the tautology that durable things are durable, and not that ancient people were rock-centric, rock-focused, into rocks.

Let's say a modern seafront village gets washed away by a tsunami, Bruno said, leaving crumbling concrete and twisted rebar as the only traces of the people who had been living there. The anthropologists come along, and they examine the remains of this tsunami-destroyed community and conclude that there had once flourished, in this washed-away place, a culture whose religious idols were concrete and rebar.

No culture can be understood, nor should be defined, by what doesn't wash away. The durable traces, the rock or rebar, are real, but they are time-disfigured nubs, as strange and unrecognizable to the people who left them behind as they seem to us. We must learn to leave room for the rest, for the vast and vanished world of which durable traces form only a tiny part.

The old story about Thal, Bruno said, was that he hunted only slower terrestrial prey that was easy to catch. It was believed that the fastest-moving non-terrestrial creatures—birds and fish—were far beyond Thal's grasp.

But over the last two decades, Bruno said, there has been new evidence that Neanderthals regularly caught corvids, pigeons, and choughs. Scientists conducted an experiment in Croatia to reproduce the Neanderthal conditions for night-hunting of choughs and found there was no "hunting" involved: the birds settle down for the evening in the nooks of a cave. The scientists went into the cave with headlamps and began picking up sleeping choughs and placing them in a basket. In their findings they reported that picking up these birds, one by one, was like picking apples from the low branches of an apple tree.

Bruno said that Italian scientists had just published a paper establishing that a cache of wing bones from corvids had been worked by Thals to remove their feathers. Ornithologists and behavior scientists at a cave in Gibraltar made a similar finding, that the wings of golden eagles, which offer little to no meat, had knife marks that were the result of feather removal, suggesting a decorative or perhaps religious use of such feathers. Thals, catching golden eagles! A creature with an eight-foot wingspan, whose talons and beaks are blades designed to shred and slice. An eagle was no apple you put in a basket. The scientists in Gibraltar speculated that Neanderthals made a blind in which to hide and wait, and set a trap of carrion, having learned the eagles' seasonal and hunting patterns. Their theories challenged multiple stereotypes at once: that Thals did not hunt birds, that Thals did not have a sophisticated sense of seasons, and thus of time, and that Thals' cognition was too basic for beliefs and rituals.

It had long been assumed that Thals did not fish, Bruno said, simply because there were no fish bones at dig sites. The reason fish bones were not found at dig sites was simply that fish bones do not last; they are rare to archeological sites.

This is faulty reasoning, but we needed them not to have fished, Bruno said, because fishing requires skill and cunning and people had already decided Thals lacked both. Until an inconvenient fact emerged: fish grease was found on cutting tools at a dig site in the Rhône valley, Bruno said, and the tools were too old to belong to *sapiens*. With more sophisticated sieving, archeologists could now better detect fish residue. The possibility that Neanderthals ate fish was becoming harder to suppress. But some still trotted out questions about method, such as, If we aren't finding lures and hooks and harpoons, how do we know these Neanderthals were catching fish? Might they have stumbled upon a salmon run so dense that fish sprang up onto a riverbank and were eaten?

This is an actual postulation in a paper I've read, Bruno said. Trained thinkers, asking if fish *all but flopped into the mouths of Neanderthals*, because such a miracle is more comfortable for academics to conjure than the idea that Thal had skills, and that he fished.

Here is where my own work, if I may call it work, Bruno said, becomes instructive. Just as anthropologists were mystified by the behavior of smoke in a cave, while I was never mystified by the behavior of smoke in a cave, since I live in a cave, and keep an active hearth, those who believe that Neanderthals could not have caught fish without specialized tools have never learned to fish without such tools. If you have not learned to handfish, it is difficult to grasp a scenario in which human hands become lure and hook and also net.

———

Bruno had started to fish with his bare hands long before he had taken up contemplation of early people, long before he'd retreated to life in a cave.

During the war, when he had lived with the old woman in the country, he'd watched a small furry animal, a pine marten, patiently holding its snout in the water of a stream, in between two rocks. It did not seem to be drinking. A young perch moved downstream and settled in between the rocks near the animal's snout. The pine marten held still. The perch was also still, sidled up against the face of the pine marten, as water purled around this odd pair. What is going on here, Bruno had wondered, and then this brown furry pine martin lifted its head in a kind of slow motion, and bit down, also in a kind of slow motion. The fish flapped; the animal held on.

After observing this strange occurrence once more, Bruno surmised that the animal was using touch, perhaps its whiskers, or its nose, to tickle the fish. The fish, he guessed, was responding to this sensation by going still, as if paralyzed, rendering itself catchable, killable, eatable.

Bruno tried putting his hand in the creek, in between two rocks, just as he'd seen the pine marten do with its snout. He waited. This was in spring, and the water was frigid. His hand ached, but he vowed to use patience the way this little creature had. Two long afternoons, nothing happened except he lost feeling in his hand. But he kept at it. Eventually a fish rested at the juncture between submerged rocks. He felt its side, the texture of its scales, making contact with the tips of his fingers. His heart began to pound, and the pounding of his heart warmed his blood and gave him the resolve to stay still. The fish very slowly adjusted itself so that its side was brushing against Bruno's hand. All at once he closed his hand and dug his fingernails into its gills.

He lost that fish.

What he came to understand, as he tried again and again to fish by hand, was that the final movement, the kill, could not be sudden. There must be no swift movements. He learned to close his hand slowly but forcefully, to extinguish the life of the fish.

Bruno spent the last year of the war neck-deep in the waterways of the southern Corrèze, his face tilted up to breathe, the waterline at his chin and his ears, his hands low, down in the depths. He would remain in this demanding position for hours, waiting for a bream or a perch or a brown trout, the holiest of catches.

Now that I am old, Bruno said, I no longer fish. My age and my resolve have reduced and simplified my dietary needs. I have taken already my fill from the rivers and lakes and streams. What stays with me, and perhaps informs my thinking still, is the transmission of knowledge that I learned by touch.

By touch I could tell you what kind of fish had brushed up against my hand.

By that same touch I could tell you what part of the fish's body was against my hand.

And I could tell you how large this fish was, that I was touching.

Because I learned the art of handfishing, Bruno said, I can imagine a number of ways the Thals might have caught their own fish. A number of ways by which their "technology" was artful and ingenious, but humble.

I don't have proof. I don't need proof.

What do scientists do? They look for proof. In its absence, they set up models. An experiment, such as the one they designed to figure out how Thals might have hunted choughs.

I do not set up models. What I do is live. And because of the way I have lived, I know what is possible.

HOT WEATHER STRETCHED over a series of days and sent the Moulinards off to swim in the river each afternoon, in a large group that included people I otherwise didn't interact with, the dour girls with babies, and the men who operated tractors and worked the fields.

I joined on one of these swim outings, hoping to form connections with others in the group. I was planning to target particular individuals Nadia had spoken of, such as Aurélie, one of the main people apparently opposed to me. Aurélie ran the group's stall at the local open-air markets, selling what they grew and canned. She wore overalls and work boots and shoved her hands in her front pockets in a style that was emphatically tough, but her hair, brown and shiny and falling to her waist, softened her tomboy pose.

People walked down the road toward the river in little groups. Few of them brought a towel. The men wore cutoffs. The women were in faded old bathing suits of snagged nylon and loose elastic.

Their swimming hole was the same location where Pascal and I had watched the boy who jumped from the top of the tree, the one who had impregnated his teacher.

Along one bank of the river was a limestone shelf about twenty feet up. The water underneath was deep, but opaque from mud. The shelf bulged as it neared the water. Moulinards—young men and women both, and older children—began climbing up to access the limestone shelf. They stood along it and jumped one by one, launching themselves from the ledge with gusto, in order to clear the rock and make it safely into the water below.

René went first. After him, the man and woman who ran the kitchen, and Jérôme, followed by Alexandre. Even Pascal jumped, in his camp shorts, a bit of a belly hanging over them, from his priestly work, which was sedentary. The only ones who didn't jump were the women with small children. Alexandre and Jérôme both had partners in that set, young women who sat in the grass and let the kids cover themselves in river muck. René's woman was among them. She was the mother I'd seen in the crèche with a toddler in her lap and another at her knee, crying, with food on its face. Those two children were René's, and as he emerged after jumping, they splashed toward him, naked and screaming with delight, and clamped onto him like mollusks he'd collected from the depths.

"California, you're next!"

It was Aurélie. "All Americans must jump!" she shouted. She was on a rock, squeezing water from her long hair.

I was standing on the riverbank. Burdmoore, my fellow American, was in the water on his back, his beer gut skyward like a flotation device.

I decided it would be best if I went along with Aurélie's taunt and climbed up there and jumped. Even as the idea of pushing off and plummeting into that water was not at all tempting.

I took off my shoes, planning to swim in my shorts. I had acquired a deep tan by then, and without tan lines, because I sunbathed nude on a chaise lounge in front of the Dubois house. I enjoyed the way the sun emptied my thoughts and flattened my feelings to a lizard-like drip of the minutes as they passed. I had come to suspect that the woman in Marseille, the tannest of the tanners at the private swim club, who tanned even during a windstorm, had been onto something. Submitting to the sun and letting it cook my thoughts was soothing.

Here at the swim hole, I decided to leave on my shirt as well as my shorts. My breasts and flat stomach and narrow waist, these attributes were not right for this milieu. Some of the girls were pretty, they had cute bodies, it wasn't all cellulite and faded tattoos, far from it, but my figure might be cause for disapproval—among the women, that is, while their partners, to avoid trouble, would claim not to have noticed my big firm breasts, as natural as my name. I had once overheard Jérôme vouching for me. "She's really nice," he'd said, to his girlfriend's annoyance. This is how it works. If you please the men, you will not please the women.

But if you please the women, you will not necessarily displease the men, and so I made my way up the muddy riverbank in my T-shirt and baggy shorts, followed by Burdmoore, who was primed to show Aurélie what he was made of too.

I stepped over knobbed tree roots, the roughness of which forced me into the same tender-footed postures and slow pace as everyone else as they had climbed up barefoot to reach the limestone shelf. Behind me, Burdmoore breathed heavily and slipped twice in the mud.

What I don't like about jumping from heights into water, including from diving boards—even low ones into clear water whose depth is known—is that once you've initiated your jump, you cannot change your mind. You can't turn back. I don't like irreversible decisions. I don't see the point. I always want the option of doubling back, reversing course, changing plan.

From up on the ledge, the water was a long way down.

"Go ahead, California!" Aurélie hollered.

I sensed that if I opted out, edged along the rock shelf and climbed all the way back down, instead of jumping as everyone else had, I would prove I was worthy of her dislike.

Just do it, I told myself. You're being tested. Like those kids who have to put on a bulletproof vest and be shot at point-blank range by the Camorra in order to join the Camorra. All I had to do was drop twenty feet into cold, muddy water.

I closed my eyes and leaped, hoping to clear the rock.

Because I had not wanted to jump, was stressed about jumping—I imagined hitting the rocks, not clearing the cliff—when I broke the surface, my body was stiff, my muscles tense. Water shot up into my brain as I was forced down into the river's depths. My foot grazed a slimy log on the bottom.

I struggled to climb out of the water, my feet sinking into its thick mud, which made the squelching sound of overlubricated sex with each step I took up the riverbank.

I chose a spot in the sun, on a rock near Aurélie, who was still pressing water from her several linear feet of hair.

She put her thumb up and grinned. Her grin had a sarcastic edge to it.

"Feels good, doesn't it?" she said.

"Yes," I lied. Water sloshed inside my ears. My neck hurt like I'd sprained it.

"You didn't want to jump."

"I jumped," I said, and smiled blandly, pulling at my T-shirt to de-paste it from my breasts.

"You were nervous. Your emotions come off you. They go like this," and she made a wave gesture with her hand. "You think you hide from us, but we see you."

I pretended not to understand her.

With some of them I could turn down the proficiency of my French like I was adjusting the heat on a stove, putting my language skills on medium heat instead of high, medium-low, and when I needed to, a simmer of incomprehension.

"I know you understand me," she said.

"Ah, yes," I said neutrally, as if too dumb to understand what it was I didn't understand.

I pointed up and said a-grammatically that Burdmoore was going to jump, slopping up my French.

He was on the ledge. There were jeers from below.

"I will now show you pussies how this is done," he shouted to them in English.

He turned and climbed up a series of footholds in the rock. He went up and up, and then disappeared from view. He reemerged at a much higher ledge, so far above the river it was hard to imagine it could be possible to make this jump. He was at least fifty feet above the water, higher than the entire tree from which that brazen boy had dropped, as Pascal told me about the scandal of his teacher and their affair.

Burdmoore was standing on a precipice, a tiny and treacherous outcropping of rock.

"I can't believe he's going to jump from there," I said. "I almost could not jump from the very lowest ledge. You were right." I was trying a new tactic to win over Aurélie, self-debasement instead of bravery. "I was afraid."

"I know," she said. "You should have seen your face." She was laughing.

I laughed too, not liking whatever she was referring to.

"There was this accident a few years ago in the Alps," she said, still laughing, "where a tram full of skiers plunged to the ground. It was because of an American military jet. You people wreck everything. The jet sliced the tram's cable, and the newspaper said the faces of the dead were found 'contorted in terror.' It's awful, but," ha ha ha ha, "I thought of that description, watching you. You were like this." She scrunched her face up tight.

Ha ha ha ha.

We both looked up. Burdmoore raised his arms above his head like he was going to dive, or maybe conduct an orchestra.

He sprang off the ledge with terrific force, his arms outspread. He sailed toward the water in that position, like a Christ on his cross, flying in a great arc. At the last moment, before hitting the water, he brought his hands together overhead, palm to palm, hurled his body downward, and cut into the surface, a perfect dive.

He emerged from the water, rivulets streaming off his belly, which now looked like his power source, a tank or reservoir where he kept his phenomenal courage.

"That was unbelievable," I said to Aurélie.

She shrugged.

"He does that every single time we come here. We're all a bit bored by it."

MY NEW FRIENDSHIP with Aurélie was delicate. It felt provisional.

If the women in these groups get mad, they might start comparing notes. That was what happened with Narc Cutler, who had not understood a basic rule, that if you want to evade suspicion, indiscriminately having sex with the people you're infiltrating is a bad idea.

I stayed discriminate and had sex only with René.

I had not been certain it was wise to let things continue after that first episode at the lake. In fact, it was reckless. But I got used to our secret meetings. I began to rely on them. Perhaps not unlike how I had come to rely on Bruno's letters. All the little habits one develops on a job, habits that are temporary and yet answer to something real, because even as I maintained a fraudulent persona, within that persona I found methods to meet real needs.

René came to the Dubois house. That was our arrangement, and so I had to put away and conceal all my surveillance equipment and computers and phones, my files and notebooks and research materials, high-powered binoculars, cameras, recording equipment, the weapons I kept on hand—a Glock 43X with a custom fifteen-round magazine, a Sig Sauer 365, a .22 North American Arms minirevolver, and a fixed blade everyday carry. I also had a Walther P38—classic and easy to use—that I could hand off to some self-sacrificing recruit, if escalation was called for.

In these sweeps of my headquarters prior to René's visits, I ended up washing about a hundred cups, if not carefully, to get them out of sight, and I cleared out all the empty beer cans and spent wine bottles in the living room as well, as if the dishes and my empties were further evidence I wasn't who I claimed to be.

René arrived in the later evening, usually around ten, in the battered truck that belonged to the commune.

He would park on the road in the woods beyond the house and knock twice. I would let him in and lock the door behind him with its heavy crossbar, and within minutes we'd be into something. We often did it right there in the front hall, him standing, my legs around his back. Only some men are strong enough and skilled enough to manage that. René was one of them.

In his exertions, a powerful smell was released from his armpits, which I found pleasant. (I never once thought of Lucien while I was with René, but the sweet scent of Lucien's pits, in contrast, had all but made me gag.) René's smell, which issued forth in a kind of wave, was redolent to me of hydroponic weed, and of a bust I'd helped coordinate at a massive grow facility in Idaho. That this scent of René's, so strongly like the concentrated smell of industrially farmed marijuana, was natural, animal and innocent, somehow touched me.

He would stare at me, his gaze focused and direct. This never felt intrusive, on account that it wasn't quite real. He had stared at hundreds of women, I understood, with those light-filled eyes. René knew his own beauty, used it as a tool, would have stared at whoever he was making love to in order to stir up a sense of urgency. His gaze wasn't about love. It was about him and what he was after. It had nothing to do with me.

After, I'd bring him a beer from the refrigerator.

He would sip his beer and light a cigarette and begin to talk. He had a low voice. It rumbled along, and if he had me in the crook of his arm as we lay on the sofa, my head against his bare chest, I felt the vibrations of his stories as much as I heard them. He did not ask me anything. I didn't talk much. I never drank in front of him, and he seemed not to notice that I brought cold beers only to him, and never one for me. He was like someone living in the year 1950. Pleasure was for men. Beer was for men. Talking, also for men. This was fine and kept things simple.

René was from a Hicksville town in Alsace. Before Le Moulin, he'd been living across the border in Germany, he told me in one of his spells of postcoital talking. He had worked the assembly line at a Daimler plant outside Stuttgart. He didn't speak German (as it was, he seemed barely literate in his native tongue). He said it didn't matter that he didn't speak German because few on the assembly line at Daimler did. None of them were German. The workers were mostly Greek and Turkish. René's job was to stamp metal panels that would become car doors. The panels came down a very long track, he said. At his station, a tall stamping machine swung down and pressed the metal piece, and he stood there and oversaw the process. During his shift, at some point, the assembly line would suddenly cease moving. This happened regularly. The factory floor went quiet, the machines halted, production seized. Then you heard the ambulance.

Somewhere on the line, he said, someone had lost fingers, or a hand. But in order to activate the compression for stamping, he said, you had to have both of your hands on the outside of the machine. There was no way to accidentally bring the stamper down on your own hand or arm. To get one hand into the stamper, and bring the stamper down with your other hand, this required skill, he said. These accidents, which happened every few days, could only have been planned and deliberate. People started drinking schnapps at five a.m., he said, when their shift began. They drank schnapps all day long. By the time a worker decided to pull down the stamper with a single hand, having fitted his other arm into the machine, the magic moment when this worker was ready to sacrifice a functioning limb, he was good and drunk, René said, numbed up, and he would not feel much when the stamper swung down with great and smooth and unstoppable force, to crush his hand.

Why would someone do that? I asked.

"To buy an E-Class Mercedes," René said, as if this were obvious. He sipped his beer. "With the compensation they give you, you can buy a nice car. Plus, you get a pension for life. You never have to work again."

And this was what had activated him, he said. He had looked down the assembly line and thought, if sacrificing a perfectly good hand was an improvement, if that could elevate the quality of a man's life, something was wrong.

The company was always angling to chip away break time, to lengthen shifts, to trim bonuses. The union pushed back. There were strikes. René started talking to the more political guys on the line, the strident ones. The radicals. He learned a lot. The union organized a work stoppage. It lasted a couple of weeks, and then Daimler fired everyone. By that point, he didn't give a shit. He'd become a subversive.

I HAD SURREPTITIOUSLY taken photographs of lots of the Moulinards to send to my contacts, including one of René that I did not intend to send them, but had spontaneously captured because it showed off his attributes. He was on the couch, having fallen briefly asleep before going back to Le Moulin.

Vito would appreciate René, I knew.

I texted him one night, hoping to get intel on what was happening in Marseille. I'd worried that Lucien would show up in Vantôme in some misguided attempt to surprise me. I had not heard from him since the day before. I figured he was busy with the film shoot, and that Vito would say exactly that, but Vito wasn't in Marseille. He'd left.

—I'm in Rotterdam

—why

—Conference on Jung. And I have to confess that despite being here, I don't know where Rotterdam is.

—no one does. it's a global mystery. even they don't know. the rotterdamians.

—Rotterdamerung.

—the ring cycle of geographical confusion.

—Serge and I had a fight.

—what happened?

—Lucien will tell you all about it. I was asserting a cultural value to do with my nation and my ethnic heritage and that's my final word on what happened.

That night, hoping René might show, I pretended I wasn't waiting by reading more of *The Life of Céline*. I didn't have a page marked. I opened the book at random and took in details. Céline was a leg man, obsessed with chorus girls. He once attended a dawn execution. He denounced, in addition to Jews, sloth, overeating, and "low IQ-ism." He did not drink and preferred watching sex to having it.

It was a chilly night, but I had the windows wide open, on alert for the commune truck. I'd put a six-pack of beer on the floor, cans I could slide under the bed if the truck appeared.

When Hitler's troops reached Paris, Céline and his wife, Lucette, were caught in a bombardment in the town of Gien, in the Loire Valley. As incendiary bombs rained down, leveling neighborhoods, they took refuge in a movie theater and stayed safe. Céline's good luck, like when his ship had plowed into another, seemed to be holding.

The movie house was filled with patients who had been evacuated from a psychiatric hospital, nutcases who shrieked all through the night. I was thinking I would call this "mixed luck" when my phone rang. It was Lucien. He wanted to tell me all about what had happened with Vito.

"We were scheduled to shoot in the Alpilles. We're driving up there to set up. It's a national preserve and it was closed for fire danger, so it took several days and a lot of bureaucratic layers for Amélie and her assistant to get us access. We're on our way, with Vito at the wheel—why Serge let him drive, I don't know—anyhow a black cat crosses the road. Vito stops the car and refuses to continue. There are five cars and a truck behind us, all part of the crew. What's happening, everyone wonders, fire? Accident? Road blockage? No, just an Italian man behind the wheel. Vito says it's *bad luck* to keep going after a black cat has crossed your path and that we have to wait for, get this, a *white* cat to cross the road. It's baking hot and we're blocking the road. Serge and I would have had to physically pull him out of the driver's seat. We sat there, and guess what happened?"

"A white cat crossed the road?"

"The gendarmerie fined us for blocking the road and would not let us film there, despite all our permits."

When the Vichy regime fell, and no zone in France was safe for a collaborator, Céline and Lucette fled to Germany with their cat, Bébert—a tabby with a large head; there was a portrait of him in the book. They were offered refuge at Sigmaringen Castle in the Danube Valley, unlike so many others who were turned back, sure to be arrested. (More good luck.)

But they were stuck living under the same roof with Marshal Pétain and Pierre Laval, chief of state and prime minister, respectively, of Vichy's puppet government, doomed and dishonored men who now despised each other.

Céline's wife spent her days in the castle of the disgraced teaching modern dance to the wives of the Nazi administrators. (The book had a photo of her at her ballet barre, her lumpy physique reminding me of the woman who did yoga on public access TV in the 1980s of my American childhood.) Nightly, everyone gathered—even Laval and Pétain despite their animus—to listen to transmissions from Paris, in order to find out who among them, huddled by the radio at Sigmaringen, was listed next for public execution. (Céline never did hear his own name announced over that radio: very good luck.)

I put the book down and looked out the window. I heard wind, and no truck driving up the road.

Part of attraction is the unpredictable nature of everything, the manner in which you wait, and want.

Good for you, I thought at René, for reducing me to those who wait. But also, go to hell.

Having decided he was not coming, I finished the final two cans of my six-pack and went to sleep.

ON ANOTHER SWIMMING EXCURSION with the group, I was walking alongside Aurélie as she chatted with two commune members, Sophie and Paul, when they fell to whispering.

I had been around for a month at this point. My friendship with Aurélie was helping to expand my credibility, but I suspected holdouts.

At the river, Aurélie and I sat on a rock together in the sun.

"I'm sorry about that," she said. "It's a strange kind of snobbery, in my opinion. A fear of foreigners."

"It's good to be cautious," I said, being cautious myself. "They don't know me. I'm an outsider."

"You're not an outsider. It is obvious Pascal likes you and respects you. Sophie and Paul, they were just being rude. There is no reason to keep a secret. I'm sure you're aware that we object to the Tayssac reservoir, and to what is happening to the water of the Guyenne. We are planning to make our feelings known at the agricultural fair, by blocking the entrance and staging a protest."

She said the hope was that it would be big. "And that's why it's ridiculous for them to act like that. You'll know. Everyone is going to know."

I had started seeing posters for this fair.

They were on the side of the road as I drove from the house to Le Moulin. They were outside Leader Price in Boulière, where I shopped weekly for supplies. Naïs was putting one up in the bar in Vantôme when I went in, alone, for no reason but to have another look at her. I'd ordered a coffee and listened to the old men, who were talking about the fair and who was entering what animal or bringing an antique tractor, and they were each calling the other's old contraption a junk pile that would not make it down the D79.

The fair was a couple of weeks from now, in mid-September, and would take place at the local lake, mine and René's, where the fishermen sat with their carp poles, a lake that might itself be sacrificed to the megabasin.

At the river that afternoon, amid the usual scene—Moulinards jumping from the limestone shelf, toddlers covered in mud, Burdmoore making his pronouncement and his big leap—I noticed, on the opposite bank of the river, the boy with the braids and the cross around his neck, the one who had knocked up his teacher.

I immediately recognized him, even from a distance.

Pascal had never said his name, but Franck was how I had begun to think of him. Even as he wasn't the Franck from the Italian documentary. He was the Franck from this place, Franck of Vantôme.

Imagine being from Vantôme.

Imagine having thirty-one Facebook friends and a stock advertisement for Lamborghini as your banner photo.

But Franck, I mean this Franck, he looked really happy. He looked different now than when I'd seen him that first day with Pascal. He was not with his group of rowdy boys, boys among whom he was a natural leader, a central figure, performing for the others, lording over them his courage and his tan body, the cross at his neck and his long braids, the trouble he'd made for the commune.

Franck looked more innocent now, more like a child. His Franckness, a kind of confidence, was still there, and yet it wasn't mean. It was sweet. He was with family, his parents, I assumed, and his comportment with them was different than how he'd been with the other boys. French hippies was my impression of the parents, the father with long dark hair and a thick beard. They sat on a blanket with a toddler while Franck ran back and forth from the river with offerings for the toddler, pebbles, a branch, a piece of a broken toy he'd found lodged in the silty shallows. Franck held up the broken toy and the baby smiled and reached for it eagerly. Franck smiled too. He set down the toy and ran back to the water. He hollered to the baby. Did a handstand, fell over, did another handstand, to the baby's squeals of pleasure.

If you didn't know the story, you would think he was the adoring older brother, dedicated to the much younger one, the parents looking on, having had one early, a love child, say, and the other late, an accident, and look how the older one helped out. Look how he doted on his baby brother.

You would never guess from seeing them that the thirteen-year-old was the father of the two-year-old. But that's how it was.

These hippies were raising the baby. Fatherhood, for Franck, was doing goofy handstands and making the baby clap.

But seeing Franck bring the baby pebbles like this task was the most important thing in the world, like his reason for being was to delight that baby, I got a feeling like envy.

Franck was involved in something pure. He loved someone totally, not because his parents said be nice to your brother, be a good big brother, be gentle, be kind, but because the child was his. There seemed enormous mystery to this arrangement, a child blessed to have an even smaller child of his own.

"That kid is a complete asshole," Aurélie said, watching me watch Franck.

VII

LES BABIES

UPON RETURNING TO the Dubois place that night, I reported to my contacts that Pascal and the Moulinards were planning to disrupt the agricultural fair here, in two weeks.

From there, things accelerated.

In less than forty-eight hours, I was informed that Deputy Minister Platon would make a visit to this fair—unannounced, and with little security. It seemed that my contacts had moles inside the Ministry of Rural Coherence who were able to arrange this. As if Platon were a pawn they could move here and there, and not a man with his own agency and autonomy.

My job was to let the Moulinards know that Platon would be coming.

If Pascal Balmy was to attempt to harm Platon, I was told, that would be best.

He's not capable of it, I responded. He's not reckless.

But someone there is, they said.

They were sending Platon in, and they wanted a trap set for him.

On the night I got this message, it had grown quite cold, as if the end of summer—it was the first of September—were a steep drop-off, a ledge from which we had fallen.

There was wood in a box by the hearth and so I built a fire with the help of *Paris Match* pages crushed into loose balls and tucked between logs. I thought I had opened the chimney flue, but instead it seemed that I'd closed it. Smoke exited the fireplace like a devil's breath, curling over the mantel and up the wall, leaving a soot stain in its path.

I aired out the room and figured out how to operate the flue. It had an iron lever, which thunked open when slid to the right.

With no updraft, the paper I'd stuffed between logs had burned up but the wood had not caught. I needed more kindling and decided on the Céline biography, having finished it. Or having read enough I felt I was "done." I lit the pages. Céline's face on that garish cover curled and shrank as he was immolated.

My fire strong, I stood over the hearth, letting the heat baste the front of my jeans, considering this job and its risks. In certain ways it had been easier to work for federal agencies. Going private meant a rogue world where you didn't have backup. You didn't even know who you were working for.

I let the heat absorb into my legs as I thought over the question of who, among these people, could be convinced to attack subminister Platon.

The logs sizzled. An occasional air bubble in the wood combusted, making a loud crack. My jeans were starting to burn my legs, so I closed the flue. The flames went low. When I thunked the flue back open, they stretched upward.

First, for elimination, I reviewed the inner circle.

None of the library boys.

And not René, who, I had come to understand, was Pascal's most faithful warrior, a company man, a commune man to the core. (What we did together was separate, in its own silo.)

Florence: no. In love with Pascal, or why would she allow him to treat her so poorly.

I needed someone with a grudge, comfortable with the idea of a mutinous plan, one that Pascal had not sanctioned.

Pascal could be so rude, as he'd been to that couple, and to Nadia. I had initially hoped Nadia's salt could be mined, but the qualities Pascal disliked in her, her will and obduracy and depth of experience, were the same ones that made her difficult to manipulate.

Burdmoore was a possibility. The record was promising. But it wasn't clear if Pascal's treatment of him was friendly hazing, an understanding between them, or something more like abuse.

I clunked the flue open and closed as I ruminated on this, and then the flue clunked open and stayed open.

It was jammed, the lever stuck.

When I got up the next morning, wind was swirling down the chimney, blowing ashes from the cold fire into the living room. I heard thunder that sounded like metal dumpsters sent tumbling. It started to rain, and heavily. Water streamed down the inside walls of the chimney, making a porridge of the ashes in the belly of the hearth.

AURÉLIE WAS CORRECT that everyone would know. Over the next few days, Le Moulin was converted to a hubbub of excitement, people having split into committees, to coordinate and to spread the word in the greater Guyenne of a blockade of the fair, in protest of the government's plan to steal their water and give it to corporate farmers, their plan to ruin this valley.

If there was a secret cadre who would escalate the protest into a battle with police (and surely there was), those details were not shared with me.

This was fine. I would be patient. It is better to let people come to you than to go to them, and this is as true of the people you are surveilling as it might be of someone you want to seduce. Like Bruno's childhood technique of fishing, you keep your hand in the water and you wait.

My contacts informed me that Platon would be without a substantial security presence at the agricultural fair, and that the local gendarmerie would not be aware of his visit.

I had twice been to these sorts of fairs, once in the US and once in Europe.

In Nebraska I followed anti-Monsanto activists to a "Beef Days" festival that had a hay-bale-throwing contest, six-pound steaks that were free for anyone who could finish eating one, and a band that performed Lynyrd Skynyrd covers. In Switzerland, I attended an ag fair with a group that was there to protest John Deere's contracts with the Israeli government. The Swiss agricultural fair had a tractor pull sponsored by John Deere, which was also my own covert sponsor.

I had believed that Swiss people were reserved, moderate, moderately wealthy, and discreet. Mild about everything but their excessive environmental regulations. But the Swiss agricultural fair was on the level of a Las Vegas–style monster truck rally, or above that.

Men and boys in full-face helmets wheelied giant tractors as an announcer yelled over a PA in a hickish-sounding dialect of Swiss German. (This was in Schaffhausen, on the upper Rhine, John Deere's international headquarters.) Each tractor pulled a metal sled that contained weights. As the tractor pulled the sled, a winch cranked the weights on the sled forward, increasing resistance so that the tractor's motor was strained, and progress became more and more difficult. To keep pulling the weighted sled through the mud, each driver downshifted and goosed his accelerator, coal rolling the arena audience with thick and dirty smoke that flumed from the exhaust pipe on the hood of his tractor. One guy's exhaust pipe sent up thirty-foot flames, as a special trick.

These people made Nebraskan Beef Days look like an Amish prayer circle.

The activist group I was infiltrating had come to Schaffhausen in hopes of sabotaging John Deere equipment, to express their anger that Israel was using the company's machines to illegally bulldoze Palestinian lands and homes and sometimes people. They were self-serious city folk from Zurich, consumed by a situation far away from here, from this tractor pull whose contestants seemed so much happier than the activists glumly pretending to spectate.

Some of them peeled off while prizes were given and winners were announced. (The grand champions were a team of two mulleted brothers with wide-set eyes.) They planned to damage a set of gleaming yellow John Deere prototypes while the crowd was focused on the awards ceremony.

Originally, these activists had thought to put sugar in the gas tanks of the prototypes. That's an urban legend, I told them. "If you want to ruin a tractor," I'd instructed, "use bleach. Glug a gallon of it into the tank with a funnel."

They were arrested while attempting this. I myself was in the crowd, clapping for the brothers, who stood on a podium, the sun flashing from their broad foreheads, shiny with sweat.

A French politician appearing at an ag fair was a typical publicity stunt. Platon had recently made an appearance at a fair in the Camargue. The photos had telegraphed his conviction that he could connect with bull breeders, despite his artificial hair and his mantle of arrogance.

He would come to the Guyenne to shake hands with farmers, pat their prize Prim'Holsteins, pose for photos.

A heavy security apparatus at such an event was inappropriate for the building of trust with country people, whose support was needed for the ministry's plan to wreck the ancient way of farming in the greater Guyenne. This was the reason Platon would be traveling to Vantôme with only his driver (not yet confirmed to be Georges, but very likely Georges) and a single bodyguard (very likely the Serb, who irritated Platon, but so many of the other state security employees were not white, and for connecting with farmers, a North African would not do).

A friend would accompany him, I was informed.

I assumed friend meant mistress: the woman from Vincennes.

Identity of friend? I asked my contacts.

Michel Thomas, they replied.

Not the mistress. Michel Thomas was a famous French novelist, perhaps the only one who was a genuine celebrity. Even French people who never read novels, or books at all, would know who he was. He had a flair for staying in the public eye by associating with controversial sorts, and giving inflammatory statements to the media, and so it made a certain odd sense he'd team up with a reviled figure like Paul Platon.

I googled and found an interview with him on YouTube. The video was from one of those talk shows they have only in France, where people think writers are interesting. Michel Thomas was promoting his novel *The Pareto Effect*. He was smoking on TV, as he talked about a main theme of the book—the injustice that twenty percent of the men were bagging eighty percent of the women.

He inhaled, holding his cigarette between his third and fourth fingers, these lesser-used digits distancing him from the act of smoking, as if he were holding his cigarette with tongs.

I thought of Bruno's discourse on fingers and why they curled: from a time before we were human, and climbed trees. What makes us human, he said, is that we have used this atavistic curvature for a startling range of activities, employing our curved fingers for precisely those things that later transformed us into creatures *who do not climb trees*.

Michel Thomas smiled, and I could see that he was wearing dentures. They looked like he had them in wrong, or they were the wrong size. His tear troughs were sunken and dark. His fraying hair looked like it had been clamped in an electric iron turned up high. I imagined the sound of burning hay, the smell of burning hair.

He told the host he was not a nihilist, despite his reputation, and instead the opposite—a man with high standards for humanity. But our current distance from those standards, he told the host, and the devolution of western civilization into ruin, had left him brokenhearted.

The pursuit of a man who has lost hope in the world is a desperate business, and I could imagine that his defeated air made Michel Thomas the target of a particular type of female, a woman not simply testing her ability to seduce, but showing this man that not all was lost, that there was something to live for.

I pictured viragos fighting over Michel Thomas, never mind that he had the sexual energy of a grandmother with bone density issues. His fragile and depleted air would be his unique strategy as a cocksman. I guessed he preferred meek young girls but would give in to the virago when she was at the point of forcing him to sleep with her. Finally, he would submit, but shrugging all the while.

Vito sent me a photo of Lucien and Serge and Amélie while I was watching the Michel Thomas interview. I hit pause and pressed like.

—you're back in marseille?

—Yes. But things are different. As you can see from this photo.

—you're not in that photo.

—Exactly. I'm the odd one out. They formed a cabal in my absence. One I plan to ignore instead of penetrate. The mutual projection of their rapport will be short-lived.

—have you read the pareto effect

—No. Wanted to. But worth a fight? Serge hates that guy. He's not a nice man.

—does serge prefer books by nice men

I sent him a photo I'd taken of the Céline biography before I burned it.

—My Celine is a fashion house. Historical. Parisian.

—this celine is also historical and parisian. known for his wit and hatreds. not thousand dollar dresses.

—Sadie . . . you cannot get a Celine dress for 1K.
—i can get one for free.
—Because Lucien will buy it for you. Serge would buy me one too. I mean if I wanted a Celine dress. He got me a YSL suit designed by Hedi Slimane. We met him at the fitting!

It's obvious that Vito loves Serge and is not using him for a clothes budget. But he wants to impress me by pretending that he is.

This kind of play that I engage in with Vito had been helpful when I was trapped with them in Marseille, and before that, trapped with them in various social situations in Paris. It was a release valve, to pretend I was a gold digger instead of someone whose motives Vito would not comprehend.

Michel Thomas was now telling the talk show host how pleased he was—if he could claim to be "pleased" about anything—that his novels were sold at Carrefour, Casino, Franprix, Monoprix, Intermarché, Leader Price, and Super U, but that until the housewares chain Mr. Bricolage agreed to a distribution deal—and as of yet, they had not—he would feel he had not quite "arrived" to the pantheon of French letters.

He said that in Japan, they sold used schoolgirls' underwear in train station vending machines, catering to a subcategory of pervert, the panty sniffer on the go. A practical idea, and so why not sell novels by Michel Thomas in vending machines? Weren't those who read novels fetishists of their own subcategory? He would never be so self-inflating as to expect his books might share status with the used underpants of schoolgirls, but he might as well allow himself such a hope, when there was so little to hope for in this life.

The host pointed out that Michel Thomas had won every big literary prize and was considered the most successful living French novelist.

The author was unmoved. "That kind of success is for losers," he said. "I aspire to something more. To be base and ubiquitous. You can't plan for that. You can only dream of it."

He stubbed out his cigarette in the tray between him and the host.

His hands now free, the author wrapped his arms around his own chest. His narrow shoulders jutted upward like two clothespins, like he was hanging from a laundry line.

ONE NIGHT I WAS WITH a large group of Moulinards who decamped to the bar of the Café de la Route for an evening of drinking and song.

As we arrived on the square, I spotted those two tramps, the couple in their Mao caps. They were seated on a bench as if it were their post, watching us as we filed into the bar to drink and laugh and enjoy ourselves. I was surprised they would still be in the area, after their brutal rejection by Pascal.

René played the accordion for us that night. I knew about some other skills of his, but not this one. The sounds he produced were serene and wistful, his lateral compression of the instrument like thick, slow ocean waves, rolling in and receding. Later, Florence and some others sang. Mr. Crouzel and his friends were at the bar, loud and animated, and Crouzel insisted Pascal join them for a drink. I noticed that the old guys didn't seem familiar with the other Moulinards in quite the same way. As if Pascal were the emissary from the commune, the one the locals acknowledged, and with whom they were willing to raise a glass.

Amid the revelry, Naïs poured drinks and performed other duties with stoic tolerance.

Bruno had left Paris and his radical milieu before Naïs was born. He had moved to the country and raised a country daughter, whose life was work, chores, weather, bills, and other pragmatic cycles and routines. A daughter who had lost her younger sister as a girl.

I watched as she stacked dirty glasses, her expression dour. Perhaps she was a hostage to that event, her sister killed by a tractor. A death that was a mistake. Siblings are parallels, meant to be equal recipients of distributed attention, competitors for love in a formula where equality is paramount. But in this case, one sister lives, while the other has to die. The parents, once happy, despair. Nothing is the same.

An old woman pushed her way into the bar and joined Crouzel and his friends. Someone said she was Crouzel's mother. Crouzel was in his late seventies. His mother must have been ninety-five at minimum. She was sturdy, dressed in moth-eaten layers and compression socks with the kind of orthopedic sandals you purchase in a pharmacy. She spoke loudly, and in Occitan. The men ordered her a pastis. As she drank it, she told a story that sent them into peals of laughter. They ribbed Crouzel, who smiled sheepishly. His mother finished her drink and left, with a lot of shouting and joviality between her and Crouzel's buddies.

When our own group emerged it was past dark, maybe ten p.m. The couple in their Mao caps was still in the square. They watched us as we got into cars and left.

I took note of this, the intent way that they watched us, watched me, as I walked past them arm in arm with Aurélie, Aurélie whose position in the commune they would be aware of, as she ran the market stall and drove the commune's larger farm truck and was a public face of the group, even as Pascal was its central figure.

The next day, sitting around the library with Jérôme and Alexandre, I said I needed my notes from home and would swing back to get them.

What I wanted wasn't my notes but to stage an encounter, a reencounter, with those two tramps.

I was on a bench in view of the Café de la Route, which was closed up for the afternoon, when the couple appeared on the square, still burdened by those huge backpacks.

They were in the same clothes as the night before, the man in his safari vest and the woman in black with her leather wrist-cuffs, both in their Mao caps, each holding a vape contraption. In their unchanged appearance, I had the sense they were waiting to be activated, to be given a purpose.

I saw them notice me and share a glance.

I waved at them.

The man—"Mao I" as I'd dubbed him—pointed at himself in a questioning manner.

I beckoned him with my hand.

He started walking toward me.

The woman—"Mao II"—followed him toward me across the square, but more slowly. Her halting steps were like those of a stray cat that has smelled food a stranger holds out: the cat wants the food, is going to eat the food, but thinks that its slow pace will protect it from the danger it moves toward.

So she was the cautious one.

I introduced myself to Maos I and II as the wife of Pascal's oldest friend, and a comrade working with Le Moulin.

"Yes, of course," the man said.

They were like the Moulinards in this way: You're meant to know things. And even if you don't know them, you act like you do.

"I don't have much time, so I'll be direct," I said. "Things are shifting at Le Moulin. And we might need your help."

"*Our* help?" the woman asked doubtfully. She was now standing just behind the man, her pack looming over her.

"We came all the way here from Bussoleno," she said. "We came as comrades. Pascal did not treat us as comrades."

The man turned and put his hand on her arm, an ancient gesture employed in every epoch of history by gullible men attempting to calm strident women beset by reasonable doubts.

"Pascal has to use caution," he said to her. "It's like I told you. They've been burned. It's difficult for him to know who to trust."

"That's true," I said. "There are people watching the commune. Watching everything."

I thought of Lemon Incest speaking to the gendarmerie in Tayssac, Lemon Incest and his implausible car, to enhance the truth effect of my point, that they should be discreet, that there were suspicious people around. Even as I was those suspicious people.

"The guy in the convertible on the square that day, before I met with Pascal, he was seen talking to police. We have to be careful," I said. "An action is being planned."

Mao I and Mao II had names: He was Denis. She was Françoise.

They had hitchhiked here all the way from the Italian border, down out of the Alps. It had taken them weeks, because so few vehicles were headed to the remote Guyenne, and especially this part of it, so far from major highways. Their funds had dropped to nothing by the time they reached Sazerac. From Sazerac, they walked. They had arrived in Vantôme on foot, exhausted and destitute, only to be shunned by Pascal. They were camping, and waiting for the autumn grape harvest to begin, so that they could earn some money and perhaps make their way to Grenoble, where they might stay awhile, because Françoise had an adult son who lived there.

I said I knew they were respected veterans of the struggles in the Susa Valley. I said others knew this as well.

"Yes, we were in the valley," Françoise said, "for the occupation of Maddalena, to prevent the military from taking the land, to stop the TAV train. We liberated that place."

"The police surrounded us," Denis added.

"Denis was arrested and charged," Françoise said. "He spent a year in Italian prison."

"A very difficult year for both of us," Denis said, looking at Françoise with gratitude and remorse.

These two were a study in codependency.

When Denis was released from prison, the Italian and French governments both placed a territorial interdiction on him: Denis was forbidden from the entire region of the Susa Valley. They had no choice but to leave.

"We have comrades in the valley," Françoise said. "But if we return there, they'll send Denis back to prison. And he can't survive it. At his age, it's too difficult. And so we have had to become sojourners, fugitives, looking for someplace to settle, to make a new life."

She was in tears. "We came here to share knowledge, to contribute," she said, shaking her head. "Pascal was a real shit to us."

"You aren't the first to have that experience of him," I said.

"You saw it," she said, her eyes red, her cheeks wet. "That day we tried to talk to him on the square. It was humiliating. I had not yet faced up to things."

Watching her, I had the thought that when people cry, their most rudimentary tools of self-comfort, from their deepest and earliest self, are called upon.

"You hear this stuff about Le Moulin," she said in a steadier voice, as she wiped tears and sniffed, putting her crying self away, back on its shelf.

"People say, 'they're really doing it, making something happen, creating their own society,' all of this, but then you also hear that Pascal can be a prick and a chauvinist. Someone had warned us that the whole project is about youth, that there's a kind of ageism, in assessing people, and whether they want you, whether you're useful to them as an *able body*. And if you're older, and you aren't from their inner circle, good luck."

Up close, they were older than I had realized. She was maybe sixty. And he could have been a decade beyond that.

"We should have listened," Denis said, cracking a smile.

Françoise was not smiling. "He rejected us like draft horses that can no longer pull their load!"

I shook my head. "We won't make it as a cult of personality," I said, channeling Nadia's discourse on leaders. "Le Moulin is not a fiefdom.

"It's a confusing time for the group," I went on. I was thinking of them watching us last night, as we filed into the bar, me among that group, inside it.

"Because we suddenly don't know who to trust. There's a fear that someone at Le Moulin is talking to the authorities," I said. "It might be Pascal," I added.

Françoise was so wounded by his rejection that I might get away with this.

"I don't believe that," Denis said. "Impossible."

"Denis, anything is possible," Françoise said.

"I didn't believe it either," I said. "And I'm still not sure. There is a small group of us who feel we need to watch out for the larger community, and not set us up for arrest."

I named a bunch of people, including Aurélie, who were in on our plan. I cautioned to please say nothing.

"We knew it was Moulinards who set fire to that equipment at the reservoir," Françoise said. "And because of that, we removed the SIM cards in our phones in Sazerac, before we arrived in town. You don't show up and make yourself traceable when you're already under a certain amount of heat, as we are. We are not sloppy."

They told me they had set up a tent in a stand of woods on a hill behind a bus shelter off the D79. I arranged to meet them there in a few days' time.

"WHAT WERE YOU TALKING TO THOSE FOLKS from Susa about?"

It was Nadia, emerging from the church as I walked to my Škoda.

She must have parked in some hidden spot. I had not noticed her car. Was I the one becoming sloppy?

"We need people to support the action in the works," I said.

Sometimes it feels so good to be honest. Especially when it's in service to a lie.

"What action?" Flames licked up into her eyes, and I could see that the old wound of being rejected was there with us now.

"I don't know much."

"Bullshit," she said.

I told her about the mass disruption planned for the fair. I said that it would be a large-scale protest and that Pascal's pick-me method of including people didn't adhere. This was a question of bodies. The more of them the better.

"So that the cannon fodder will get kettled, I'm certain!" she said. "Hauled off in buses, for mass arrest. Hmmf! No thanks, Québécois! Those two will learn the hard way that Pascal doesn't reject people and treat them like dirt only to pick them back up for no reason. He's a user to the core! But far be it from me to interfere. They should know better. But they're too in thrall to Pascal to give up on Le Moulin and see the truth. If they were smart, they'd get the hell out of here, which is what I'm doing."

She said she and Bernadette were headed down to the Vaucluse, whose truffle season would be starting soon, and from there, they would work their way back north.

We said our goodbyes.

A FEW TIMES, exchanges between Pascal and the library boys fell to silence when I arrived, as if my presence were a candle snuffer, depriving their talk of air.

And once, as I joined Aurélie's table in the mess hall, a conversation she was having with another woman dropped off upon my arrival. They both looked at their food. Unlike that day at our swim hole when Sophie and Paul had whispered, she did not later apologize.

Either these silences indicated that people were planning a melee, as I hoped, or the silences meant I was under suspicion. Whether they were promising or ominous, I pretended not to notice them, and not to notice the inconsistencies in the Moulinards' treatment of me.

Pascal was always including or excluding people in little conversations and moments; this was how he moved through the social atmosphere of Le Moulin. And if he and the boys occasionally went mum on my arrival, there were times when Pascal seemed to shun them and favor me.

One evening he invited me, and right in front of Jérôme and Alexandre, to visit Jean, to discuss plans for the fair, which was seven days away.

Pascal and I were leaving to walk to Jean's place—he lived outside the village—when Burdmoore appeared.

"Are we taking off for Jean's?"

There might not have been a particular reason Pascal didn't want Burdmoore joining us, but Burdmoore's insistence on coming along was reason enough for Pascal to try to shed him.

"I don't want to impose on him," Pascal said, "by showing up with a bunch of people. I think it's best if it's just me and Sadie."

"It's not 'a bunch' of people. It's me. I saw him yesterday and he invited me."

I'd had my eye on the dynamic between Burdmoore and Pascal, still uncertain if it was based on mutual affection or some kind of enmity. It was seeming like the latter.

Jean's place was a twenty-minute walk from Le Moulin, on the other side of Vantôme, where the village gave way to a patchwork of small hilly farms. The three of us set out.

"'I'm a dream in seek of a dreamer,'" Burdmoore recited. "That's Jean. Something he wrote in '68."

"He wrote that much earlier," Pascal said.

"Well, he wrote it, is my point. And it took on a life of its own. Fah-Q heard about it. Put it all over the Lower East Side. Fah-Q was like Debord," Burdmoore added for me, "but the Puerto Rican version. With guns."

Pascal inhaled, as if steeling himself to stay quiet.

I heard a car behind us.

Pascal turned around.

It's not her, I didn't say, knowing he feared this could be Nadia Derain, who had already left for the Vaucluse.

It was Crouzel's ancient mother, in a dusty Peugeot hatchback, tut-tutting from the town square. She rolled down her window and yelled that Crouzel was behind her, warning us to make room.

A giant tractor appeared, with Crouzel perched in its high seat, in faded overalls and work gloves. We filed to the side of the narrow road. Crouzel put on his brakes and yelled to Pascal over the shuddering racket of the tractor engine. He was doing trail clearance, he said. They finished their exchange and Crouzel moved past us at a slow clattering roar.

"The secret to a peasant's survival," Pascal said, "is the little assignments he gets from the canton."

He said Crouzel was paid by the state to maintain public walking trails. The trails were part of what was called "the green belt," which no one used except tourists, and in this part of the Guyenne, there weren't any tourists. Crouzel and his friends fought every year over who got the assignment to maintain the green belt, Pascal said, but Crouzel always ended up with it, and some people suspected it was because his mother went into the canton's administrative headquarters ready to go to blows over the issue.

We sat at a picnic table on the deck of Jean's small ramshackle house. Jean sucked on a cigarette and poured us eau-de-vie from a plastic gallon jug. Pascal didn't touch his. I sipped mine, but only to be polite; eau-de-vie is poison. Burdmoore and Jean both downed theirs and refilled their cups.

Some of the dairy farmers were planning to block the entrance to the fair from the D79, Jean said. They would empty their milk tanks. Not all of the farmers were on board to participate, he said, as there were a lot of internal disputes in the dairy union. But he guessed it would be at least thirty breeders, and thirty tankers.

"Each tank holds six thousand gallons. You can do the math if you want, but the point is: we are talking about a megabasin of milk."

Jean suggested that the Moulinards might create a human barrier beyond the tractors and the tanker trucks, to prevent the police from getting through. They could assist with a milk giveaway, which the Périgourdine farmers had done, in addition to their milk dump. A giveaway did not contradict a dump, Jean said. A giveaway, connecting one tanker to a hose and filling gallon jugs and handing them out to anyone and everyone, this flooded the market with free milk simultaneous to flooding the roads with wasted milk.

I'd heard a rumor, I said, that a government official from Paris was coming to the fair.

Pascal and Jean both looked at me.

I was not on script. This was real-time, and I had to make quick decisions. I had to act.

"Paul Platon is making a surprise appearance at the fair." I said this in French, though we had been speaking in English, on account of Burdmoore's presence. But I wanted Jean to understand me perfectly.

"Platon is that deputy minister they chased out of Nantes, no?" Jean asked Pascal.

Pascal said it was. "This could be quite the moment. No one likes that guy! He's truly repugnant. Does he think he's going to seduce the people around here with a PR campaign? Hilarious!"

"But how do you know this," Jean asked me, "if it is not announced?"

Was this a stumble? It was too late.

I took a sip of alcohol. It tasted like nail polish remover. To set the mood, I visualized that maid in Vincennes, kicking the little white dogs that belonged to Platon's mistress. I would have kicked those dogs too.

"When I first got to Paris, I walked dogs for a living."

"Lucien told me this," Pascal said, and added, smiling, "he said you don't even like dogs."

"That's true," I said, laughing. "But I had no work papers, and it was a cash job. I had a client out in Vincennes, this woman Hélène de Marche. Sometimes she asked me to stay for an aperitif when she returned from work. She had a lover, but he was married, and this was her great lament. The lover was Paul Platon. I had to hear all about it from her. After the affair was made public, he stopped coming to see her. These people, they pay you to walk their dogs, but really, it's counseling on the cheap. Now Hélène is frantic, because she thinks Platon has a new mistress. She told me that he's bringing her to the Guyenne."

"But how would she know?" Jean asked, confused. A bit too reasonably confused for my comfort level, but Pascal dealt with Jean's question, and better even than I could.

"A jealous woman," Pascal said, "is on a fact-finding frenzy. Her mission in life is to know, and no obstacle will deter her knowing."

"I had mentioned to her that I would be in this part of France," I said, "at Lucien's family place. They've never met, but it's like I'm her only friend or something. When I saw her number on my phone yesterday, I was hesitant to take the call."

All of this took place in French, while Burdmoore refilled his cup with liquor. He seemed aware that something important was being discussed, but he did not speak the language well enough to follow.

"Are you certain about this?" Jean asked me. "It might call for a change of plans," he said to Pascal. Jean should let the farmers know about this development.

At which point Pascal once again did my work for me, without any prompting on my part.

"Jean, you cannot say anything to them! This has to be secret. If Platon finds out that news of his appearance has been leaked, my guess is he'll call it off. He doesn't want another Nantes. He thinks he's coming here to drum up popular support for the megabasins."

Jean was convinced.

For now, Platon's appearance at the fair would be kept quiet.

"At least until we figure out how to use it," Pascal said. "If, for instance, the dairy farmers formed a line beyond the fair, after his arrival, Platon would be trapped."

"And a lot of people would be injured and arrested or worse," Jean said, "when the state arrives with a massive show of force."

"Or so many people will join us, take our side, that we make a zone of occupation and push the police out."

Jean and Burdmoore had drained the last of the eau-de-vie. Jean padded inside in his destroyed espadrilles and emerged with a bottle of pastis in one arm and a large wooden crate in the other.

It was getting dark. I felt the evening was over, as a private objective had been met, to get them excited about a confrontation with Platon—perhaps they would even plan something risky all on their own, without any suggestions from me—but Jean was focused on showing us, or showing me, as the guest, what was in this box, which contained prehistoric relics he had found while digging in his yard.

"You don't have to go live in a cave to be in touch with the past around here," he said as he set down the box. "Live in a cave, and then send *long emails* about it."

"Jean," Pascal said with gentle scorn.

"I'm too busy working in my garden to bother with sending emails. If someone wants to see me, they come up to the house. If they want my opinion, they ask."

I felt a little sad for Bruno, who wasn't here to defend himself against his old rival.

Jean arranged the contents from the box on the table's surface with a haste bred from familiarity, like a chess master setting up his board. Or a boy putting out his toy army guys or his Lego pieces.

Jean said that if he ever got desperate, he would sell these things to the big museum up in the Périgord.

He had sorted his dirty relics by what looked like size but turned out to be epoch. The largest tool was the oldest. He picked it up.

"This is six hundred thousand years old. A paleontologist visiting from Montpellier confirmed it."

It was a big misshapen rock. I said it was hard to imagine what it had been used for.

Burdmoore picked it up. "This tool has been engineered," he said, palming the rock, "for a specific use."

"What use is that?" Pascal asked flatly. He had a way of addressing Burdmoore that suggested Burdmoore's contributions were not welcome.

Burdmoore weighed the rock in his hand. "This is what our ancestors would have referred to, in their language, as head-smashing equipment."

I thought it was funny, but Pascal insulted Burdmoore to Jean, quickly and in French.

"What did you say?" Burdmoore was gripping the rock. "Did you just call me an idiot? What gives, Pascal?"

"Part of what I appreciate about you, Burdmoore, is your directness and your simplicity of mind."

"Fuck you, Pascal," Burdmoore said.

He was drunk from the gasoline water.

"Lately, I've noticed you think it's amusing to insult me. It's not amusing and I'm tired of it. And I'm to the point at this moment where I gotta make a choice. Either bash your head with this rock or walk away."

He walked away from Jean's yard and disappeared into the dark.

"I'll talk to him," I said, getting up. "With a lot of Americans, feelings get buried, and result in these . . . outbursts."

Pascal nodded. "He's become a powder keg."

"Go talk to him," Jean said to me, and then to Pascal, "If you alienate him, I won't have anyone to drink with. And our movement needs, shall we say, fermenters."

"He took off with your six-hundred-thousand-year-old rock, Jean."

"Ah, shit! No, but you know what? It's just a rock I dug up and put in the collection. That's a bunch of crap about the paleontologist."

They were still laughing about that as I left.

THERE ARE NO LIGHTS outside Vantôme. The moon had not yet risen.

I caught up to Burdmoore.

As we walked in the dark, the church bells sounded the twelve chimes of midnight. When they ceased their clamoring, Burdmoore spoke.

"I've been at this a long time."

"At . . . what?"

As I waited for him to answer, I mentally recited his rap sheet. There were trial transcripts, and other detailed accounts online of the armed group he'd been a part of in the late 1960s, a history described in lurid detail in a book—there were excerpts on Google Preview—put out by some grubby left-wing press.

"Don't play dumb, sister," he said. "Something is going down at that fair, with that minister. And most of us won't have any idea what we're walking into."

I said nothing, a generally effective method for getting people to continue to speak.

"When I arrived here, I figured, you know, it takes time. To find out what's going on. But the longer I'm here, the less Pascal tells me, and the more grunt work I somehow end up doing. And suddenly some shit happens, and no one admits anything. They torched that equipment in Tayssac. And they put everyone on the commune at risk. See, we get all the risk and none of the glory. And if there's going to be a showdown, I want in. I want to know what we're doing."

"Can you keep a secret? Keep what I tell you to yourself?"

It was so dark that I could not see his face as I waited for him to respond.

Instead of answering my question, he said that he hadn't realized how lonely he was. How culturally different these people were, until I showed up. How drawn to me he'd felt. Not in some sleazy way, he assured me. A sisterly way.

"They aren't like us," he said. "There's just some difference you can't get around. Even with you. Sure, you speak their language, but you're more like me than you are like them. So maybe Pascal has indoctrinated me to his 'affective layer' bullshit." He laughed. "Yes, I can keep a secret."

"There might be something brewing that Pascal is not involved in," I said.

"Is that right."

Without seeing him, I felt him cogitating next to me in the dark. Focusing himself. Sobering up a little.

"A plan of action," I said, testing the waters.

More cogitations. The sense he was open.

"Does Jean know about this?"

"No."

The moon, still unseen, had announced itself in a quaking halo of yellow light along the line of the hills.

"When you showed up, I had this strong feeling. I told myself, this chick is looking for trouble. Turns out I was right."

"You don't want trouble," I said. "I get it. We can pretend we never had this conversation."

The moon had advanced. It brimmed over the hill, pouring its yellow light.

"How about you give me the details," Burdmoore said, "and maybe I *will* choose trouble. Or I won't. But you leave it to me, sister, to decide what I want."

IF YOU WERE FROM THE DRUNK TANK, the holding cell, the reform school, the orphanage, or the streets, you had a leg up with Guy Debord. There were a few, in that crowd around Debord, Bruno wrote, who came and went from the prisons, and one guy who had been in a penal colony for murdering a guard.

There were the criminals and delinquents on the one hand, and on the other the intellectuals like Guy. Guy was committed to rejecting society, while the hoodlums lived their rejection instead of thinking about it.

At the end of the war, young Bruno had been transported to Paris to be reunited with his family. After it was confirmed that he had no family, he was shuttled among institutions. This went on for several years. Finally, he opted to flee. He didn't look back, and no one came in search of him. There was a community, he said, of boys like him, kids who looked out for one another and made their home on the streets of Paris.

The Moulinards had asked about his early history in that storied era, the 1950s on the Left Bank. Bruno told them he was fifteen when he first met Debord. That was in '53. Guy was older by six years, and this gap—between a fifteen-year-old orphan living by his wits, and a twenty-one-year-old Guy, who was enormously cultivated, with a lot of opinions, a nice apartment on rue Racine, a girlfriend with a car—was a chasm.

Guy was mysterious and bookish. Bruno had no interest in books. He felt there was no need, he told the Moulinards, to bother with books, given that Guy read them all the time, and Guy tended to relay to Bruno when there was something in those books that Bruno should know about. In exchange, Bruno taught Guy about the fundamentals of hoodlum survival.

The girls Bruno's age, who had been similarly heaved up parentless onto the shores of postwar Paris, whether from concentration camps or from safekeeping in the countryside, these girls were housed in orphanages managed by strict nuns. The boys who were out on the streets were the lucky ones, Bruno said, and so they tried to share their good luck with the girls, by helping them escape these grim nunneries so that they, too, could enjoy their fundamental disposition as vagrants. It is bad enough to be a vagrant, Bruno said. But to be locked into a nunnery, and barred from enjoying your vagrancy? This was worse.

Some of them, both girls and boys, made their home at tables and chairs outside the Café Dupont-Latin, on the Boulevard Saint-Michel. It was there that Bruno first met Guy and was exposed to the fad of existentialism, popular among the old bar philosophers. Bruno took to their hobby of drinking, but not philosophy. Sometimes the younger ones, bored by existentialism, would ditch the bar for some house whose owners were at work or out of town, where they drank stolen dry wines like Entre-Deux-Mers and stolen sweet wines like Banyuls, and if they weren't sweet enough for the youngest orphans, it was Bruno's job to add sugar.

Trauma twists us, Bruno said, and because of my guilt over my family—my brother, especially, murdered by the Nazis at age twelve—I felt a certain protective obligation to the little ones. I became their older brother, and I stirred the sugar in their drinks.

The Dupont-Latin, Bruno said, was merely a point of embarkation, the gateway to a strange journey whose next destination, around the time of his seventeenth birthday, was a different bar, the Mabillon, on the Boulevard Saint-Germain.

You asked about the early days, he said, and this is how they went: In the morning, we drank in the streets. In the evenings, we drank at the Mabillon. For multi-hour stretches, Guy disappeared, presumably to go read books. Meanwhile, I panhandled and stole, to have money to buy drinks. And on occasion, I fell into bed with someone I coveted.

Arrested for petty theft, Bruno was sent to a reformatory where boys punched each other from morning until night. Bruno would lie in his bunk and dream of being eighteen, so that he could be sent to a proper prison. That was how blinkered my mind was, he said, by the war, by the loss of my family, by the reckless abandon that was my guiding principle.

After the reformatory, he rejoined Debord and the rest, who were now at Chez Moineau on the Rue du Four. This was 1955. The scene was more intellectual by then, Bruno said. They had a journal, even.

Guy believed that true art never devolved into actual art, it had to be lived as a gesture, like going into Notre Dame Cathedral and yelling "God is dead," or stumbling home drunk, on foot, because there was a rail strike, and declaring that your drunken meandering was a new way of mapping the city. If you sold art or published under your own name or had a job, you were considered a lowlife. I was as guilty as Guy, Bruno said, for my pretentions in this regard. The rules for inclusion in our group were arbitrary and strict, and there were purges.

The value of us non-thinkers in the group, Bruno wrote to the Moulinards, was measured by how much we drank and how much we stole, whether it was bottles of wine from the cellar of the Brasserie Lipp, or a car on a side street that was waiting to be hot-wired. Bruno said his specialty was rifling hotel rooms.

In that era, so long before your time, he told the Moulinards, you had to lock the door of a hotel. It didn't lock automatically. Many people would forget to lock their room once they returned to it. The rooms that Bruno entered were generally occupied by people he hoped were sleeping.

I got very good at making no noise and at seeing in the dark, he said. I admit with some chagrin that perhaps I originally learned to see with my fingers, to see by touch, not in the caves, but in dark hotel rooms where strangers slept, as I felt for items to steal.

The results were random and inconsistent. A shoehorn. An ice bucket. A woman's toiletry case. Or he would get lucky and find a wallet or purse. Once, he grabbed a velvet bag that felt to have metal parts inside, which turned out to be a disassembled MAC 50, a French army pistol.

Some of the others who stole got more ambitious. They began to pilfer lead from the lamps in the Catacombs, not unlike the way people today steal copper wire, Bruno said. Lead then, like copper now, was valuable and could be resold. From there, for the more serious thieves, it was jewelry stores, armed stickups, arrest, and then a choice: prison or the Foreign Legion.

Watching the others go to prison, or to Algeria to fight for colonial France, Bruno had a revelation that he could change course, that his own commitment to mayhem was not inevitable, not total. He stopped thieving. He gave up drinking. He got a job punching tickets in the metro, rented a maid's room out in the nineteenth. He made plans to enroll in school. He was still a teenager. Guy Debord shunned him, and the others followed suit. Working, enrolling in school, these things were just not done. You were meant to reject society completely, to fling yourself headlong into a world without the old structures.

Bruno punched tickets in the metro by day, and by night, he took up reading. At the age of twenty, he left Paris to study earth science in Lyon.

Upon graduating, he was contracted to teach high school students in the city of Rodez, famous, he told the Moulinards, for its enormous cathedral, and also for its mental hospital, which had once housed the playwright Antonin Artaud.

He was not aware, until he arrived there for his first day of work, that it was a reform school. The pedagogical principles were punishment and cruelty, which brought Bruno back to his own childhood, fighting bare-knuckled to survive in the reformatory. It was not by accident, he told the Moulinards, that he had somehow landed at this awful school in Rodez. Bruno was certain it was fate.

While the other teachers beat their students with a closed fist or a belt or a cane, Bruno vowed a gentle approach. He treated his students like peers, like equals. They worked together, and a communal feeling took hold. It was this spirit, he said, that formed who he is now.

The sentimental education he underwent in Rodez had created in him, he wrote to the Moulinards, a deep belief that life is precious, and that when it is treated as precious, it is made so.

The lessons that I took as a teacher in Rodez, he said, have outlasted everything else, all the twists and turns through my history. The ideas that I developed are in fact one idea, he said: Children will choose love over brutality, if given the chance. Adults will do the same, if given the chance.

All acts of savagery originate with authority, he wrote.

The work to be done, he told them, is a refusal of savagery.

Pascal (he rarely singled out Pascal in these emails, and so I took particular note), you will undoubtedly find my position "romantic," and even "hopelessly" so.

I have been called worse. And I'll admit that what I find romantic is your continued interest in the mystique of Debord. And yet I've surely been no help in undoing that mystique, and instead, I have probably even built him up a little more in your eyes. You are excused because you are young enough to know only the legend, and not the reality. I don't disavow my own history, my association with Debord. At the same time, I shudder to think of those who keep the flame, manage the legend, who believe that the twin hobbies of drinking and denunciating are signs of life. They are signs of death. But never mind. I left that milieu not to reject it but to find something else. And your question has led me back to Rodez and to a promise I made and that I've kept.

I have never been opposed to property destruction, to principled direct action. The Guyenne is under threat and it must be protected. In this we agree. But intimations I get—and here, you'll have a harsher word for me, perhaps, than "romantic"—but things I hear on cave frequency suggest to me that there is something up ahead, a plan in the offing, over which you and I are not united. If this plan risks the safety, the lives, of people—*no matter who they are*—you will be making a mistake. A wrong turn.

I want to make myself clear to you, that I deplore violence in all of its forms.

I HAD READ THAT EMAIL from Bruno with a certain investment. The occasions when he went into his personal history were special. They were special occasions.

With a little distance, I had the thought that what Bruno was hearing on his "cave frequency," that someone might be hurt—surely plain old intuition, but whatever, people are strange, and where *does* intuitive knowledge originate?—in any case this notion he had was correct, and if he blamed Pascal, all the better.

In the few days since that email, there had been no new correspondence between Bruno and the Moulinards. Perhaps Pascal was stewing over what Bruno said about violence, or the accusation it was Pascal who was the romantic, and not Bruno.

I started to derive childish satisfaction from the prospect that Bruno would blame Pascal and the Moulinards for violence, and not me. As if they were the bad children, and I was the good one. They were acting from fancy, from affectation, acting out. While I was just doing my job. Just trying to get by. To live, and to be.

I now possessed subminister Platon's full travel itinerary. He would make his appearance at the agricultural fair at the lake in Vantôme at 13:00 hours on the appointed day, one week from now.

His security would be the Serb and only the Serb. He would be driven by Georges. Georges who was reaching retirement age. Georges who despised the subminister. In a pinch he'd peel off to save himself, that Georges.

With the itinerary were vehicle details. Platon would arrive in a black Citroën DS 7 Crossback, this year's model, a state car.

He would shake hands with those breeders who had won top fair prizes, taste a regional dish or two, and at 13:30 he would leave the fair.

According to Platon's itinerary, the DS 7 Crossback's next destination would be the department Lot-et-Garonne.

I kept my contacts updated on the plans at Le Moulin and among the farmers.

I warned my contacts that I could not guarantee these plans would not leak. If Platon got word from his own intelligence that there was going to be a big demonstration, I assumed he would cancel. I conveyed this.

We *are* his intelligence, they said in reply.

What I had depicted to Burdmoore that night on the dark open road was a classical "black bloc" tactic, of masked people who would create an offensive line and lob projectiles at the police.

I had given him no names. Instead, Burdmoore gave names to me, when we had a moment alone at Le Moulin, walking under the walnut trees: the two people who ran the kitchen. Felix, who oversaw the walnut operation.

"You should think about letting them in on this," he said. "I know who is up for rabble-rousing. People are ready to split off from Pascal. There are people who think he's talking to the cops."

I wondered if what I'd said to Mao I and Mao II concerning Pascal had spread, as if by underground waterway.

I didn't want or need Felix or the two who ran the kitchen. I needed only Burdmoore, and now was the time to see how far he was willing to go.

I said the plan was to charge Platon. I didn't mention that he would have an armed escort.

"Physically attack him? What's the point? Why him?"

"Because he's the one who's coming here," I said.

Whatever stooge from Paris shows up to the Guyenne, I said, will be made to understand that their power is limited, and even meaningless. That the Guyenne is autonomous.

I felt a bit stirred up myself, in talking like this. An image flashed into my mind of the peasants and Cagots, armed and in great numbers, sending the nobles running for their lives.

I had finished speaking. Burdmoore was examining my face, his bloodshot eyes darting between my own. I didn't like it. But when he spoke, I liked what he said.

"I have a secret I'm going to share with you. Something no one here knows about me. I've got a bad liver."

He patted the cloth of his T-shirt over his big hard belly, as if his liver condition were the cause of the gut.

"It's a casualty of my generation. Hep C. Nothing in life is fair, is it, California? The secret is that I don't have much time left. I've seen what happens when people try to hang on. It's not pretty. It is ugly. And I'm not going for miracle cures."

TODAY WAS SUNDAY, and with the fair less than a week away, Jean and Pascal had gone to a planning meeting with some of the dairy farmers in Sazerac.

It was just me and Jérôme in the library, but we weren't working. We were doing what European activists spend hours and hours doing: simply talking. I asked Jérôme about Bruno. I called him "Lacombe" like they did, and the word felt foreign in my mouth, a coyness that Bruno and I were in on, this distancing by formal address.

"We have had this loyalty," Jérôme responded. "It's been a challenge to face up to things."

Face up to things?

Jérôme said there were growing questions among them about Lacombe's relevance and, frankly, his coherence as a thinker. He went to retrieve a stack of papers and put them on the table.

"You can read these if you want to."

Printouts of Bruno's emails.

"We always felt like there was something to honor in the clandestine nature of our communications with him but it's wearing off."

There was a time, he said, when a communiqué from Lacombe would come through and they'd all gather around the printer like supplicants, to read these emails full of outré declarations about cave bears and cavemen. But that time had passed.

"My position, and Pascal knows this, it's not anything I've kept hidden, is that you can't go back. To live in a cave and renounce technology, renounce everything, that's like"—he laughed—"about the most *modern* thing a person could ever do."

I asked how so. It was fine to be curious. I was curious.

"A caveman isn't rejecting what's around him. That's for intellectuals, people who have overthought everything. You have to deal with life as it is. This guy is talking about half a million years ago, but he's writing about it on a computer. He's a crudivore, renouncing the cooked, while people have been eating cooked food forever, and he's renounced agriculture, which the people in this area have been practicing for twelve thousand years."

He's not against fire, I didn't say. He just keeps his small.

"He thinks the future is in tiny clans. What about genetic diversity? What about cities, and culture? Pascal, me, Alexandre, we were trained to love the classics. What about poetry, and what about art?"

I pictured the footprints in moon milk, as Bruno called it. The white cave. Prints he suspected were a child's.

"Lacombe thinks he can short-circuit history by denying the world. Some of the stuff he writes . . . he said he was hearing radio broadcasts from the 1940s, secret Resistance transmissions. He claims his cave is a temporal labyrinth that holds answers to the great riddles. At first, we all got kind of sucked in. But when you pull away, it starts to seem like madness."

Jean had made fun of Bruno that night when he showed us his rock collection, and Pascal had laughed. Pascal enjoyed it when people devoted to him weren't devoted to each other.

Bruno himself had spoken about this rift he had with Jean, in the email declaring his position on violence.

Bruno had gone on to say that his old comrade Jean Violaine took quite different positions from his own. Their formations were not the same. Certainly, they had both long ago rejected official state communism, such as the Soviet Union, but Jean still believed in the possibility that capitalism would be dismantled, or would collapse on its own, and be replaced by some form of communism—a lowercase *c* communism, as Bruno put it.

Bruno understood the need for hope. He said that this need alone, quite human, must have accounted for Jean's ability to convince himself that when farmers campaigned for market protections it was revolutionary. It wasn't. Bruno said he sensed danger ahead. He hated to see Pascal get drawn into a pattern of defeats.

What Jean envisions, Bruno said, is the same old dreary world, which Jean believes people should struggle toward with unions and strikes and collective bargaining—a fight they will lose. Deep down, Jean, too, knows they will lose. But he pours himself another drink and enjoys his camaraderie with the old farmers, his camaraderie with his young disciples.

I feel a sympathy for Jean, Bruno wrote, but I won't mince words. Whether in a rural outpost or an urban core, trying to dismantle capitalism from within capitalism is a <u>dead end</u>. (It was the first time I'd noticed his use of underlining.)

It is not unlike waiting for Jesus to arrive, to both abolish and fulfill biblical law. In both cases, Bruno said, the waiting is the thing, and the commitment to waiting is bound up with a refusal to acknowledge that what you wait for is *not coming* (he was back to his italics).

Whether Christian or communist, the real goal of believing, falsely, in a better world, was to energize people to keep going, to *keep on trucking* (he wrote this phrase in English, suggesting Bruno was fluent in our cultural idioms). Keep on trucking, he repeated, toward the return of our Lord and Savior. Toward a future that will draw away from you, in lockstep with your advance.

Even if you "win" a battle with the state over the question of water, Bruno wrote to Pascal, the farmers of the Guyenne are dependent on the state. The state is their lifeblood. They cannot compete in an open market! They depend on state subsidies and price protections.

You fight for a lost status quo, he said, and your victory is what? A slightly more functional capitalist relation. That's all.

But, he said, I understand that Jean's way, the tireless organizing, the debates, the little victories, is more straightforward than what I might propose, than what might constitute "my way." Plumbing the depths inside yourself is not easy work. It is difficult work. But I am convinced, he said, that the way to break free of what we are is to find out who we *might have been*, and to try to restore some kernel of our lost essence.

Bruno did not call this essence that was deep inside of people the salt, but it was what he meant. He was talking about the salt.

I HAD BEEN STUDYING a map of the lake, the parking lots, the D79 and its connecting routes, the hills above the lake. I had added elements: the dairy farmers' blockade; the direction from which police would come, when they learned that a state official was caught behind a line of protesters; the location where Platon's driver, Georges, would park the car and wait; the route I myself would take, once Platon was trapped and my work was done, to get out, out of Vantôme, and out of the Guyenne.

I had found, on Google Earth, what looked like a steep fire lane that went from the lake straight uphill, and then connected to the D79 farther up. It was marked on the map as Chemin des Pêcheurs or "fishermen's path."

I would need a clean escape as police descended. I was hoping to hide the Škoda on this little fire lane I'd located on Google Earth, so that it waited for me while I finished my job. When everyone at the fair was trapped and kettled, just as Nadia predicted, I planned to be far away, on a major highway, fleeing north.

I visited the site, disappointed to discover logs and branches had fallen across it, and there were deep ruts that looked impassable. I walked the length of the road, surveying the work that would have to be done to get access. I needed Crouzel to clear it with his tractor. Whatever the canton paid him, I could do him better, but Crouzel was on the inside with Pascal. Between him and his ubiquitous mother, they were not keeping any secrets.

Along the flatter, lower part was an old logging site, with huge piles of stacked logs. A sign warned that climbing the logs was prohibited. The sign was accompanied by an illustration of a person being crushed by tumbling logs. It had been designed as a visual warning that could be understood in any language, but in French read "DANGER: it is prohibited to climb on logs."

On both sides of this old lane, under its pines, were patches of wild nasturtiums. A wind came through, stirring them. Their circular leaves, like large green faces, nodded "yes" in the wind. But in the next gust, those same leaves jiggled and jostled from side to side, saying "no."

I continued toward the lake, where I'd parked the Škoda.

It was twilight, and the tall grasses in the meadow that wrapped around the backside of the water were in shadow. As I neared the grassy field and the bench where I'd sat with René, I was mesmerized by these tiny white clumps hugging each blade of the tall grass. They looked like little lice on thick strands of green hair. I thought of what Bruno had said about his own lice: problems leave when they are ready to go.

This wild grass, bending in all directions as wind swept through, was covered with them. Upon close inspection, the tiny white blobs were small snails attached to the grass blades. They had overtaken the meadow like invading aliens.

My vision was focused low, on these little snails, and I hadn't noticed that there was someone seated on that bench, mine and René's.

It was an old man, facing the lake. He had white hair to his shoulders. The old-timers here do not have hair to their shoulders.

I stared at him. As if he sensed my presence, he stood from the bench and turned to face me. My heart was pounding.

He looked like Bruno Lacombe. The long hair. The serene face. But his gaze was penetrating, and not serene. He turned, his hands in his pockets, and walked toward the parking lot. He headed right, going slowly down the D79 on foot.

I went to my car and got in and made a right onto the road.

He was walking along the shoulder.

I slowed as I approached, with no plan for what I would say.

I put on my brakes and lowered the passenger window.

"Good evening, sir."

"Good evening," he replied. He had stopped walking.

The photo of Bruno on the back of his book was twenty years out of date. I could not be certain. But I was already sure in a way that didn't allow me to conjure a scenario in which this man was not him.

"Sir?"

"Yes?"

"You live nearby?"

"Not so close, no."

My car idled, the window down. This man looked like Bruno.

"In the hills above the lake?"

He shook his head. He had the comb-over.

"Sir, you are not Bruno?"

He shook his head.

"But you know who I mean? Bruno Lacombe?"

"No, I'm sorry. I am Frederic Peyrol. I live in Le Petit Sazerac." He pointed down the road as if pointing homeward.

He nodded goodbye and set off at his slow pace.

I watched him, my car stopped there on the road. He did not look back.

IT WAS WEDNESDAY MORNING—the fair was three days away—when I sent an email to the Moulinards' shared account and said I wasn't feeling good and would not be there today.

I was feeling great, actually. The morning was overcast and cool, perfect weather for my plans. I locked up the house and drove to a gardening and hardware outlet in Boulière, purchased the equipment on the list I'd made, and headed toward Vantôme.

Passing along the lake, I was alert for the man who might be Bruno on the side of the road, but I saw no one.

I parked next to the bus shelter on the D79. (I had never once seen any bus, or anyone waiting for a bus in this shelter.) I walked off the road, up into a wooded area.

I had a job for the old draft horses, Denis and Françoise. And at a much better rate than they would make working the grape harvest.

They were at their encampment, seated at a small fire, pouring heated milk from a pan into their tin cups, and adding packets of instant coffee. "We don't have another cup," Françoise said. I assured her I was fine.

I sat cross-legged, mirroring how they sat, and gazed into their fire in the blank-faced manner that they did, as if much of what coursed through our minds could not be converted to words (and even if it could be, it shouldn't).

In the firelight, under shadowy woods on this gray day, their two faces, weathered and creased, took on a medieval character.

Françoise broke the silence.

"We saw him."

"Who?"

"The man in the car that doesn't have a top."

"Is that so," I said.

"Yesterday he passed the bus shelter on the D79. An hour later, he passed by again, going in the other direction. And then he went by once more."

It was just a ruse I'd put them on, to create a feeling of paranoia, mentioning the man in his Chrysler Sebring. I was impatient to redirect them to why I was here.

"You can't risk arrest, and this is well understood. Still, there is a role for you. Should you want to join us. This is a critical moment for Le Moulin, and for the small farmers who need our help. Your help."

They stared at each other for a beat beyond my own comfort.

"The woman from Brittany warned us," Denis said, "about all this. About you and the Moulinards."

He meant Nadia, I assumed.

"But she is a bit touched in the head I think," Françoise said to Denis.

Denis shrugged. "Perhaps. That doesn't mean she's wrong. She said the action will be a trap and that a lot of people will be arrested."

"I think Pascal might intend that," I said. "But others of us, Aurélie, Burdmoore, René, Sophie, Paul, Felix, Florence, certain others that I cannot name, we have a different plan. Which is that no one will be arrested. Even if there's a police kettle."

I said we had divided in order to conquer. And my job was to clear a road. I described the fishermen's route, from the meadow on the far side of the lake, currently impassible. I said we would have vehicles there, shuttling people to safety, and how comical and great it would be, when we all escaped the police kettle. But to achieve this, the road needed clearance.

"Can you two help me do this work?"

I said we had taken up a collection, and that myself and Aurélie—it was my instinct that they liked hearing her name, the invocation of someone who looked so legitimate and capable, with her long hair and her overalls, the way she commanded the farm truck—that we wanted them to be able to pick back up and move on, to find their way to Grenoble. I said I had relayed their situation, and that everyone was sympathetic. People felt it was critical to acknowledge elders and their achievements in opposing state violence. Who are we, I said, if we treat our elders as disposable? This had been yet one more example of Pascal's failure of vision, I told them, his inability to lead and to uphold the ethics of the group. I unzipped a fanny pack at my waist and took out an envelope that contained one thousand euros.

"But that's a lot!" Françoise said.

"Some of them are from rich families," I said. "Take it."

Françoise pocketed the envelope.

We walked to my Škoda, whose hatchback contained axes, shovels, a chain saw, two wheelbarrows, and ropes for pulling logs.

Denis and Françoise were both rugged and impressively hardy despite their age. They did not tire. Françoise barely even sweated. Denis was an expert with the chain saw. The two of them had a way of communicating that was purely physical, an understanding of who would pick up the heavier end of a log. Who would swing and who would step back. Neither complained.

I enjoyed those long hours of brute physical labor the three of us did together to clear that road, a day spent working like dogs. Its rewards were not unlike lying in the sun, emptying the mind, except that the more one puts in, the more one reaps, and this form of mind emptying left me wrung out in a way that was blissful.

Back at the house, thirsty and tired, I drank a forty, a *formidable* as the French call that large size of beer bottle, made myself a salami sandwich, and went upstairs to lie down in my room, the baby chamber.

Lucien had texted while I was working with the two Maos.

Robert the Comatose had died.

I replied that I was sorry to hear it.

—You have a big heart, Sadie.

Even simulating the role of his girlfriend, I didn't convey bigheartedness. Was Lucien onto me?

—Can't wait to see you. We wrap shooting early. As soon as a week from now.

—that's such great news

It didn't matter to me when he finished shooting, as long it wasn't before the fair on Saturday.

My contacts reconfirmed that Platon would be traveling with Georges, the Serb, and the author Michel Thomas, of the frayed hair and ill-fitting dentures, who was touring this area as research for "an agronomy novel"—whatever that was.

I checked Bruno's email. The Moulinards had sent him nothing. He had not written them either.

I was working on preliminary materials for my next job when I got a Google Alert for Nancy, an alert that tended to produce many false positives—references to Nancy that were not Nancy, just some person with her name, first and last.

I assumed this was that.

I clicked the link, which led me to a very long article on a news site known for whistleblowing.

The government had just released, after nine years, twenty-five hundred documents concerning the court cases of Nancy and the boy, in response to their lawyers' persistent Freedom of Information Act requests. The article suggested that among the documents was exculpatory evidence of illegal government surveillance by an undercover agent known by the alias "Amy."

In having screwed over Nancy and the boy, "Amy" was a symptom of government intrusion, in the form of spying and worse. What kind of person would manipulate and frame young people with utopian hopes and principles? How many Amys were out there, pressuring activists into committing illegal acts, and then disappearing, untraceable and scot-free?

It seemed that all they had was this generic first name, an alias I'd discarded long ago. But I didn't feel much relief.

The FBI might try to scapegoat me. They had done this, recently, to a former agent. The agent was theirs, and following their orders, but to avoid negative attention, the Feds charged him as a rogue. He had testified at a trial without revealing the methods he'd used to collect evidence. They convicted him of perjury, and he went to prison.

The federal statute of limitations for perjury is five years. It had expired, I reassured myself as I retrieved another *formidable*.

I opened it, took a sip, and put it on the bedside table covered with Les Babies stickers.

Overthinking things, I reminded myself, goes with the territory of my profession, a profession for which there could be a Les Babies sticker: the Baby Spy.

WHEN I WOKE UP the next morning, the Baby Spy was the Hungover Spy, perhaps from not hydrating sufficiently while clearing the road, and not eating, and the stress of that Google Alert. Those two forty-ounce bottles of what I thought was beer turned out to have been malt liquor, twenty proof.

My contacts had sent messages repeatedly. They wanted Platon "neutralized." That was their term.

I am not a hit man, I responded.

Having a hangover can be useful in that it cuts away the need to soft-pedal things. One is encouraged to speak the truth, because the buffers that allow for subtleties and dissimulation are replaced by splitting headache.

You're not comprehending, was the reply. *They* will do it.

Stop acting pious, I told myself. Admit it: you knew all along that they were setting up Platon for something grievous. You knew in Marseille. You knew six months ago, when they had you following the guy around Spanish villages.

It was time to pull back and negotiate.

I upped my price to an absurdly high number. My own worth is an existential metric. It is not determined by the market.

I was certain they would balk.

They agreed to the price.

And suddenly, my purpose here was to get these people to kill a man.

No one cares about Paul Platon, I reassured myself.

The average French person, embodied in his driver, and in his own bodyguard, would not care if Paul Platon disappeared, never to be heard from again. And this was the very reason I had studied his driver and guard: for apathy.

And so why should *I* care, I reasoned, talking to myself in loud thoughts that banged around my head, which hurt, as I paced Chez Dubois looking for my Advil supply.

I understand that you "deplore violence in all its forms," I thought at Bruno, as if he were here in the house with me. But what about in the case of a man who is universally reviled?

And why should I, in particular, be *more concerned* with this man's fate than the average French person? Than his own driver?

Bruno, why should I care more about Platon's life than the man who is *officially tasked with safeguarding it*?

I could not find the Advil.

MY HEAD HURT SO BADLY that I was forced to pound a beer as medicine. It was seven a.m., and I don't drink in the morning, but this one time I allowed it.

I stopped at the gas station in the little village between the house and Vantôme. I filled the Škoda's tank, slipped into a bar next to the station, and ordered a whiskey. Now that I had started, it was prudent to have a second dose of medicine before I got to Le Moulin.

When I emerged from the bar, I heard amplified music.

That guy in his Chrysler Sebring, Lemon Incest, was pulling in next to the pumps. The most unlikely vehicle in the Guyenne if not all of southern France. The car without a top, as Françoise had said.

I'd sent her and Denis chasing a mirage, by suggesting he was a cop. But was the mirage chasing me?

Today it was different music, crass and symphonic. It sounded like it had been scored for a James Bond movie.

The man was pumping his gas. As I walked to my car, he turned his head, observing me.

I got in the Škoda and was about to drive away, but thought better of it and killed the motor. I got out and approached him.

If this guy was somehow watching me, I was going to put a stop to it right now.

"What do you think you're doing?"

"I'm putting fuel in my car," he replied. "I drive it, which causes the tank to empty. Then it has to be refilled."

"I saw you in Vantôme," I said.

"Vantôme? I have been to Vantôme. But not frequently."

He put the nozzle back in its resting position on the pump and closed his gas cap.

"Are you following me?" I asked.

His smile did not change. Mild, inscrutable. The kind of smile that could drive a person to rage.

"But why would I follow you?" he asked in a soft voice, as if he had lowered it so others would not hear.

"You tell me," I said.

"You're a stranger to me, madame. I have no recollection of you. I have never followed you. I do not know you. But I think I know your type."

"What type is that?"

"You are paranoid," he said with a demonically neutral smile.

He got into his car and started it, commencing that hideous movie music. As he drove away, I realized he was correct about my mild and temporary paranoia, which had already lifted.

I felt relieved. I felt glad. Glad to be paranoid instead of followed and watched.

Today was Thursday, and instead of translation work at Le Moulin, we were all involved in planning. The fair was two days away. The Moulinards would set up a staging area from which to descend onto the D79 after Platon arrived.

"How on earth will this guy *not* know about the protest?" Aurélie asked a group of us at lunch.

Because French intelligence is withholding that vital information from him, I did not say.

I was leaving lunch when Pascal pulled me aside. He asked if I'd heard anything more from Hélène de Marche.

I said I had not.

He asked how long I'd worked for her, and where she lived.

As I answered, I saw the little boutiques of Vincennes, the nannies pushing strollers, the young people walking dogs for hire, all of which I'd observed, and so I was able to insert myself in a familiar scene and depict it casually. I described my days, my route through the park, where I ate my lunch, the bookstore I stopped in sometimes, before I got on the metro to go back to Lucien's.

I was doing a lot of work, more work than I should have to. But I felt Pascal wanted this display from me, needed to believe he could trust me.

He listened as I rehearsed my dog walker's bona fides. My Vincennes bona fides.

"It's strange," he said, just as I thought my trial was over, and I could relax.

It would have been nice to have another beer. I'd put some in my car.

"What is?" I asked.

"It's a striking coincidence. Platon coming here. And you knowing about it."

"What I've always appreciated about this concept of coincidence," I said, "is how it reifies our search for causality, our need to establish logical connections among disparate events."

Pascal himself was always making these kinds of statements, magisterial claims that didn't mean anything if you examined them.

He bit his lip, thinking on this.

"But one thing I've come to understand as causal, not a coincidence," I went on, "about the people whose dogs I walked, about a certain layer of Parisian society, and honestly, about what I have gotten myself involved with—Lucien, his family, and frankly you're part of that world, Pascal—what I've come to understand is that when people like you and Lucien know someone powerful, it's not a coincidence at all."

"I've never tried to hide what I come from," he said.

"You know judges and captains of industry. While I know some woman who waits for a lowly bureaucrat. Actually, I know her dog."

The comment about the dog made him laugh. But as I said it, I saw myself bending down on a winter sidewalk to pick up dog shit. Working part-time for some bimbo way out in Vincennes. While Pascal sat snug in the bar at the Hotel Meurice and I thought, Fuck you, Pascal.

"Having you here has meant a lot to me," Pascal said.

Like most people, he was unable to read minds.

"You're good at transposing our ideas and, frankly, I like having you around. After this book will come another, we have a lot of the material for it already. All we need is to convince Lucien to give up on the mediocre and compromised world of film, see it for what it is, and move here."

Lucien and I would come and live on the commune, he said. René and his crew would build us a house.

Perhaps Lucien and I would have children, Pascal said. I might discover an aspect of life, and of myself, that was waiting to emerge.

The only baby I'd ever have is the one I'd find in a dumpster, left where no one else could hear it cry.

Since that will never happen, I will remain forever childless, and in the meantime nurse only beer, like the ones I had put in the trunk of the Škoda.

"GOD'S WAY OF REMAINING ANONYMOUS," Pascal might say of the phenomenon of coincidence, in explaining to himself why Deputy Minister Paul Platon was coming here, and how it could be that I'd been informed of such a thing in advance, and secretly.

But, Pascal, a coincidence is not God's way of remaining anonymous.

"Coincidence" is a term you choose for the good work it does to cover what some part of you knows, but a part that cannot be allowed to speak.

The coincidence, as an explanation for things that are mysteriously aligned, is hiding what is not a coincidence, Pascal, and is instead a plot.

LATER THAT AFTERNOON I peeked into the woodshop. René wasn't there. Burdmoore and I were graced with a moment of privacy.

Burdmoore had done much more than was on his toilet-roll-long rap sheet. He told me he'd robbed twelve bank branches in the New York Tri-State area and had killed a drug dealer, an act of goodness, he said, to remove harmful elements from the Lower East Side in the late 1960s. He was adept with firearms, but old-fashioned ones, guns that people don't use much anymore. It was perfect that I had the P38, which I planned to give him on Saturday.

He had mentioned his experience with guns as an aside, part of his general braggadocio, but now I made clear that the confrontation with Platon, which I had previously outlined only in vague terms, involved weapons.

"Some of us," I said, "are going all the way with this. Platon signifies the ruination of this place. Not just as a place, but as a chance for people to live without the constant incursions of the state. Farmers are killing themselves, as you know. They feel there is no future. We must push back, and with everything we have."

He said nothing. I kept going.

"A lot of people talk. But when push comes to shove, they aren't willing to risk anything. Most people don't have the will or the experience to execute a serious plan. You do."

"That's probably true," he said, "that most don't have the guts or the training. When I think of all the mistakes, the dreams, the fifty lives

I've led, I have to ask myself, what does it mean if I let it all go, if I just fade out, ingloriously, in some hospital in a foreign country?"

I was headed to the Škoda. Not just for a secret beer. I had an errand to run.

I went to the town square. I parked behind the church and stayed in my car.

I watched as Naïs wound the handle of the torn old cloth awning, which retracted inward like the pleats of an accordion. She locked the café doors. Rolled down the metal shutter with muscular efficiency. Loaded bags of groceries into her car.

I assumed she was bringing these home to Bruno. I pictured him in the kitchen of the house, on a visit from the deep, to enjoy a stew that Naïs had prepared. Bruno at a little table, dipping bread into this stew, the two of them talking very little or not at all.

She got behind the wheel and set off. I followed at a safe distance.

She took the D79, as I had anticipated. She turned left at a crossroads after the lake, a traverse that went upward in switchback.

She took another left. I arrived at that turn: a narrow gravel road, not much more than a walking lane that went through dense woods. I watched as her little hatchback rambled along, listening with my windows down to the mealy sound of her tires on the gravel. Her brake lights bloomed (her one brake light; the other was out). Her car turned right.

Thank you, Naïs.

Thank you for showing me the way to Bruno's.

Having made a mental map of this route, I returned to Le Moulin.

I joined a group assigned to make banners and listened as people shared news of various developments: Crouzel and some other farmers around Vantôme would open gates and turn off electric fences, and drive their cattle down toward the lake, to collect on the D79, behind the tractors and milk tankers.

At dinnertime, the discussions and planning continued. As I entered the dining hall, I saw that René and his woman were seated together in the back of the room. She looked up at me. I got a plate, put rice on it, ladled some kind of stewed meat over the rice, and sat down with the people on my banner-making committee. As I ate, I noticed that René and his woman weren't speaking. They chewed glumly, and then he got up to clear his plate and left. Perhaps they were having an argument.

I carried my dish to the washtubs, slid what I hadn't eaten into a compost bucket, and double-dipped my plate. I heard Burdmoore telling someone a story in broken English. His method for being understood was to speak English as if it were his second language, clipping off definite articles, voice loud, repeating himself.

As I left the building, René's woman—what was her name, I could not recall, hadn't bothered to learn it—caught up to me.

"I need to speak to you," she said. "You have something with René?"

"Sorry?"

"You are seeing my partner, René? He goes to your house?"

"No," I said.

She walked next to me, quiet, trying to figure out how to respond in the face of my flat denial.

I thought of René driving forty minutes on winding roads to see me, like he had indicated he would tonight. I saw him lifting me up, my legs wrapping around his back.

I was thinking of that as I walked toward my car with her alongside, and I guess I didn't realize I was smiling.

"There's something the matter with you."

I turned the flame of my French skills to low. "Sorry? Can you . . . repeat?"

"I . . . don't . . . like . . . *you*."

René likes me just fine, I thought at her.

Or at least I remembered it that way, but later I understood that I must have said it out loud.

IT WAS TEN P.M. when I heard the commune truck come up the little road and stop in the woods. René. I let him in.

He pushed me against the wall, more roughly than usual. His open hand clapped up against my face and head.

It really hurt. That's something people don't realize about a slap. They think, *not as bad as a punch*. But a slap can hurt quite a lot.

My face was stinging. My ears rang. My head was vibrating, rattled from the force of his huge, open hand.

I tried to get some distance from him, but he pinned me again and gathered my hair in his fist.

I didn't want to let on he was hurting me. He meant to hurt me.

He squeezed the handful of my hair harder. His other hand was on my neck. I saw from his expression how angry he was. His woman had made trouble for him, trouble he was extending to me.

His hand tightened around my neck, making it difficult for me to breathe. One of my eyes was starting to twitch, my vision fraying at the edges.

He let go and stepped back.

"I'm leaving."

He said this dramatically, like it was a further punishment, beyond choking me and trying to detach my scalp.

But he didn't leave. He stood there with his face full of petulant sadness, as if his own outburst were a kind of hardship he was suffering, worse for him than it was for me. Perhaps I should even apologize, for having left him no choice but to rough me up.

"If you ever come here again," I said, "I will jam a knife in your skull."

It just slipped out.

I started laughing. I couldn't stifle it. I was thinking of Bruno's description of the skull with the stalagmite, stalactite, whichever, a mineral growth shooting upward like the horn of a unicorn.

We always picture, Bruno said, our picturing is ceaseless. We pick up things along the way, he said, that are of no use at all. They return as images that flash into our thoughts. The trick, he said, is to acknowledge these images, let them float past.

René said something I didn't quite hear. Something like "You crazy bitch."

Being choked had brought on a vascular event. Worse than usual. Full-blown. The edges of my vision were fractured oscillations. I could still see if I looked straight ahead.

Peering through my tunnel of functional vision, I watched him leave.

It was fun while it lasted, René. But you didn't know this was temporary.

You people are not real to me. No one is.

The door was open to the night air. Despite my marbling vision, I managed to shut it and slide the crossbar.

An hour later I noticed that I could see.

It's always like that. I am not aware of the moment when the problem subsides, and instead I'm suddenly aware that for a while I've been fine.

It was eleven p.m. I washed my face and did a couple of things on the computer. The fair was thirty-six hours from now. No changes to the plan, or so I was told by my contacts.

I reread the article about the document trove the Feds had released to the lawyers of Nancy and the boy. There were photographs of both of them illustrating the article (the boy was still sporting the chin-line beard, which gave him a Founding Fathers solemnity) but no image of "Amy" who had done them dirty. Googling around, it seemed there was nothing beyond the one article. Their Freedom of Information bounty would take time to sift through. Have fun reading twenty-five hundred government documents, guys.

I checked Bruno's email once more, as I did every night before closing my computer.

There was a new letter in his sent folder.

THE MOULINARDS had emailed no new question.

He was writing into the void, a follow-up to his previous letter about the Debord years, after the war, and his beliefs on violence, his disagreements with Jean.

I wondered if he was trying to pretend the Moulinards weren't ignoring him, and within this pretense, hoping to reengage them.

―――――

He had just read an article, he told them, which suggested a new theory, that the great beasts knocking horns in charcoal and ocher on cave walls in the Guyenne and the Dordogne and the Aude could have been drawn by *Homo sapiens* for a purpose that was rather separate from *H. sapiens*'s hunting and his killing, his material claims on the natural world.

If these new theories were accurate, Bruno said, *H. sapiens* may have been a better artist than Bruno had previously thought. These depicted beasts on cave walls, long regarded as deities of the hunt, might instead have been deities of the sky. Not the animals that man hoped to trap and kill and skin and eat, but those animals that shone as arrangements of stars in the celestial heavens, wondrously out of reach.

The depictions on the walls and ceiling of places like Lascaux and Combarelles in the Périgord, recently discovered Chauvet in the Ardèche, the caves of the Guyenne, if these painted animals were not hunted beasts but star maps, meant to anticipate the movements of the heavens, this indicated quite a few things about *H. sapiens*, in terms of his sophistication.

The famous red hands we find in various caves, he said, that arch overhead, hand over hand stamped up a wall like rising heat—like a migraine, he said, that blots your vision (Bruno, I was having one an hour ago!)—no one knew what these handprints were. Some now suspected they represented the Milky Way. Dung beetles take their cues from the Milky Way, to find their way back to their nests. Odysseus could not have sailed home without Ursa Major, which he kept on his left as he traveled eastward. The Great Bear and Little Bear circle the north celestial pole. The star farthest north seems to stand still as the rest of the night sky turns, Bruno said. This is Polaris, he said, the lodestar or steering star.

I want you to go outside, he said, and find that star.

If it is not yet night as you read my letter, cease reading until night falls. When it is dark, start here again.

Go out under the night sky. You'll see the Big Dipper. Even under a full moon you will see it, and now, in late summer, know that its handle points up. The dipper's cup, which to me has always looked like a cart without wheels, has two stars that form its front. Draw a mental line between those two stars that form the front of the cart, and extend upward, to the first bright star that intersects with your line. That is Polaris. Learn this, and it will be something you carry with you.

Go now, he said, and do this.

It was a plain request, a simple demand, to go outside and look up.

The letter had been sent tonight. Would Pascal or any of them do as he said? Jérôme would not. Perhaps none of them would.

I did.

I put down the computer and walked out the front door of the Dubois house.

It was a moonless night, and the black heavens were ablaze with stars. It hurt my neck to look up at them, so I lay on the ground, facing the night sky. It felt close instead of far, a black dome right above me.

I found the Big Dipper, a stark pattern that seemed so human, of our design. It did look like a cart without wheels. Something a vagabond might push, a tinker selling his wares.

I followed Bruno's instructions. I drew an imaginary line from the two front corners of the tinker's cart to the next star above. This was Polaris.

I had assumed the North Star was the brightest star in the sky, but it wasn't. It was just a star, but one with special powers. That I had located it, and it wasn't obvious, made me proud.

Bruno, I found it.

I went back inside.

Our standard story, Bruno said, is that seafaring would not have been possible without that North Star you've just gone out to locate and behold, to ponder a little.

But a certain eighteenth-century Polynesian shows us this is wrong.

The man's name was Tupaia, Bruno said, and I need to delve a bit into his story for context, so that you can appreciate what he taught us.

Tupaia was a high priest and artist. He fled his own island for Tahiti, where he ingratiated himself with Tahiti's high chieftess, a woman named Purea. They were lovers. Around the time the English explorer Captain Cook landed in Tahiti, Purea's power was undermined. The benefits of being her lover had vanished, and so Tupaia asked Captain Cook to take him on board Captain Cook's ship, the *Endeavour*, when it departed. Captain Cook agreed. They sailed south, all the way to New Zealand, where Captain Cook watched Tupaia address the local native chiefs and speak easily to them, and in Tupaia's own language.

Captain Cook and his men could not speak to Frenchmen across the English Channel, and yet Tupaia and these Māori, half an ocean away, somehow shared one language.

And strangely, Bruno wrote, they also shared fishing techniques, stone tools, canoe type, hut construction, food preparation, clothing style, jewelry, and tattoo art, even lovemaking preference—outdoors, in fresh air.

And yet, between the island that Tupaia was from and the island where the Māori lived stretched a quarter of the globe's surface. It seemed impossible to Captain Cook that these people shared a culture.

The price for sex with the Māori women was the same, Captain Cook noticed, as it had been for women in Hawaii and in Bora Bora and Tahiti and Easter Island: one iron carpenter's nail per union. Captain Cook had threatened to shackle his crew, Bruno wrote, in order to stop his men from prying all the nails out of the *Endeavour*, reducing their own vessel to scrap in order to pay for love.

Some of the ship's crewmembers, Bruno wrote, were convinced that Tupaia's ability to talk to the Māori was proof of God, who had created all people from molds or templates, but each island people in its location, so that they developed quite similarly and yet without contact or intermingling, consistent as a single variety of perennial, flowers from seeds scattered near and far.

Captain Cook sensed this wasn't true—that separate from God's intent, there *had* been contact among these people, over a huge watery stretch. Tupaia had guided them to New Zealand and seemed capable of navigating over the whole of Polynesia, and yet he was from a culture with no charts or maps or any of the navigational instruments that Captain Cook and his crew possessed.

Captain Cook asked Tupaia to draw him a map of the Pacific, Bruno said, and Tupaia did. But Tupaia never explained the map, and then he died from fever in an illness-riddled port.

Captain Cook made his own copy of Tupaia's map and brought it to London. It exists still, in a library. For two hundred years, Bruno said, it was considered an oddity. The islands of the Pacific were in all the wrong places. Had Polynesians really been seafarers, as Cook had been convinced? Historians decided that if they had traveled long distances across the Pacific, they were landing hither and yon by accident and luck.

But we are beginning to understand, Bruno wrote, that historians did not know how to read Tupaia's map.

Captain Cook had added compass directions and a scale to the copy of the map he had drawn. To Captain Cook, a map was a bird's-eye view of fixed landmasses that were overlaid with longitude and latitude. With such a map, and his knowledge of maritime astronomy, his sextant, quadrant, and telescope, a navigator like Cook would be able to chart a reliable course *so long as the map was correct*. This is our own culture still, Bruno said. It's what a map is to us as well. But Tupaia's map was not this kind of map. It was not wrong. It was made wrong by the addition of cardinal directions, by the assumption it was a map in a European tradition.

Now we know, Bruno told the Moulinards, that the Polynesians were not landing hither and yon. They were the world's most advanced sailors. They sailed much of the globe, long before the Europeans had achieved any such thing. They went all the way to the Americas, and before Columbus. We know they did it, Bruno said, but how, and how their maps functioned, remain something of a mystery, but there are theories. These theories suggest new directions for all of us, Bruno said, using lost skills that these Polynesians cultivated for charting their course.

The North Star upon which I have asked you to gaze—and I can lead a horse to water, Bruno wrote, but drinking is up to you—if you drank in the location of our lodestar, you have beheld the most critical point in the sky for seafaring, but only in the Northern Hemisphere. This star is not visible in the Southern Hemisphere, Bruno said. They have no North Star. So how did the Polynesians sail?

Some think they used "a star path," of stars that rise and set on the horizon in succession, and that they aimed their canoes toward this series of stars. But, Bruno said, they used more than mere stars. They used all of their senses. The smell and taste of the sea. The shapes and position of clouds. The direction of waves as they broke over the prow of a boat. If Polynesian sailors could not see the waves approaching their canoe, on account of fog or nighttime darkness, they stood up in their boat, their legs apart, so as to interpret swell patterns, Bruno said, by the sway of their own testicles.

Go ahead and laugh, Bruno told the Moulinards (told me). But these people settled six million square miles of ocean.

Bruno said that Tupaia and sailors like him would have been taught navigation as babies. These sailor-priests, as Bruno referred to them, were steeped in knowledge handed down over thousands of years. They lived alone from the age of three, in a tent-pole structure whose roof was a model of the cosmos, for learning star position and sea lane. To look up and grasp and locate and know would be second nature to a sailor-priest-in-training, whose domestic world was a model of the sky.

When you look at stars, Bruno said, you merge into the flow of time, the right-now and the before and the to-come.

If it were true, Bruno said, that instead of greedy dreams of conquest, *H. sapiens* had been drawing star constellations on the walls and ceilings of caves, surfaces whose curved lineaments became a model of the heavens, this could recast Bruno's views on early man, or rather late man, *Homo tardissimus*.

Sailor-priests-in-training had plied the heavens on the fabric of their tent ceilings. And perhaps Tardie had been engaged in a similar study, but more abstract and less schematic: Tardie had coded the stars as earthly creatures, had projected into the heavens a wild menagerie of beasts. His intention, to navigate not the seas but the zodiac.

Of astrology, Bruno said it touched him that long ago people had thought up categories of human "type" and attempted to map those types to the universe, a universe that *did* involve us, pertain to us. They had that part right, he said. To look up and see stars is to look inward and see ourselves.

All attempts to categorize people, Bruno said, whether by astrology or anthropology or blood, answer to a root desire: to know the future. And by knowing it, we hope that we might prepare for it, or even control it.

If astrology was built upon myths, Bruno was now coming to see that he himself had clung to a different set of myths, painful as it was for him to admit it. He had looked to species to locate where we'd gone wrong. He had believed it was Better Before, and he was beginning to suspect that this was a kind of reverse teleology, a mystification of the past, and a presumption that progress is bad, that progress itself is not progress.

He had been vaguely aware of a flaw in his thinking. But the logical "fix" was not an embrace of outcomes, to love the shiny driverless car headed toward extinction, and to presume that the technological prowess that had designed the car could design a viable future, solve the nihilism of progress with yet more progress.

Was it Better Before? I honestly can't say, he wrote. In looking back, what I really wanted was to know how we navigate with the knowledge we have. What future do we imagine for our present?

When I reframe, he said, and think of *Homo sapiens* putting star maps on his cave ceilings, his attempt to imagine *his* own future, and of Neanderthals, with their handprints of the Milky Way, doing the same, my insistence on difference dissolves. These two iterations of human were both beset, and deeply, by a need to know, the same need that plagues me, now.

No sailor-priest am I, he said. In fact, I have altogether forsaken the sky, and thus the future, in my attempts to sort the past.

In my reassessments, he said, I have lost my bearings, and I will have to find new ones.

With that, he signed off.

I lay down on my bed and looked out the open window.

A wind had come up, creating a rushing sound as it gusted, pushing the trees. Stars were coming in and out of view as the tree boughs separated and moved. In the dark dynamism of wind and trees and night, I wanted to address Bruno. To tell him he was not alone.

"Bruno."

I said his name out loud. I shouldn't have.

"Bruno, I feel that way too."

The act of speaking, of hearing a voice, my own, in this empty house, pulled some kind of stopper.

It let something into the room, some kind of feeling. The feeling was mine, even as I observed it, watched myself as if from above, from up near the ceiling of this room, a room I would soon leave forever, as I would leave this false life.

There was a girl below, on the bed, in this room.

She had tears on her face, this girl. And her face was my face, and her tears were my tears.

THE FIRST PERSON I SAW when I arrived at Le Moulin the next morning was René's woman. She was standing in the area where I parked my Škoda, as if she was waiting for me.

She watched me get out and walk past. Dimples of satisfaction showed around her mouth. She said nothing. There was no need. She'd gotten things under control. René could now slap her around instead of me, choke her instead of me.

Everything was harmonious at Le Moulin that day, my last. It was Friday. The fair was tomorrow. If there were secrets to their planning, it seemed to me they were ready, had done their preparations, and the work now was simply to wait.

At lunchtime, I headed to my car.

"Not joining us?" Pascal asked.

I said that Lucien's uncle had died. I said something about paperwork at the house that the family needed. We were all to meet in the morning at Le Moulin, before descending on the fair.

And then I was operating on a kind of autopilot, as I traced the route I'd seen Naïs take yesterday, the difference being that Naïs, I knew, was busy now at her taps, and Bruno, if he was home, would be there alone.

The road dead-ended at an unfenced property, a little stone farmhouse and rambling barn in the shadows of fir and chestnut trees. I parked and got out. The wind was still strong, as it had been last night, with gusts coming through and pushing the trees.

Here was Bruno's barn, vines mounting its sills, windows broken and boarded. This was it, the structure to which he had expelled himself. I peered in. Cavernous, a space that looked to be both empty and a mess. I heard chickens, closed up in a pen somewhere inside the barn.

The house had heavy curtains drawn over its windows. From a vent pipe location, I guessed where the kitchen was, which Bruno had mentioned in one of his letters, the table where he wrote to Pascal and the others on Naïs's computer, which she used for the café's bookkeeping. A small satellite dish was nailed to the roof, near the front door. Under it was a jumbled woodpile, an old blue tarp thrown on top, rainwater collected in its folds.

Naïs's wood, or Bruno's, was mostly scrap, with old nails sticking out. Warped plastic farm trays were thrown in a disordered stack near the front door. There was a bucket of rotting compost, a crate filled with moldy-looking garlics. A wheelbarrow with a puddle of standing water at its base, furred in orange rust. Bags of chicken feed, one split and leaking, rain spoiled.

The country life.

I'd once been hired to entrap an American couple with a beautiful estate in the Hudson River Valley north of New York City. The owners were fine art dealers. Their place was on a plateau with a view of West Point Military Academy, iconic across the metal gleam of the Hudson. A competitor of this couple had hired me to sell them forged Picasso drawings. I was invited to their estate, decorated by these art dealers, a married gay couple, in impeccable furnishings and textiles. They were subdued men of aristocratic bearing, with the kind of manners that don't police, that simply model. Woven into their refinement were glints of cutting wit, and thus of great intelligence.

We'd lunched on the terrace. Playing collector, I'd worn tailored English clothes, what Ralph Lauren-né-Lipschitz attempts to copy in the stuff he markets to the masses, but the real version, on expense account, a camel blazer with buttery suede elbow reinforcements and polished riding boots.

After lunch, they had given me a tour of the grounds. They showed me flowering trees of rare origin and lanes of exotic moss—thick, electric green, and meant to be walked on, the couple explained, needing to be walked on, the weight of human steps rousing the mosses, stimulating them to grow. My riding boots, the men said, were perfect for the moss. They encouraged me to step on it. So-and-so in her spike heels—a collector whom the men named—was not allowed on their moss.

I'd been to their competitor's yacht on Long Island for what he said would be a small gathering, my presence meant to establish my identity as an art adviser. The gathering on this yacht featured champagne magnums and shiny shrimp on tiered platters, guests chatting over piped-in hit songs. The competitor bobbed his head to the music as if he could not help but enjoy it.

The dealers over the Hudson turned down the drawings. They were polite and didn't suggest there was any question of these drawings' source, but it was clear to me that they could spot a fake a mile away, whether a Picasso or a woman in riding boots.

Teams of gardeners had tended the grounds of that country estate, trimming and sculpting its hedged order. The roses were fed, sprayed, watered, pruned, and mulched, as if each bush were an elite military cadet. The hickory logs on the terrace where we'd lunched were quartered precisely and stacked just so.

Naïs was too busy and too poor for such order. As I inspected her dilapidated place, I had the thought that it was as ordered as it needed to be, and no more. Its disorder spoke of use.

Confident she would be at the bar awhile yet before closing up, I wandered.

Yellow leaves rustled underfoot and drifted downward as wind sifted through the trees. Autumn was upon us, a transition the Guyenne fair was meant to mark. As it would mark the end of my time here.

I saw the permaculture plot Bruno had mentioned, tended by him and Naïs, uneven rows of old chard or some other fall green. I saw the little stone hut he'd lived in after his daughter's death.

Beyond the hut, the land sloped downward. There was an enormous rock lodged in the lower aspect like a giant tooth. Bruno had described this rock. At its base lay the entrance to his cave.

I walked down the slope toward the rock.

I'd thought about this place enough that it seemed already familiar to me, a parcel where I had a right of trespass.

I lost my footing on the descent, unsteady, perhaps from drinking more than usual the past couple of days.

There it was, a dark opening in the base of the rock, about five feet high: the entry that the previous owner had boarded, and Bruno had unboarded and explored.

I ducked and entered, using my pocket Olight, wonderfully bright for its tiny size. This cave was shallow. At its end was a gap between the rocks, a crevice a person might squeeze into. Bruno now used a different passage, I knew from his emails. He was vague about where it was. But I was certain this was the gap he'd originally passed through.

It was narrow enough that if you got in, you might not get back out. As Bruno told it, he had reached into the gap. Felt airflow. Suspected a larger cavity below. Went down to find out. From there, discovered a world of more and more underground spaces, a vast network in the earth. Some were dry, some wet, some narrow, others spacious, like underground palaces, or churches, and they went and went and went.

I aimed my light down into the gap. I saw metal anchors drilled into the wall, a rope looped through them.

"Bruno," I said.

There was no reply. I said it again.

The rope was there to guide you down. I reached my hand in. The walls were cold. I felt the rope. I heard the sound of a car, louder and louder, and then the motor killed. A door open and shut.

I ducked out and started walking swiftly up the hill. Swiftly, that is, but casually, like someone with nothing to hide.

The car was actually a large truck. A man stood next to it. Not Bruno. My age. Dressed in the utilitarian clothes of a state worker. This must have been the son.

A feeling of nervous excitement overtook me.

I tamped it as I conjured an explanation. He'd expect to know why I was on his father's property. I said I was looking for the place I was meant to stay. I'd realized, when I took a look around, that this was not my vacation rental.

"Who are you renting from?" he asked.

I said I could not remember their name, but that it was near the Château de Gaume.

"If you turn back to the D79 and continue north you will pass the road to that place. This is the property of Madame Quercy."

Quercy? Perhaps it was the ex-wife's name. It could have been why I never found a property record for Bruno. But why would his son call it that?

"There's an outage here," he said, "because of the winds." He opened a panel on the side of his truck, and I saw that it was a Telecom truck.

I SPENT THE AFTERNOON at the Dubois place, packing up equipment and planning for my next job, an assignment on the island of Malta.

I sorted my clothes and put them in my suitcase, the clothes of Sadie Smith, simple outfits, jeans and T-shirts and sweaters that I was sick of. I could dump this stuff before I returned the car and got on a plane.

In the evening, there were new Google Alerts. The news about the document dump and "Amy" had spread like lice looking for a host. Some of the articles speculated on who this federal agent was. Had she infiltrated other movements and scenes? Is this what the FBI was spending tax revenue on? "Amy" had been paid sixty-five thousand dollars for entrapping these people, one article claimed. (Actually, it was more.)

"Amy" was an example of the illegal and immoral and wrongheaded surveillance of leftist activists in the United States. Nancy was the self-appointed expert and martyr on this topic, even as the boy had served more time than she had. There was a video of them being interviewed. She did all the talking. As he looked at her and nodded with his serious beard, I was reminded of how he had looked at me, and I felt a twinge of nostalgia.

In the video, she says they are pursuing a civil case against me, now that they know my true identity.

My true identity?

I took a Xanax to calm my nerves. I washed it down with red, which I'd been forced to drink because I didn't have any white and I had run out of beer.

I reminded myself that right now, today, this moment, my "true identity" was Sadie Smith, and as her, I had a job to do.

I loaded the gun I planned to give to Burdmoore tomorrow, so he could sacrifice himself. I put it on the side table next to the bed.

I held off on a second Xanax. It was important that I sleep defensively, which is similar to driving defensively, a modality of heightened anticipation, ready to waken at the slightest disturbance.

But I needed sleep, and it wasn't coming. I felt like all the lights had been turned on inside me, bright as a twenty-four-hour office building.

I gave in and took the second Xanax and also an Ambien and set my alarm.

OR I THOUGHT I SET MY ALARM.

I woke with a start, but by no external stimulus.

It was eleven a.m.

My heart pounded from disorientation and drugged sleep. The Lucien phone, which I would soon scrub, scrub and return to factory settings, was stacked with messages.

Vito, texting.

—I have news.

—Lucien is with someone.

—It's not a fling it's a relationship.

—I was wrong about the cabal. It was two not three.

—It's Amélie.

—(In case you didn't already guess.)

I was behind schedule. I gave myself twelve minutes to make coffee and pack up the Škoda and get going. I was putting on my clothes when Vito started texting again.

—Sadie?

—Do you not care??

This guy had no sense of what my concerns were at the moment.

—Sadie?

I powered off that phone.

NO, VITO, I DO NOT CARE.

I TORE OUT. Left that house open like an old, unlaced shoe.

I was headed in the direction of the lake in Vantôme, intent on stashing my car on its little escape route and getting to the boat dock, where I was to meet Burdmoore.

The rest of the Moulinards would be in their staging area, waiting for the moment to descend onto the D79 and set up their blockade. Would Pascal notice I wasn't among them? Naturally. But the plan would be in motion. He'd figure, she's just a translator. She doesn't want to involve herself in this. She's with Lucien, after all. My mediocre friend. Like him, she's got the heart of a good bourgeois. Even if she didn't seem exactly "good." What did she seem? There was an emptiness to her. A sense her lack of affect went all the way down.

He'd think all that, or he wouldn't, and it didn't matter.

I would get there on time, despite having grossly overslept. My grogginess was wearing off, helped by the beauty of this day, sunny and fresh. The sky was a deep blue and decorated with storybook clouds, clean and round and puffy, scudding over the valley and creating cool shadows on the green hills.

As I neared the lake, there were cars full of fairgoers backed up the little D79, normally so empty. This was the big event. Once a year. People from all over the region. Vehicles were parked along both sides of the shoulder as far as I could see, with families streaming down the road in groups toward the fair. The main lots for the lake were already full, with cars turning in to park on a field. I inched forward, the road bumper to bumper.

Along the meadow next to the lake were displays of old tractors and food trucks in rows. A band was setting up their equipment on a soundstage.

I got through the chaotic lake entrance and kept on the D79 past the fair, as I headed toward the little connector where I planned to deposit the Škoda.

From this section of the D79, cars were traveling in only one direction, toward the fair. I was on the other side, which was empty, as I backed onto the secret road, the little route the Maos and I had cleared. I reversed more than halfway down and parked the Škoda so that it was positioned for a quick escape, by the time cops of every kind stormed this place.

———

I walked down the D79 toward the fair. I passed the displays of antique tractors and the rows of concessions and picnic tables. The Moulinards would be off-site still, coordinating, as I was meant to be, as a group, with subgroups. I wasn't afraid of encountering them here because I knew they would not be here. But also, I already felt free of them.

I passed the old heifer scale, a metal plate on the ground with a wood awning built over it. A farmer was threatening to weigh his thick-waisted wife, picking her up, as she feistily demanded he put her down.

I felt the buzz of an alert. I had been getting updates on Platon's coordinates; they'd put a tracking device in his car. The phone was in the outer pocket of my fanny pack, whose inner compartment contained my Glock and minirevolver, as well as the vintage pistol for good old Burdmoore.

I unzipped the outer pocket and snuck a glance at the alert. Platon was on schedule.

Old men in cardigan sweaters and shirts and slacks in monochrome acrylic, outfits they didn't intend to look ironic and hip, and instead were their "Sunday best," lined up for high-powered gasoline water. Their wives, with dyed hair of unnatural hues that were not intended to look edgy, their village beauty parlor best, waited at picnic tables for the husbands to bring them their booze. Younger people stood in lines for fried fish or hamburgers or ice cream. There was a vendor advertising marinated bear meat, and a sweaty man over a grill, flipping this bear meat with tongs.

I was meant to connect with Burdmoore at the boat dock, beyond the last booth, which offered cuisine from the West Indies. The young man and two women running it were the first non-white people I'd seen since leaving Marseille a month ago. Their banner said "NOT SPICY" in huge letters. They had no customers.

I sat down on the concrete and waited.

Burdmoore knew the plan. He would separate Platon and his bodyguard from the crowds, walk these two men to the edge of the lake, and shoot them.

He was supposed to be here at noon.

He wasn't.

An update came through on Platon's coordinates:

"He is early."

I stood on the dock's concrete embankment to get a better look.

The Crossback appeared on the road, ink black, with a spinning blue light on its roof, indicating state provenance, official business.

Dusty old farmers' cars were moving over to let it pass.

The fair's official greeting committee, old men in special red vests and berets, understood the car as important and began to clear a lane for it in the parking lot, close to the fair's entrance. The car pulled in and parked, its blue light spinning. Fair officials surrounded it, looking pleased and excited. It was a rural functionary's dream to have a surprise visit like this by state officials, and all the way from Paris!

The Serb got out of the car. He spoke to two of the red-vested men.

Platon's driver, Georges, was next. Georges went around to open the rear door, but in no hurry, with his hallmark attitude of dutiful contempt.

Paul Platon emerged from the car, his nose up, sniffing the air for his photo opportunity.

Where was Burdmoore?

Michel Thomas stood from the opposite rear door. The celebrated author, French national treasure, with his strange wig of destroyed hair, his sunken features, but the sharp gaze of an eagle.

The men in their red vests spoke into walkie-talkies. Summoning the prizewinners to meet Platon, I assumed. They nodded eagerly at the deputy minister. This was their big moment. They didn't seem to understand who Michel Thomas was and he didn't look to them like someone to whom special treatment at the Guyenne Agricultural Exposition should be bestowed.

I watched the author as he took in the scene, the booths, the old tractors, made notes on a little pad. I could see that he was primed to soak in the environment, deploy it in one of his books and thereby fix himself in posterity, instead of disappear like people are meant to. He'd be in libraries, the rest of us dust or mulch, an unkempt headstone.

Where was Burdmoore?

Georges leaned against the Crossback, putting tobacco in his pipe, waiting, which was what drivers like him actually do. Sometimes they drive, but mostly they wait.

I heard the bwap bwap of an off-road motorcycle. Its rider was splitting lanes between cars, coming down the D79. The rider turned into the lake entrance, coasting with his clutch in, loudly and obnoxiously revving the motor for no reason but to create a disturbance. Some arrogant local youth.

The rider straddled his cycle and flipped up the visor on his motocross helmet, surveying the crowd. It was Franck.

Vantôme Franck. Being a kid, free to roam, despite having a kid.

I watched from the boat dock as officials ushered Platon into the fair. Michel Thomas paused to light a cigarette. The group kept walking.

The Serb was behind Platon and the fair officials. He'd been lifting weights, I could see, his muscles testing the stretch of his suit.

A band was about to begin their set as I lurked near the stage, keeping Platon in sight, and an eye out for Burdmoore. They launched into their first number. It was a cover of "Used to Love Her" by Guns N' Roses. The singer wore a do-rag like he thought he was Axl. He held the microphone and moved like Axl. He even did the little muttered preamble over drumstick clicks, and the high-pitched coyote howl.

I used to love her. But I had to kill her.

Where was Burdmoore?

Officials had cleared a center lane between the food stands. A farmer was being guided toward the little party of Platon and his red-vested handlers. The Serb was behind them, looking bored and inattentive.

I used to love her. (Ooh yeaah.) But I had to kill her.

The farmer summoned to meet Platon had boils all over his face, as if someone had hastily sculpted his visage from lumps of clay. He led a piebald cow with a glossy blue ribbon around its neck toward the deputy minister. Fair officials looked on proudly.

Two teenage girls passed by, long-limbed and golden, in very short shorts, and the Serb turned to watch them. One of the girls caught his eye, and nudged the other. The two girls stopped walking and consorted. Anyone new, anyone in a suit, was someone to flirt with.

Where was Burdmoore?

The Serb, with native fluency in Jailbait, was chatting up the girls. He was focused on them as if his primary duty was not to guard the subminister but to get into the pants of one of the girls (while no doubt using his security credentials to loosen them both up). The Serb's heavy brow was less severe, I noticed, now that he was grinning.

The subminister shook the farmer's hand, pretending not to be offended that the man's face was studded with boils. He pretended to pet the farmer's prizewinning cow. Everyone seemed uncomfortable, especially the farmer. A red-vested official took photos.

The two girls walked off and the Serb followed, as if they'd just made some kind of agreement. One kept turning her head. The Serb smiled, eager on their heels. He'd forgotten all about Paul Platon. This was just a bullshit assignment anyhow. An ag fair in the sticks. Might as well try to have a little fun.

The band finished "Used to Love Her" and started in on "Sweet Child O' Mine." The guitar player wasn't skilled, but he managed to crank out the blistering opening melody in a way that was at least recognizable.

Young mothers in halter tops and exposed midriffs were dancing in front of the stage, young men in T-shirts advertising farm equipment or Red Bull moving their heads to "Sweet Child O' Mine." A toddler stood alone and bopped its knees stiffly to the rhythm, the best it could do to dance. Like that baby, I find it impossible not to love Guns N' Roses.

The Serb and the girls had gone off behind a mobile generator.

I heard chanting and cheering. Mr. Crouzel was coming down the road on his tractor. Aurélie and a bunch of other Moulinards followed the tractor on foot, holding banners. Banners I'd watched them make. "Water for All." "Megabasins No." I saw the mirror-flash of milk tankers.

The protest was starting. Platon would be trapped. The Serb was gone. And Burdmoore, to my relief, was walking toward me.

There was no point scolding him for being late. I quickly passed him the P38. He reacted like a baby boomer being handed the keys to a 1965 Ford Mustang.

"Wow," he said. "This thing takes me back."

He held the P38 and discreetly cocked its hammer, then slipped it into the pocket of the jacket he wore.

Protesters were swelling into the parking lot, in front of the Crossback. Georges the chauffeur took in the scene and quickly got into the car.

Crouzel shut off his tractor. Aurélie, with a bullhorn, guided the protesters in chant. They descended onto the grounds of the fair. People stepped back to make room for them.

Burdmoore raised his voice, so that I would hear him over the din of protesters and "Sweet Child O' Mine."

"You want me to use this thing? On this guy Paul Platon?"

Something was off.

"Just walk up on him, firing?"

The ribboned cow had started to stomp and kick. The old farmer lost control of its halter.

Two of the men in red vests pulled Platon out of the way of the cow.

The tankers were starting to flood the D79 with milk. It splashed out from their tanks, filled the irrigation trenches next to the road, and poured down into the parking lot, sending people running.

"Do you think I left my brain in a trash can someplace?"

"What?"

"Do you think I'm seriously going to run at this guy, in front of all these people, with cops bearing down, and fucking shoot him? Are you nuts?"

The band had stopped playing. I heard police sirens, impotent, trapped behind the milk tankers.

"But thanks for this, sister." Burdmoore patted the jacket pocket where he'd put the gun.

"I'll keep it as a souvenir. It'll remind me of that time some crazy chick came to Le Moulin and tried to stir up a bunch of shit and no one went for it."

He walked off toward the protesters.

"THIS IS YOUR FAIR, this is your land, this is our life! Protect it! These people are your enemies!"

"Megabasins, no! Farmers, yes!"

I heard vehicle doors opening and more sirens. There was a showdown on the road. People in black, their faces masked, but Moulinards no doubt, had formed an offensive line.

Behind that line, police started firing tear-gas canisters. People were screaming and running to avoid getting gassed.

I followed Platon and the two fair officials who were trying, with no script or plan, to escort him to safety.

They headed toward the back side of the lake, away from the crowd. It was the same direction I needed to go, toward the fishermen's road to freedom.

Things had not gone as planned. My priority was to get out of here regardless.

I heard a bwap bwap. It was Franck on his motocross bike. He was going this way also. Teenage boys are clever like that.

But it seemed he wasn't attempting to flee the melee like everyone else. He was trailing Platon and the two fair officials, going slow, standing on his foot pegs.

He pulled in the clutch and let his cycle idle. And then he lurched ahead, toward Platon and the old men. He accelerated between them, knocking both of these old men to the ground. Or perhaps the loud sound of his motorcycle had startled them and caused them to lose their balance. Franck really was an asshole.

He skidded to a stop and set upon Platon, circling him and revving his motor. Platon looked panicked, a man far from home, far from what he knew. No one here to protect him.

"Stop this!" he shouted at Franck.

Platon was trying to get away from Franck's motorcycle, but in each direction he moved, Franck cut him off.

Platon ran toward one of the huge log piles in the clearing. Safe harbor. An escape. A motorcycle cannot climb a stack of logs.

When Platon's foot made contact with the third or fourth log, this log he had stepped on shifted, transferring weight from the log above it. Platon attempted to get clear of the falling log by going higher. He was wearing city shoes, dress shoes with hard leather soles, and as he tried to avoid the moving log, he slipped and proceeded to set even more logs moving. He lost his balance and fell. The logs laddered down from the top of the pile. They rolled over him. The pile collapsed, with Platon underneath.

Franck took off. Wanted no part. He opened his throttle and surged away.

I don't blame you, Franck.

I ran up the little road, toward my car, my route of escape.

AS I TRAVELED NORTH on the D79, headed for a highway that would take me to a main autoroute, a fast and efficient toll road toward Paris, rural police and riot police and other police were passing me, streaming in the opposite direction. Fire trucks. A weird flat-front vehicle I understood to be a water cannon. Gendarmerie buses, one after another, empty, as if they were going to arrest the entire rural population of the greater Guyenne.

VIII

URSA MINOR

THEY PAID ME the exorbitant price I'd named.

Paid it without inquiries as to how things went.

An accident, declared as much officially, was more than good enough.

I blew off Malta.

Something had to change, and the good luck I'd been dealt had sealed it for me.

Instead of getting on a plane at Charles de Gaulle, after receiving my money I bought a car and drove it to Spain. And not a shitty Škoda, either, which, where were those cars even from?

I bought an E-Class Mercedes.

Pull the stamper or lose a hand. I'd pulled the stamper, and I was done pulling the stamper.

I shot right through Palafrugell, birthplace of the deceased sub-minister Pablo Platon y Platon. Poor Paul.

I could still hear his final high-pitched scream as the logs had crushed him.

I continued onward from Palafrugell to a tiny village on the rim of a cove that felt like a secret.

Clear turquoise water and soft yellow sand, limestone cliffs and stone pines, their branches sculpted by wind. The sand wasn't soft. It had the consistency of marbles. I bought water shoes to protect my feet.

It was mid-October now. The tourist season was over. I was the lone occupant of the only hotel in this tiny village, whose clerks wore lavender jackets and stood behind a huge white desk. The floors were tile, also white. I walked around barefoot. It was that kind of place, built for people to enjoy the sea, and not to be formal.

I had been there a month and was friendly with the clerks, especially a young Catalonian woman with large sloe eyes and bleached hair, a husky voice. We had an agreement. She would tell me if anyone came around asking after someone who might be me. So far, no one had.

Every morning I swam, the only person in the cove. And every morning a cormorant sat on a little rock above the waterline. We each had a routine. In the silvery dawn light, the sea was as smooth and still as cast silicone, and so salt-rich that I floated almost out of the water. If you were pitched from a ship into water like this, you could live a long time. The salt would hold you. I lay on my back.

Me and my cormorant and the rock, we were like figures suspended in the silicone.

If the later day brought wind that riffled the surface of the sea, dawn was always the same. A reset. The silicone poured smooth.

It was an off-season hotel, the bathing Spaniards gone, back at work in Barcelona, but it was fishing season, and I watched as boats appeared, rusted old vessels that men and boys dragged up the beach.

I spent my afternoons on the hotel terrace, eating squid and drinking beer. But then I gave up the beer. Gave up drinking. Just stopped. That was it. No, it was not easy. But I did it.

Few things worth doing are easy.

Any habit that offers pleasure becomes a hassle if you need it to get from hour to hour.

I read the news.

The French papers, and the Spanish ones, too, had all but snickered about Platon's fatal accident, and about the posted signs next to the logs, with pictures warning of danger.

Can he not interpret a pictogram? Designed to warn even those who cannot read?

But they had not been there, at the scene of his death. They didn't know. It was Franck's fault.

The protest at the lake in Vantôme had become a full-scale melee. Two hundred and fifty-eight people were arrested, including union leaders, Moulinards, anarchists who had traveled down from Tarnac, in the Corrèze, and the singer from the rock band who had been performing at the fair, who was accused of running at a cop with his microphone stand.

Michel Thomas had been injured in the riot. He'd gotten a projectile to the face, resulting in a black eye, as could be seen in news photos all over the internet. It helped to confirm his reputation for uncanny timing, for prescience. Notorious and nonpartisan, Thomas was always at the scene of the crime, a bystander and observer to society's convulsions. Cagey, a likely reactionary, but most of all, a writer with no affiliations, with a talent for washing up on the shores of chaos.

The state was going after Pascal Balmy. There were photos of him and Jérôme and Alexandre in the paper. Their families had hired the finest lawyers in Paris to represent them. The police had launched a massive raid of Le Moulin, and as evidence they cleared out every last volume from their library of five thousand books.

Jean was under investigation. Bruno's name also came up, as a "bizarre survivalist" who had mentored the group, but they had found no evidence of illegality so far.

Bruno had changed his email password. I could no longer hack his account. This hurt, but I understood.

There were long debates on French TV over whether, juridically, these people could be held accountable for the death of Platon.

Meanwhile Nancy was getting her attention, making her case. Someone had scanned and uploaded to the internet the twenty-five hundred FBI documents that the Feds had released to Nancy and the boy. An activist with hours and hours to kill might sift through them and come up with information about me. I myself had no instinct to do that work, or to glance at even a single page of those documents. There was nothing in them for me to learn.

What had Bruno said about the future?

When we face our need to control it, we are better able to resist that need, and to live in the present.

I stopped reading news articles. I stopped watching videos. My new rule about drinking had been an attempt to rid myself of a crippling attachment. The internet was yet another crippling attachment, and so I banned it.

I walked for hours each afternoon on knobby paths along the cliffs above the sea.

I walked to a lighthouse and watched its magnificent crystal flash and turn.

There's that old myth about the humble lighthouse and the giant battleship. The ship has mistaken the lighthouse for a boat, a little pissant boat that better get out of its way. The captain of the battleship comes on the radio, to command the little boat to move, a boat that he doesn't understand is a lighthouse on a rock. The captain believes he is in a power struggle with the thing in his path and that the more forceful and arrogant he is, the more likely it will yield. He is not wrong that he is engaged in a struggle for dominance. He's only wrong that he'll win.

The hotel would close soon for the winter. My friend, the sloe-eyed clerk, told me about a small house I could rent cheaply, on a bluff above the cliffs beyond the little village.

My first night in the new house, I went out on the veranda and lay down and looked up at the deep.

I proceeded as Bruno had taught me:

First, locate the Big Dipper, by the four points of its cart.

There it was. The tinker's cart. A cart he fills with wares to be sold and pushes across the sky. The cart of an eternal traveler.

Form a line from the bottom corner of the front of the cart, Bruno had said, to the star at the upper corner. Continue that line upward, to Polaris.

Polaris does move, Bruno had explained, as the earth's axis shifts, in a cycle that lasts twenty-six thousand years. Just a little less than the gap of time between us, he had said, and the mysterious people who put their pictures on the walls of Lascaux, who put a reflecting pool of the night sky in the lightless chambers of the earth.

I can't intuit their reasons, Bruno had said. But I can be certain they studied the sky. And that we must, as well.

Polaris glowed, the steadfast star, Bruno had called it. Reliable and fixed, and yet the sailor-priests of Polynesia had managed without it.

A key principle of their navigation, Bruno had explained, was an inversion of movement: destinations *arrived toward sailors*, rather than sailors moving toward destinations.

This concept of seafaring was called etak, Bruno had instructed, or "moving island"—in which a sailor in a canoe traveling the open ocean, whether standing with his legs apart feeling wave-swell, or seated and rowing, or seated and not rowing, this sailor was himself *stationary*, while waves and the occasional landmass flowed past his boat.

These sailors weren't stupid, Bruno had said. They knew they were not actually standing still. They were employing a special form of cognition, a skill that was crucial to getting somewhere.

You and I, Bruno had said, don't live in their world. Our own earth, our version of it, is fitted with Cartesian coordinates, a straitjacket of plumb lines and cross-stitches. The sky is no longer visible in most places. Our stars have been replaced by satellites, whose clocks tell atomic time.

With GPS you can know your location without looking out the window, he had said.

You can know your location without knowing your location.

You can know things without knowing anything.

We often proceed as if we know things without a sense of what knowledge even is, Bruno had said.

The earth is turning, for instance: sure, we know that because we've memorized it. But our knowledge of the earth's turn is false, it is knowledge without context, disconnected from the rest of the universe.

When the sun rises, we think *it's rising*. When it sets, we think *it's setting*.

The sun is not rising, and it is not setting. The sun, my friends, has no daily orbit.

He had called them his friends.

Bruno, they were not your friends.

It is us, he had gone on, who are moving. The earth is turning, and we don't sense it.

We've ceased to locate ourselves in a larger system, a grand design. We've cut the rope, my children.

His children.

They don't deserve to be your children, Bruno.

Here, perched over the dark, calm bed of the Spanish sea, the sky was the same as a Guyenne sky.

When you engage the heavens, Bruno had said, you merge into the flow of time, the right-now and the before and the to-come.

You join a continuum, an ever-present. You see through your eyes, and the eyes of others. Difference dissolves. But you stay you.

As I looked up from my veranda, my new house, following Bruno's star instructions, I felt distances dissolve between him and me.

I had a sensation of floating, not unlike floating on the salty swells, as if I were borne aloft, as if I were held by this lake of stars.

But then I sensed odd movement on the edges of the sky, the peripheral regions of my vision.

Was I having a vascular event? I had mostly stopped having them when I gave up alcohol.

The movement was real. A star was pawing its way among the other stars, moving, but too slow to be a shooting star.

As I lay there, I saw another of these little stars crawling along, and another, and then another.

They were satellites. The sky was full of them.

That I had relied on satellite technology did nothing to mute my sense of offense. The sky was polluted with these things. The whole glittering dark dome above was alive with them, moving here and there. They were little electric lice. Lice crawling over the cosmos like it was a warm head.

These lice were yet another sign of Bruno, a child running free in the ravages of war. That was Little Bruno. And then Big Bruno had lived to tell.

I never even got to meet him. Unless that had been him at the lake in Vantôme, and I had missed my chance.

You are not Bruno?

I am not.

I went in and lay down in my new house, empty except for a bed I'd had delivered that morning.

There was no ambient light up here. The room was dark.

I looked into the dark. I began to see things. They were from inside my mind.

What I saw was those babies, like the ones in the Dubois house, moseying into view. Les Babies.

We are all sieves, Bruno had said. We catch and hold on to things along the way. We say hello to these things, these distractions, and we let them float past.

The fortnight Bruno had experimented with darkness, he had told the Moulinards that in the heart of blackest blackness, he had experienced a visual hallucination of opalescent lava in a magnificent volcano-spill. The volcano, he said, had morphed into a magical bread oven that spit golden loaves, loaves that rolled from the oven as if on a conveyor. These scenes, the lava and the bread oven and the gold loaves, had then morphed into little cartoon images that were familiar to him: they were the debased advertising logo of a brand of factory cookies, mass-produced, something from his own childhood.

The experience was a reminder, he said, that when you attempt to escape the world, to leave it behind, you bring things with you.

Understand that you can never leave purely, he said. We want to escape what ails us, into some idyll, but know that when you go, you travel with cargo, stowaways, souvenirs from the old world. Don't be afraid of them.

Instead, say hello. Be friendly. Be patient. These things you've brought along will pass. Say hello and watch them go.

I lay and watched Les Babies. Naked and classical. Babies in chef's hats. Babies in aprons.

They floated by and faded out.

I said goodbye to them, the only babies I would ever have, and that I hoped they'd be back.

As autumn progressed, the Big Dipper was sinking. Each evening, it was tipped a little lower on the horizon, the tinker angling his cart, a sky tinker pushing his sky cart on a frictionless journey, with no need of wheels.

On a night with no moon, I drew the line from the two front stars on the tinker's cart upward to Polaris.

Polaris, Bruno had said, connects the Big and the Little Dipper. It forms the end of the handle of the Little Dipper. This is the Difficult

Dipper, he had said, the one you will not see unless the sky is suitably dark.

There it was, a flipped cart, upside down, standing on its handle.

There they were. Both dippers, and their linking star, their guiding star, and Bruno's, and mine.

Nights, I lay on my veranda, my star deck, and looked up. Days, I looked at the sea. Or I read. Or I walked.

My sloe-eyed friend came to visit sometimes. She spoke to me in Catalan, which I wanted to learn. I spoke to her in French.

But mostly I was alone.

Come December, a new work inquiry arrived. Someone in the UK.

I had been turning down all offers of work, and so I had mostly stopped getting them. I responded to this one as I had to all the others.

I have retired to Priest Valley, I wrote.

Priest Valley? Where is that? they asked.

Exactly, I replied.

ACKNOWLEDGMENTS

Thank you to Jason Smith for his encouragement and wisdom, and his influence on tone, theme, and world. To Nan Graham for the grandness of her vision and her meticulous and spirited attention to this book. To Susan Golomb, as always, for her amazing and tireless support. To early readers Francisco Goldman, Ben Lerner, Marisa Silver, and Dana Spiotta. To Remy Smith Kushner for his knowledge of the caves of the Guyenne. Tovey Halleck for his skill and expertise at catching fish with bare hands. To Katherine Monaghan, Sabrina Pyun, Stuart Smith, Brianna Yamashita, Lauren Dooley, Kassandra Rhoads, Hannah Mouschabeck, Katie Rizzo, Jaya Miceli, Wendy Sheanin, Jonathan Karp, and everyone at Scribner and Simon & Schuster. To Maja Nikolic and Sasha Landauer at Writers House. Finally, my heartfelt thanks to the Civitella Ranieri Foundation, the Maison Dora Maar, the Ucross Foundation, and MacDowell.